The Road To
# APPLE DUMPLING BRIDGE

The Road To
# APPLE DUMPLING BRIDGE

K. L. Knowles

CHAPLIN BOOKS

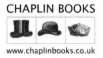

www.chaplinbooks.co.uk

First published in 2019 by Chaplin Books

ISBN: 978-1-911105-44-2

Map illustrations by K L Knowles

Printed by Imprint Digital

A CIP catalogue record for this book is available at the British Library

Chaplin Books
5 Carlton Way
Gosport PO12 1LN
Tel: 023 9252 9020

www.chaplinbooks.co.uk
www.appledumplingbridge.co.uk

# CONTENTS

*For my family*

# FOREWORD

*H* *idden safe somewhere in the corner of the world lies a holy relic carved by the paws of the Animal God himself. A mystic Acorn fashioned from the wood of a tree that grew in the Alver Valley in the Country of Gosport, its possession guarantees eternal life, peace and happiness. Generations of animals have hunted far and wide for the Acorn, religious wars have raged and quests have been founded by mighty kings. But not everyone who seeks the Acorn does so for the right reasons. Although the animals of Gosport hold fast to what Hudsonicus Holozoa, their God, taught them – that kindness is everything – they know that others hunger for more.*

*Everyone likes to think that the Acorn is hidden in their own little corner of the world. But perhaps it is right here in southern England, where the map of the coast wiggles up and down to form a harbour – a city on one side and a town on the other? If so, then who can prevent the Acorn from falling into the paws of evil?*

*The animals will receive no help from humankind: generations before, cholera spread through the lands, killing the people, leaving another kind to evolve and take their place, to live in their houses, run their businesses, farm the land, fish the seas, protect the shores, and govern their countries.*

*Our story begins in 1939 in a world that you never knew existed. A world under threat that only a Chosen One can save.*

# PART ONE

# GOSPORT

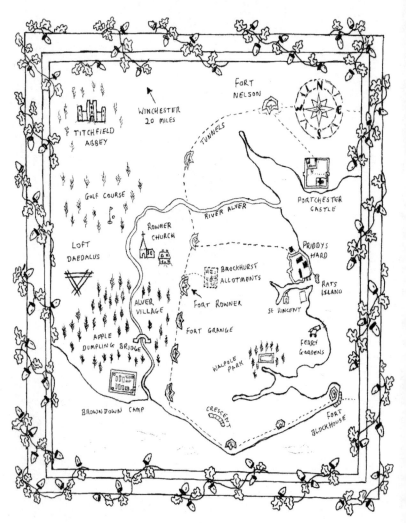

**GOD'S PORT - OUR HAVEN**

## Chapter 1

# THE GREATEST SHOW IN TOWN

$E$ very year throughout Gosport, grand celebrations took place to mark the start of the summer season. Lashings of food were served, together with wine made from every berry, and the animal folk gathered to enjoy great feasts and entertainment. Fort Rowner was the venue for one of the largest of these celebrations and drew animals from far and wide.

Led by Lady Ellen Prideaux-Brune, a bubbly badger, the Doe-hen Institute of Ladies prepared diligently, almost as if it were a military operation. For some it was the highlight of their social calendar and a feather in the cap of the D.I. but for Lady Prideaux-Brune it was more about upholding tradition. With her brother, Brigadier Brune, she had inherited land throughout Gosport; both were wealthy but generous to those in need. Lady Prideaux-Brune was full of community spirit and was never too proper to get stuck in. Indeed, if she saw that there was a job to do she would simply get on and do it, rallying everyone around her to help, of course. A no-nonsense, paws-on old gal, she was eccentric to the core. Her whiskery brother was equally well respected within the community, who thought him loveable and jolly, though Lady Prideaux-Brune made no bones about her views – she thought him a bumbling old fool at times, forever twittering on about battles gone by.

"Marvelous!" declared Brigadier Brune sitting at his table surrounded by a feast. "Absolutely scrumptious. Well done, ladies." He patted his stomach and drank more from his goblet of elderberry wine.

The fort was buzzing with activity for the 1939 festivities – there was music, dancing, D.I. competitions and bake sales, games for the children, laughter and fun. It was a day for little ones to remember and for their parents to relax.

Through the throng of the crowd came two old friends walking together carrying plates of food in their paws towards the table where their families were waiting.

"I hear that Jane Priddy is buying more land for additional dock space," said Mary Camper, a rather pompous red squirrel who was overfond of a bit of gossip, to her friend Gertie Nicholson.

"Well yes, I heard that too. But I also heard that she only had to pay Bernard Hardway a couple of farthings and a smile for it," replied Gertie as they joined Mary's husband at the table.

"Well, it makes you wonder, doesn't it?" said Mary. "Pass the salt, dear," she asked her husband.

"What are we wondering about this time?" said the gentleman squirrel in a despairing tone.

Ignoring her husband, Mary added: "Well, he always did have a soft spot for Jane and for other fieldmice in general. I'll never understand it. I mean, she is practically a recluse on that big old estate of hers. When was the last time we saw her at a D.I. meeting – 1935 wasn't it? And what does it say about him – carrying on like that?"

"Oh I agree, dreadful business," said Gertie, utterly compliant as always.

Breaking up the gossip was the squeaky voice of Ethel Knight, one of the few grey squirrels in their community, declaring a magic show and introducing her best friend and conjurer, Agatha Mumby. Of course Mary and Gertie had something to say about that.

"Oh really, why does she insist on putting on this dreadful show each year?" said Mary, twitching her tail in indignation. "We really must discuss this at next month's meeting. How are we to pass on the traditional animal ways when Agatha dresses like a wizard? It simply will not do."

"Ladies and gentleman, gather round, gather round!" said Ethel to the crowd, struggling to make herself heard. "You are about to see the greatest show in town. You won't believe your eyes, folks. Please welcome the greatest conjurer of them all – Aggy Mystic Mumby!"

Agatha, who had donned an oversized wizard's cloak and pointy hat over her red squirrel fur, was welcomed with rapturous applause. She took up her position next to a big haphazard-looking wooden contraption with a large handle on the side of it.

"Thank you, and thank you to my apprentice friend, Ethel. I will now attempt something you have never seen before. For your viewing pleasure I will make Ethel disappear. Please do not try this at home." The crowd played along, 'ooh-ing and aah-ing' in all the right places. The little ones who had gathered at the front were loving the spectacle. "Ladies and gentleman, for this to work we must all say the magic words together: – 'Magical-is, Disappear-is, Ethel-is'."

"Oh please," mocked Mary Camper.

"Ethel, if you will, stand on the 'Disapearis Apparatus Generator' and on my word, everyone, shout as loud as possible – one, two, three, Magical-is, Disappear-is, Ethel-is." Agatha began turning the crank at the side of the machine as fast as she could. "Repeat the words!" she cried to the crowd of woodland creatures.

3

"MAGICALIS, DISAPPEARIS, ETHELIS
MAGICALIS, DISAPPEARIS, ETHELIS
MAGICALIS, DISAPPEARIS, ETHELIS."

Suddenly there was a loud bang like a cannon and a huge puff of smoke formed around Agatha's machine. It silenced the crowd. They were not sure if it was part of the show or something they should be worried about. Agatha rushed to the back of the rumbling machine to try and find Ethel. The explosion had flung her into the air and when she landed she had rolled into one of the tunnels of the fort at the back.

"I knew we had used too much gunpowder, Agatha," said Ethel getting to her feet and dusting off her grey fur. Agatha ran back for her applause from the crowd as the smoke cleared.

"Thank you, thank you – I will now attempt to bring her back."

Ethel scampered undetected up the side of the fort to the covered way – a high grassy platform overlooking the festivities. Agatha cranked the machine once more and worked the crowd again. Again there was a bang followed by a huge puff of smoke. Agatha pointed to the covered way where Ethel was standing above the crowd waving. The crowd broke into even more rapturous applause. As they watched, she pointed to the sky behind them. All the creatures turned and the tannoy introduced The Red Sparrows in a magnificent display.

"You can't beat The Red Sparrows," declared Brigadier Brune. "Fantastic squadron, brave men. Good soliders too, you know."

As the crowds settled back to their tables to enjoy the rest of the summer evening, Agatha and Ethel began packing away the machine.

Lady Prideaux-Brune bustled up. "Fantastic show, Agatha. Well done," she said. "Will we be seeing you at the next D.I. meeting? Important issues to discuss and next year's festivities to plan. I want more explosions, more dancing and music. And baking of course, which reminds me I must remember to collect a slice of that scrumptious walnut loaf before I leave. Anyway, must dash – a competition to judge and I have a couple of farthings on the snails today." Lady Prideaux-Brune had always liked a flutter on the snails.

"Oh Agatha! Is that really something we should pursue as entertainment?" asked Mary Camper as she approached with Gertie Nicholson trailing behind her.

"What's wrong with it, Mary?"

"Well, it wouldn't surprise me if a little too much 'baking powder', shall we say, was used. It should be left to the menfolk. It's far too dangerous and it's unbecoming. I for one intend to see to it that such forms of entertainment are never seen in these festivities again. Wouldn't you agree, Gertie?"

"Well, yes absolutely," said Gertie, who always agreed with Mary. "We have so many other things for you to do for the Doe-hen Institute – organising competitions for example." Gertie failed to realise that, as a tom-boy, Agatha was not the sort to be interested in boring bake sales or competitions.

"No thank you, Gertie," said Agatha, "and thank you, Mary, for your concern but please leave me to my mechanics and I will leave you to your baking soda quantities. Speaking of which, you may want to concern yourself with Lady Prideaux-Brune who is at your table stand now, I believe, judging the competition." With that, both Mary and Gertie scuttled off to the other side of the fort.

"They're such busy-bodies, Agatha," said Ethel, as she dismantled the handle of the machine.

"I know. Just ignore them. In fact I think Lady Prideaux-Brune has the right idea. Next year we will make it even more spectacular. They will surely have something to say about it then. I think I could make the explosions bigger without knocking you off your feet. I could rig up some flashing lights, create more smoke and perhaps even have some music playing from the tannoy." Agatha was a gadget and gizmo enthusiast but her enthusiasm did not necessarily mean her inventions always worked. Her intentions were good and she always had numerous unfinished projects on the go. She lived in the cottage next to the Parish Church of Rowner with her father Peter who was the churchkeeper. Peter had always divided his time between keeping the church and teaching his daughter about the world. A good creature of faith, he was educated in the country of Winchester in his youth and injured out of the Great War of 1914 as a young squirrel. He was brought home to Gosport to live a peaceful life, where he furthered his studies while employed as a carpenter, later joining the church as its keeper. He had met and fallen in love with June Ayling, a strong character with gumption and a particularly attractive red tail. They married in 1920 and had Agatha the same year. June worked as a nurse at the War Memorial Veterinary Hospital in Bury but was killed in a motorcar accident in 1925 as she walked across a busy road from the chemist's to catch a bus. Peter never remarried and brought up his daughter by himself.

With the help of Doris Cruikshank, an amiable but timid red squirrel, Agatha and Ethel finished packing up and headed to the marquee where the beer festival was underway. It was always a popular tent.

"Agatha! We can't go in there!" said Doris, surprised at

where she had found herself.

"Come on, Doris," said Agatha, not breaking her stride.

"You know what they say, Doris. If you can't beat them, join them," said Ethel as she followed Agatha into the tent.

Doris reflected on this comment for a moment then glanced over at the food tent entitled 'Strawberry Days Are Here Again' where she saw Mary Camper and Gertie Nicholson trying awfully hard to impress Lady Prideaux-Brune. Indeed she even headed that way for a second until she heard Agatha and Ethel laughing in the beer tent, clinking their glasses together and having so much fun. She covertly changed her direction to join them, hoping to go unnoticed as she did.

"Hey, Doris! Over here, Doris!" shouted Agatha, waving her paw above her head. As Doris approached, Agatha thrust a beer into her paw, clinked it and downed hers in one. With that the big band struck up and Agatha and Ethel began dancing, joining paws, and swirling their tails and each other around. Doris sat down on a table and started swinging her legs to the music and watching her friends as she drank the beer given to her by Agatha. It was something she had never tasted before. She sipped it cautiously at first, holding the glass with both paws, and found herself rather enjoying it.

Time elapsed and soon the early evening sun was beaming the last of its rays into the old Fort. The crowd was still strong. Of course some of the little ones had dispersed, but there was still a whole evening of dancing, big-band music from The Squeakeasies, drinking and singing to come.

"There's nothing like a good old Fort Festival is there, Ethel?" said Agatha, sounding rather out of breath as they had just finished half an hour of non-stop dancing. They approached the table to rejoin Doris, who had surprisingly struck up a conversation with Henry Paget, a rather dapper red squirrel dressed in casual trousers, flannel shirt and braces.

"Indeed," replied Ethel as they both looked at each other in delight at their friend, and giggled. "There's definitely nothing quite like a Fort Festival."

"Mind if we join you, Doris?" asked Agatha as they playfully interrupted Ethel's conversation by sitting down at their table and drinking another beer or two. "How's the cricket, Henry?"

"Not so good, I'm afraid. We lost the last innings. Pipped at the post we were, by the Brazen Badgers. But I have to say, talking to Miss Cruickshank here, I'm thinking of setting up ventures new. Perhaps a little tennis or maybe badminton. What say you, Doris?"

"Oh well, yes. I really don't know. Yes, badminton is nice and of course tennis is too."

Agatha and Ethel exchanged looks again, giggling behind their paws at their friend who had clearly been caught by surprise at the charming advances of one Mr Henry Paget.

Just then, as Agatha was sipping her drink, she glanced through the bottom of her glass and saw Brigadier Brune at another table drinking and laughing. His eyes were shiny from the sauce he had been drinking and he was being as loud as ever, telling stories to all those who would listen and a few who would not. Agatha jumped from her seat with an idea.

"Brigadier! Brigadier!" she called out, as always less than formal. "How's that supply of 'baking soda' looking? Ready for next year?"

The Brigadier cleared his throat before responding. "Well, as you know, I like my cooking but I dare say there will be enough left over for one such as yourself." The Brigadier was an avid collector of army surplus, including gunpowder. "What are you working on at the moment then, Agatha?"

"Oh, the usual. Actually, Jane Priddy has commissioned my services to build a new loading dock." She was conscious that a tone of pride had entered her voice.

"Expecting trade, is she? Interesting. You know, Priddy's is a fine business and Jane is a fine mouse who works very hard. She is an astute businesswoman. I knew her brother. Fought in the Great War. Fine fellow. Tragic business. One could learn a lot from Jane Priddy. She is not an easy pet to know. Her squeak is worse than her bite though. You'll see."

"Agatha!" called Ethel. "You really need to see Doris and Henry – he's teaching her how to dance."

The pair cheered their friend who appeared to have lost her inhibitions along with several glasses of beer: the empties on her table were being collected by a couple of moles. The music was simply too good to say no to, so Agatha and Ethel joined them on the packed dance floor.

Doris called out as she swung past Agatha and Ethel: "there really is nothing like a good old fort festival!" With that, who should walk passed the entrance of the marquee but Mary Camper, closely followed by Gertie. They both stopped for a second to peer inside disapprovingly before strutting off. Agatha, Ethel and Doris fell about laughing and carried on dancing.

Just then, as the crowds were enjoying themselves, a loud and deep humming sound thought to be from another air display could be heard in the distance heading towards Fort Rowner. It was the Pigeon Bombers flying past in formation. Everyone rushed out of the marquees to see the spectacle.

"Wow!" said Doris innocently, "they haven't been seen this far out for years." She smiled toothily.

"They're a bit too far out from Loft Daedalus for my liking," said Agatha astutely.

"What's all this? Let me see here," said Brigadier Brune as he left the tent still holding his beer in one paw, and a cake in the other, with a table napkin tucked into the top of his shirt.

As the crowd watched the rare sight in awe, the Red Sparrows also flew past them. Suddenly a Red Sparrow spun out of control and fell to the ground in the fort, sliding towards the marquees. The crowd was silenced for a moment. Then above them flew over a couple of Starlings from Portsmouth, then some more, and then some Gull Bombers. Suddenly there appeared a great battle in the sky and the crowds ran for cover. It was utter chaos: there were feathers and wounded Sparrows everywhere, a marquee collapsed and Pigeons and animal folk in the fort were trapped and scared. Agatha, Ethel and Doris ran over to the back wall of the fort while Brigadier Brune stood just outside the beer tent looking up into the skies. Seeing a Red Sparrow hurtling towards the old badger, Agatha ran back towards him, grabbed his arm and pulled him to the ground just in time. The Sparrow crashed into the tent, which collapsed with animals still inside. Gosport was under attack.

\*

Portsmouth was a dark grey country and looked like one giant city built entirely of cobbled streets. There were plenty of old taverns, crime, decay and poverty. It was insular and unknown, a place fortified by walls and towers. Secrets were kept locked inside. It was supposedly governed by

Prime Minister Denis Delaney, a well-mannered stoat, but he was simply a puppet for another's story.

The crowds gathered in the Guildhall Square, hundreds of thousands in formation waiting for their Admiral Gizor's commands. The hum of the crowd was silenced when the doors of the great Guildhall were opened and out walked the Admiral in his uniform, proud and strong with grey coat and tail shining gloriously. With outstretched paws he walked towards the podium on the steps to greet his faithful audience.

"Animals of Portsmouth," he began, "I speak to you today as two breeds. Lord Admiral Grey, High Commander of the Fleet of Ratufinee – protector of our land and shores – and as a humble breed of Pedigree, Jean De Gizor. A grey squirrel who has wanted nothing more than to preserve our ways, banish evil from our shores and take back what is rightfully ours. To gather justice by the paws and to fight tooth and tail for it.

"Too long have another kind taken our trade, fished our seas, taught in our schools, stolen our status, left us bereft, and governed our lands without decree. They have taken God's Port – half of heaven's land – and re-named it. They have taken our allies too and polluted their minds with their Red ways. They have paid no regard to those of grey colour and fur. For too long has this poison been allowed."

He nodded to one of his acolytes, who unfurled a banner showing a cartoon of a red squirrel, thin and mangy-looking, with a scowl on its face. Gathered in its dirty paws was a great pile of money, gold, silver and treasures.

"Mark my words," he said, "for I have seen their evil doings. They tempted me from my path but my way has been regained and I am found – fearing nothing in the pursuit of Pure Blood and preservation. And it is this that I swore to safeguard and it is this that I am now reminded to

11

protect when I have been faced with years of utter contempt in the face of reason. My message now is clear, and it is one that I now provide to you – it has been Heaven's Light, Our Guide but it is you who are the light, and I who am your guide." A huge cheer erupted from the crowd.

"Will you follow me in battle? Will you fight with me as I fight for you?"

A second cheer from the crowd erupted: "HAIL GIZOR!"

"Yesterday evening, my final message was delivered to Gosport – that reason should prevail and that we intend to reclaim what is rightfully ours. A response from the Alverstocracy of Gosport is still awaited. Too long have I been patient and reasonable with nothing in return, and therefore again my message is final and clear – there will be no negotiation, no deal of trade or profit. The Reds do not and have never belonged there. We must rebuild our empire and reclaim our land. We will not be content with just half a Harbour. We are a strong nation – one that opposes injustice and one that will free our allies from the poison and dirt that courses through the veins of the Reds, bleaching their fur and tainting their skin red.

"The Reds have taken your jobs, taken your security. Now, Prime Minister Delaney promises to return that security to you, for your children's, children's, children and I – Gizor – will deliver it with every breath I have and every soldier and sailor that will follow me. I swear to you now, I will guide those in dark to the light and take heaven away from those who belong in hell.

"Will you follow me to re-join this Harbour and reclaim Our Pedigree, Our Place, THIS PORTSMOUTH?"

This time, the cheer was deafening.

\*

Gathered in the opulent Crescent of Alverstoke for their monthly meeting were the ladies of the Doe-hen Institute, led by Lady Prideaux-Brune. The committee included Mary Camper, recorder Gertie Nicholson, Molly Siskin – a small dormouse – and Elizabeth Stanley, a hedgehog prickly in both senses of the word. The meeting was always well attended by the pretentious upper echelons of Gosport society and included water voles, red squirrels, moles and wrens. The meeting was opened with the traditional rendition of *God's Port, Our Haven* sung in the somewhat doleful key of A minor, with all standing and accompanied perfectly on the piano by Gertie as always.

"Right-o ladies, after this week's attack we must remain strong and show some spirit and determination," said Lady Prideaux-Brune quite loudly. "We'll show 'em. We won't let the barmy Pompeys get us down."

"Huh-hmm," interrupted Mary Camper with a deliberate cough. She liked to bring her own sense of control and order to proceedings. "That said, and of course said well, Lady Prideaux-Brune …"

"Of course," replied Lady Prideaux-Brune with a wry smile. She was no fool and knew Mary of old. Some believed she only attended the meetings to watch, with quiet delight, Mary biting her own tongue.

"…We must trust that the menfolk will provide a peaceful solution to the troubles. I'm certain that with a few discussions this whole matter can be resolved and there will be no need for panic," declared Mary pompously.

"Quite right!" said Elizabeth Stanley, who was sitting next to Mary at the front of the hall.

"Oh, that's right then is it, Elizabeth?" asked a heckler at the back.

"Who …?" said Mary, straining her neck to see who had made such a challenge, "I can't quite see who …"

"Don't worry, Mary, I'll stand for you all to see." Agatha stood up on her hind legs at the back to declare herself.

"Is there a problem, Agatha?" asked Mary.

"Not in your world there isn't. But in mine there is a very big problem brewing the other side of the harbour."

"Well yes, but as I've already said, I'm sure the Alverstocracy will seek a peaceful remedy and we will be advised of exactly what that is in due course. Until then we must each do our duty and support the effort. Now back to the agenda …"

But Agatha would not be stopped. "What 'effort' exactly are we supporting?" she cried, indignantly. "It's been three days since the attack and nothing has been done. The Alverstocracy hasn't said a word. I shouldn't be surprised if they just roll over and agree to any demands, not that we even know about any. Your husband has a seat on the Ward of Anglesey, Mary – what is being done?"

Agatha's captive audience muttered their agreement, forcing Mary to respond.

"My husband assures me that all avenues are being explored." Mary was clearly flustered and kept looking down at her neatly trimmed claws. "Every effort is being made to …"

"It doesn't sound like you know very much at all, Mary. They're still cleaning out the Fort, for goodness sake. We've lost half our fighters. That was not exactly a declaration of continued peace."

Mary struggled to respond, so did the only thing she knew how to do and that was to carry on regardless.

"On the agenda today we have Mrs Temperton's prize-winning lettuce to discuss," she said, looking across at the brown rabbit.

"Actually, Mary," said Mrs Temperton bravely, "I don't

14

want to talk about my prize-winning vegetables today."

"People want to talk about what happened, Mary," declared Agatha forcefully, but Mary continued undeterred.

"And we have Mrs Appleby's collected poems about the life cycle of the flea to hear, plus our Standing Items, and of course we need to elect a new treasurer with Mrs White sadly standing down at the end of the month. Now, as Mrs Temperton has withdrawn her item from today's agenda, Mrs Appleby – the stage is yours."

Relieved to be passing the meeting over, Mary took her seat nearly as quickly as she had spoken, only to find she had sat somewhat uncomfortably, on her tail. She adjusted it surreptitiously. The ladies of the D.I. were silenced for a moment until the wooden floor of the hall was scuffed gently by the legs of a single chair and up stood Mrs Appleby, a tiny little dormouse.

"Ode to a flea. ..." she began, with blind innocence. Agatha lifted her front paws up in despair and let them fall loudly to her side before walking out in disgust and frustration.

## Chapter 2
# THE RESISTANCE

G osport was governed by the Alverstocracy, which consisted of the elected members of its seventeen Wards and was headed by First Minister Theodore Forton, a solemnly spoken and kind water vole who had entered politics quite without intention. A shipbuilder by trade, he had successfully negotiated commerce between Gosport and its neighbouring Country of Fareham, which in turn had secured the relative free flow of trade between them since 1912.

"I have here," said Theodore Forton in his reedy voice, "a letter from Prime Minister Denis Delaney of Portsmouth, signed by him and counter-signed by Lord Admiral Grey, High Commander of the Fleet of Ratufinee Jean De Gizor, he too of Portsmouth. It is dated yesterday, the twenty-second of May nineteen thirty nine and reads:

> *Dear Sirs,*
> *It will always be the misfortune of others to ignore the greater good, as it has been your misfortune of late. Times of hardship, though, may pass with cooperation fully expected and necessary for deeds to be pardoned. Of course, our more stringent capabilities have not yet been*

*tested. I dare say there will be no end to those who
volunteer to test them. Our reach is far.*

*I am grateful to you, however, for your cooperation
and will of course reward such assistance where evidenced,
with the same riches in keeping with your current existence.
In this regard I have ensured your safekeeping as a gesture
of my thanks and goodwill.*

*In the following days and weeks our advance will
be robust and expedient. Any wavering in your assistance
will not go unpunished. You have my assurance that the
Peoples of Gosport will remain unharmed if they fully
cooperate and contribute to the greater good their services
to Portsmouth.*

*Yours faithfully*

*Prime Minister D Delaney*

First Minister Forton placed his reading glasses on the
lectern in front of him and took a long, slow, deep breath.
He then looked up at his Ward Ministers and said somberly:
"So you see. There are no demands. No deal to be had.
Nothing to be done."

\*

Agatha woke to the gentle burbling of animals outside in the
street. She couldn't quite hear what was being said and was
unconcerned, so turned onto her side to catch a few more
minutes of rest before having to get ready for Sunday
service. It was a glorious warm sunny morning. As she
woke for the second time, she sat up in bed, stretched out
her paws, yawned, swung her legs round and stood up with
her eyes initially still closed. She dressed hurriedly, ran a

brush through her fur, walked downstairs, had a berry cereal and a quick cup of apple juice, and walked to the front door to leave, wearing her Sunday best (Agatha style and therefore scruffy, of course). As she was about to leave, she saw that the morning's post had already arrived. Among the bills and many letters for her father was an unfamiliar-looking envelope that bore the postmark of Portsmouth. Agatha placed the rest of the post on the stand in the hallway while examining the mysterious envelope that was addressed 'to the Red occupier'. As she left the cottage, she opened the letter and began reading:

### *BY COMMAND of PRIME MINISTER DENIS DELANEY*
#### *And*
### *BY ORDER OF ADMIRAL JEAN DE GIZOR, HIGH COMMANDER OF THE FLEET OF RATUFINEE*
#### *Portsmouth*
#### *are hereby granted an*
### *OCCUPATION ORDER*

*BY THE stroke of midday on the Twenty-Fifth of June Nineteen Thirty-Nine all red squirrel occupiers of Gosport are to vacate their dwellings.*

*IT IS ORDERED, the following:*

*\* Vacate your illegal dwelling.*
*\* Take only what you can carry and of that which is valuable to you.*
*\* One suitcase per squirrel is permitted only.*
*\* Travel south to Camp Browndown, Gosport, where you will be met by the Gizor Army.*

18

*Limited transportation will be provided for those impaired or infirm.*

*ALL Red Squirrels are to be temporarily housed by Portsmouth in Camp Browndown by midday on the twenty-fifth day of June. Until this day, there will be a curfew of 6pm to 6am every day.*

**FAILURE TO COMPLY WITH THE TERMS SET OUT IN THIS ORDER WILL BE MET WITH THE PENALTY OF DEATH.**

*Endorsed By First Minister of the Alverstocracy, Theodore Forton of Gosport.*

*Signed: PM D. Delaney 23rd May 1939*

*Signed: Admiral Gizor 23rd May 1939*

With the order in her paw, Agatha swung open the garden gate, which then banged against the picket fence, and ran as fast as she could towards the church where early hymns had already begun. As she did so, she observed notices pinned to trees, lamp-posts and fences. The notices said much the same and were coloured red. Agatha burst into the church just as the Reverend Edward Stapland, a red squirrel wearing a cassock and holding a prayer book, was saying to his congregation: "let us pray." Agatha's entrance was far from quiet and the heavy old ornate oak door to the church slammed behind her, echoing to the rafters. Prayers were not disturbed, however. Animals were weeping quietly and comforting each other and the atmosphere within the church was solemn and troubled.

The gathering was more of an impromptu village meeting than a church service. But comfort was clearly being drawn from the old church whose ancient walls had listened to the prayers of the faithful for so many years. Agatha realised that she was not breaking the news and instead, due to her tardiness, she was late to the outcry. Reverend Stapland took to the lectern to allay fears – his own as well as those of his congregation – as best he could.

"It is in times of ruin that the greatest of strength is borne," he said. "Our Lord Hudsonicus Holozoa in the book of Rodentia teaches us the lessons of humility and tolerance in the face of adversity, a lesson we are to remember always and one that will forever guide our path. The Silver Acorn placed upon our person reminds us of the poisoned bread – the greatest sacrifice of our Lord Hudsonicus Holozoa. And we honour him with all our encounters. Lord we pray to you, this day with Orders upon us we look to you for answers. Lord, provide us with the strength to rally our humility and give unto others your orders just the same. Keep safe those of your Will and Power."

Agatha was still standing at the back re-reading the Occupation Order clutched in her paw. She walked down the aisle and up to her father who was perched on a pew at the front, near to the Reverend.

"Papa, what word from the Alverstocracy?" she whispered.

"Agatha, service!" scalded Peter Mumby, angered by his daughter's intrusion.

"Sorry, papa," she said sheepishly and quickly took her seat.

When the service was over, many stayed behind to seek comfort in continued prayer. As Agatha walked out of the church, her father remaining behind for his duties, she and the remaining congregation observed around thirty Grey Squirrel soldiers marching past the church in formation, along Rowner Lane. As they did so, they trampled over anything in their way, including Doris Cruickshank who was crossing the road to greet Agatha. She was flung back and had to time her exit most carefully to get through the tightly packed rows of marchers.

"Hey!" shouted Agatha angrily to the soldiers, as she helped steady Doris.

"Little pup," said a condescending Gizor Officer who walked over to Agatha and Doris. He towered over them both, his feet and ears looking monstrous. "You are either brave or stupid," he said. The officer waited for a response from Agatha but she said nothing. "Well? Which is it?"

Doris covered Agatha's mouth with her paw and answered for her. "Stupid, sir,' she squeaked.

The officer smirked and glanced around him at the church folk who had begun to line the street as they left the service. He looked down again at Agatha who had still not replied to him and advised: "Be careful, little pup. This world isn't yours anymore." The officer then re-joined his soldiers to direct their march, having lost interest in pursuing anything other than what he had just created – fear and dominance over the two little red doe squirrels before him.

*

The sound of drums and trumpets announced the arrival of Admiral Gizor who was travelling by motorcade to the Guildhall Square accompanied by Prime Minister Delaney. The Portsmouth crowds were twenty-deep in places and lined the streets towards the Guildhall where even more had gathered and where a huge blaze had been set. The blaze was fierce and rose up into the evening sky, blowing its embers west with the wind towards Gosport.

"I don't know what I enjoy more – the fortuitous wind

21

blowing west or the burning of the Red tainted word," remarked Admiral Gizor to Denis Delaney. He turned to the cheering crowds, looking severe and powerful. "More books I say! BURN THEM ALL!" he shouted. "I do hope they wash their hands afterwards," he commented to Delaney, referring to those tossing books into the fire. As Admiral Gizor's path was cleared by his troops, he approached the Guildhall steps and walked up towards his podium to begin his speech to the people. He began:

"My Portsmouth comrades,

"Just as these flames rise higher with each Red book we burn, we become stronger and unpolluted from the stains of others. We burn these books as a sign of riddance. The rid of disease and spell. We are unbound and freed by our own actions. And saved are we, from the evil Reds. Their 'good' Lord Hudsonicus was nothing more than a vermin traveller who outstayed his welcome, pitched his place along the River Alver and claimed to have created heaven's port. The Alvish are simple folk and the Red Squirrel a pest that plagues their growth. They will be well rid of them.

"We have begun our righteous path to pedigree and the re-occupation of Gosport. No threat of extinction of our people will stop the extinction of their actions towards us any longer. Our pure path is set. No sympathiser will learn if they cannot be taught and therefore they too will face the extinction of their tainted words.

"Blessed are the people of Portsmouth of pure grey colour and fur, and wretched is the Red Squirrel riddled with disease and evil. Portsmouth will rise again with every book we burn and every sacrifice we take. We will be victorious in our followed path. Their God will soon abandon Red faith and follow Gizor's Law. Bless all of Portsmouth strength and battle and bless the Gizor spirit of MIGHTY PORTSMOUTH."

A huge cheer erupted as the books continued to burn high into the night sky.

"That ought to do it, don't you think, Delaney?" commented Admiral Gizor, glancing down to his left at his Prime Minister, a weak and small figure in comparison to the burly build of the Admiral, even though this weak and small figure was supposed to be in charge.

As Gizor left the steps of the Guildhall and entered the crowd, a grey pup squirrel with soft fur and big eyes blocked his path. The pup stretched out his paws towards the Admiral, a book held in his claws. Gizor soldiers responded quickly to what they perceived as a threat, but were signalled to stand down by their High Commander. Recognising the pup's enthusiasm and spirit, Gizor took the book and walked towards the fire. He signalled to one of the guards for a cloth to cover his mouth and nose from the smoke and stench of the wretched Red blaze. He glanced at the pup to his right, held the book in the air for the crowd to see, listened to the sweet chant of 'Hail Gizor, Hail Gizor, Hail Gizor' and tossed the book into the burning flames for all to see. He was magnificent in his glory.

*

Agatha had always cycled everywhere and was not about to stop now. Nor would she change her normal routine against the better judgement and advice of those around her. Indeed, she thought nothing of cycling quickly past marching Gizor soldiers daily in the run-up to Occupation Day, and even rang her bicycle bell to signal her intention to do so. At times she even blew them a mocking kiss as she passed by. On those occasions, however, she pedalled past rather faster. And where was Agatha Mumby going every day on her bicycle? To work, of course. No silly Gizor invasion was going to stop her from finishing a good job for Jane Priddy.

As Agatha approached the entrance gates to Priddy's Hard she observed a grey squirrel officer dressed in a long black trenchcoat and black hat and gloves standing at a doorway speaking to Mrs Priddy. She observed a similarly dressed officer directing some Gizor soldiers, pointing at various supplies and equipment. One of the soldiers had a clipboard and appeared to be marking off items as they travelled through the yard. Although Agatha could not hear what was being said at the doorway, the conversation appeared tense. She watched the officer hand Mrs Priddy a note of some kind. A few curt exchanges were heard and at one point Mrs Priddy was forced to stand back when she attempted to stop the Gizor soldiers from loading equipment into their truck. Just as Agatha was about to put her foot back on to the pedal of her bicycle to ride to her aid, she observed Mr Bernard Hardway emerge from the side gate and stride towards the officer who had manhandled his good neighbour.

"I say!" shouted the fieldmouse. "Remove your paws from the good lady Priddy at once. Who do you think you are to lay a print on her arm?" He puffed himself up as much as his small frame would allow.

"It's OK, Mr Hardway," said Jane Priddy, attempting to keep the peace.

"Who I am is not any of your concern or business," snapped the officer, looking down at Bernard Hardway. He turned back to Jane Priddy. "There is an understanding, is there not, 'good lady Priddy'?" said the officer, mocking Mr Hardway's pitiful defence.

"Yes, that's right – an understanding," said Jane, uncharacteristically submissive but astute. Her nose had become more pink than usual, the only sign that she was slightly flustered. She raised her paw in anticipation that she would need to attempt to stop Mr Hardway from advancing.

"Well, I …" began Mr Hardway but was interrupted by the officer.

"You will be wise, Mr Hardway to shut your squeaker." He walked away towards the Gizor truck. As he did so, he observed Agatha at the gates. He turned back to face Mrs Priddy and from a distance said: "I trust your sympathies are with the Pompey Gizor, Mrs Priddy?" Jane did not reply. The officer placed one foot on the Gizor truck and held onto its frame as it was leaving the yard. "The list is to be prepared for collection next week," he added, as the truck passed the two mice, tipping his hat with disdainful respect.

Agatha had no time to put her feet back onto her pedals as the truck sped towards her so instead had to waddle with the bicycle to get out of the way. As she did so, the truck clipped the back wheel and Agatha went flying head over tail onto the ground along with her beloved bicycle. The officers in the truck could be heard laughing at her misfortune. She quickly scrambled to her feet as she watched the Gizor truck go out of sight. Mr Hardway and Mrs Priddy came running to Agatha's aid.

"Who were they, Mrs Priddy? I've not seen officers like that before," said Agatha as she dusted herself off.

"You've seen one, you've seen them all," said Mr Hardway as he picked up Agatha's bicycle. "That's had it, I'm afraid," he added as he examined the twisted back wheel.

"I'll fix it, Mr Hardway," said Agatha proudly. "Who were they, Mrs Priddy?"

"Gizor Collectors – The G.C." Jane Priddy stared at her treasured yard with sadness. The soldiers had left it in a bit of a mess.

"Well I don't care who they are. No one puts a print on

Mrs Priddy, I say," said Mr Hardway, believing he had defended her honour if nothing else.

"Thank you, Mr Hardway," said Mrs Priddy. "I am most grateful."

"Well, I'll send over some of my fieldmice and a couple of voles to sort this mess out. We'll have it ship-shape in no time."

"Thank you for the kind offer, Mr Hardway, but no – I'm fine thank you. I can sort this out myself."

"Nonsense."

"No really, Bernard, I would rather," pleaded Mrs Priddy.

"Well, right you are. If you're sure?" He always softened when she mentioned his first name.

"Quite sure. Thank you." Jane knew how to handle her neighbour.

With that he left the yard, offering of course his services whenever required. He always had a soft spot for Jane Priddy of Priddy's Hard.

"I think I have a spare bicycle wheel somewhere in the yard you can have, Agatha, if you wish to hunt around for it?" she said.

"Yes, thank you, Mrs Priddy. I'll keep my eyes out for it while I'm working on the dock," said Agatha.

"Good, good. Right then." said Mrs Priddy as she walked off into the yard to properly survey the damage. She wasn't one to engage in idle chit-chat.

Agatha travelled through the yard to the edge of Forton Creek, reviewing her work on the dock. She looked out over to Portsmouth in the far distance and observed the billowing smoke and smog above its walls. The creek that travelled west behind St Vincent Barracks had a limited entrance to shipping due to Burrow Island, known locally as Rats Island, located in the centre of its mouth. The small tidal island, used as a burial ground for convicts from afar, was a no-man's-land for the peoples of Gosport – unused for decades, it was now home to a rabble of rogue and ne'er-do-well rats. Agatha continued her work on the dock occasionally hearing Mrs Priddy squeaking her orders at her employees. She was an astute businesswoman, focused and firm – a widow who had decided to continue her late husband's metal merchant business with much success. She had found that she had a nose for managing manufacture and trade. She lived alone on the huge yard that formed the estate and employed some eight hundred workers.

\*

As Agatha travelled back to Rowner cottage after a hard day's work at the dock and having fixed her bicycle, she saw two Gizor Fighter Starlings fly overhead, appearing to practise manoeuvres. They were both travelling too fast and there appeared to be little communication between them, which ultimately resulted in them crashing into each other, both spiralling out of control. Agatha saw them in the distance as they hurtled towards the ground, landing behind a line of trees. She pedalled as fast as she could across the green where local cricket was played to the crash site, where a small crowd had gathered opposite Rowner Church and cottage. As Agatha approached, it was clear that the fighter birds were dead. It was also clear from the smell of them that they had both been drinking large quantities of alcohol.

"Instead of standing there, Agatha, help us carry them to the church," said Peter Mumby to his daughter.

"Papa?" replied Agatha.

He ignored her protest. "Grab one end. Come on. You there!" he said, pointing to a strapping young vole in the crowd. "Grab the other."

"Papa, I don't understand," said Agatha.

"There is nothing to understand. We are going to bury them. Hurry."

Overhearing Peter's answer, the vole stopped immediately and dropped the wing he was holding. "I'm not helping to bury a Pompey in a Holozoa church," he said and walked off, leaving Peter and Agatha to carry the bird the remaining distance to the churchyard themselves as well as having to go back for the other starling.

At the back of the churchyard, the Reverend Edward Stapland was overseeing a couple of church moles dig two graves for the fallen birds and had his prayer book open ready to commence a short service for them.

"For reasons of your Will, my Lord, these Gizor Fighters have found themselves grounded upon your land, and with your power we will protect them in death and forgive all sins. Bless them, Our Lord Hudsonicus Holozoa, and bless the land they lie in." One of the church moles then placed a wooden cross to mark each grave carved with the words "The Red Fallen Blessed" and dated a whole month prior to their actual deaths. Just as the last of the earth was being moved, making a mound on top of the burial plot, the small group was silenced when a couple of Gizor soldiers walked past the church in the distance, unaware of the hasty funeral taking place for their comrades only yards away from them.

Following the short ceremony, Peter approached his daughter who was standing over the burial plot. He placed a paw upon her shoulder and said: "Humility, Agatha. Humility will protect us all."

\*

With the weakening of Gosport's air defences following the Battle of Fort Festival, Loft Daedalus airfield – home of the Red Air Force – was vulnerable to capture. It was easily taken without a fight by the Gizor Army. As the airfield was overtaken, the G.C. gave instructions for all Gosport service personnel to gather for parade.

"I say, old chap, the wings of those have seen better days," commented a Pigeon Bomber to his comrade, referring to the Gull Bombers from Portsmouth who had just arrived at the airfield. "His landing was atrocious – all over the place, it was."

The Gull Bombers were equally critical of their would-be counterparts.

"Look at their pathetic wingspan. No wonder we flew rings around 'em," said one.

"Yeah, but look at their facilities, Mandible – they got it good 'ere," replied Herman.

"A big loft space and somewhere to stretch your wings don't make the garlic juice any different," said Mandible, a tough-as-nails bulked-up seagull full of grit and salt.

"What's that?" called a scrawny Gull Bomber landing awkwardly near to his more experienced colleagues and running up to join them. "I like garlic juice."

"You would, Beaky, you pigeon fancier," responded Mandible unpleasantly, laughing at the youngster before him.

"'Ere they are, the Arrows," mocked Herman, referring to The Red Sparrows who had just entered the parade line.

"Don't know their left wing from their right," said Mandible offensively.

"Ey up!" warned Herman, nudging his friends as Flight Lieutenant Laraday arrived.

Lt Laraday, a nasty looking crow, held himself in such a way that always commanded attention and bestowed him power. He approached the parade of Alvish flock assembled to be inspected.

"In all my years of seafaring flight I have never seen such a Trafalgar rabble of inbred useless Bombers and Fighters," he said, walking up and down the parade line with his wings crossed behind him. "The Red country has provided Gosport with no means of suitable defence – none that I see before me in any event. You will, of course, be aware of the Gizor Occupation Order of Gosport and the Alverstocracy endorsement of that order. To that end, the Red Air Force now belongs to Portsmouth and you will be controlled by the Gizor Air Force commanders and used accordingly to serve your new country." The parade line shuffled slightly with the news. "You will obey the G.A.F at all times, take your orders only from them, and serve the animals of Portsmouth. HAIL GIZOR!"

The parade of Alvish birds were then directed to line up outside the north blister hangar for identification rings to be fitted to their legs. The hangars were huge structures and dwarfed the R.A.F. personnel.

"Name?" asked a Gizor officer to each Pigeon Bomber, Red Sparrow and air personnel at the recording station inside the hangar where they were organising the identification process of the flock.

"Look at them thinking they're all that and a bag of crumbs," observed Herman from a distance.

The airfield had never been busier with pigeons, sparrows, gulls and starlings, Gizor crows and magpies. Fieldmice were rallying, others were ordering, the Portsmouth flag had been raised and Loft Daedalus was now, without a doubt, Gizor territory.

*

Everyone in Gosport knew that Occupation Day was fast approaching. Old friends would have to part and families would have to abandon their beloved homes and businesses. The red squirrels would be stripped of their rights. Of course, there were some animals in Gosport that had, without order or prompting, risen to defend their country in the absence of the Alverstocracy doing so, and small pockets of resistance were in place hidden in and around Gosport. Unfortunately, their few successes were no match for the organised mass onslaught and awesome firepower of the Portsmouth Gizor. They continued just the same and vowed never to give in or surrender. The Alvish heart was strong and spirited. As the days and nights passed closer towards Occupation Day, the summer sun continued to shine on Gosport and its leafy paths, its brightness at odds with the ominous feeling.

Agatha was cycling as quickly as she could from Priddy's Hard to home, having lost track of the time – she was in danger of breaking the Gizor curfew. As she cycled down Avery Lane and onto Station Road, she knew her time was up and quickly had to duck for cover beside the railway line to avoid the passing Gizor patrol. She hid in the brambles on the edge of the path. She was halfway home. As she looked up from her hiding place and a foot patrol passed her position, she saw some Gizor Magpies searching the skies and the ground below them. Agatha had no option but to stay where she was for a while.

When the time was right, she thought it best to leave her bicycle in the undergrowth and travel by foot and claw. She knew to keep away from the roadside and therefore climbed discreetly over the fence of Brockhurst Allotments and hid between the carrots and turnips. As she travelled through, trying her best to avoid trampling on the home-grown produce, the light was beginning to fade. As it did, she could make out the shadow of a rabbit across the way in the distance. She watched it as it hopped past the cabbages and carrots towards a shed. The rabbit stopped and looked around to see if anyone was watching before it knocked on the door. Agatha observed that it wasn't the knock you'd usually use if visiting someone – perhaps it was a signal? The shed itself appeared to be in darkness but the door soon opened and light spilled out on to the ground of the allotment and shone in Agatha's eyes. She ducked for cover. The rabbit quickly disappeared inside, and the shed was once again in darkness. Agatha looked around to see if it was safe to move and started to slowly and carefully approach the shed. As she reached it, she stood flat with her back against its wall, hoping she would not be seen by the Gizor Magpie flying overhead. She stretched out her paw, hovered her fist over the door and knocked quietly, using the same signal as the rabbit had just done. As she waited for an answer she saw the Gizor patrol heading closer to her position. She closed her eyes in the hope that the situation she found herself in was going to get better somehow by doing so. As the seconds passed, she closed her eyes tighter and tighter until suddenly the door opened, and Agatha was pulled into the shed. The door closed behind her in a flash.

"Who are you?" said a voice in the dark. Agatha had not yet opened her eyes. "Who are you?" repeated the voice, holding on to the scruff of her overalls. As Agatha began to open her eyes, she found the light was pointed directly at her and as a result had to squint to see. All she could make out was the small silhouette of a mole and standing beside him, the rabbit she had just followed. "How did you get here? Who brought you here? Who are you with?" There were too many questions fired at Agatha all at once for her to answer straight away.

"I'm Agatha. I was hiding from the Gizor and saw you

enter this shed," she said, pointing at the rabbit.

"Oh, Flop Head, how many times has the boss said – always check before you knock?" said the mole to the rabbit.

"But Berry, I did. I did check, I tell you," said the rabbit.

Berry released Agatha from his grip and moved the light away from her eyes to reveal an ordinary-looking shed with various gardening tools scattered around and a smell of fence paint, creosote and topsoil. The rabbit was revealed as being white and a bit dopey-looking. The mole was just a mole, but he did seem to have a grumpy expression.

"Suppose you better meet the others," said the mole.

"Others?"

Berry walked over to the back of the shed, opened what appeared to be an old kitchen unit, jumped in and disappeared down a small hole closely followed by the rabbit. Agatha hesitated for a second, peered into the cupboard and down the hole and heard an echoing voice call up to her: "turn the light off before you come down, will you?" She saw that the darkened hole that they had both jumped into had a ladder attached to it, which she carefully began to climb down. Climbing was not one of Agatha's talents.

She had heard of the Resistance Movement but had never seen any groups or knew anyone involved with them. She knew what she had stumbled upon and knew that she was climbing down to a company of kin – brave and strong. They would be battle-scarred and worn but determined, plotting further missions. She desperately wanted to be part of it. She reached the bottom of the hole and saw that she had to scramble through a low tunnel from where a faint but warm light was emanating. At one stage the tunnel was so low and tight that she had to crawl through it on her paws and knees. She didn't mind. She was excited at the thought of being part of something that could make a difference. What she found, however, was not what she had anticipated.

As she approached a bend in the tunnel she found herself able to stand slightly and as she did so she could hear the mumblings of animals in the near distance, their voices incoherent until she got closer.

"We head north," said an echoing voice.

"No, I say we head south to the Camp," said another.

"What good are we in the south when we need to let Fareham know in the north?" responded another.

Agatha reached the end of the tunnel and saw Flop Head and Berry waiting for her ahead. The tunnel had opened into a bricked cavern lit by old brass lanterns attached to its walls.

"What was your name again?" queried Berry.

"Agatha."

"OK then, Agatha, up you go," said Berry as he directed her up some narrow-stoned stairs with Flop Head excitedly hopping closely behind.

Agatha climbed the steps, which opened into what she worked out to be the right caponier of Fort Rowner – a covered passage that led across the moat of the fort. The crowd of some thirty to forty animals before her were debating and chatting in groups, looking at maps and writing up plans on the damp stone walls. There was rubble and old broken bits of furniture scattered about the place. She found herself standing in the middle of the caponier, which was large and had many candlelit rooms situated to its sides and a darkened tunnel ahead, which appeared closed off. Above her was a stone spiral staircase leading to a balcony overlooking the main floor. As she looked at her surroundings, Agatha did not notice the small squirrel coming towards her.

"What's your name and where do you come from, dear?" asked Rosie, a sweet, motherly-looking red squirrel who had taken it upon herself to feed and warm those who worked, plotted and sought shelter with the Resistance.

"I'm Agatha. I live in the Parish of Rowner."

"Come on in and sit yourself down, lovey. Would you like a custard cream, dear?" asked Rosie, directing Agatha to a tatty old comfy chair.

"Leave her be, Rosie. Stop fussing," said Berry.

"Berry? Berry?" said Flop Head excitedly. "Shall we tell her, shall we tell her?"

"I wish you wouldn't repeat yourself all the time, Floppy," replied Berry, looking irritated.

"Yeah but shall we tell her? Shall we tell her?" said Floppy, ignoring the advice.

Berry looked down at Agatha and then whispered to Floppy: "The boss ain't back yet. Might not be best pleased. Better wait and see."

"Here's your tea, dearie," said Rosie to Agatha, "and I've given you an extra biscuit. Just for you."

"Thank you." Agatha reached up her paw for the tea cup while trying to hear what Berry was whispering. She noted that Berry addressed Flop Head as 'Floppy', so perhaps they were close friends.

As Agatha continued looking around quietly while sipping her tea, she heard a commotion coming from the tunnel she had just travelled through. There was the sound of running paws coming towards the caponier, a sound that alarmed her at first, thinking it might be Gizor soldiers. Others around her, however, did not appear startled so Agatha stayed small in her comfy chair preparing herself just in case she was right to be alarmed. She watched as the crowd turned their heads towards the stone steps at the back. Suddenly a small and slightly dishevelled group of red

35

squirrels, together with a couple of mice and robins, burst through the gap in the floor up into the caponier. The group looked worn out and bedraggled but exhilarated and jubilant. As they were welcomed home, and Rosie began providing fresh towels, first aid and of course pouring more tea, one onlooker asked: "So how did it go? Tell us!"

"How did it go? How did it go, he asks?" said the excited voice of a red doe squirrel to the crowd and her motley crew. Agatha stood up from her chair but couldn't quite see through the crowd. "Well I'll tell you how it went! We took 'em by surprise. We made 'em squirm like worms. We were stealthy like wagtails. Weren't we, crew?"

"Yeah!" said the crew.

"We told 'em we were coming for 'em and we came. We looked 'em straight in the eyes and put fear in their cold hearts." said the doe squirrel with passion. As she recounted her story she scampered up the spiral staircase and spoke with gusto. "We gave 'em what for. They were shaking their tails. And we told them we'd be coming back for more. They ran away like sheep." Agatha could see her clearly now. She was wearing a red bandana, an old Gosport Army jacket that was torn and battered, and had war paint on her face. "This is God's Port and Our Haven will never be Portsmouth's." A cheer went up from the crowd. "From the Alver Valley to the Gosport Gardens, from the Crescent to the Peel Common, from Priddy's to Elson, Our Haven belongs to Our Alvish – OUR GOSPORT."

Agatha saw Floppy beside her hopping with excitement and cheering his leader. Agatha grabbed his arm and asked with wonder: "Who is that?"

"That's Hertha Marks. Hertha Marks, that is," he said as they both watched the leader shaking paws with her comrades, who were congratulating each other and retelling their stories to the crowd.

As Hertha walked down the stairs to get some much-needed tea and biscuits from Rosie, she noticed Agatha at the back of the room.

"Who are you?" she called out, her voice echoing against the stone walls. The room went silent.

"Ah, well that's what I wanted to talk to you about, H," said Berry, slightly nervously.

"Please tell me she's been initiated," said Hertha, walking towards Agatha.

"Er, well no, not in the … er initiation sense of … er … well no. She hasn't."

"But look Hertha, look Hertha," said Floppy, pointing at Agatha. "She's a Red."

"Yes, thank you, Flop Head," replied Hertha, stroking him on the head affectionately as he hopped to her side. She reached Agatha. "So, what do they call you?"

"Agatha."

"Well Agatha, you've seen our operation here and you've seen how we work. But how do we know we can trust that you won't blab under interrogation?"

"Because I want to join you," said Agatha proudly, thinking that such a declaration would bring instant membership to a Company of Resistance. The group laughed at her.

"No, no," said Hertha, smiling at her band of followers. "Let's give her a chance. Let's see what she can bring to the table, shall we?"

Agatha thought to herself for a second before saying: "I have information."

"Don't we all?" mocked Hertha. She was full of passion for the cause and always fighting for justice, but could never resist playing to her audience.

"Two Starling fighters are missing. The Gizor are looking for them," said Agatha.

"So?" said Hertha, pretending to be uninterested.

"I know where they are," declared Agatha.

"Where?"

"Dead. I helped bury them two nights ago."

"Oh dearie me, my love," remarked Rosie, dunking a custard cream biscuit into her tea with a delicate paw.

"And?" asked Hertha, wanting more information.

"And …" added Agatha, "I know that The G.C. are interested in Priddy's Hard and will be collecting in a couple of days."

Hertha stared at the squirrel before her as the crowd waited for her approval or condemnation. She walked round Agatha sizing her up, before eventually breaking her silence and saying: "You'll need a jacket."

## Chapter 3
# THE STEEL OF PRIDDY'S

Agatha burst into the printing press room to find her friend Ethel hard at work producing the *Gosport Crier*. The heavy machinery with its cranks, pedals, dials, ink, and moving parts was very noisy and drowned out the sound of Agatha rushing in.

"Ethel!" shouted Agatha to her friend who at first could not hear her. "Ethel!"

The sound of the machine slowed as Ethel removed her foot from one of the pedals. "Can't you see I'm working, Agatha?"

"Here's the mock-up for you to have a look at," said Agatha, holding out a piece of paper.

Ethel took the notice from Agatha's paws and reviewed its content. "Agatha, I can't print this. I told you, I can't help. I'm sorry."

"But it's for the effort."

"If I print this, what do you think is going to happen? I'll tell you, the Gizor will shut this place down. Then there'll be no notices. No news. Nothing." Ethel looked at her friend's disappointed face. "I can't. You know I can't. I'm sorry."

"This is news, Ethel."

"No organised march in the High Street is going to stop this sorry situation from playing out."

"It sounds to me like you don't even care," said Agatha, angrily.

"That's not fair, Agatha. You and I both know that notices like this will only inflame the situation further."

Agatha looked at her friend in utter astonishment as if she had just learnt that she didn't know her at all. "Yeah, well maybe it's easier for you to stay out of the shadows when your fur ain't red," she said.

Ethel ignored the response and carried on with her work, with the printing press starting to whirr up again.

*

"Come on, Floppy, we'll be late!" called Agatha to her new friend as they ran towards St Mary's Church in Gosport High Street. They were carrying long branches for their placards and red bandanas to give out to the crowds. They ran down the side of the church and into a community hall at the back where the Resistance Movement were waiting. The march had already begun down the High Street with hundreds of locals – squirrels, voles, stoats, badgers, mice, rabbits and hedgehogs – forming a united front in support of the Red Squirrel. While Gizor troops were present – watching, laughing, and permitting the fruitless charade to take place along the street – the Resistance had grander ideas and had plotted a rally that would go down in history.

"You're late, Agatha. Come on!" said Hertha as she hurried them into the hall to prepare. "Where are the flyers?"

"I couldn't get them."

"OK, we'll do without. Have you got the flea darts?"

"Check," said Agatha, tapping the breast pocket of her jacket.

"Right, are we ready? Remember, people – maximum impact. Join in and spread out. Meet you back at the shed. Good luck."

As the march approached, on its way to Walpole Park, the group scattered into the procession. The Gizor were also scattered along the route and – as predicted – were failing to take the peaceful message seriously. Instead they simply mocked the parade as it passed.

"Look at the poor pathetic creatures. YOU BELONG IN THE WOODLANDS!" called out one Gizor Officer trying to impress his men, who were laughing. Another took to sticking his foot out to trip up unsuspecting protestors as they passed. Others threw peanut shells and crumbs. As the protestors reached Walpole Park, the Gizor army deliberately amplified their national anthem through the tannoy to drown out the demonstrators.

Agatha and members of the Resistance had other plans and knew their first move had to be to take out the tannoy. They all reached their designated positions in the park and all tried to keep low and inconspicuous – flea darts at the ready. It was on Hertha's signal that they blew the darts towards their intended targets, knocking out unsuspecting Gizor soldiers who had surrounded the park. This gave Hertha a chance to stop the music abruptly and call out: "GODS PORT, THE ALVER HAVEN – KEEP THE GIZOR OUT! KEEP THE GIZOR OUT!" Gizor soldiers were soon running towards her position. As they did so, Hertha hoisted the Gosport flag so it was positioned at the top of the tannoy pole. The flag flew gloriously in the breeze like the sail of the ship it featured. The chants continued from the crowd as Hertha slid down the pole: "GOSPORT! GOSPORT! GOSPORT!" She scampered into the crowd for cover as the soldiers ran towards her. The others scattered on her command and the crowd quickly

41

dispersed, as the parade had become the firing ground for the Gizor Army in search of Hertha and her crew.

*

Admiral Jean De Gizor stood alone in the Semaphore Tower in Portsmouth Dockyard overlooking the harbour, with his arms crossed behind him, staring over towards Gosport. He noticed Prime Minister Delaney enter the room but did not react and stayed fixed at the window.

"Tell me, Denis," he said. "Would a king train his servants? Or a craftsman, make his tools?" Gizor glanced at Denis Delaney to his left. He did not wait for a response and Denis knew he would not want one. He breathed in deeply, turned back towards the window, and continued his reflection. "I hear the Gosport air is suburban. I also hear – and perhaps you can confirm this, Prime Minister – that the air has mixed with foul. I hear, for example, that despite the first two thousand soldiers sent for Founder's Phase, they have not quashed the resistance but just stood by and watched it happen?"

"I believe the trouble, Jean, is that they ..." Delaney began, weakly.

"The trouble, Denis, is sheer incompetence," replied Gizor raising his voice and twitching his tail in annoyance. "I will not be made a fool. There will be no 'Resistance' that challenges our core. And such resistance will be extinguished immediately. Have my expectations not been clear? Bring me those responsible."

"Sir?"

"Bring me those responsible, so that I may teach the strength of Gizor Law and test their resolve against mine."

"But sir ..."

"Damn it, Denis!" shouted Gizor. "Bring me the

officers in charge of the chaos in Walpole."

As Delaney left the tower and approached the main gates with pace and purpose, wearing his black suit and bowler hat, with umbrella in paw as always – even on the hottest of days – he observed G.C. officers entering the dockyard in convoy. The busy dockyard was full of soldiers, sailors and air force crew preparing arms and manoeuvres for battle and occupation. Delaney scurried out of the gates onto the bustling grey cobbled streets of Portsmouth. He was immediately approached by the fishermen – mostly stoats and voles – selling their fresh catches of the day from the small boats shored up just outside the main gates. Delaney's stomach rumbled: the smell of the fish was tempting, but he walked on. Next he was approached by peasant folk and fowl, beggars and traders, including Pompey Lil' the notorious seller of lucky heather. She was a haggard old grey squirrel with barely any teeth and a pointy chin that curled into her lower jaw. She was dressed in an old moth-eaten fancy faded frock. Delaney politely ignored her sales-pitch and walked with purpose to his waiting escort – he had orders to observe.

From the Semaphore Tower, having watched Delaney leave, Gizor turned to the south east and looked down at his men scurrying about the dockyard, busying themselves attempting to satisfy their great leader. His gaze rose a little and he looked out over Portsmouth, observing the slums, the cobbled streets, the grey rooftops and smoky land all contained within his proud stone walls. He then turned back towards the west to look out towards leafy Gosport and allowed a slight wry smile to reflect in the window. Gosport would be his. It was inevitable.

*

Flying on the back of a Portsmouth Crow, Delaney was able to truly see for the first time all the territory they were invading. As they approached Loft Daedalus he could see the airfield bustling with activity but as they landed, Delaney also observed servicemen looking far too relaxed, smoking on the side of the runway and evidence of drinking and gambling to the sides of the blister hangars.

"Prime Minister sir," greeted Flight Lieutenant Laraday, rushing over with a salute. The impromptu visit had sent the air and ground crew scrambling about behind him trying to re-establish some order.

"Any news, Lieutenant?" asked Delaney in his calm and reserved manner.

"No, sir. The locals appear rather tight-lipped."

"Hmm. Well, keep looking. Someone must know something. They can't just disappear."

"Yes, sir, of course. We do have one or two leads – one being a little parish in Rowner."

"Can't say I approve of this," commented Delaney as they walked past clear evidence of an abandoned game of poker.

"No, sir. Just a way to relax I suppose, sir."

"I wonder what our Lord Admiral's views on that would be," said Delaney, leaning on the wrath of Gizor for effect. "How have the Gosport Army settled?"

"The Gizor Law has settled them well, sir, as expected."

"I see," said Delaney as he observed the wings of Gosport birds being clipped in the distance. He was slightly shocked by what he was seeing – a barbaric act – but maintained pretence. He cleared his throat before informing Laraday as to the reasons for his visit. "Yes … well … the reason I have flown in today is to talk about the Walpole chaos."

"Yes, rather an embarrassment by all accounts, sir," replied Laraday.

"Yes, and one not gone unnoticed by the Lord Admiral."

As the two discussed their instructions, the ground crew and service birds were busying themselves in the airfield. The Gosport Army was being segregated within one area of the field and put to work in others. Para-mice were practising base jumps, the Gull Bombers were practising their take offs and landings and the Starling Fighters were sprucing up their feathers and wings, helped of course by some reluctant wrens and robins.

*

Agatha rode her bicycle as fast as she could towards Priddy's Hard in support of Jane Priddy who was at the gates of the yard making a symbolic gesture by locking them securely and standing fast, with her fieldmice, voles and squirrels behind her. Agatha dropped her bicycle outside and scrambled over the gates to join them. The G.C. were on their way. Jane and her workforce stood in total silence, united by their pride in Priddy's – a yard that had secured employment for hundreds of workers for many long and glorious years. They pricked up their ears as they heard the sound of trucks and marching soldiers. As the trucks appeared in the distance, Jane took a step back to join her line of workers and joined arms as if to rally defiance, however fruitless.

On arrival, a G.C. officer walked up to the locked gates. He had a thin face and mean little eyes.

"By Order of Admiral Gizor, High Commander of the Fleet of Ratufinee, protector of Portsmouth to whom this land now belongs, I hereby declare this yard and its trade to be in our keeping. HAIL GIZOR!" he said. This was met with steadfast silence from Jane and her workers. The officer twitched his whiskers in annoyance. "Anyone who disagrees with said Order will be shot," he said. "I suggest, therefore, that you open the gates."

The silence was palpable and there was not a single shuffle in the crowd. Met with such defiance, the officer signalled to his men to smash open the entrance to Priddy's. Agatha, who was standing at the front in line with Jane, could feel the arms of those beside her tense. As the truck rammed through the gates, the crowd – still arm-in-arm – were forced to swing to the side. As the grand entrance gate fell to the ground and the remaining trucks and infantry squirrels clambered over it to enter the yard, the G.C. officer approached Jane.

"What is a little fieldmouse doing with such a big yard, I wonder?" he said. "And all these workers? I do not understand you, little mouse. What do they owe you that they repay you with their lives?" He strutted up and down the front line of workers and back towards Jane, "No, no, little one. An order is an order." With that he reached for his side pistol and shot a fieldmouse dead from the line. The sound of the gunshot rang out across the harbour.

As the Gizor army marched on through the yard, Jane and her workers still stood in line. A few whimpers could be heard for their fallen brother and their fear caused a nervous shuffling.

"Now it appears I have lost a worker because of your silliness, little Captain," said the officer. "Do you have the list?" Jane passed him a clipboard and he flipped through the pages attached to it. "Ah, yes. You will keep your jobs and your lives if you simply follow the rules." He stepped back to address the Priddy's folk. "You will all be serving Portsmouth with your skills here at Priddy's. You shall work for Gizor and construct the plans to the letter. Do you understand?"

Jane stepped forward. "My workforce is strong and dedicated ..." she said, "... and at Gizor's mercy."

"Good," replied the officer. "Now show me the collection of metal works." Jane walked the officer into the yard while Gizor soldiers shoved the workers backwards towards a work hall to organise them.

*

Days passed and the workers at Priddy's were producing huge steel frames and girders as ordered by the Gizor army. Each section of each frame was carefully moulded, placed on loading trucks and driven away. They worked long hours for little rest. They were permitted to go home each night but had to arrive early each morning to repeat the day. Rest was punished and quality was inspected vigorously. Pushed to the brink of exhaustion, they still carried on. Jane was permitted to care for her workers by providing them with water every couple of hours as a relief from the heat of the furnaces and the sun.

On one particular day a Gizor jeep delivered an unexpected visitor – Prime Minister Delaney. A Gizor officer greeted him with a salute as he stepped out of the jeep with his bowler hat and umbrella in tow. He had brought with him two officers under court-martial. The officers were taken through the yard by Gizor personnel while Prime Minister Delaney was given a conducted tour.

Agatha, being Agatha, couldn't resist moving closer to the Prime Minister to eavesdrop.

"Ah, I see the constructions are going well," said Delaney to his tour guide.

"Yes, sir. On target and on time, sir."

47

"Good, good. Where are the boats then?" asked Delaney, looking around.

"This way, sir," said the guide, directing his guest towards the back of the yard.

At this moment Agatha smiled knowingly, glanced up towards the bell tower situated on the work hall, and signalled to Floppy who had climbed up behind it. He hopped up and down with excitement and began ringing the bell ferociously. With that, Hertha and her resistance fighters charged through the gates with pellet guns and swords. The Gizor Army were taken by surprise but fought back, outnumbering the Resistance. Prime Minister Delaney and the two court-martialled officers were bundled onto the jetty and into a boat that quickly rowed off down Forton Creek and into the Harbour. Agatha and Hertha reached the jetty too late to stop them and could only watch the Prime Minister float away while a battle raged on behind them.

\*

Portsmouth Harbour was choppy and the boat very small, leaving Prime Minister Delaney to reflect that perhaps a flight on the back of a Crow would have been better in hindsight. As he approached Portsmouth dockyard, he held tightly onto his bowler hat. Navy service squirrels were there to pull the boat into dry dock and escort the two court-martialled officers away.

"Admiral Gizor?" asked Delaney to a guard who helped him off the boat.

"Parade, sir," replied the guard.

Delaney walked to the parade ground where Admiral Gizor was about to address his Army.

"Founder's Phase is almost complete," said Gizor. "Our successes will depend on the will of our forces to unite and fight against oppression and injustice. The Gizor directive is clear and robust. This mighty army before me of solid steel will defeat the brittle oak of Gosport and purge it of its rot." The admiral paused and observed the small figure of Delaney take his seat behind him. Gizor paced up and down for a moment before returning to the lectern. "But there is rot within these very walls," he declared. "Rot that can infest a weak mind. There is no room for weakness in my army and my resolve is strong, very strong and my rules clear." Gizor signalled to the guards who brought out the two court-martialled officers who had been in charge of the Walpole chaos.

"You see here before you the rot in this army," he said, waving his paw at the two, who had their arms tied behind them and their heads held down in shame. "But no more shall there be any occasion for weakness. Steel does not rot." He walked over to the officers. "Am I not a fair leader? Do I not present you with orders to follow – instructions to help you in your role? Have I not provided you with prospects and silver in your pockets?" The two officers nodded but did not raise their eyes to him. "Then why – I would like to know – do you defy me?" Admiral Gizor turned to face his audience. "These officers were placed in charge of overseeing a fruitless parade of Red supporters. Yet they allowed an infraction of this march to convey the message of resistance." He swung round to confront them again. "How do you plead?"

"Sir?" The two officers did not want to admit their guilt and feared their punishment.

Gizor moved closer to the face of the officer on the left. "Is this man opposite you a guilty one?" he asked. There was silence from the parade in anticipation of the officer's answer.

"Yes, sir," replied the panic-stricken officer.

Gizor signalled to a guard for a pistol and told him to untie the prisoner. He offered the gun to the court-martialled officer.

"Shoot him."

"Sir?"

"Shoot or I will hand the pistol to him."

The officer trembled as he took the gun from Admiral Gizor. It visibly shook in his paw as he raised it towards his comrade who was standing opposite, only five feet away. He closed his eyes for a moment, put his claw on the trigger, and without a word of apology to his comrade shot him between the eyes.

"Some steel left in you yet, I see," said Gizor, sniggering. He took the gun and pointed it directly at the officer's head. "But alas not enough," he said and shot him at point-blank range. Gizor turned to face his parade. "Nothing less than solid steel will be accepted in my army."

*

Only the dark rainy night observed Gizor, shrouded in a cloak, approaching the gates of Kingston Prison. The doors immediately opened for him. It was one of his weekly visits, always shrouded in secrecy. He travelled there alone to be counselled by a rather unorthodox prisoner known as Lillian Francis. His visits were never documented in any official records kept by the prison and he signed the visitor's book simply 'Jean'. He was escorted by a mole through the cobbled corridors towards a bolted oak door. The guard unlocked the door, revealing a spiral staircase leading down to the prison cellar. It was the darkest of places – damp and cold. The walls glistened with only the candlelight that lit their path. He travelled along the corridor where the guard unlocked a poky old cell and then left Gizor with the prisoner.

Gizor stood still for a moment looking at the back of an old squirrel with long red fur who was sitting in a chair at her writing desk with only the dim glow of candlelight to see by. She was scrawling her many musings on to paper and mumbling to herself. Many years of imprisonment for witchcraft had sent the old woman crazier than what she had been accused of when she had her freedom.

"I seek your counsel tonight," said Gizor in an unusually respectful tone. He had himself imprisoned Lillian for witchcraft many years before and would never openly admit to fearing her words.

"The chestnuts?" requested Lillian, still with her back to him, absorbed in her writing.

Gizor walked over to a dusty shelf to reach an old jar and pass it to Lillian. She did not respond, so he began impatiently to untwist the lid. Lillian's chair was flung backwards as she stood suddenly, which startled Gizor and stopped him in his tracks. He handed the unopened jar to Lillian who turned to face him with disapproval. He lowered his head in shame and regret.

"Hold out your paw!" Gizor did as he was told and reached out his arm towards her. Lillian emptied the contents of the jar into his paw, scattering the small fragments of chestnuts. She examined how the contents had positioned themselves and the patterns they had formed. She looked down at his paw then suddenly up to his face and placed her paw on the top of his head. She peered into his eyes intensely then closed hers for a few seconds. She began chanting, removed her paw from his head and started swaying and twirling around the cell, her red tail gleaming in the candlelight. She stopped suddenly and declared: "I see a shadow on your soul. A burden. Some apprehension." She spun around again, chanting deliriously, then suddenly grabbed Gizor's paw with both of hers and opened his palm wider and flatter so she could read more. She peered back into his eyes intensely.

"What is it? What do you see?" asked Gizor.

"I have seen great death."

"Mine?"

"I have seen honour and triumph. I see a ship, a battle, death, and the hills – the great Downs. Loss. Great loss and great triumph."

"What does it mean? I need more!"

"The mighty will win. The Guide will lead," replied Lillian who then knocked the fragments out of Gizor's paw and returned to her desk, muttering to herself.

Gizor stood there for a second, returned the jar to its shelf and walked away. His plan would work, and the Occupation would begin.

## Chapter 4

# TUPPENCE-WORTH OF CHESTNUTS

F irst Minister Theodore Forton was at Bury Hall in his reading chamber surrounded by official documents on his writing desk. He took off his glasses to rub his tired eyes and breathed in deeply. He put the glasses back on, reached for his quill pen, and dabbed it gently in the ink well, making alterations to a document. He replaced the pen and picked up the document, looking over to his right where a small vole pointed at him and counted down from five, signalling to Theodore to speak to his listening wireless audience. Reception was poor but Theodore's solemn-toned slow-paced voice could still be heard through the distant crackle:

"I speak to you this evening, seated here in The Alvara Chambers of the Great Bury Hall, a Parliament started by the Will of this people. And I speak to you this evening – should you recognise my voice – with my paws laid bare and bereft for you to search as I have done so myself these past few weeks. And I am left – my mind lost and yet my heart still heavy with responsibility – with few answers and many prayers. I am left, as we all are, to carry the burdens of our stories. And it is my burden now to learn too late that we fail to recognise the field when we hold on to a single blade of grass. My burden here in this life will now be in exile. The Alverstocracy rests today, its last day. My only hope and comfort is that our lives – those of the creatures of Gosport – will be remembered in the stories passed on, and in the bravery created in our adversity. A Will that does not divide but is a Will to live. A Will intended to survive. Lord, bless us and keep us safe."

*

The *Gosport Crier*, usually a weekly periodical, was becoming a daily one with its readers' demand for news. First Minister Forton's wireless message was the front-page story and copies of the *Crier* were selling out fast.

Mary Camper was at the corner shop, quietly gathering a few bits in her basket for supper. She was standing in the aisle at the back when a young sweet-faced red squirrel entered the shop. The bell of the door sounded as she did so. The two female shopkeepers, both grey squirrels, peered over at her from their perch next to the till.

"Could I have tuppence-worth of chestnuts please?" asked the young doe as she eagerly approached the counter. She could barely see over the top of it but had her pennies ready to hand over, stretching out her paw.

"What do you think, Margaret – should we sell this red doe some chestnuts?" called Frances to her colleague as she sat filing her claws behind the counter.

"Well I think we're terribly busy, Frances. I know I simply cannot spare the time." She flicked over the pages of her magazine without actually reading them. "Besides, I think we've run out," she added.

"But I can see them on the top shelf just there," replied the young doe innocently, pointing to behind where the shopkeepers were sitting.

"Oh no, you are clearly mistaken," replied Frances.

"No. Look. There they are!"

With that, Frances stood up from her stool, clearly irritated. "Look 'ere," she said forcefully, "we haven't got any. You're being very rude and I'm afraid we shall have to ask you to leave now."

"But …"

"But nothing. Now I've asked you to leave and leave you should. Go on now. And try not to touch anything as you go with your filthy paws. Shoo!" She came out from behind the counter to usher the young one out of the shop.

The two shop assistants continued their conversation as if nothing had just happened, "It says here that every whisker that falls out never grows back the same," said Margaret. "I can believe that, can't you, Frances?"

"Josephine down my way believes it brings you luck. She wishes on each one she loses." She walked back to the counter to continue filing her claws.

Mary, still at the back of the shop, observed the awful treatment of the youngster and fearing a similar fate started replacing the items that were in her basket.

"Can we help you, love?" called out Frances, hearing someone was at the back of the shop.

"Err, no err, quite OK thank you," replied Mary flustered, turning so that her tail would not be visible where it poked out from beneath her cloak.

"We have a special offer on the bread rolls today if you're interested. And we have some lovely chestnuts," called out Frances as she walked towards the back of the shop.

With that, Mary placed her basket on the floor and shuffled quickly out of the door, leaving the two shopkeepers to jeer at the sight of her tail as she left. They had not realised she was a Red. As she left, and in such a hurry, she accidentally bumped into a passer-by on the street. The chicken looked at her in disgust and knocked her backwards slightly, causing her to bump into a brown rabbit who looked in horror at the colour of her fur. Mary quickly wrapped her cloak tightly round her for comfort and hurried away towards home.

\*

In the dark of the caponier, the Resistance met by candlelight.

"It's not enough to just protest and cause a stir. We must lead from the front," declared Hertha Marks to her motley crew. "With Parliament in hiding, a new one must emerge. If there is a 'Will intended to survive', then risen are we." The crew of tired bandits cheered in agreement. "We need organisation. Floppy, did you bring the maps?"

Floppy hopped over, holding in his paws and under his arms a bundle of rolled-up old maps of Gosport. "I did, Hertha, I did," he said. In his excitement he bumped into the table, knocking creatures' drinks over, and dumped the maps down in a haphazard manner. "See I told you I did, I told you I'd bring the mappies."

Hertha reached for one of the maps and rolled it out flat onto the table, grabbing a few cups to hold it in place in each corner. She leant over the table. "Right, we know we have positions in Priddy's Hard, which is obviously of some strategic importance to the enemy, and we know we have positions at …" As Hertha tried to plan and show her crew important Resistance bases, she was continually interrupted by Rosie trying to clear up the mess that had been caused when Floppy bumped into the table.

"Let me just get this spot for you, my dearie," said Rosie, lifting up the map to clean under it. "Oh and here. Missed a spot. That will never do now, will it?"

Hertha looked up and glared at Rosie. "As I was saying, we know ..."

"Biscuit, dear?" asked Rosie.

"No," replied Hertha, starting to get annoyed. "No thank you, Rosie."

"Biscuit? Biscuit? I'll have a biscuit, Mrs Rosie," said Floppy.

"Right, Floppy – get your biscuit. Rosie – I think I noticed some grease marks on the balcony up there," said Hertha, trying to occupy those distracting her.

"Right you are, my lovey. Don't worry about a thing. I shall have that cleaned up in no time."

"Thank you. Now, I've heard from the Town Ward, but has anyone heard from the Anglesey Ward?"

"Shouldn't we hear from the Grange Ward Resistance?" asked Agatha.

"Interesting. Why do you ask?" replied Hertha, leaning on the table studying her plans.

"Well, because of Occupation Day." Agatha was startled that the group weren't discussing it.

"To be frank, we don't have the animal power to stand at Browndown to watch them close the gates, Agatha."

"But we can't sit back and let that happen. We're the Resistance!"

"We have to choose our battles wisely. We can't save an entire country from the Camps. For one, where would they all hide? No. We would put them all at greater risk. We must plan our attacks for the coastal wards near to Portsmouth, close to the source."

"What's that, my dearie, you want some sauce?" asked Rosie, eager to please and listening to only half a conversation.

"NO!" shouted both Hertha and Agatha at the same time in pure frustration.

Agatha pressed her point: "But we could save some, surely?"

"Agatha, we are only a few. We must concentrate our efforts on strategy. We must gather information and be one step ahead and plan our actions for the greater good."

"... and do what with it? We gather all this information for what? Where does it go if we are so few?"

"Agatha please, I'm trying to plan."

Agatha stood up from her seat at the table and physically distanced herself from the group.

"Biscuit, dear?" asked Rosie. Agatha just shook her head and walked away.

As she left via the shed door and into the allotments, dusk was fast approaching. As she walked through the allotments, grabbing a carrot to munch on, all she could see were roads of trucks and marching Gizor soldiers preparing for curfew. She picked up her bicycle on the edge of the allotments and cycled home, muttering to herself, feeling hurt, dumbfounded and frustrated by the words of the 'Great' Hertha Marks.

\*

Agatha walked into the cottage, placed her hat and bicycle clips on the side in the entrance hall, peered into the sitting room to see if her father was about, then quietly started to walk upstairs to her room. However, her father was in his study and called out to her.

"Agatha? Is that you?"

"Yes, papa."

"It's very late," said Peter Mumby as he continued reading his book at his desk. Agatha appeared at the doorway behind him.

"Yes, papa. Sorry."

"I worry about the curfew and your tardiness."

"Yes, papa, I know. I shall try to do better next time."

"Supper is in the pantry. Did you manage to post my letters?"

"Thank you, father. Yes," replied Agatha who was not at all hungry.

"I wonder what it is that takes you suddenly longer to get home from Priddy's these days?" he asked, turning in his chair to face his daughter.

"Papa?" replied Agatha, trying to present an air of innocence. Her father knew her better than she knew herself.

"Priddy's is a different place now, I hear," he declared astutely. "Be careful, Agatha."

"Yes, papa," she said, heading for the stairs. "Goodnight."

Agatha couldn't sleep. Ideas were racing through her mind. She knew Hertha was right but also knew that Browndown was important and wanted to know more about the Camp before being forced to go to it – which she had no intention of doing in any event.

She woke early, and with the curfew still in place, left the cottage, grabbed her bike and cycled towards Grange, being careful to avoid the Gizor soldiers.

As the curfew was lifted at 6am, she began to cycle along the main roads towards Browndown, but discovered that all the roads towards it had been sealed off by the Gizor. She decided to hide her bike in some bushes and go by foot through the Alver Valley woods. The woodlands were largely deserted, vacated by the Gizor some weeks before. She travelled further into the dense woods to reach a clearing, wishing – not for the first time – that she was good at climbing. She began to hear the bustle of trucks and Gizor soldiers in the distance. She scrambled up the old motte and bailey to get a vantage point and stayed low to the ground to avoid detection. In the distance through the trees she could see the camp, which was a hive of activity. Gizor trucks and personnel were busying themselves behind the walls of the Camp. They appeared to be installing high fencing within the camp walls, and there were endless deliveries of huge metal structures and bricks. Agatha knew that the metal works were from Priddy's and wanted to get closer. However, as she did so, she slipped down the hill and let out a yelp as she went. She quickly picked herself up, dusted herself off, and ran back into the woods to hide in the cover of the thick undergrowth.

She had bumped her head on the way down and was a little disoriented, so she lost her way back to where she had left her bicycle. She did not realise that she had entered Grange Farm with its outbuildings, stables, barn and old farmhouse.

As she approached the property she walked passed bold warning signs saying 'Private Land, Keep Off'. Agatha didn't really know much about the farm, who owned it or its inhabitants. She didn't know very much at all about its history other than that her father had always told her never to venture there. She didn't know why. She wanted to get to the muddy lane that led to the house, to follow it out and get back on the right track to take her home. Having approached from the back of the property, she had to walk to the side to get to the beaten track ahead of her. As she stepped into the open, an old hedgehog dressed in scullery maid's uniform, holding a basket of clothes, quickly approached her.

"You there, shoo! Go on now. You can't be 'ere. The master won't like it. Shoo now, I say!"

"Hello," said Agatha to the hedgehog in blind ignorance.

"I told you, you must leave, and leave you must quickly now. Go on!"

"I'm just trying to get home."

The old hedgehog kept looking around her, shooing Agatha away as she did. "Go, I say. For your own sake. Ain't no place to be."

With that, a tall, dishevelled, miserable-looking badger swung open the farmhouse door carrying his rifle with him.

"What's this? Who be there?" he said. He clearly had a temper to match his looks: he was also very hard of hearing and his sight was not much better. Farmer 'Rabbit Skin' Jack he had been nicknamed by the locals and he didn't mind the connotation – however untrue. Rural myths have always circulated amongst the locals and the stories have often been as wild as the tell-tales themselves. "Now see here, scarper I tell you. This is private property. Whoever you are, ain't nothing here for you and you'll feel the back of my paw if you don't. I likes me a hanging, I do," he shouted as he raised his rifle, aimed at whatever was moving in the blurry distance and fired his gun. Agatha ducked and dived as she ran swiftly away towards the muddy path. She now knew why her father had told her never to venture to the farm.

As she ran further away, she could still hear Rabbit Skin Jack shouting out and moaning about people trespassing on his land. She had begun to slow her pace when she heard a truck approaching. She dived into the undergrowth to the side of the track as the Gizor whizzed past her position. They were heading to the farm. She was too intrigued by it not to start following it. As she approached the farm again, she hid carefully in some bushes. She could see a grey squirrel officer talking to Farmer Jack, and one harassing the scullery maid who appeared uncomfortable at his unwanted advances. Agatha looked above the officer's head: she could see they were standing under an oak tree. She looked beside her and picked up a stone and threw it at the officer's head, only appearing out of the bushes for a few seconds to do so.

"Ouch!" said the officer, rubbing his sore head. Luckily for Agatha, he had assumed whatever struck his head was from the tree above him. Agatha watched him walk back to his comrade, talking to Farmer Jack.

"So, you will see to it that the apples are prepared again for next week?" said the officer to Farmer Jack.

"Aye, I will. I still haven't received my letter though, I'll have you know. I ain't too happy about that. So, I put it to you Mr soldier-sailor, where is my letter? Cos I ain't in the business of doing no deal with pesky thieves. Do you 'ear me? There won't be one apple prepared and nothing in the Keep for you to take if I don't gets me my letter. You take that back to your Gizors, you 'ear?" replied Farmer Jack, who was clearly strong willed.

"You will receive your documentation, Mr Jack, when we collect the fruits and pastries," replied the officer.

Farmer Jack was not happy with the response he received and stepped forward towards the officer and grabbed him by the lapels of his greatcoat. "You listen 'ere, and you listen good," he said. Both officers were taken aback by the badger. After a startled second, the other officer attempted to grab Farmer Jack and pull him away from his comrade but Farmer Jack was too strong and simply pushed the officer so hard that he fell to the ground. "I am a badger of my word. You squirrel animals may not understand the farmer ways but I can soon teach you – should you like."

"That will not be necessary, Mr Jack. I'm certain we can provide you with the letter by the afternoon," replied the officer, still being restrained by the farmer.

Farmer Jack slowly released his grip. "Right you are then," he said. "Be on your way."

*

Agatha ran back to her bicycle and cycled as fast as she could to the allotments with the information she had gathered. She barged into the caponier, making quite a noise.

"Hertha!" she cried out, "Hertha!"

Hertha was standing, looking into a tall broken mirror that was leant against a slippery wall. Her arms were outstretched, with Rosie repairing her jacket with patches. Others members of the crew were studying maps, drinking elderberry wine and playing cards.

"Hertha. I have information about the Camp and of Grange Farm ..." said Agatha excitedly.

"Agatha, I told you not to go fishing there. Our operation cannot reach that far."

"But Hertha, they are making large structures of steel from Priddy's and reinforcing the walls. I saw pipes, and iron, and communal sleeping quarters."

"I do hope they have biscuit and cake for the townspeople when they get there," said Rosie.

"Agatha, they are preparing the camp as they said they would. It's nothing we don't already know," said Hertha.

"I also stumbled upon Farmer Jack at his farm and the G.C. visiting him wanting great quantities of food prepared."

Hertha immediately turned to face Agatha. "Farmer Jack has never been part of Gosport. It does not surprise me that he has sold his soul and his land to the Gizor. Leave well alone, Agatha."

Floppy started jumping up and down crying out:

"Rabbit Skin Jack, Rabbit Skin Jack. He be a-feared. I be afraid of Farmer Jack, I be. I don't want to go there, Agatha. No, not Farmer Jack. I don't want to go there."

"Now see what you've done!" said Hertha. "It's OK, Floppy, we're not going there. Farmer Jack won't get you."

Hertha looked down at her newly repaired jacket, turned around to her followers, and walked up a few steps of the spiral staircase to address them as their leader.

"With only a few days left before Occupation Day, we must remain strong and united," she urged. "I can keep each of you from surrender if we remain strong as one. Our aim? To message the world and build a stronger front, and to show Gizor that we did not surrender and that if we fall, we fell fighting." Hertha stepped higher to the balcony and continued her rally to the troops. "And if we should die, the world will know the cause of our deaths, and that we died with honour and valour without falter or fear. For we, the Resistance, broke our chains and refused to lie down and surrender. God's Port Our Haven in soul, spirit and fight will never be Portsmouth's." Hertha broke into a rousing chant with her troops: "GOSPORT! GOSPORT! GOSPORT!"

As the chants continued, Hertha signalled for Agatha to climb the stairs to the balcony. "You see, Agatha, we will fight the battles we can win. Our job now is to raise the word to the world. That's the plan. We spread our crew across the outskirts and alert the world, which is blinded by boundary. We break down those boundaries. Therein lays salvation and hope." Hertha placed a paw on Agatha's shoulder, "Are you with me, Agatha?"

Agatha was transfixed by the charismatic leader before her. "Yes," she replied, "Yes I am, Hertha."

*

The summer rain was heavy on the roof of the church as the Reverend Edward Stapland helped Peter Mumby lay out the Hudsonicus Books along each pew ready for the next morning's service.

"How's Agatha, Peter?" asked the Reverend.

"Yes, well Agatha will be Agatha as you know, Reverend. Just like her mother, she is."

"Quite. I remember when she stood up to sing God's Port Our Haven and belted out her version of it and the choir had to change theirs from that day on. The choirmaster was not happy as I recall. Rehearsals were never quite the same after that."

Just as the pair were chatting away, there was a loud knock on the oak church door. The Reverend placed the remainder of his books on a pew and walked to the back of the church to open the door. He was greeted by Gizor soldiers in dark grey ponchos soaked through to the fur. One solider stepped forward into the church doorway. "Reverend Edward Stapland?" he enquired.

"Why yes. That is I. Can I help you?" replied Edward.

The soldier stepped further into the church and thrust a shovel into the Reverend's paw without saying a word. Another soldier brushed passed him and grabbed Peter's arm, ushering them both out of the church. As they entered the churchyard, they could see a group of red squirrels standing in the pouring rain lined up with wheelbarrows, shovels and sledgehammers. Edward and Peter were pushed further into the graveyard.

"I say, could I ask what this is all about?" said Edward.

"Quiet. No questions. Dig." The solider pushed and shoved the pair and pointed down to a headstone in the cemetery. "You remove the stones, place in the barrow."

"But this is sacred land – you couldn't possibly ask me to do this."

"You will remove the stones and place them in the barrow or I will shoot your friend here," replied the solider, pointing at Peter. "Your choice, Mr Reverend," he mocked.

The small group of squirrels worked into the night removing all the headstones in the cemetery, carrying them to the wheelbarrows and trucks. Peter observed one of the soldiers approach the two wooden crosses at the back of the graveyard where they had some weeks ago buried two Gizor fighters. Peter signalled silently to the Reverend.

"You there!" shouted one of the soldiers to the Reverend. "What is this?"

"It's a recent burial," said Edward.

The soldier started kicking at the dirt mound. "Where is the headstone?" he asked.

The Reverend did not know how to reply. Peter stepped in and calmly said: "The family have yet to choose a headstone."

"There are two graves here? Unusual, is it not?" enquired the soldier.

"Two brothers from the Gosport Army," replied a quick-thinking Peter.

"Brothers? What did they die of, to have both died together?" asked the soldier.

He continued kicking up some of the dirt. Peter could see that this had kicked up a Gizor badge from one of the fighter's uniforms. He quickly stepped forward, kicking dirt over to hide it. "I think it was cholera, sir," he said calmly.

The soldier immediately stepped back and wiped his boot on some nearby grass in disgust and fear of what he might catch.

As they finished loading the trucks, the Reverend bravely asked what the headstones were to be used for.

"A muddy lane," said one of the soldiers and laughed as he walked off. "Blame the rain, Mr Reverend."

The pounding rain was fierce that night – the creatures of Gosport slept anxiously in their beds, wondering what the new world tomorrow would look like. Across the land and roads of Gosport marched the Gizor army, positioning themselves ready for the early wake. Little ones were tucked up sound asleep while their parents were huddled together and still packing their valuables in suitcases, silently crying, and preparing themselves for what morning would bring.

"Agatha?" called out Peter to his daughter as he searched his writing desk, "have you seen my old notebook?"

"Yes, it's here, papa," replied Agatha as she found it on his desk right in front of him.

"Ah good. Can't leave without this, now can I? Are you packed, Agatha?" He continued searching for precious things to take.

Agatha stood looking at her father pack away his things. She needed to tell him that she wasn't going with him, "Father …?"

"You will need a warm coat, remember," interrupted Peter, "We don't know how long we will be in the camp for. Could be a few weeks, could be a few months until they re-home us all. Need to be prepared."

"Papa …"

"I do believe there was talk of setting up a school for the little ones and a church. I shall have to pack some books, I suppose." He was a wise old man and knew full well that his daughter had no intention of going to the camps.

"Father …"

"And of course, the church will need a keeper."

"Father, please!"

Peter stopped in his tracks and looked up at his daughter. They starred at each other in silence for a moment.

"You will need a long coat, Agatha," Peter said solemnly to his daughter.

"Yes, father."

"And a sturdy strong bag. You will find one in the shed, I'm sure." Peter sighed and fell silent for a moment. "I've done my best with what I had to give to you, Agatha. I speak to your mother every day and I'm sure she listens to my ramblings. I could only teach you what I knew and nothing more. Your mother is ever present. I see her every day in you. You are strong like her and I am proud of that. I am proud of who you are and what you have become. I understand your path and that you cannot follow me, any more than I can follow you. I ask only that you keep safe yourself and guard your open heart for others to see without trespass for we are the writers of our destiny and the narrators of history." He looked down at his writing desk and picked up an old leather-bound notebook. "Here," he said as he placed the empty notebook into her paw. "May you write your own, and may it be kind."

# PART TWO

# PORTSMOUTH

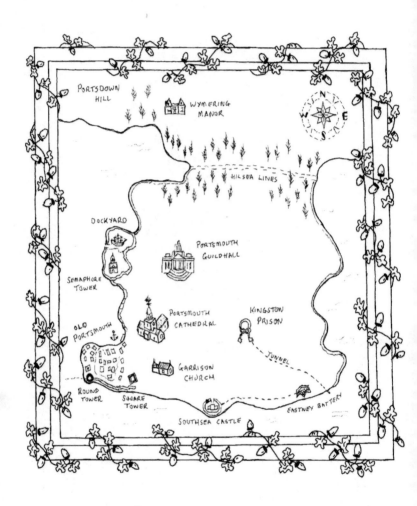

## HEAVEN'S LIGHT - OUR GUIDE

## Chapter 5
# AN ISLAND FOR
# A CASTLE

J une 25th 1939, Occupation Day, was dark and soggy
with ominous clouds. Organised by the Gizor Army,
all red squirrels and their sympathisers were to be moved to
Browndown Camp. Their homes were to be requisitioned
by Gizor officers, personnel, and Portsmouth creatures
selected for re-settlement in Gosport. There was no
common courtesy to be shown – the move would be swift
and immediate. As animal folk left their dwellings for the
Camp, their new owners walked past to refill them.

The roads were busy with trucks, loading wagons,
trailers, and lines of red squirrels walking in procession
towards Browndown carrying their suitcases and all that
they could to keep with them. It was a sorry sight. Thick
mud was only prevented by the headstones that had been
freshly laid along the path. Scores of animals were arriving
at the gates on Browndown Road and were being organised
by the Gizor Army who were selecting and separating them
all. Families who had arrived together were put into
different sections of the camp, their belongings taken from
them for 'safe keeping'. Each creature was ushered into
registration tents and stamped to the skin with the crest of
Portsmouth – a crescent moon lying flat under a star. They
were asked basic details about themselves – name,

profession, and skills. They were handed a new set of clothes, a uniform of sorts. They were immediately told to change into the clothes and abandon theirs in the huge containers supplied for them. The organisation was likened by one as an assembly line in a factory. It was brutal and cold-hearted – no regard or courtesy was given. The Camp was situated on the coast next to Stokes Bay Town, its boundaries fenced as they joined the shore, with the beach forbidden to passers-by. The Camp contained quarter barracks – their walls painted lime green and their roofs corrugated – constructed in organised military lines and blocks, with parade areas, a few brick buildings, and a grand old house situated in the middle for the officer in charge. The Gizor Army had constructed additional outposts to each corner of the site, guarding its fencing. In the middle of the Camp was a huge wooden outpost raised above the entire site with guards watching from above.

Lady Prideaux-Brune had been easily identified by the Gizor as a Red sympathiser and ushered through the gates. She stood out from the crowd, not just because of her size, her long rain mac and colourfully eccentric summer bonnet but because she was full of spirit, walking proudly beside those who were mocked for the colour of their fur. After changing her clothes and graciously requesting that she keep her hat, she walked out of the holding tent and onto a parade square where thousands of animals were lined up.

A Gizor officer dressed in a grey long coat stepped forward onto the parade ground, walked up to the first row of animal folk and paced along the line, inspecting the assortment of red squirrels, badgers, voles, stoats, rabbits and hedgehogs. He walked with his paws crossed behind him and exuded an air of authority. He went back towards the front of the parade and stepped up to a raised podium to address the prisoners.

"I am Colonel Fratton," he said. "Remember my name. I am in charge of this camp. If you obey the rules, you will live. If you fail to obey the rules, you will die. You will remain in the camp until such time we have decided where to place you. You will be put to work and serve your camp. You may have acquired certain skills and these skills will be used where appropriate and where required. I will not be disturbed by trivial questions or complaints. There are clear rules to follow and I have nothing more to say. Hail Gizor!" The Colonel saluted the air and walked off.

There was a shuffle and muttering in the crowd.

"Well, I never," commented Lady Prideaux-Brune. "There's a squirrel of few words if ever I heard one."

"Silence!" shouted another officer who appeared at the podium. "When called, step forward in line. My name is Corporal Milton. You will address me as such. And I will address you as I see fit." The officer peered to his right towards a Sergeant and signalled to begin a roll call.

"Step forward D Cruikshank, G Nicholson, M Appleby." The Sergeant continued calling out names and those called stepped forward. Officers grabbed them and shuffled them forwards to the front of the parade. Once a group of thirty had been assembled, it was marched away, and the roll call began again. Lady Prideaux-Brune's turn soon came around. She stepped forward, as did Mary Camper who she had not noticed before because she had been standing a few rows in front and to the side of her. Mary Camper had taken her time to respond to her name, and as a result was manhandled out of the line in frustration by one of the officers. "Silly little Red," said the officer.

They were ushered to the front of the parade awaiting a few others to join them and then marched off to a brick building, where they were lined up in a queue at the entrance. As they did so, they noticed other groups that had just entered the building were now leaving. They were sobbing and unrecognisable. Their fur had been shaved entirely off. Lady Prideaux-Brune was taken aback by the sight but coughed to clear her throat and declared to her group: "Oh well, ladies, it will soon grow back." With a nervous paw, she smoothed the white stripe of fur that ran down her forehead to her nose.

*

Makeshift bunks had been made on the floors of the caponier for a rabble of Resistance. The den was dimly lit by candlelight and filled with those muttering plots and schemes. They were in it for the long haul and had committed each to a life of exile – a covert existence. Of course, Rosie was still there, having found her calling. She would not take part in the battles but made it her business to feed the troops and ensure the den was as cosy as possible for them all.

"Here you go, my lovey, a nice warm mug of elderberry tea for you and an extra biscuit, my dearie," she said to Agatha.

"Thank you, Rosie."

"You got dearie ones in the camps, my lovey?"

"My papa, yes."

"Well, at least you know where he is, my lovey. The same can't be said about you for him now, can it?" said Rosie, astutely.

"No, I suppose you are right." Agatha felt sad at the thought of her father worrying.

"Anyone else for a cup of tea?" asked Rosie as she walked off to warm the stove again for another round.

"I will, Mrs Rosie, Mrs Rosie I will." Floppy hopped from his bunk over to the stove to pinch another biscuit from her. She could never refuse him a little treat.

"Right, we need to figure out a way of reaching word to Fareham," declared Hertha, deep in thought at a table where she was studying her maps and plans.

"What about using Priddy's? The docks?" suggested Agatha.

"They have the outer rim of the creek guarded. If we were to use the boats to travel up, we would need to do it under cover of darkness. Even so, the moon might break our cover. Any other ideas?"

"Travel by paw in the open would be just as dangerous and slower," remarked one of the motley crew.

"Saint Vincent's?" suggested Agatha again. "The quay on Forton Creek, the other side of Priddy's, might be better and unexpected."

"I like your thinking, Agatha," said Hertha. "What's the state of play with St Vincent's at the moment, anyone?"

"I should reckon the Gizors are using it," replied Berry, knowing that the barracks there would hold a thousand troops or more.

"Even better then – take 'em by surprise. Take their boats from them and travel up to the castle." declared Hertha passionately.

"The castle?" queried Agatha.

"The castle! The castle!" said Floppy. "I ain't ever been to the castle castle."

"That's it then – we'll leave at sundown." Hertha thumped her paw on the table where she was studying her maps.

"Portchester Castle?" queried Agatha again.

"It's the closest we'll get to Fareham to spread word to the Abbeystocracy at Titchfield."

"But the Priory Monks are isolated – no one goes in and no one goes out. What word can they spread?"

"It's our only hope – that they'll listen. Right, here's the plan."

*

A small rabble of Resistance took their place in the shrubbery and undergrowth behind St Vincent Barracks, unseen by the swarm of Gizor Military parading the square within. From her position on the ground, Hertha signalled to her group to keep their eyes on the tall outpost tower overlooking the creek, with a couple of soldiers on guard. Quite frankly their watch seemed more focused on the poker game they were playing on top of the tower than on the ground below them. The group, led by Hertha, ran one by one towards the legs of the tower, before moving again to another clump of undergrowth, then to the back wall of the barracks themselves. Pressed flat against the wall, they were able to escape the bright gaze of floodlights moving across the grounds. Urban myth had it that if the clock strikes thirteen at midnight, then the ghosts of all creatures who paraded its square would parade again. The chimes began to ring. Hertha and her gang seized the opportunity and ran towards the creek and down the bank, quickly untying the anchor lines as they did so and stealing two rowing boats. They all clambered in – Hertha and Berry in one boat, and Agatha and Floppy in the other. They rowed off silently, initially keeping close to the banks so as not to be noticed. They approached the mouth of the creek, with Rats Island to their left, and rowed into the still waters of the harbour. The pace was slow and steady. Agatha had not realised she had rowed into a stretch of water bound by chains linked to the bank. The boat creaked as the wood scraped across the jagged chains, making a small hole through which seawater immediately began to bubble up.

Floppy began jumping up and down in panic. As the boat began sinking, they both had no choice but to jump into the murky water. Hertha and Berry rowed back towards them. Floppy was able to reach them first and clambered into their boat, shaking the water off his white fur. Agatha, however, had drifted too far from them with the tide, and the Gizor were patrolling the outskirts of the barracks. Without saying a word, Agatha swam away from her chance of rescue – towards Rats Island.

Bedraggled and worn out, she reached the shore of the small island and collapsed onto the pebbles between the jagged rocks and stones. The moon was her only means of light. She could see St Vincent's in the distance and to the north could just about make out three of her comrades in a small boat heading out to the Castle in the far distance in the harbour. Hertha had been right about the moon.

Agatha sat on the shore and squeezed the water out of her tail with her paws. She looked around and behind her. The way was steep. It looked as though she would have to climb the rocks to reach the shelter of the trees. She wasn't the greatest climber despite being a squirrel, but she was even less of a fan of ne'er-do-well rats – particularly convict rats who had committed heinous crimes. She couldn't stay where she was, so had little choice but to climb.

She reached the top, water still dripping into her eyes, and found a dense canopy of trees. She thought it best to stick to the shoreline and follow it round towards the direction of Priddy's rather than enter the island stronghold itself. She reached the north edge of the island overlooking Priddy's but the tide was too high for her to tread the sand dunes back to the mainland and the thought of another swim was exhausting. She would wait for low tide.

She found cover as best she could to dry off and tried to sleep, but every noise and rustle made her sleep with her eyes half closed, constantly on the alert. Halfway through the night she was woken by a shriek and a gnawing sound. She adjusted her position and tried to keep low in the undergrowth. The gnawing and rustling sound was coming closer. She closed her eyes tight in fear and tried to keep silent, but her breathing was too heavy. Suddenly she was grabbed from behind, bundled into a net and dragged through the woods. She pleaded with her captors to no avail. The short and bumpy journey saw her taken to the centre of the island and through a large crowd of smelly, rotten rats jeering at her and squabbling between themselves. The net was loosened, and she was thrust out to stand before a rabble of flea-infested convicts. She looked around her and could see groups of rats singing sea shanties and others drinking and fighting amongst themselves. They were all dishevelled with yellow teeth, old scars and half-bitten-off ears. The smell of them was overwhelming. Agatha placed a paw to her nose as she looked around. Just as she did so, a scrawny rat approached her and tried to grab at her paws, and another pushed him away. "'Ere she's mine," said the first rat.

"She's a funny looking rat," called out another to raucous laughter.

"Think you're funny do ya, Squidge?" replied another.

"Yeah I do's as it happens," said the rabid-looking rat.

Agatha, frozen with fear, stood silently, her heart racing, moving her eyes rapidly around her immediate space to see if anyone else would grab at her.

"Well, well, well, what do we have 'ere?" came a voice from the crowd. The mob of rats that had surrounded Agatha began to part, and a tall scrawny and deformed rat with torn ears and patchy flea-ridden fur pushed and shoved his way through the disorganised crowd. He spoke at a slow and menacing pace. "We are in a spot of bother, ain't we?"

The rat started slowly circling Agatha, sizing her up. He whispered as he circled: "Ain't had me a little red meat in a long time."

"Please!" begged Agatha.

"Shut it!" replied the angry rat. "This 'ere is our place. Ain't no place for you."

"Please!" repeated Agatha.

"I said shut it!" The commanding rat continued to circle Agatha with his rabble of men looking on, sneering at Agatha's fear.

"How shall we kill her, Weevil?" called out one of the rats from the crowd.

"You must forgive my men. They 'ungry, you see. We ain't eaten in days. And when we ain't eaten we tend to get a little … carnivorous as you poshies like to say. Well, you on the wrong land, little do-si-doe. This 'ere is my island and who dares to tread it belongs to me." Weevil turned to his crowd of followers and declared: "A roast tonight, boys!"

The crowd cheered, and a huge bonfire lit up the centre of the island.

"This world isn't yours anymore," declared Agatha bravely, quoting what a Gizor officer had once remarked to her.

Weevil grabbed her by the throat. His grip was tight. "You what, you filthy scum?" he said.

"This island. Your island." Agatha coughed, trying to catch her breath with Weevil still holding tight her throat. "It won't be yours for much longer. Maybe not even by tomorrow."

Weevil loosened his grip. "Explain," he demanded.

"The Gizor. Gizor is coming."

"What are they?"

"The Gizor fleet. The Army. Portsmouth. They've taken

Gosport. This island is theirs. It'll be next. They're coming."

"Scaremongering," snubbed Weevil as he tightened his grip once more.

"No. Priddy's has been taken already," replied Agatha, trying to convince Weevil.

"Look 'ere. No one is coming, just like no one is coming to rescue you, ya filthy vermin."

"Cook her in the fire pot!" shouted one of the rats.

"Look over to the Barracks, look over to Priddy's. Go to Priddy's. They're over there. Please, you must believe me. They will take your island."

Weevil loosened his grip again, pulled Agatha closer, and stared intensely at her. "Waldheim? Bandicoot?" He beckoned for his men with his free paw. "Go check the walls. Yersinia? Fetch the spit iron. We havin' a roastin'."

"Please," begged Agatha.

"Listen 'ere. We ain't afraid of no army. The army be afraid of us. Couldn't keep us in their walls, could they? No, they put us 'ere on this island 'cos they were too scared to lock us up and feed us through the bars. Bunch of cowards."

"'Ere ya are. Weevil," said Yersinia handing him the spit iron.

Weevil teased his young prisoner with the scalding hot iron, pointing it at her face as he walked round her once more. "No do-si-doe walks onto my land and tells me that they've run out of rat poison," he said. "Next you'll be asking us for help." The crowd scoffed and jeered.

"They WILL take your land."

"Shut your face, doe scum."

"Weevil! Weevil!" called Bandicoot, returning from the south side of the island. "There's something going on over there. Can't make it out though."

"Sames, Weevil," said Waldheim. "Over at Priddy's. I

80

sees some grey soldiers. I sees 'em standing on the dock looking over."

"Right you pond scum, get the island covered. Now!" barked Weevil to his band of rats who scampered off in all directions in panic and preparation. He turned to face Agatha, released his grip and allowed Agatha to scurry off into the trees. All she could hear behind her was panic from the band of villains, and Weevil barking his orders to the rabble of convicts around him.

Agatha ran to the north shoreline. The tide was now low. She clambered down the rocks and on to the sand dunes. She didn't look back. She scuttled across the damp boggy dunes towards Priddy's. Sunrise was approaching fast and she made for temporary cover under one of the docks she had constructed for Jane.

*

The small rowing boat carrying the three companions made its way silently up the still waters of the harbour towards Portchester Castle. As they approached from the south, the perimeter walls towered above them. They pulled the boat inwards to anchor it on the gravel shore. From there they travelled by foot, staying close to the walls of the castle along the shoreline towards the gates to the north. The fortress was lit only by the dull light of wrought iron torches attached to its inner walls. Hertha called out a 'hello' through the portcullis gates that were firmly closed. There was no response.

"Look, Hertha! Look, Hertha! A rope!" Floppy waved the rope he had just found, which was attached to the side of the entrance. As he did so, the bell rang out. Hertha quickly pulled the rope taut to stop the chimes.

"Be careful, Floppy. Try not to touch anything. We

want to be as quiet as possible, don't we?" said Hertha.

"I be as quiet as a mousey, Hertha. A mousey I be," whispered Floppy to his leader. "I found the rope, didn't I Berry? I found it, I did."

"You need to be quiet, Floppy," replied Berry, peering inside to see if anyone would come.

Floppy, still proud of his discovery and smiling to himself with satisfaction, did not notice what the others were seeing as they looked through the portcullis. In the distance, a cloaked figure was approaching. What kind of creature it was, they could not see.

"State your purpose this late hour of our Lord's creation," said the figure.

"We bring a message from Gosport," replied Hertha.

"Patience," said the figure, walking away.

Hertha raised her paws in frustration and shook her head, "Where's he going?"

"I be afraid of that one, Hertha, I be," whispered Floppy, standing to the side in the shadows.

The cloaked figure shortly returned to the gates. "We bid you good morrow and blessings," it said.

"But wait," said Hertha, puzzled at the response. "We have a message to share."

"Good morrow my fellows, blessings be with you," repeated the monk.

"I demand to be heard! Our message must be shared. Open the gates!" said Hertha.

"But it is Compline," stated the monk, indicating that the castle could not be disturbed during prayers.

"But we bring news – terrible news. A message must be given to your people."

"A message we have, a message we do," said Floppy from the shadows, hopping a little. The monk gasped in shock at the sight of the white rabbit before him. He

82

scurried to the side of the entrance and opened the gates.

Hertha and Berry looked at Floppy, then at each other. Confused, they entered the gatehouse and observed the cloaked figure kneeling beside them, his head bowed as they slowly walked past him and into the grounds of the castle.

"What was that all about?" Berry asked Hertha.

"I have no idea but stay close, Floppy."

"I be scared, Hertha I be. I be scared."

"Just stay close," said Hertha, holding out a reassuring paw for him to hold.

The three companions slowly walked the path towards the plainsong chanting they had started to hear in the distance. The ethereal, haunting sounds were emanating from the small church that stood in the south-east corner of the grounds. Whilst the Sisters of St Mary's choir sang, the Priory Monks could be heard chanting in prayer:

*"HUD-SONNN-ICUS, HUD-SONNN-ICUS, HUD-SONNN-ICUS."*

As they walked, the cloaked figure that had allowed them in suddenly scurried past them towards the church, revealing by its tail to be a vole.

As the three reached the church gates, a myriad of monks spilled out to greet them. All cloaked, with their heads bowed, they remained controlled, silent, and did not touch the visitors. Intimidated by their presence, Floppy attempted to hide himself behind Hertha – rather unsuccessfully given his size.

Hertha stepped forward to break the silence. "We have a message," she declared.

An elder stepped forward from the gathered voles. "Our Father Lord Hudsonicus Holozoa brings to thee his promise today," he said. "It is a blessing." He raised his hands in praise and jubilation.

"The Gizor Army have invaded Gosport," said Hertha quickly.

Ignoring her words, the elder walked closer to Floppy. "The promise is true," he said in wonder. "You have appeared for thee."

"What is going on?" Hertha asked Berry under her breath.

"I can't be sure, but I think they think Floppy is some sort of God," said Berry.

"Thy light of Rodentia, our prayers of light appear. Thy White One has cometh," declared the elder.

"Err, yeah. They definitely think he's a God."

Floppy squeezed Hertha's paw in fear.

"Apologies, my dear friends," said the elder. "Come, you must be hungry. Let us feed you supper this Holy night."

"Supper?" said Floppy loosening his grip on Hertha's paw, "I like supper, I do."

The elder led the three from the church grounds towards the castle.

"But we have come to deliver a message," said Hertha to the elder who had ignored her.

"Yes, yes. We can discuss many things. You must forgive our joy. We are simple creatures of prayer and devotion. Come. Join us this night." He led them into a great hall where a feast had been prepared. "I am Pontius Perseus, by the way."

Berry and Hertha cautiously sat down at the huge banquet table but Floppy jumped into his chair and immediately began stuffing his face with carrots.

"Ask me your question," said Pontius, realising that the companions had no idea why the monks were worshipping Floppy.

"Who is he to you?" asked Hertha, picking up some

bread and passing it to Floppy.

"These walls keep safe more than just the prayers of some devoted servants," said Pontius.

Hertha looked at the elder and repeated her question: "Who is he to you?"

"The walls keep us safe with our devotion to them. These walls, built by the great Aurelius, keep a promise: that which is spoken by the Prophet will be sacred and adored at the castle, bestowing eternal life."

"Hang on, you believe that if you live here you will live forever?" asked Hertha.

"Walk with me," said the monk. "In devotion resides hope, and hope is eternal."

"What's this got to do with a white rabbit?" asked Hertha, infuriated, leaving Berry to stay with Floppy as he scoffed his food.

"In the study of Hudsonicus, the White Rabbit appears at the gates of Rodentia – innocent and begging pardon for crimes not committed," said Pontius. "The rabbit is not pardoned and is not helped. The rabbit is cruelly treated and dies a bloody death. It is believed that the rabbit will return one day and pardon the innocent, the devoted, and the enslaved."

"You can't seriously believe that Floppy is the white rabbit, can you?" said Hertha mockingly as they climbed the spiral staircase of the Keep.

"Let me ask you this," said Pontius as he opened the tower hatch and climbed out on to the roof. "What do you see when you look above the trees?" He pointed out towards the harbour where the view was broad and both Gosport and Portsmouth could be seen together.

"I see my world. A world that I need to get back to."

"We only see the moon because of the sun," replied Pontius, turning towards Hertha who was trying to prise open the hatch, uninterested in carrying on the elder's indulgence. "You believe he is limited by innocence when in fact he is devoted by hope and more powerful than you will ever realise."

Hertha looked out over the Keep and across to Portsmouth. She then turned to face Pontius and as she did so she caught a glimpse of a flag behind him that was gently unfolding with the breeze to reveal the Gizor insignia.

"If you'll excuse me," said Hertha trying to remain calm and wanting to get back to her friends. She began climbing down the uneven spiral stairs and headed back towards the great hall.

"It will always be the smallest of lights that will burn your eyes – just like the sun," said Pontius, walking swiftly behind her. "His devotion to you is misplaced." She turned to face the vole.

"Listen here. You know nothing about us. You know nothing about him. You talk of devotion and hope, but achieve nothing by prayer. We came to seek your help, but you ignore our message and prattle on about eternal life. You seem content with a life of ignorance. Well that's fine, but it doesn't involve us." She walked off into the great hall. "Come on. We're leaving," she called out to her companions. Berry immediately stood up from his chair quickly followed by Floppy. "These animals cannot help us."

"I'm sorry you feel that way," replied Pontius. "Sir Roderick will be displeased."

"Who's Sir Roderick?" asked Berry to Hertha as they gathered their things.

"I don't know, and I don't care," replied Hertha, helping Floppy to gather his belongings. "Let's just get out of here."

Hertha tried to open the door, but it was locked. "Why

is this locked? Let us out!" she said.

"I'm afraid you cannot leave," replied Pontius.

Hertha grabbed hold of Floppy's paw and pulled him behind her. "Fine, we'll find another way."

"I'm afraid the way is locked."

"Why?"

"My friends, if you will only be seated. Finish your meals and we will provide you with the comforts of warmth and shelter."

"We wish to leave."

"That will not be possible. Please return to your meals, my friends. You are safe here. There is nothing to alarm you."

"You cannot hold us here against our will."

"And I ask for your patience," snapped the vole. "Please finish your meals," he added, gesturing to the table.

"And then we can leave?" asked Hertha.

"It will be of Sir Roderick's choosing whether you leave this place or not."

"Well, where is this Roderick?"

"Wymering Manor, I suspect. He will be here by morning. Until then I suggest you get some much-needed rest. Lucius will show you to your quarters." He left the room.

"This way, my friends," said Lucius, stepping forward to guide them. A grey squirrel, he was well-spoken with a kindly demeanour. Having little other option, Hertha and her companions reluctantly followed him.

"Who is this Roderick?" asked Hertha as Lucius led them through the castle, past its many rooms and along its many corridors.

"Sir Roderick of Portchester. He leads our faith and bestows our blessings. He keeps us safe."

Hertha rolled her eyes. Lucius had sounded like he was

87

reading from a script. "So, I suppose you believe you will live forever?" she said mockingly.

Not expecting any form of reply, certainly not one she would be interested in, Hertha was surprised by the grey squirrel's response as he showed them to their darkened 'cell' and locked the door behind them. "I am not Pontius Perseus," he said.

"Wait! Lucius!" called out Hertha with a glimmer of hope. He did not respond. "We bed here for the night and find our way out in the morning," she said to her comrades, looking around at her darkened surroundings and trying not to reveal her panic. "We'll meet with this Roderick and see what he has to say for himself," she said with bravado, as if she had any other choice.

*

Each day, more and more red squirrels and red sympathisers arrived at Browndown Camp – those who had until then escaped Occupation Day. They arrived beaten and tired from their treatment. They suffered the same fate as the others – being branded and sheared and put to work in the camp, which was now almost full. Yet more and more kept arriving.

"I do hope the re-homing process won't be as ill-prepared as this camp appears to be," said Mary Camper to Gertie Nicholson as they walked across the parade square.

"Well, yes I couldn't agree more, Mary."

"I see a new batch has arrived," called out Lady Prideaux-Brune. She was leaning over a tin bath scrubbing pots clean and passing them to others to stack.

"I am utterly bewildered," said Mary walking towards Lady Ellen, "by the menial tasks that we are being forced to carry out when such tasks are better placed in the paws of those labourers accustomed to doing them."

"Surely now, Mary, washing a few tin pots is not above your skills-set?" mocked Lady Ellen.

"My point is that they would be well advised to order some semblance of production and efficiency."

"I will leave you to *advise* them of that then, Mary," replied Lady Ellen, looking up towards Mary and signalling with a nod and a smile that a Gizor commandant was passing by. In response, Mary quickly grabbed a mess tin from Lady Ellen and passed it to others in line to stack.

*

Agatha, still covered in mud and sand, her red fur almost unrecognisable, woke from her short slumber on the shore beneath the dock of Priddy's. The sun was pouring through the wooden slats as she lay on the wet shore. She clambered out and looked over to Rats Island where she had been only a few hours before – a place from which she felt lucky to have escaped. It was hard to believe that such a villainous army resided there. She could see no activity on the island, which was largely covered by a beautiful canopy of trees. She hoped her comrades were safe and their mission successful at the castle.

She decided to risk the run through Priddy's. She figured that her fur was matted and sufficiently grey looking, so she grabbed a hessian overlay that she had used to cover some of the rubble when she was building the dock, pulled it over her shoulders and walked towards the yard in the hope she would go unnoticed. Whenever a soldier appeared, she would turn away towards the surplus supply stores throughout the yard and pretend to work.

"It is impossible without them," said Jane Priddy as she stepped out into the yard following a Gizor officer.

"What would you have me do, little one?" asked the officer as he turned to face Jane.

"I need more workers. We cannot provide the order without them." The officer looked at the little mouse before him, scoffed and started walking away. "Look at my workers!" She pointed to those scattered around the yard. "They are ill with work. The demands are too great."

"And your solution?"

Jane noticed Agatha behind the officer in the distance, attempting to hide herself by appearing to be busy moving and stacking various supplies, "Half my workforce is gone. Occupation Day saw to that," replied Jane. "We cannot meet the demand."

"Your precious workers will have to do better then, won't they Mrs Priddy?"

"And if we can't deliver?" She knew she held a degree of power over the situation – however small – as hers was the only steel and metal plant in Gosport.

"Do you wish for me to report your failings? I suspect not," said the officer who noticed that Jane had briefly looked beyond him at something in the distance. He turned as if to walk towards Agatha's position.

"It will be your failing too …" said Jane, attempting to turn him around. The officer looked angry and walked menacingly back towards her. "… and your success," she added.

The officer paused for a second, then gave a wry smile.

"You will get your workers, Mrs Priddy."

*

Officers and infantry gathered early in certain pomp and ceremony at Southsea Castle on the south side of Portsmouth in readiness for a VIP visitor. His motorcade arrived from the north, a relatively short distance from the Dockyard. Admiral Gizor stepped out of his car to a throng of well-wishers and those in awe of his leadership. They were proud of the decorated squirrel taking their Country forward and restoring their wealth and honour.

He waved to the crowd as he was escorted through the gates of the castle. "Any word from Fareham?" he asked his henchman, Hilsea, a broad-shouldered weasel.

"No current word as yet, sir, but Roderick is a fine choice." He led Gizor through to the Keep and into a war room.

Argumentative as always, Gizor took immediate offence at the comment. "And are you a fine choice, Captain Hilsea?" he asked as he walked towards the large table where officers were surveying their captured land and reviewing their strategic strongholds.

Hilsea thought it best not to reply directly, so pretended to brush a crumb from his whiskers to play for time. "As you can see, sir, we have secured the camp and Founder's Phase is complete," he said, directing his leader's focus away from him and towards the table.

Gizor peered at the scaled map of his two countries – Portsmouth and Gosport. He remained silent for some moments, carefully studying the map before delivering his verdict to the nervous creatures gathered around the table. "Good," he said. The feeling of relief in the room was palpable. It was high praise indeed from the Admiral.

As he continued studying the map with much interest, Prime Minister Denis Delaney flung open the doors and almost fell into the war room. Doffing his bowler hat and holding his closed umbrella, he tried to pull out some papers from his briefcase as he rushed towards Gizor. The briefcase fell open and his documents fell to the floor. He scrambled about trying to gather them up.

"Admiral, sir … we seem to have a problem, sir."

Uninterested in problems, Gizor ignored Delaney's entrance. "And these positions here?" he enquired, pointing at various pins on the map.

"Yes, Admiral, those are of particular importance," said Hilsea. "Priddy's allows an excellent vantage point and depot, and Daedalus, sir, a small airfield. All taken."

"Admiral, sir?" repeated Delaney, still collecting his papers from the floor.

"Denis, have you seen this?" said Gizor still ignoring the Prime Minister's plea to be heard.

"Yes, Admiral. It is most impressive, but I have a most pressing issue, sir." Delaney flung his briefcase onto the edge of the table and started rifling through his papers.

"Issue?" asked Gizor, still looking at the map. Delaney attempted to hand Gizor a most important report but his outstretched paw was ignored.

"Yes, sir. The camp – it is at capacity, Admiral."

"Capacity?" asked Gizor, still largely uninterested in the 'issue'.

"Yes sir, there has been an underestimate."

"Of how many?"

"Thousands, sir."

Delaney's response was initially met with silence from Gizor with those around him waiting for his reply,

"And this is to scale correct?" asked Gizor, gesturing to the map.

"Yes, sir," said Hilsea.

"Thousands you say?" asked Gizor finally.

"Yes. You'll see that the initial estimate did not include sympathisers and I fear we did not have a full appreciation of the sheer number of those sympathisers and of the Red Squirrels themselves," gabbled Delaney.

Gizor began walking round the table surveying his

land, one paw folded behind him. He turned to review the many prints, photographs, diagrams and plans on the walls of the room. "Is this the camp?" he asked as he pulled an aerial photograph from the wall.

"Yes, Admiral, I believe it is," answered Delaney.

"Copnor, your progress?" asked Gizor to another of his henchmen.

"Sir, we cannot move the deadline forward ..." Observing Gizor's displeasure at this comment, Copnor added "... not without a significant breach of detail and unrest in the camp." Gizor just glared at Copnor in response. "Give me two weeks, Admiral?"

"Sir, I don't understand. If I could be privy to some of these plans," asked Delaney, who had not understood the exchange between Gizor and Copnor.

"Military matters are not your concern, Mr Prime Minister," replied Gizor and returned to studying the table.

\*

Portchester Castle looked glorious in the morning sun, its outer walls adorned with Gizor flags. Such insignia had gone unnoticed by Hertha and her companions in the dark of night. They woke to the beams of spotted sunlight shining through the narrow-barred windows of their cell within the Keep and the sound of footsteps walking along the corridor. Hertha jumped up and nudged Floppy and Berry to do the same. The cell door was flung open.

"Your presence is requested, my friends," said the hooded figure at the door. The three companions shuffled backwards as the figure entered their cell. "Morning prayers are due."

"We demand to speak to Roderick!" said Hertha.

"All in good time."

The three were led out into the corridor, through the Great Hall and out into the courtyard where the Priory Monks had gathered. Pontius Perseus stood forward from the crowd.

"Good morning my friends," he said. "I trust you slept well? Will you join us for morning prayer?"

"Where is this Roderick you speak of?" asked Hertha, uninterested in morning prayer.

"Sir Roderick has been informed of your arrival. He will join us shortly. Please, observe our prayer. Come."

The companions had little choice but to follow the monks as they left the courtyard, entered the grounds of the castle and walked towards the church in the corner. Hertha, as Floppy's protector, retained a tight grip on his ear. She took careful stock of their surroundings as they walked the path towards the church. She could see the east entrance of the castle, which was gated and locked. She could see through the portcullis and out into the harbour where she surmised they had anchored their boat the night before. The way appeared fortified and impossible to breach. Berry too, was standing on his hind legs, looking around to find some way of escape. Floppy, on the other hand, appeared blissfully unaware of their hopes to plan an escape but all the same copied his friends by looking around him.

They entered the church of St Mary. The Priory Monks took to their pews, while others gathered hymn books and passed them down each row to the congregation. The Sisters of St Mary's began their angelic song, and the monks began their Hudsonicus chants and observation of prayer and devotion.

Pontius passed the companions to Lucius who was waiting to show them to their seats, while he continued to the altar at the centre of the church. He began intoning in a fluting voice:

*"Thine is the kingdom, the spirit of life*
*The fruits of our Lord grow still to this day and the next*
*So that we shall forage no more a slave*
*That which is given, is given by him*
*For a new dawn is passing*
*That which the prophet may say*

*New light of Rodentia, bring down to thee your rays*
*Here today and forever we pray*
*In the Glory of your coming*
*Your message is our solace*
*Our comfort and giving to you*
*Forever and ever."*

Hertha, Berry and Floppy sat fidgeting in silence, observing the service while still searching their surroundings but hemmed in by those around them.

"It is our prayers that bring us here today to welcome new friends – those of the Lord's teaching. And the Lord brought to thee his heavy heart and he was repentant this day, and we worship his teachings," continued Pontius.

Hertha couldn't help herself any longer and stood up from her pew and declared: "We wish to leave." Her brave voice echoed through the old Norman church.

"Leave?" replied a dark, cloaked figure at the back of the church. He slowly walked down the aisle towards the altar. Hertha watched the subservient response from the monks around him, bowing their heads and moving out of his way. He was a tall burly grey squirrel: clearly this must be Roderick. He was wearing almost princely robes becoming of his title but certainly not becoming of his character. He snarled as he walked the aisle, was unsteady on his feet, appeared dishevelled and was stuffing his face with berries and spitting the pips out on to the church floor.

This was the squirrel of inherited title, whose family owned most of Portchester's land, but a shameful character with little honour or care for anyone other than himself: an offensive squire with no moral standing.

"Sir Roderick," said Pontius, bowing his head as his leader approached.

Roderick missed his footing as he attempted to step up to the altar but recovered himself by clutching onto the lectern. He swung round and attempted to focus his eyes on Hertha, who was still standing, looking at the spectacle.

"Is he drunk?" whispered Berry to Hertha.

Roderick balanced himself upright by leaning on the lectern. He stared at Hertha and surveyed his congregation, swaying slightly.

"Leave?" he repeated. "You enter my castle in the dead of night [hiccup] and expect to what – [hiccup] to tell us of your woes?" He paused for a moment, steadying himself. He leered behind him at the shuffling of feet where the Sisters of St Mary's were moving from the choir stalls to the pews, as was the tradition in the service. He ogled them as they walked behind him – looking them up and down, following their path as they walked, fancying his chances no doubt. He turned back towards the congregation. "Your woes are no different [hiccup] to a thousand woes." He scuffed his claws on the wooden floor. "And I grow easily tired of hearing about them." Releasing his grip from the lectern, he stepped forward, "Bring me the rabbit!" he demanded. Before Hertha could grab hold of Floppy's paw a couple of monks had dragged Floppy from the pew and shoved him in front of Roderick. Hertha tried to escape from the narrow pew to help him, but without luck. She was pushed back down into her seat by Lucius who grabbed her paw to keep her in her seat. Unseen by anyone else, Lucius passed a small folded piece of cloth in his paw to Hertha.

They exchanged a look and Hertha realised that he was helping them. She had no time or way of examining the cloth but saw it was inscribed – a message.

Floppy stood shaking with fear in front of Roderick who asked his name.

"Floppy I am, Floppy."

"Your real name boy?"

"Floptiers, your majesty."

"Your full name, Mr White Rabbit?"

"Floptiers Burrows-Warren the Third, your majesty, sir."

"My oh my, a rabbit of kin [hiccup]. Thou shalt bow ordinarily I suppose. But alas, there are too many Thirds for there to be a Fourth," said Roderick, removing his side pistol, swinging round and pointing it at Floppy. "I dare you to show us who they believe you are." The monks gasped in horror.

"But I'm not a king," replied Floppy, misunderstanding Roderick's words.

"He doesn't understand!" shouted Hertha, standing up.

Roderick, still drunk and swaying in the aisle, turned and pointed the gun at Hertha. He fired, missing Hertha who had ducked, resulting in the bullet ricocheting off the old walls of the church. Some chaos ensued as the animal congregation scrambled around. This was Hertha's and her friends' chance of escape. She and Berry scrambled over the pews and ran towards Floppy. Roderick fired again, killing a monk. They couldn't get to Floppy who was rigid with fear with his eyes closed tight. Suddenly, amongst the chaos he was grabbed and pulled away towards the vestry.

"Run rabbit run!" shouted Roderick who mocked the chaos and continued firing into the crowd as if it was a game and he had targets to hit.

Hertha and Berry, kneeling behind a pew, watched

97

through the crowd as Floppy was dragged into the vestry by a small figure in a monk's habit. Hertha and Berry timed their retreat and made for the vestry. The firing continued within the church. They entered the little room and scampered towards its door to the side. They ran out of the vestry and headed towards the boundary walls of the churchyard. Priory monks and the Sisters of St Mary's, who had by that time fled the church and were running towards the Keep, were scattered around the castle grounds. Roderick could be seen coming out of the church waving his pistol, still unsteady on his feet and appearing dizzy, pointing his gun at anything resembling the three prisoners. Hertha and Berry, hidden behind a gravestone, desperately looked around for Floppy but couldn't see him anywhere. Their position was not as hidden as they had hoped, as a couple of Priory monks were running towards them. Hertha scrambled over the wall of the churchyard, pulling Berry up behind her, and they ran to the east entrance of the castle walls. Still there was no sign of Floppy. The Priory monks quickly apprehended the pair, but not they made a last-ditch attempt at escape by attacking their captors and trying to wriggle free from their grip. Hertha tried to scramble up the stone steps to the right of the entrance but was soon pulled back. They were brought out kicking and squealing. Hertha looked up during her struggle and saw Pontius Perseus standing in front of them.

"Where is he?" asked Pontius. Roderick was still some distance away scanning the field himself.

Hertha had no answer and just as the question had been asked, she saw that behind Pontius, Roderick was aiming his pistol upright and at an angle, following a target. Hertha followed his aim with her eyes and could see the monks scattered around the grounds all pointing to the walls of the castle. Pontius, with his back to the commotion, turned to follow Hertha's gaze. They all observed Floppy following his rescuer, running and hopping along the castle walls towards the Keep.

"Run, Floppy, run fast!" cried out Hertha as Roderick started shooting. Floppy, guided by his new companion, scrambled over crumbling walls and turrets to reach the outer wall of the lower chamber of the Keep known as Ashton's Tower. The crowd watched as the two jumped for cover by entering the tower through a narrow door and disappearing.

## Chapter 6
# THE KINDNESS OF BEAKY

D aedalus airfield was a hive of activity. Flocks of new Gizor Air birds came and went daily carrying messages about military plans and operations; and large squadrons of seagulls returned from bombing raids throughout Gosport and further afield. Gizor's advance was strong.

"Two pair – I win," said Beaky, a Gull Bomber, who was playing poker at a table just outside the north blister hangar.

"Beaky! Get your wings over 'ere, you pigeon fancier!" shouted Mandible, who disapproved of Beaky's opponent – a pigeon messenger from the R.A.F. Beaky hopped over to his comrade. "What have we said to you about consorting?"

"Yeah, but I win every time."

"Lieutenant Laraday wants someone to scout Grange Farm. I told him you would be the perfect candidate," said Mandible, knowing that the assignment was boring but that it would get Beaky out from under his feet.

"Yeah, yeah, I can do that, and what – report back?"

"Consult your manual, Beaky," said Mandible in a mocking tone. "It's a scouting mission. Of course, you report back, dopey."

"Yeah, yeah, I can do that. What am I looking for?"

"Oh, just some flowers and dandelions. What do you

think? Resistance, Beaky – anything suspicious."

"Right, I'm on it." Without hesitation Beaky ran to the edge of the runway and got himself into position for take-off. He flapped his wings, ruffled his feathers in preparation then stopped and cried out: "What's the mission called?"

Mandible rolled his eyes. "Call it what you want!" he said.

"Operation Beaky Grange it is then," said Beaky, feeling proud of his important assignment as he started down the runway and flew into the sky. He flew a short circuit of the airfield and dropped back down towards Mandible. "How do I get there? What's it look like?"

*

"Right-o, ladies," said Lady Prideaux-Brune to her assembled D.I. Institute. She was not about to let being in a Gizor Camp do away with their monthly meetings. "Much to discuss, much to do. Now, I propose a dance. Liven the place up a little."

Mary Camper shook her head in disapproval. "I really feel that a dance in the camp would be most inappropriate and I very much doubt in any case it would be approved," she said.

"Yes, yes, but no harm in trying. Keep the spirits up, no?"

"Well, I'm just pointing out that it won't be approved."

"Mary, perhaps you can help in getting it approved then?" said Lady Ellen with a sly smile. Mary simply turned her head and tutted in disgust at the suggestion.

Just then the Camp siren blurted out and Gizor officers prepared to open the gates for the arrival of a truck, the kind commonly used for transporting large animals. More arrivals were entering the camp.

101

"Not pigs, surely?" said Lady Ellen, wrinkling her nose. They watched the truck pull into the entrance, and then Jane Priddy jumped down from the cab of the vehicle and was greeted by some officers. She was shuffled into a side office.

"Was that Jane Priddy I just saw?" asked Mary.

"I believe it was, or someone awfully similar," said Lady Ellen.

"How on earth does she see over the steering wheel? She's so tiny."

"I think one of her badger workers does the driving."

Just as their interest was sparked, Brigadier Brune came out from the crowd, gesturing with his walking stick and issuing orders to the Camp. "Line up chappies, parade in two minutes I'm told," he barked. "Be in your finest, unruffled. Spick 'n' span. Show 'em our best." The Brigadier had adapted well to life at the Camp despite his age and frailty. It took him back to battles gone by and despite being captive he rather liked the regimental rules of the Camp and was making the most of it.

As the parade assembled in the square, Gizor officers began inspecting the lines of prisoners. Jane appeared, standing next to an officer at the front. She stood with a clipboard and passed it to the officer who began calling out identification numbers. As the numbers were called, officers grabbed each animal in turn, pulled them from the line and began shackling their ankles together and marching them off in small groups towards the transport truck.

*

Beaky flew above Browndown Camp to get his bearings. He could see the parade line of thousands of animals and those being loaded into the truck. As instructed he began

102

flying almost back on himself, heading north to find Grange Farm. He followed the Alver river and circled the outbuildings and farmhouse of Grange Farm then observed to the north of the site some smoke rising from the trees. He could smell delicious apple dumplings and naturally flew closer. He spied a little village hidden under the canopy of trees – only the smoke from a wood fire and the smell of food revealed its location. Beaky made his decent, circling as he did so. Although mindful of the fact that he was on a scouting mission his stomach had other ideas. He landed haphazardly as usual, on a path to the east of the village. To the south he could just make out the farmhouse roof of Grange Farm, he turned and began walking away from it down the path towards the smell of dumplings. As he wobbled down the path, his awkward webbed feet kicked up the dirt beneath him – conspicuous as ever. He had never been in the woods before, for a seagull's place is in the sky along the coast and not in the woodlands. He followed the winding path, which sloped slightly leading down towards the thatched cottages. He could hear beautiful music – the sounds of old penny whistles, light drums and bells. As he grew closer, a small hedgehog child, gathering some twigs in the distance, caught sight of the seagull walking towards him. He immediately dropped his twigs and scurried as fast as he could into the little village. The music stopped. Beaky quickened his pace as the smell of scrumptious dumplings became stronger. As he entered the village, its occupants were scurrying around in panic.

"Err, can I have some pie?" asked Beaky, ever direct.

In response, a brave little fieldmouse dressed in scullery uniform approached him. He towered over her. She was holding a plate out towards Beaky while curtseying and bowing her head. She was hoping with all her might that he would accept the offering and then leave. The villagers were watching from their homes, trying to hide and hoping the same.

"Take the food from the lassie," whispered Morag to herself as she stood in the distance at the water pump, holding on to the shoulders of a small child hedgehog to keep him safe. Morag was a feisty little hedgehog who ran the village that served the farm beside it.

Beaky took the dumpling and scoffed it quickly. "Mmm, this is delicious," he responded gratefully. "Got any more?"

Morag had seen enough. "Look 'ere, laddie," she said, stepping forward slightly and calling out. "You's cannae be 'ere so best be away with ya now."

"What was that music I heard? It was good," said Beaky, seemingly unaware that he was unwelcome. He couldn't quite understand the hedgehog's funny accent but she didn't seem to be threatening him.

"Farmer Jack will have your guts for garters if he finds you 'ere," warned Morag.

"Farmer Jack?"

"Aye, Farmer Jack don't like visitors – best be on your way now, laddie."

Beaky was blissfully unaware of the power he had over the little villagers and stepped closer to Morag.

"Whoa there, laddie!" said Morag, panicking and stretching both paws out in front of her in immediate defence as the villagers around her shuffled deeper into their hiding spaces and some instantly scrunched into small round balls – as hedgehogs do.

"I likes it here," commented Beaky looking around the village. "Never been in the woods."

"You've had your food, now you must be on your way."

"Can't I stay just a bit longer?"

Morag, conscious that this was a Gizor Gull and so he would do very much as he wanted, was taken aback. "No," she replied eventually, somewhat confused.

"I won't be no bother."

Morag realised she was dealing with an empty acorn shell, as did the rest of the village who came out of hiding and began their daily chores – weaving cloth, chopping wood, making barrels, and embroidering. She approached Beaky. "What d'ya want, boy? Why are yous 'ere, laddie?"

Beaky quickly stood up straight and shuffled his feathers proudly. "I'm on a mission," he squawked.

"Oh aye?"

"Yep, a scouting mission," added Beaky still looking around the village, fascinated by what the villagers were doing. He could see in one corner laundry being pressed and in another, tools being sharpened and food prepared.

"Is it not a secret mission?" asked Morag, knowing full well it probably should have been.

"Err, well, I suppose so." Beaky didn't know how to respond.

"It's OK, sonny lad. Your secret's safe with us. Nothing to see here, though – just a little village. No Reds, no mutiny here."

"Well that's OK then."

Morag walked closer to Beaky and tried to lead him out of the village with a guiding paw, but could only reach up as far as his leg.

"So, do you all live here in the woods like?" asked Beaky, ignoring Morag's paw and turning back round to check out the tools they were sharpening.

"Aye we do. We've lived here for generations. We serve the land, laddie. But you must leave as Farmer Jack won't be best pleased to find yous here."

"OK, but can I come back?" asked Beaky.

"I donae think so." She started walking Beaky out of the village.

Beaky looked sad at the response he got, especially when he could see villagers putting up bunting, setting out cakes, bringing out ale, and preparing a bonfire. Morag began to soften towards him.

"I'm Beaky," he said, turning to face Morag and stretching his wing out to shake her paw.

"Well perhaps we'll meet again, Beaky, after all this bother's done with," she replied as he slowly walked out of the village.

"*Perhaps* is better than never, my mamma always said."

"Be careful with ya now, Beaky," called out Morag as he went.

"Shall we tell Farmer Jack?" asked Jasper, a woodpecker in charge of woodcutting for the village. He stood behind Morag, wearing an apron covered in wood chips, as they watched Beaky waddling off down the track.

"No, we keep this one to ourselves for now."

"He may bring others back," warned Jasper.

"Aye and if he does, we'll be ready."

*

The animal transport truck arrived at Priddy's gates full of workers. Agatha had waited for its arrival. She kept low and hidden in one of the outer stores and watched from a distance as the animals were unloaded and put to work immediately. As she watched, she saw her old friend Doris being unloaded and given a huge hessian bag to carry to the store.

"Psst," whispered Agatha, trying discreetly to get her attention. "Psst. Over here."

"Agatha?" replied Doris, turning around and looking into the corner of the store where Agatha was crouching.

"Yes. Act as if you are busy. Don't turn around. Carry on working."

"Agatha, I'm so pleased to see you," she whispered, giving a toothy smile. "Are you OK?"

"Yes. Are you? What is the Camp like? Have you seen my papa?"

"No, I haven't seen him yet, but the Camp is divided up. We are not all together and more keep arriving every day – too many. It's overrun." She hoisted the hessian bag onto her back. "Agatha, where have you been?" she asked. As she did so, an officer approached her with more bags for her to load into huge containers. Agatha crouched lower and hid in the shadows.

"Quicker!" he shouted.

"Yes, sir," replied Doris docilely as the officer walked off.

"Listen. No time to explain," said Agatha. "I'll meet you here when I can, for word from the Camp. We'll get you out of there soon, I promise."

\*

As more arrived at Browndown each day, the work increased at the Camp itself. Animals were put to work sorting out endless collected belongings, jewellery, clothing, currency, and photographs. Huge rooms had been set up for the workers to sort through the treasured belongings of those in the Camp – belongings that had been taken from them immediately they arrived.

"Faster!" shouted an officer to one long line of workers seated at a table. But the pace did not increase to his satisfaction. The officer signalled to one of the supervisors, who grabbed the slowest worker out of the line and dragged her outside. She was an elderly weasel, worn out and frailer than the rest. Some shouting could be heard before she was dragged away and never seen again. This prompted everyone to keep their heads down and quicken their pace despite their exhaustion.

"The arthritis in my paws is playing me up something chronic," said Gertie, who was trying her best to sort through the belongings as fast as she could.

"Here – use this," replied Lady Ellen, passing her a rag and discreetly wrapping it tight round Gertie's wrist for support.

"I much preferred washing out the mess tins than this."

"Well at least we're sitting down and out of the midday sun," replied Lady Ellen, ever-jovial.

"And when for heaven's sake will the re-homing begin?" asked Mary rhetorically.

*

Agatha made her way back to the safety of the caponier. As she travelled she could not help but think of her friends – those in the Camp and those she had watched drift off towards Portchester Castle. It had been three days since she had seen them and still there was no word. She hoped she would find them back at base with an army of rallied support from Fareham. She clambered over the fencing and into the allotments towards the shed, to find the door ajar and the cupboard wide open. She scanned the allotment for Gizor personnel before climbing down the tunnel and heading towards base. As she approached the entrance, she found herself having to shift rubble and broken furniture out of her way to gain entry. She thought the worst. Either her band of resistance was trapped inside or had been captured.

Her heart began racing as she managed to shift the last piece of wood out of her way. The caponier was silent, dark and thick with dust, which she wafted away from her eyes with her paws in order to see. As she slowly walked around, she knocked an old tin with her foot and it spun around, making a noise. It was Rosie's old biscuit tin. She picked it up, along with her easy chair, which she placed carefully upright. The caponier was empty and destroyed. Plans had been ripped from the walls and torn to shreds and there was evidence of a scuffle – a small battle had taken place there. She called out "hello?" but there was no reply. She sat down on the easy chair, grabbed hold of Rosie's biscuit tin and hugged it close for comfort.

\*

A truck approached the entrance of Kingston Prison in Portsmouth and waited for the gates to open. It moved speedily into an enclosed yard where officers greeted it. Hertha and Berry were bundled out of the truck, a sack over their heads, and their paws chained. They were marched off into the prison itself. They were both battered and bruised and had no idea where they were.

"Put these two in the cellar!" called out a voice.

The two comrades could hear the clanging of metal doors being shut and locked as they were shoved down the spiral steps, along a cobbled damp-smelling corridor and through to their cell. The officers removed the chains from their paws, locked the bars of the cell and walked off. Hertha and Berry immediately pulled off the sacks from over their heads. It took a few moments for their eyes to adjust to their dark surroundings.

"Where are we, H?" asked Berry, testing to see if the doors had been locked behind them. Of course, they had been.

Hertha looked around and immediately went to the only light available in the cell – the barred window, which was small and narrow and into which only a faint light shone slightly from the other side. She couldn't see out: the window wasn't designed that way. In fact, it was barely a window at all but instead a hole in the wall that sloped up a few yards to reveal sunlight, but barred either end, with drops of remaining rainwater falling into the damp cell.

Hertha started sniffing the foul air through the bars. "Portsmouth," she said, sighing to herself. She held onto the bars, staring up at the sky, and felt desperate and empty of ideas. Berry didn't have any either. The bars were too closely spaced even for a mole to escape, but he continued pushing and pulling at them for some signs of give.

Their silence was abruptly ended by the sound of footsteps walking slowly down the spiral staircase towards their dungeon. Hertha swung round, and Berry released his grip on the bars. They could hear only one set of footsteps approaching. Hertha clenched her paws as if ready for a fight. Berry grabbed one of the sacks that had been put over their heads and twisted it tight to make it strong and noose-like. All that could be heard was their breath and the footsteps. As the sound grew closer, Hertha edged nearer to Berry.

A figure in a dark grey cloak and hood walked almost serenely past their cell, stopped in front for a second, turning its head only slightly towards the two prisoners, before continuing to walk down the corridor. The figure made no attempt to speak.

"Hey!" Hertha called out. There was no response. "You there!"

The figure simply ignored her. Hertha grabbed hold of the bars and attempted to look along the corridor to see the stranger, but the angle would not allow her. The footsteps then stopped and there was silence once more.

"We need to get out of here as quickly as possible," she said, staring at the now empty corridor before them.

"In Floppy's words – I be afraid, I be," said Berry.

Hertha quickly ran back to the light and sat down on the cold damp floor, curling her tail around her for warmth. Berry turned to watch. She frantically tried to pull off one of her boots and reluctantly had to untie its long bootlace to do so. She then removed her old tatty sock and searched inside it. Berry stepped closer to see what she was doing.

"The note," she said, with a glimmer of hope in her voice. "He gave me a note. Remember? Lucius handed it to me in the church a few days ago. I hid it in my sock. The Gizor didn't look there." Hertha pulled out the small piece of cloth. She could barely see it in the poor light. She crawled to the window on all fours and moved the cloth around to get a clearer look.

"What is it? What are those markings?" asked Berry standing over her.

"I don't know. It makes no sense."

"Is it an old map of some kind?" asked Berry, who couldn't read.

Hertha dropped the cloth to the cold floor and held it taut to examine it further.

*By design to aid our task*
*Travels the direction of our path*
*A mighty ship of glory be*
*Forged above the windy sea*
*Move first, the Fourth, elude deceit*
*And follow thee*
*Serves to glory those in need.*

*Scattered rust and wood of rot*
*We wait the dank*
*Shored by the dock*

*Of our path, our puzzle be*
*We seal these walls*
*And start with thee*

*Of brick and stone are brittle bones*
*To test a puzzled mind*
*Stone dungeon deep*
*As chained, we sleep*
*Charts the stars above the sky*

*To beckon craft, O summon thee*
*Heaven's light, our Guide to see*
*No sound of fog will blindfold thee.*
*One word to gather, to believe*
*Our Great, Our Mighty, come to thee.*

"Oh, just what we need – a riddle. As if we didn't have it easy enough, hey H? Doesn't mention anything about a key by any chance, does it?" said Berry mockingly, returning to push and pull at the cell bars and to try and squeeze himself through. Hertha continued sitting on the floor studying the piece of cloth, trying to work out what it meant and scratching her head with her claw to stimulate her tired brain.

*

Agatha spent days by herself, manically sifting through old maps and taping plans back together in the dim candlelight of the deserted caponier. Unsure of her next move, she needed to find Hertha's map of other pockets of resistance located in Gosport. She started creating her own map based on what she knew – where the Gizor troops were, their strength in numbers, and locations she knew they would be interested in. She also pieced together small fragments of Hertha's map that had been torn to bits and laid it out on to the table. She used Rosie's old biscuit tin and a couple of mugs to fasten it flat.

"Right," she said to herself. "Now, if I'm here, the Camp is here, Priddy's there. Hmm, the airfield is wide open. I bet that's been taken." She studied the map and it suddenly dawned on her that the airfield would be the main base of operation. "I need to get to Daedalus," she said, quickly grabbing her jacket (the one that Hertha had given her). She stuffed a few biscuits into its pockets, folded the map and held it by her teeth while simultaneously tying their signature red bandana round her head. One ear kept getting in the way but eventually she got the bandana at the right angle. She grabbed the map and tucked it securely inside her jacket. As she was about to leave, she stopped to look at herself in the broken mirror leaning up against the wall. "You can do this, Agatha," she said to her reflection.

\*

"Oi, Beaky!" shouted Mandible from across the airfield, "get yourself 'ere."

"Yes, Mandible?" Beaky ran eagerly across the airstrip. Mandible rolled his eyes as Beaky hadn't realised he had just caused the crash of two Starling fighters preparing for take-off.

"You like garlic juice, don't ya? Well, make yourself busy. Go and see if you can help out at Blister North," he ordered.

113

"Yes, Mandible," replied Beaky enthusiastically. "Oh boy! Blister North!" He was proud of getting more and more responsibility as he saw it and waddled off to the north of the airfield for his orders.

"Sergeant, sir? Private Beaky reporting for duty, sir," he shouted with a salute to a commanding officer.

He was immediately put to work supervising a factory line of pigeons that were sorting through jewellery that had been delivered from Browndown Camp. A group of magpie officers were seated at the end of each line inspecting the items for their quality and worth.

"Here, boy!" called out a Magpie officer in his harsh voice to Beaky. He was holding two wedding bands in his raised foot. "Can you tell the difference?" he asked, thrusting the rings towards Beaky.

"Well, they're both shiny."

"Feel the weight of them, boy."

Beaky took them awkwardly from the officer, balancing them on his beak. "Both heavy too," he observed.

"This is why I'm a magpie and you're … well … you. It may be subtle but there is a difference. This one is fake and this one is solid silver. Melted down, worth even more."

"Oh right," replied Beaky, passing the rings back to the officer. "So, where did all this stuff come from then?"

"The Camp, of course."

Beaky looked around at the heaps of jewellery being rifled through by the Pigeon Bombers, some wrens and robins. "So, they didn't want 'em anymore then?" he asked innocently. The magpie laughed and walked off without replying, pushing along a tray of solid silver with his feet. Beaky was puzzled as to why the officer was laughing but dismissed it from his mind and started making idle chit chat with the workers.

"Hi there, I'm Beaky. Do you need a new sorting tray or maybe some garlic juice?" he asked. A small water vole carrying a tray towards the table brushed against him. The water vole quickly ran back to get some garlic juice. The animals and birds in the factory line clearly thought that this Gull Bomber was playing with his prey, as a Gizor soldier would. They were submissive and eager to serve.

"Here!" said the magpie officer from a distance. Beaky turned around. "Catch!" said the officer, throwing him a piece of jewellery that Beaky caught in his mouth. "You can keep that one for yourself – worth a worm or two," he said laughing.

Beaky looked down at the piece of jewellery. It was an old battered medallion – a talisman – with an inscription on the back: '*Kindness is everything in life*'. He wondered why anyone would want to give up such a nice piece of jewellery.

Just then, the airfield siren rang out signalling the end of the day. Beaky placed the medallion in his handkerchief, wrapped it up and tucked it safely away in his jacket pocket. The assembly line stood up from their stations and in an orderly queue marched out of the blister hangar, bowing their heads in subservience.

Beaky followed the marching line out onto the airfield where he observed them being ushered into a penned area. One of the wrens, who was weak from work, fell to the ground. Beaky ran to help her up. She was shocked by his kindness and nodded her appreciation before re-joining the line. Beaky thought to himself: "yes, kindness really *is* everything."

## Chapter 7
# A TRICK OF
# THE LIGHT

Hertha and Berry, still trapped in their cell, were fed only leftover scraps and were more than a little hungry. Berry (who liked his food) was particularly suffering and as a result was very grouchy.

"I wish you'd throw that old rag away," he said, gesturing at the piece of cloth. "Ain't no help to anyone. You've been staring at it for days."

Ignoring his grouchiness, Hertha replied: "I think it's a sign. Something we have to look out for."

"Oh, and clearly we have such a lovely view that we're at risk of missing it because there's so much to look at."

"Oh, so you wanna give up then, Berry? You only see the moon because of the sun," she said.

"What's that supposed to mean?" said Berry, folding his arms in annoyance.

"It's something Pontius Perseus said."

"Why on earth would you listen to that brainwashed fool?" asked Berry flinging the hessian sack around as if it was a whip. He was hungry and bored.

Just as the pair began arguing, they heard footsteps again on the stone staircase. Berry, who had been leaning against the bars, shuffled further into the room and turned around to face the corridor. Hertha sat up. Both watched as the ghostly figure walked past their cell again without a word.

"That's every night!" Berry stood up and shouted. "I've had enough of this. Oi! You! Come back here! Roaming around like some sort of ghost. Who are you?"

"Berry! Shush!"

"'No, I'm sick of this," replied Berry holding the bars and trying to peek around the corner. "'Show yourself, you coward."

"'Berry, don't."

Just as she asked him to stop bringing attention to them there was an almighty howling noise, like a gust of wind, which blew down the cobbled corridor. The dim candlelight began to flicker. The howling grew louder and more intense. Suddenly the gust of wind became so strong that Berry was forced away from the bars and his fur pushed flush to his face. Hertha struggled to get up from the floor but as she did so she looked up towards the bars to see the strange cloaked figure spinning around in front of their cell, howling and chanting. It was the first time that they had got a clear glimpse of the figure, which was clearly female.

"Stop!" shouted Hertha as she got to her feet and grabbed the bars. "Stop, you old ghost!"

The ghost did indeed stop. She stopped with her back to their cell, still cloaked and with her hood over her head. Her cloak was made of old faded crimson patchwork and was moth-eaten and torn, with threads hanging to the floor.

"You're no ghost, are you?" asked Hertha quietly.

"Ghost?" said the figure in a frail old voice and began cackling manically to herself.

"You're more like a witch."

With that the witch stopped laughing and slowly turned her head to the right. There was silence.

"Well? Which is it?" asked Hertha.

The witch let out an almighty high-pitched scream, suddenly turned sharply, and grabbed hold of the bars while raising her head to the sky. "A WITCH!" she screamed. The hood over her head fell back to reveal an old red squirrel.

"She's a red, Hertha. The Red Witch," said Berry who immediately backed off to the rear wall of the cell. They had both heard legends about the Red Witch. Everyone had. Stories that had been passed down from generation to generation. Witches that could turn you into a snail with a single look, cast spells to make you go crazy, and ones that could give you a lifetime of horrible bad luck. Witches lived in dark places in the woods where only the unfortunate stumbled upon them. Yet they found themselves looking at one in front of their very eyes.

"Stay back, witch!" shouted Berry, brandishing his taut hessian hood as a weapon. "Stay back, I tells ya."

"Who ARE you?" asked Hertha bravely.

"Don't ask her questions. She will turn you into a spider and pull off all your legs," warned Berry.

"Silent treatment, eh?" said Hertha to the witch who stood in silence looking up at what would be the sky if they hadn't been in the depths of a deep dungeon. "A witch with no name? And I thought all witches had a name?" Hertha was afraid deep down but refused to show it. Plus she figured had nothing to lose by seeking answers and perhaps teasing the witch a little to reveal something. Anything.

The witch slowly lowered her head in an almost eerie manner and responded: "You only see the moon because of the sun." She immediately followed this with a screech-like cackle.

"Are you a prisoner?" asked Hertha. "You've been listening to us, haven't you? I dare you to tell us who you are."

The witch stood silent for a few moments as if to

118

ponder a reply.

"The ways your path will turn to water, dust and chalk, north the harbour," she eventually replied.

"Do you even have a name? Or have you forgotten it?" This last question was met with deathly silence. "You've been here too long. That's it, isn't it? You've been here so long as a prisoner you don't even know your own name any more? They've locked you up and you've forgotten everything. Trusted to wander the halls and good for nothing. You're trapped with no magic at all!"

With this remark, the witch grabbed Hertha's face in a tight clench with her paws between the bars and looked her straight in the eyes. "The smallest of light will burn your eyes."

Berry stood forward in immediate defence. "Get off her, witch!" he said, grabbing the witch's paws from behind his friend. As he did so, the Red Witch screamed. It was a deathly high-pitched scream that sent her and Hertha flying backwards towards their respective walls – the witch in the corridor and Hertha in the cell. Berry rushed to help his friend up off the floor. Hertha dusted herself off and both looked up to find the witch had disappeared.

*

Agatha made her way on foot through the edge of Cherque Common – a wooded area between the village of Rowner and Loft Daedalus. She cut through Shoot Lane, being careful not to be noticed. Through the trees, she could hear golf being played, and clubs being swung. She wondered how anyone could be playing games at a time of war.

"Fore!" shouted someone on the green. Agatha ducked just as a golf ball flew passed her head and landed in the brambles.

"It's got to be around here somewhere," said a voice a short time later. The voice came nearer and a paw reached down into the undergrowth next to Agatha, feeling for the ball. She looked up. It was John Robinson, a landowner born of a wealthy family who had always spent most of his days at the golf course with his fellow Alverstocracy members or at the Lee-on-Solent sailing club. He was an otter who enjoyed a whiskey or two. He was always in competition with others such as Brigadier Brune, Lady Ellen, Bernard Hardway and of course Jane Priddy. Yet, his competitors had a charm about them, whereas Mr Robinson was ruthless with a reputation for coldness. One thing was for certain: he was no sympathiser. As he bent down, leaning on his club, he caught a glimpse of Agatha. They looked at each other. He paused for a second, said nothing, retrieved his ball and walked back to the green where he was joined by a Portsmouth grey squirrel dressed in tweed golfing gear with Argyle socks pulled up to his knees and a Burberry cap.

"So tell me, Burrfields. If the Camp is already full where do they intend to put them all – all those still out there hiding?" asked Mr Robinson.

"Well, I know nothing about the resettlement process, but I do know there are no homes to be had," replied the grey squirrel. "They will be found and taken to the Camp, I suppose," Burrfields continued as he took a swing. "Disposed of, I suspect."

"Disposed of?"

"Well, Gizor wants his pure breed, so I would imagine the cull will be in operation soon."

"I see." He tried to hide his shock at what he had just heard.

"Well, can't have vermin back on the streets now, can we?" They walked away.

Agatha was in turmoil at hearing their conversation – one deliberately staged by Mr Robinson for her benefit. It was the only kind thing he had ever done. She scrunched up the mud and grass in her paws in desperation. The 'C' of 'G.C.' stood for Cull, not Collectors. Agatha felt a fool. She decided to ditch her plan to go to the airfield and instead started her way carefully back to the caponier so she could collect her thoughts.

*

The Camp at Browndown was very much a divided one. The animals were separated from loved ones, were put to work and driven to the point of exhaustion. There was no regard for age or fragility. But this was of no concern to the Gizor troops.

"I do believe the re-homing process has finally started," commented Mary Camper, sitting outside with Lady Ellen, Gertie and others to eat their meagre rations after a long day's work. "And I see they are installing de-fleaing stations for us all at last. About time too, I should think."

"Yes, it was getting a little overcrowded I must say, Mary," said Gertie.

"I do hope that they re-home accordingly."

"Accordingly, Mary?" enquired Lady Ellen.

"Yes, well you know – according to our already established positions within the community," said Mary rather pompously. "It is only right and proper, after all."

"Yes," agreed Gertie. "Only right and proper."

"Oh, do be quiet, Gertie," said Mary.

Lady Ellen listened to their nonsense chatter but made no passing comment on this occasion. She was quite tired today. She heard Peter Mumby across the way banging a tin pot to signal the start of church service and the little group got up to make their way over. The animals used one of the barracks as their makeshift church.

"Ah, Doris," said Lady Ellen seeing her walk into the barracks, "any more word from Agatha?""

"Not hide nor hair," said Doris, perching on the side of one of the beds.

"I do hope she is OK. Mind you, she has done very well so far not to have been captured."

"Pointless exercise if you ask me," interrupted Mary. "She ought to just hand herself in to the appropriate authorities in my opinion."

"Well no one actually asked for your opinion, Mrs Camper," replied Doris.

"She's just like her mother was. Never listens to reason. Always has her own ideas," added Mary.

"The world would be a boring place if we all shared the same view, Mrs Camper," said Peter Mumby, who had been listening to the conversation about his daughter. "And to challenge is to learn, is it not? To ask questions and seek reason in this mad world and learn for the next?"

The vicar moved to the front. "Good evening, my fellow congregation," started Reverend Stapland. "Let us pray." The room fell silent. "We gather here in small devotion yet in stout heart and thank thee for our strength – that which you have given, and that which you have laid beside us – always. We pray for our new homes – a new place to settle with new opportunity. We know you will allow us to remain strong and begin a new world where this community of brethren will remain devoted to your teachings. Your words reflect all forgiveness and we obey in kind – to your greater power, guidance and purpose – a new start, we will begin."

Just as the Reverend had finished, the door to the barrack burst open.

"Marjorie! Has anyone seen my Marjorie?" called out Francis Appleby, a red squirrel in a frantic panic looking for his wife.

"Oh, dear me no," replied someone in the congregation. "I haven't seen her since late morning." There was a mumbling of chatter from the crowd, asking each other when they had last seen Marjorie Appleby.

"Perhaps she's been moved to the other side of the Camp?" queried another.

Just as the congregation continued firing suggestions as to her whereabouts, an excited young buck squirrel came rushing through the doors. "It's snowing!" he declared.

The crowd looked at each other confused. "Snowing? In June?" They all rushed outside to see what the young buck was referring to.

While the day had lost almost all its light, the moon appeared to light up the camp as the animals piled out of the barrack and on to the parade square. The buck child had not been the only one to have noticed the 'snow'. All the inhabitants of the Camp appeared from their barracks. Looking up into the sky the snow was falling beautifully on to the parade square and floating hypnotically through the air. Animals reached out their paws in bewilderment. It was neither cold nor the season. Some cried a miracle had taken place – a sign of hope – that anything was possible if it could snow in the summer. A gust of strong wind appeared to scoop up some of the flakes from the ground and whirl them around. Some of the animals began dancing with each other in an impromptu celebration. Others held their paws to cover their noses because as the wind circled, a wretched smell was uncovered. Soon the entire Camp could smell something most foul and acrid in the air and covered their faces to protect themselves from it.

The crowd was being watched by two guards above

them in one of the outposts. "Silly vermin," they said, laughing.

*

The Semaphore Tower stood austere against the dark summer sky. Gizor enjoyed its position at the centre of Portsmouth Dockyard, where it towered over both his lands. The door was closed and guarded. It was late. The two soldiers at the door could hear laughter coming from Gizor's office – something they had never heard from their Admiral. They briefly looked at each other, unsure if they should go in to check on their Commander-in-Chief. They thought better of it.

Through the door were two distant cousins – Jean De Gizor and Sir Roderick of Portchester who had grown up together – along with a couple of commanders, all smoking, drinking and playing a game of poker. It seemed that the relationship between Jean and 'Reckless Roddy' was such that a submissive game be played for the sake of their leader was not necessary. Reckless Roddy was out to win.

"So, Sir Roderick, if I give you Wymering Manor will you give me Portchester Castle?" mocked Gizor, who knew he was ultimately in control of his cousin and his land.

"If I give you my Castle, Jean, will you give me yours?" he replied referring to Southsea Castle on the Common.

"Ah," he replied, chuckling to himself. They were both very drunk. "Only if I am allowed to keep the Sisters of St Mary's."

"That's no deal, cousin Gizor. I cannot give up my Sisters. They mean too much to me."

"Defection in the ranks!" shouted Gizor as he slammed his fist on to the table in jest and gulped his whisky down.

"You always drove a hard bargain."

"I learnt it from you, cousin."

Gizor drunkenly peered into his near-empty whisky glass as the others continued their game. Gizor had suddenly lost interest. He staggered up onto his feet and walked over to the south window. "See the view, Roderick?"

Roderick grabbed his drink and walked over to his cousin.

"What I want is further than I can see. I want the Ark," said Gizor.

"And you will have it, cousin Jean."

*

Agatha reached the relative safety of the caponier. She scrambled around looking for some chalk and paper in the dark, lighting a couple of candles to guide her. She right-sided a chair and sat down at what had been the 'planning table' used by Hertha. She began writing a notice. She was not immediately satisfied with it, so scrunched it up in her paws and began again. She did this several times. She needed to get this right. She had a plan, albeit one she would have to carry out herself as the only member of the Resistance left, it would seem. She worked through the night. As she continued drafting her notices, she heard a noise in the far corner towards the centre of the fort itself. Rubble was being moved from the outside. She quickly picked up a notice and stuffed it into her jacket pocket, grabbed a bread knife, blew out the candle and hid herself in the corner, her tail wrapped around her. She was ready for anything. She was still angry from what she had learnt and wasn't prepared to die until she had spread the word. The sound of moving rubble was getting louder: they were breaking through. Agatha tensed and prepared for battle.

From the shadows in her corner, she snuck a peek at the moving rubble to her left. A ray of morning light began to shine through. She was ready. She worried she might be outnumbered, but it was too late to get to the other side of the caponier to make her escape back up to the shed. She had only two options left – to hide or strike before they all bundled into the room. Perhaps if she struck one of the Gizor she would have time to make a run for the shed. Her breathing was heavy. "Think, Agatha. Think," she whispered to herself. She heard the accent of a Gizor soldier.

"Here, let me," said the voice as if to take over from another. They broke through: a soldier entered the caponier, wafted the dust away from his face and immediately began coughing as a result. Despite the morning light, the caponier was still a shadowy place.

Agatha could only seem to hear two sets of footsteps and therefore made a quick decision to strike. She ran out from her corner, yielding the knife in her paw. She lunged at the grey figure standing at the broken entrance. She lost her footing slightly, tripping on some rubble, which made her advance weaker than she had intended, yet she still struck the solider, catching him on the arm. They both fell to the floor, the knife was flung out of her paw and lost among the rubble. She began hitting the figure on the floor as hard as she could to keep him down.

"Hertha! Hertha!" cried a voice.

Agatha stopped in her tracks. "Floppy?" she cried in shock. There was no time to think: "Floppy, grab him. Get him!" she shouted as she continued hitting the prone figure.

"Aggy?" Floppy realised it wasn't Hertha he was talking to, it was Agatha. "Aggy, leave him. Leave him, Aggy," said Floppy as he pulled her off the prone figure.

126

She slumped backwards on the floor.

"Floppy? What's going on?"

"Lucius! Lucius!" he cried, as he rushed to the side of the grey squirrel and sat him up.

"Floppy, what's going on? Where's Hertha and Berry? Who's this?"

"This is my friend Lucius," said Floppy attending to him. "Lucius is good. Lucius won't harm you."

Agatha watched Floppy support his friend by propping him up against a wall, "Floppy, he's a Grey. He's a Pompey. He's not your friend."

"But he is, Agatha. He is, I tell you."

Agatha was not convinced. She had worked herself up and was still so angry. She picked herself up off the floor, grabbed her knife and asked: "Who are you?"

"I am Lucius Uvedale," he replied weakly, clutching his right arm, which was bleeding. "I come from the Castle."

"Where's Hertha? Where's Berry?" asked Agatha, still suspicious. "What have you done with them?" She pointed the knife at the 'villain' on the floor, grabbed Floppy by the paw and pulled him away from his so-called friend.

"It's OK, Floptiers," he said, gently trying to reassure Floppy who couldn't understand where his loyalties lay. "Your friends will be safe for now." He staggered to his feet, using the wall for support. He was clearly in some pain from his wound. Agatha moved her knife closer towards the 'enemy'.

"What do you mean 'for now'? Where are they?"

Lucius staggered over to the planning table ignoring Agatha's bravado. He almost collapsed into the chair, wincing as he did. "They will have been taken to Kingston Prison," he said. "I'm sure of it."

"What?" Agatha was confused. She last saw her friends

rowing towards Portchester Castle. "What's happened, Floppy? What is he talking about?"

"Them's bad monks in the Castle, Aggy. They locked us up, they did. And the bad man came. He was mad. He was worse than Ponty Pinty. The bad man shot at me, he did. But I escaped because I'm a White Rabbit. I ran, and I ran. Just like Hertha told me to. I was brave. It was dark, and we went through tunnels. We crawled, and we crawled. Sometimes we ran and sometimes we walked. I was scared but I was brave. Wasn't I, Lucius?"

Lucius gave a gentle sigh. "Yes Floptiers," he said, "you were very brave, my friend."

Agatha lowered her knife, trying to piece together what she was hearing.

"Where's Rosie?" Floppy asked as it suddenly dawned on him that the base was empty and ruined.

Agatha ignored Floppy and sat down at the table, wanting to know more from Lucius but she didn't know where to begin.

"Your friends will have been taken to the Prison," he said to Agatha again. "We had hoped they had escaped and that we would find them here. He kept talking about this place – his home, his friends."

Agatha suddenly realised she had hurt someone and felt enormous guilt. She had never hurt anyone in her life apart from Sandy Pickton, a stout red squirrel at school who used to bully her. She grabbed the cleanest cloth she could find, shook it free of dust and attempted to wrap it round Lucius' wound.

"Tell me everything," she urged.

*

The Gizor Cull – no more to be known as the Gizor Collectors – could be seen ushering the new arrivals to Browndown Camp off the animal transport trucks and through the usual checks – shaving their fur and stamping their skin with a permanent Pompey crest. Their belongings were taken from them and piled high in one corner where campmates were assigned to load them into huge trolleys and cart them off to various sorting barracks. Every day, there was an endless supply of belongings to sift through as new arrivals continued to appear.

"This is ridiculous," declared Mary Camper at the sheer amount of work to be done. "I'm still waiting for my flea treatment." She scratched her side with her back leg. Her once-smooth pelt was growing back patchily. "These conditions simply will not do."

"You!" shouted an officer who had overheard her displeasure. "Stand up!" Mary did as she was ordered. "You have a problem?"

"Well, yes. Yes, I do as a matter of fact," replied Mary. The others watched while trying to look busy working.

"You want flea treatment?" asked the officer.

"Yes, yes I do." Mary caught a glimpse of her fellow workers looking almost relieved that it was not them standing up in front of a Gizor officer. "It's only right to offer some basic amenities in these conditions," she replied pompously.

"And you have not been offered treatment?"

"No, none of us have," replied Mary, believing she was making some progress pointing out the injustice.

"Would it please you, little squirrel, if I arrange the treatment for you and your comrades?" said the officer, taking note of her serial number.

"Well of course."

He walked away from Mary, "Very good," he said.

"You will get your flea treatment."

Mary returned to her sorting table. "Well, if I had known it was going to be that easy I would have asked days ago," she commented to her friends.

*

Agatha had hatched a small plan and now had the support of Floppy and their new friend Lucius to carry it out. Lucius was a particularly useful ally, given that he was a grey squirrel: it enabled the three to get closer to the enemy. Agatha and Floppy were hidden in a large wicker basket attached to the back of Agatha's old bicycle, which Lucius was riding without challenge through the streets occupied by Gizor troops.

"HUMANIKOS PERSONIKAS! HUMANIKOS PERSONIKAS! Beware the Humaniki will cometh! They rise again!" shouted a group of alternative preachers, as Lucius rode through the streets of Brockhurst and into the town of Bridgemary. Agatha lifted the lid of the basket ever so slightly as they passed, to see Gizor soldiers wrestling the would-be prophets of doom to the ground.

"Silly prophets," said Agatha.

"What's the Humanikos, Aggy?" asked Floppy.

"An old wives' tale. They went extinct about 65 million years ago if they existed at all. They're not coming back, Floppy, so don't worry about that."

"Are they dragons? Because I be afraid of dragons, Aggy."

"No, they're not dragons, Floppy. They're nothing to worry about. Besides, you're a White Rabbit remember – brave as brave can be." Floppy puffed out his chest and smiled to himself proudly.

Lucius rode the bicycle up to a tall fenced area. He

briefly got off to open the gate then rode into a small courtyard, closing the gate behind him. He parked the bicycle and looked around to see if it was safe for Agatha and Floppy to get out of the basket. "OK," he said. They climbed out of the basket and kept low and quiet just in case.

"She always keeps a key under the plant pot to the left of the door somewhere," said Agatha as they hunted for it.

"I found the key, Aggy. I found the key," said Floppy excitedly.

"Well done Floppy. We need to be quiet, though."

"Oh, I know – quiet as a mousey I can be," whispered Floppy, remembering how quiet he'd had to be when he was at the Castle with Hertha and Berry.

The three of them snuck into the printing press room and closed the door behind them. They pulled down the blinds and turned a few lights on.

"We need to find the main switch," said Agatha, who wasn't sure what she was doing or how the infernal machine worked. She had only seen her friend Ethel work the dials and crank some gears. They spent about an hour trying to work it all out until finally the machine started whirring and Agatha ran to Ethel's seat and began copying what she had seen her friend do. Soon Agatha's notices were rolling off the press in huge volumes. Lucius took himself off and stood outside the door, watching to see if the noise of the machine was attracting any attention, while Floppy gathered up the printed papers. Agatha pedalled as fast as she could, as they didn't know how much time they would have. It turned out they didn't have much time at all. Lucius signalled an alert with a whistle.

"Go! Go!" shouted Agatha to Floppy as she quickly stopped the machine, climbed off the apparatus and grabbed the notices from Floppy. They both hid under a table, moving some boxes to cover their position.

They heard a high voice speaking to Lucius. "You shouldn't be here. Why are you here?" it said.

"I was cycling by and saw a light on," replied Lucius.

The door of the printing room opened. "Hello?" The machine was still whirring as it cooled down. "I know you're here. Show yourself or I'll call the Gizor," said the voice.

Floppy was immediately rattled and looked at Agatha in desperation. But Agatha recognised the voice. "Ethel?" she called out.

"Agatha?" replied Ethel. Agatha shifted the boxes to the side and crawled out from beneath the table with a bundle of notices under her arm. Floppy followed her.

"You can't be here, Agatha," replied Ethel peering in panic through the blinds behind her on to the main road. "If the Gizor catch you … And what have you done to my press?" she said, surveying the damage to the printing room.

"Do you know what they're doing, Ethel?" asked Agatha referring to the Camps.

"I know what they will do to you if they find you here – and to me. You must leave." She began resetting the dials on the press.

"You really don't care, do you Ethel?" asked Agatha angrily.

"Leave, please!"

"What's happened to you? When did you become so scared of doing the right thing?" She pulled the notices from under her arm and chucked them at Ethel. "Come on, Floppy. Let's go." The notices fell gracefully to the floor in front of Ethel. She picked one up and without reading it locked the door behind her friend. She walked back to her printing press to survey the damage. She turned the notice over in her hand and read:

132

## MASS EXTERMINATION OF THE RED SQUIRREL IN GIZOR-OCCUPIED GOSPORT
### Addressed to the Governments of the World Wildlife Federation

Published on behalf of the Red Alvish
by The Alvish Resistance, Gosport, 1939

The purpose of this document is to make public the contents and intention of The Gizor Manifesto and its Armed Forces lead by Admiral Jean De Gizor, High Commander of the Fleet of Ratufinee. It is the intention of Admiral Gizor to mislead the WWF from whom it seeks false membership and to wage a campaign of occupation throughout your Commonwealth under the pretence of fellowship and collaboration. There are no such intentions of goodwill on the part of the Admiral. however much asserted. Instead there is a veil of deceit and should this publication invite your inspection the truth will be uncovered to reveal the mass extermination of freedom and the demise of a race through torture, captivity, slavery and ultimately murder.

We, The Alvish Resistance, on behalf of its people of Gosport, invite such an investigation and do so with hope that the world can demonstrate its united civilised power against evil and tyranny. It is in this hope (and only this) that we are saved.

Yours in hope of life,
The Alvish Resistence, Gosport.

*

For days now, Beaky had been making regular visits to the hedgehog Morag and the villagers he was so fond of, despite their reticence. That said, they largely ignored the seagull because he appeared an innocent sort. He was in danger of becoming a bit of a fixture and Morag was mindful of how to manage an empty acorn that could easily bring an acorn tree of trouble their way.

"Beaky?" Morag called.

"Yes, Morag," replied Beaky, skipping down the centre of the village chomping on some worms.

"Where'd you get this trinket again?" she asked, inspecting the gift he was given by the Magpie officer.

"That? I got that from the north hangar. Precious, innit? The officer who gave it to me wasn't that bothered about it, but I thinks its proper nice, I do's. Can't believe no one wanted it."

"What do'ya mean, no one wanted it?" asked Morag.

"Well, you know. They didn't want it. There's loads they're giving away."

"Who are 'they', Beaky?"

"Err, well. I don't really know. Those lot in the camps, I s'pose."

"Do you mean to say that this here trinket belongs to some poor folk in the Camp?"

"Yeah, they didn't want it any more."

"Is that right? And I suppose you believe that bees make honey for us then, eh?" she said mockingly.

"Hey?" asked Beaky, unclear as to what she meant.

"There's always a good and a bad in this world, Beaky – those that take and never give, and those that have nothing but share what they have anyway. Make sure you're on the right-side, laddie." She handed him back the trinket.

*

Berry and Hertha were asleep when they were awoken by the jangling of keys at their cell door. Both immediately sat upright.

"Get up, ya filthy vermin!" shouted an officer as two other prison guards entered the cell and grabbed Berry and Hertha. They were marched down the corridor and up the spiral staircase, through various corridors and out into a huge prison yard. The morning light was difficult to bear as neither of the friends had seen it for days. They were joined by other creatures who had clearly experienced similar conditions. They were all put into rows and hosed down with a powerful jet of water. Some of the smaller animals fell backwards on to the ground due to the sheer force.

They were then shackled at the ankles in lines and marched off to various waiting trucks. Hertha and Berry were shackled together along with ten other prisoners, bundled into a truck and driven off. The journey was bumpy along cobbled streets. The prisoners were unable to see out of the canopied truck. Twenty minutes later, they arrived at their destination. Soldiers entered the back of the truck and put hessian sacks over the prisoners' heads and pushed them one by one off the truck. As they were all shackled together, their exit was less than smooth and if one fell to the ground, so did many of the others. They were marched in line blinded by their sacks. The foul Portsmouth air turned to sea air and the wind began to blow their blindfolds taut against their face, making them struggle to breathe at times. They were led over and down a jagged and uneven surface where finally their blindfolds were removed to reveal the harbour shore.

"It's Gosport," said Berry, looking out over the harbour towards home. They had been driven to the oldest part of the Country known as Old Portsmouth on the south-west coast. They were immediately put to work moving huge boulders and positioning sandbags along the banks as defence from any impending attack.

The day was long and the work heavy and exhausting, especially for the smaller creatures like Berry. The job appeared to be an endless one and would take days if not weeks to complete. As the guards tugged on the line of prisoners at the end of the day, pulling on their chains to get them off the bank, Hertha lost her footing and fell back down the steep bank, pulling a few of her comrades down with her.

"Pathetic vermin!" shouted a prison guard. "Get up!" As he stood at the top of the bank looking down at the rabble and shouting abuse, Hertha noticed his grey face was obscured by a shadow. It was the shadow of a ship. As the others began to re-climb the bank, she took a moment to look up at the old buildings towering over them as the sun was going down.

"Berry," she whispered as she walked behind him as the group were marched off, "I know what it means."

Berry didn't have a clue what she was talking about and simply turned his head as if to question her in silence.

"Look up," she whispered. "Look over there." She moved her head towards a tall building called Tower House. On top of its spire was an ornate weathervane with a cast-iron ship signalling the wind's direction. Berry still didn't know what she was talking about and shrugged his shoulders. Hertha rolled her eyes at him in frustration.

"You! Get a move on!" shouted an officer at Hertha, who was lagging. The officers in charge had forgotten to place sacks over the prisoners' heads to lead them back to the waiting truck and as a result, Hertha was taking it all in, frantically looking to the tops of other buildings and mapping it all out in her mind. The truck had been parked some distance away towards the Square Tower, further into

Old Portsmouth. The guards were heard arguing among themselves because of their forgetfulness. As they were bundled up into the truck again, Hertha – who was at the end of the line – observed an officer salute the wall of the Square Tower before getting into the truck. She looked up at the wall to see the Bust of Admiral Gizor in the wall itself in bronze. Just as she had observed this, she was pushed into the back of the truck and driven back to Kingston Prison.

\*

Agatha, Floppy and their new friend Lucius were busy talking in the caponier. Agatha was keen to hatch new plans and schemes. She knew they had to warn the camp and could do this from Priddy's but she also wanted to do more. She wanted to free the camp itself, but didn't know how. Her flyers had been left behind on the floor of Ethel's press, so they needed a new plan. While they wished for the WWF to rescue their world, Agatha knew they needed to rescue themselves at the same time.

"Right, I think we head south to the Camp after we've delivered the message to Doris at Priddy's," she suggested.

"But Hertha said no to that idea, Aggy. I remember, I do, and then Rosie gave me a biscuit," replied Floppy.

"Well, Hertha's not here is she, Floppy? And things have changed," replied Agatha.

"What is our plan when we reach the camp?" asked Lucius, who knew Agatha didn't have one.

Suddenly there was a noise from the entrance where Floppy and Lucius had previously broken through.

"Ssh," she warned. Agatha beckoned Floppy and Lucius over to her position and they hid in the corner quietly.

"What will this be used for?" came a Gizor voice from outside.

"I believe we have it down for destruction and the materials used to build officers' quarters, sir," replied another voice that sounded like a vole.

"I see. In the meantime, we should move the Pompey Pensioners here. They are always wanting to be useful in their old age. Their presence will bolster our occupation in this Ward," said the first voice, referring to the older generation of now-retired Gull Bombers. "And what is over here?" asked the voice, as the two Gizors could be heard walking away from the caponier.

"What do we do now, Agatha?" whispered Floppy.

"We find a new base." She stood up and grabbed her rucksack. "We pack up and we leave."

"But where, Aggy? Where do we go?" asked Floppy, half-heartedly packing some belongings in a bag.

Agatha tried to think as she packed all essentials for their journey. The entire Country of Gosport had been invaded and the Gizor were everywhere.

"Lucius, the tunnels? They led you here. How far do they go?" asked Agatha seizing some maps and laying them out on to the table once more.

"The tunnels are dangerous, Agatha," replied Lucius.

"Yes, yes, but you did get through them."

"Some were almost impassable. They are old and most have collapsed. It's very dangerous."

"I banged my head, I did. I banged it bad," said Floppy referring to his journey.

"But you did get through them. How far do they go?" asked Agatha again.

"It is rumoured – but only a rumour – that they are joined all together. All the forts from this one to the next," said Lucius.

"Then it's not a rumour. You made it from the Castle to Rowner and therefore we can do the same. Our base is now the underworld of Gosport." She placed her paws on Floppy's shoulders by way of encouragement. "We can do anything. We're the Resistance," said Agatha with gusto and excitement. "Are you with me?"

\*

Each day the animals in the Camp worked to serve their captors – always in fear and always with obedience because of that fear. The mood was despairing in the workhouse, the barracks used for sorting the Camp's belongings.

"The Camp is a lot quieter these days isn't it?" remarked someone busy working through heaps of jewellery.

"Yes, I noticed that too," remarked a wren. "Perhaps it won't be too long before we are moved."

"Where's Mary?" mouthed the dormouse Molly Siskin, leaning down towards the table and to her left to seek out her friend Gertie from the line. The group began shuffling and looking around to see if they could find her. Gertie didn't have a clue where Mary was. They resumed their work as an officer began his inspection down the line.

"The trouble with you red vermin is your chatter," remarked the officer as he walked the line. "We give you the comfort of shelter and chairs to sit on, yet you continue to be restless. I suggest no chairs."

"Remove the chairs!" shouted another officer to his men in response, who immediately obeyed by grabbing each member of the line and forcing them to stand up while the chairs were flung backwards. This prompted the workers to increase their pace almost instantly.

Just as they continued their work, Mary walked into the workhouse, to everyone's surprise and relief.

"Oh, I've had a lovely flea treatment," she said with her

139

stubbly fur softer as a result. She took her position in the line and started working alongside the others.

"I trust the treatment met with your approval, little vermin?" asked the officer, smiling to himself as he stood over Mary.

"Yes, thank you, I am most grateful to you, sir."

## Chapter 8
 # THE OLDEST ORDER OF THEM ALL

F rom Fort Rowner, they had made their way southwards through the tunnels. Lucius had spoken true of the level of decay. Their path was treacherous in parts with the walls crumbling around them, but other areas appeared largely intact and standing strong. There were many side tunnels leading off to dark places of the underworld, and then large chambers where they pitched their base. They carried their supplies from the caponier and then went back for more.

"Tell me about the Priory, Lucius," said Agatha as they rested for a while. Floppy immediately pulled up a chair beside them as if to be told an epic bedtime story. He sat excitedly with his paws resting on his podgy white cheeks in anticipation.

"What is it that you want to know?" replied Lucius, sitting on the floor leaning against a dusty wall, re-bandaging his arm from where Agatha had stabbed him a week or so ago.

"As much as possible I suppose."

Lucius sighed. "There is much to say about it. Too much for me to truly convey."

"I am a blank canvas, Lucius."

"Which Priory do you refer to?" he replied, looking up

at Agatha for a second.

Agatha was puzzled: she only knew of the Priory Monks at the Castle. "The one you don't want to talk about," she said shrewdly.

Lucius looked back down to his bandaged arm and smiled to himself. "The Portchester Priory was not always ruled over by Sir Roderick or by Pontius Perseus," he said. "The Order is of peace, formed to worship Hudsonicus Holozoa. It is not an Order of conflict or battle, and nor was it formed to cast judgement on the cultures of others. Its purpose is only to worship and to do so in peace."

"And the other?" asked Agatha.

"Worship can be for the many as well as the few. Do you know of the poisoned bread?"

"Of course. The Lord's greatest sacrifice, to die for another."

"Yes, that's right. Our Lord knew that the bread was poisoned and sacrificed himself by taking the bread that was meant for the peasant. There were those that judged him a thief who got what he deserved and others that judged him a fool for saving the beggar. But what is not known is who the peasant was and why he saved her. Have you heard of Apple Dumpling Bridge?" asked Lucius to his captive audience.

"No," replied Agatha.

"I like apple dumplings, I do," said Floppy.

"It crosses the Alver River right here in Gosport in the Alver Valley. You see, he may have been a Lord of our creation but he was believed to be a beggar – ousted for his 'sorcery'. He sought sanctuary under the bridge after taking some bread from a noble King. He was battle-scarred and wounded. The King's soldiers hunted Hudsonicus through the valley, but they could not find him. A forest woman of the woods – a brown rabbit – watched from afar as he hid beneath the bridge when the King's soldiers crossed over it.

There he stayed for many a day and night and the doe rabbit of the woods left him apple dumplings to feed upon. When his strength was regained he left the sanctuary of the bridge and tried to repay the rabbit for her kindness with an acorn carved from a silver birch, but she denied her part in his recovery and declined his gift. She was found for her crime by the King's soldiers and stood an unfair trial for treason. It was then that Hudsonicus the Brave showed himself to the crowd and stole the poisoned bread meant for the doe rabbit as her punishment. He fell to the floor with the poison racing through his body and declared 'thou shalt rise above this hate and lie always with you in kindness through the valley.' As he died, the acorn he had carved fell from his paw and was lost to the earth." Lucius stopped and looked at his friends.

"Lost?" asked Agatha.

"So, it is believed, yes."

"There is another story, isn't there?"

"The Priory is old and is as sacred as this tale itself. There will always be those who believe Hudsonicus was a thief and those who worship him as the creator of the earth itself and all its kindnesses."

"And the acorn?"

"Within the Priory of St Mary's was another Order: the Ark Rodentia."

"Who are they?"

Lucius stood up as if to walk away. "The Ark Rodentia is the oldest Order of them all," he said.

"I've never heard of them," said Agatha.

"An Ark protects, does it not? And while it protects, it keeps safe its secrets within." He walked away to continue arranging the chamber.

Agatha pulled herself up from the dusty floor. "They found the acorn, didn't they?" she said.

The night was dark and rainy once more, which suited the atmosphere of Kingston Prison. Hertha was once more studying the cloth given to her by Lucius.

"I don't know why you're bothering, H," said Berry grumpily. "Even if you're right, what good is it to us? Ain't no way of escape from this place."

Hertha ignored her grouchy cellmate and continued studying the message on the cloth, reading it out loud to herself quietly:

*By design to aid our task*
*Travels the direction of our path*
*A mighty ship of glory be*
*Forged above the windy sea*

She felt confident that she now knew what the first part meant – that the weathervanes would somehow guide them somewhere. But she didn't know when or where and was frustrated by the second phrase.

*Scattered rust and wood of rot*
*We wait the dank*
*Shored by the dock*

She sighed with frustration. "Wood doesn't rust, and if anything is shored by the dock it's going to be a boat isn't it?" she asked rhetorically. "You know what, Berry?" said Hertha, feeling in a somewhat reflective mood, "You know what I'd really like to do?"

"What's that? asked Berry, not really interested.

"I keep thinking about that bust of Gizor. You know, that statue we saw in the wall."

"Yeah?"

"I would love for that to go missing."

"You're going stir crazy in this place, Hertha."

"No, but just think of it. It would be like a small victory."

"Oh yeah, and the second you climb that wall will be the same second that they shoot you. You've got about as much chance of stealing the bust as you have of getting out of here. You might as well believe in magic."

"And what about our neighbour next door – the Red Witch? It didn't take you much to believe in her the other day," said Hertha firing back at Berry.

"Yeah well, that's different. I was taken aback. Just can't explain it is all – how she disappears like that."

"Must be a little bit of magic then, no? Wait a minute." She sat upright. "We've been missing the point. How does she disappear? It's a trick just like Agatha once told me about a machine she made which made her friend disappear. She used smoke to fool the audience." Hertha grabbed the cloth from the floor and stood up and read: "*No sound of fog will blindfold thee.*" She looked up and rushed over to the bars of the cell. "We need the witch. You there!" she called out, "The Red Witch!" There was no response. She referred back to the cloth:

*Of brick and stone are brittle bones*
*To test a puzzled mind*
*Stone dungeon deep*
*As chained, we sleep*
*Pure light ascends the night again, and*
*Charts the stars above our skies*

*To beckon craft, O summon thee*
*Heaven's light, our Guide to see*
*No sound of fog will blindfold thee.*

145

*One word to gather, to believe*
*Our Great, Our Mighty, come to thee.*

"But what's the word?" she said to herself.

"I really must say you've gone quite mad, in my opinion," said Berry, yawning.

"Berry, you're not helping."

"No, that's right I'm not helping. It's a waste of time. Stupid riddles and rhymes about ships and stars, and guiding lights. What light? There is no light. We're in a dark cell, in a prison, in Portsmouth! Stupid cloth."

"That's it. Well done, Berry. We need a light," replied Hertha as she tried to reach the lantern mounted on the wall outside their cell.

"You what?"

"Heaven's Light, Our Guide to see," she replied as she stretched her paw as far as she could through the bars to no avail. It was just out of her reach. "Berry, you try."

"Don't be ridiculous – my arms are half the length of yours," he said, sighing. "Wait a minute." He walked back to his makeshift bed and grabbed the hessian sack and once more twisted it taut. He began flicking it in the hope it would knock the lantern off its hook. It took him several tries but eventually the lantern fell to the floor and rolled towards their cell.

"Excellent!" shouted Hertha, grabbing the lantern. The bars, however, were too close together for the lantern to be pulled through. Berry could see Hertha was discouraged, so nudged her out of the way. He grabbed the top of the lantern and twisted the bottom of it away from its casing. It was hot to the touch and burned him: he dropped the base which then rolled into the middle of the cell. Hertha checked on her friend's paw. "Are you OK, Berry?" she asked but he didn't reply. He was looking upwards to the ceiling of the cell in silence, which made Hertha think he was in a lot of pain. "Berry?"

He nodded, signalling to the ceiling. Hertha turned around to find that the cell had been lit up by the flame still sitting in the base of the lantern to reveal a million painted stars on the ceiling and the word *Peggy* etched into the stone. "Peggy," she mouthed to herself. Hertha whipped round and called out through the bars of the cell into an empty dark corridor: "PEGGY!"

Suddenly they heard a deep roar of thunder that rattled the prison cell and shook the remaining lanterns hanging along the corridor. Hertha immediately stepped back from the bars as did Berry, who got up off the floor still clutching his burnt paw. Both moved towards the back wall as the sound of thunder continued and a strong wind began to whirl again through the prison. The sheer force of the wind blew out the lanterns and left the two friends in darkness. At that very instant, the thunder stopped along with the wind. Berry and Hertha remained in silence, their backs to the wall, looking at the cell door. A dim light in the corridor began to shine from the right side and grew stronger, with footsteps walking closer towards their prison cell. The candlelight began to cast a shadow on the far side of the corridor wall. It was the figure of the cloaked woman – The Red Witch. She walked serenely in silence towards their cell holding a lantern high in front of her. She turned to face them and still in silence peered into the locked cell, pushing the lantern towards the bars to light up the room.

Berry grabbed Hertha's paw and said quietly: "If she turns us into spiders I reckon we make a run for it up the drainpipe."

The Witch continued to stare into their cell, sneered then cackled. She then blew out the flame of the lantern, causing Hertha and Berry to gasp in the pitch darkness. The thunder began to roll again and suddenly the lantern came back on and the Red Witch was standing in their cell. Hertha and Berry both let out a high-pitched scream.

"WHO DARES TO SUMMON ME?"

"What are you?" asked Hertha.

"WHO DARES TO SUMMON ME?" She spoke again in a trance-like state.

"I am Hertha Marks. I summoned you."

The Red Witch started coughing and spluttering. "Oh, my achy bones," she said, holding her paw to her lower back while stretching. Berry looked at Hertha puzzled, and Hertha shrugged her shoulders. "Now, where was I? Oh yes, THEE WHO CONJURES ME, SPEAK FORTH THE WORDS TO ME," she said as though back in trance.

Hertha was unsure of how to respond. "Peggy?" she asked.

"No. No. No." She fell out of her trance once more and began pacing the cell, "You have to say the words."

"Abracadabra?"

The witch looked up at Hertha and shook her head. "I can't say them for you," she said, sighing.

"But I don't know what the words are."

The witch looked Hertha in the eyes and quickly glanced down to the floor where the cloth was lying and back up to Hertha. Hertha scurried to the floor to pick up the cloth and began to read the rhyme out loud again.

The witch sighed again and tutted to herself. "I've got better things to be doing, you know," she said.

"I don't understand, if it's not Peggy and it's not any of these words then I just don't know."

"But it's there in front of you. Oh, what's a witch to do when she's surrounded by dim-tails," she replied.

"Hey!" said Berry, "We're not dim-tails. Listen here, Peggy, we've been stuck in this prison for weeks now."

"I AM NOT PEGGY!" shouted the witch.

"Well who the heck is Peggy and who are you?" asked Berry.

"That's none of your business. Just as it was none of your business to go the Castle. I have to be going now."

"Wait!" shouted Hertha. "LUCIUS. Lucius is the word. He gave me the cloth."

"Very well," replied the witch, "Now let me see here," she said as she started walking towards the bars of the cell, "Ah yes, I remember." She placed her paws on the bars and began a chant, swaying as she did so: "STONE DUNGEON DEEP, AS CHAINED WE SLEEP, IS THIS THE WAY, GO WE." Nothing happened. "Oh. Nothing's happened," she said, perplexed, "That's odd. Oh well, try again later."

"Later?" replied Hertha. "What was supposed to happen?"

"You must understand, a conjurer can only conjure when all the cosmic stars are aligned." She plonked herself down on Berry's bed and folded her arms and legs, "They just aren't aligned at the moment."

"Well …" Berry was dumbfounded. "When will they be aligned?"

"Oh, soon I expect – nothing to worry about. Who are you again?"

"Who am I?" replied Berry, "Who are you, more like?"

"Oh goodness gracious me, I haven't introduced myself. How rude of me." The witch stood up and took Berry's paw and shook it firmly. It was his burnt paw so it stung, but he didn't like to withdraw it. "Lillian Francis, Lilly for short. How do you do?"

"Not a very witchy name," said Berry.

"A witch?" she said, outraged, "I'm not a witch. Goodness gracious me. Where on earth would you get that idea from?"

"Must have been something you did," he said, glancing over at Hertha.

"Noooo, I'm not a witch. My name is Sylvie. Josephine's the witch," she added, confusing them more. She plonked herself back down and started inspecting her claws waiting for the 'cosmic stars to align'.

*

The early evening sun was glorious in the quaint Alver Village on the edge of Grange Farm. The bunting was still flying high as always, and the penny whistles and soft drums serenaded the dancing villagers. They led a peaceful life, and one that was largely isolated from the rest of Gosport. They lived on the farm and served it well. They never had any reason to leave: their entire existence was sustainable without having to be part of Gosport, its politics, and its silly old war. Peaceful they were, and they worshipped the land. They weren't religious in any way. They were hardworking, and a strong folk. Concerned for others? Yes. And fair? Yes, to the very core. A simple folk who lived a happy village life.

Among the dancers was Beaky, stamping his webbed feet ferociously in one spot to the drums and having a wonderful time. Days had gone by and he had forgotten his mission, forgotten that he was a Soldier of Gizor and shouldn't be consorting with the Alvish. Yet he loved the little village and was fast becoming a friend. Morag, however, always held in the back of her thoughts that he was indeed a Gizor soldier. Instead of telling him the error of his ways, she knew it was best for him to make his own mind up and therefore showed him the ways of her people and the life he could have in peace.

"Go on, laddie!" she called, cheering his attempts at

dancing. As a seagull he was unfamiliar with the woods and equally unfamiliar to the rhythm of folk dancing. But he was giving it his best shot.

"Look at me, Morag!" he cawed, trying to show off some new moves as he spun around. In doing so, he became dizzy and lost his footing, falling into a table of delicious apple dumplings. The villagers laughed as did Beaky at himself. "Umm, delicious," he said as he licked the food away from his long beak.

The sound of the music would often bounce around the woods and beyond. It spilled out into the neighbouring villages and even found its way down a tunnel or two.

"What's that sound, Agatha?" asked Floppy who was munching on some carrots. The Resistance, comprising Agatha, Lucius and Floppy, had moved south under Fort Grange and were resting in a huge chamber that was now their base.

Agatha searched the air with her ears and snout. "It sounds like drums," she said.

"Sounds like jolly music to me," commented Lucius.

"Can we go see it, Agatha? Can we go see the music?" asked Floppy.

The threesome packed up some supplies for their journey and headed out of the tunnel via a drain, wearing cloaks to hide their identities. They followed the sound towards Grange Farm, a short distance from their hiding position underground. They entered the farm using the path that Agatha had previously travelled when she had met the wrath of Farmer Jack. She thought it best not to tell Floppy, who was afraid of Rabbit Skin Jack. Instead she told him to stay close behind her and as they approached the farmhouse, they made their way through some brambles to the right and down a narrow path that opened up as the music became louder. As they came closer they could hear much laughter and could smell fresh apple dumplings and other dainties.

Floppy began skipping to the music and hopping ahead of the others.

"Floppy!" Agatha called out. He innocently skipped into the village entrance whereupon the music immediately stopped. Agatha and Lucius held back.

"Whoa there, laddie!" shouted Morag, with her paws outstretched to stop the intruder. Floppy stood still in silence and didn't know quite what to do. "And who are you?" she asked of the rabbit before her.

Floppy looked back into the woods, seeking reassurance from his friends who were hiding in the distance. Lucius calmly mouthed to him his name. "I'm Floppy," he replied.

Morag noticed he had glanced back into the woodlands. "And who are you with, laddie?" Jasper the woodcutter stepped forward behind Morag, along with a few others ready in defence.

Floppy glanced again into the woods but neither Agatha nor Lucius had any direction for him. "I'm a White Rabbit," he responded.

"Beaky? Is this a friend of yours?" asked Morag, calling into the crowd while also signalling to Jasper to explore the woods for the stranger's friends.

Beaky came running out of the dancers, and waddled over to Morag. "Never seen him before."

Floppy's eyes widened with panic and fear as he realised that Beaky was a Gull Bomber from the Gizor Army, "I'm a White Rabbit," he repeated.

"Oh aye, I can see that, but what are you doing here? This is private property," she warned.

"It was the music. I liked the music."

Jasper then appeared with some other, holding Agatha and Lucius by the scruff of their necks. They were still cloaked, and their hoods remained up. They were dropped on to the ground next to Floppy. Lucius' hood fell back to reveal a grey squirrel, while Agatha remained with her head down and her hood still covering her head.

"And who are you then?" Morag asked.

Agatha got to her feet, with her head still bowed low. "We are travellers," she replied, noticing Beaky's webbed feet standing in front of her.

"Is that right? And where you travelling to?"

"We mean no harm," Agatha replied, ignoring her question.

"You just liked the music?" Morag stepped closer to Agatha, trying to size her up. As she did so she caught a glimpse of Agatha's paw protruding from her long cloak, revealing her red fur.

"We are messengers," said Lucius. "The intrusion was unintentional and without purpose."

"There's a war on, you know," said Morag. "Can't be too careful these days."

"We understand. We shall leave you," replied Lucius, grabbing Floppy's paw as if to leave, which prompted Jasper to step forwards preventing them from doing so.

"It is quite rude to leave without word of your name," replied Morag.

"Of course. This is Floppy and I am Lucius."

"And you?" asked Jasper.

"That's Agatha, that is," answered Floppy. "Aren't you, Aggy?"

Jasper was not satisfied with her lack of reply and was suspicious of her hiding under her cloak. "Have you lost your tongue as well as your manners?" he said, snarling.

"My friends, this village is not sided with troubles. We remain at peace here," reassured Morag, aware that Agatha would be reluctant to reveal her identity particularly when

153

standing in front of a Gizor Gull.

In response, Agatha lifted her paws and pulled down her hood to reveal herself as a red squirrel. She waited for a response from the crowd.

"Hello," said Beaky.

"Hello," she replied.

"My new friends, you are welcome to stay for dinner," said Morag as she signalled for the dancing and music to continue. A scurry of hedgehog maids came forward from the crowd offering plates of food to the visitors. One such maid approached Agatha and smiled kindly at her. It was the scullery maid she had helped many weeks before at the farm when two Gizor officers were pestering her. Before disappearing into the crowd, the maid whispered into Morag's ear, presumably to tell her that she had seen her before, but Agatha was too concerned about the Gizor Gull to hear what she said. "Don't worry, lassie," said Morag, thrusting a drink into Agatha's paw. "He wandered into the village like yous."

Floppy was itching to join the dancing and grab some food but was seeking Agatha's agreement. She reassured him with a nod and he ran into the dancing crowd.

"Now, Lucius, let me show you around," said Morag, leaving Agatha to stand alone until the scullery maid took her by the paw and led her into the dancing crowd. Agatha, almost forced to dance, did so while watching Lucius walk off with Morag down the village lane towards the water pump.

"Word from the Castle?" Morag asked him quietly.

"Roderick has advanced. Perseus is lost," he replied.

"Aye I always knew he would." They both appeared relaxed and familiar with each other. "And the Ark?"

"Scattered around."

"Probably best. And these two?"

"More than a worthy choice, my old friend."

*

Were the stars aligned yet? The witch was still sitting on Berry's bed, waiting. Berry and Hertha were standing in the far corner whispering to themselves.

"Whoever she is, she knows who Lucius is, which can only be a good thing, no?" said Hertha.

"I guess so. But it seems like we're waiting on some batty old squirrel who doesn't know who she is or what she's doing."

Just then, the witch jumped to her feet from the bed. "It's time," she said. "The stars have aligned."

"How do you know?" asked Berry.

"I feel it in my witchy bones. Besides, Peggy said so."

Berry and Hertha looked at each other, puzzled again. Berry was about to challenge the witch about her various names, but Hertha grabbed his arm to stop him and nodded to the witch to show them her magic.

The Witch grabbed the bars and began swaying as before and chanting: "STONE DUNGEON DEEP, AS CHAINED WE SLEEP, IS THIS THE WAY, GO WE." The light began to flicker in the corridor. "SHOW LIGHT, THE STARS. RED FLAME TO SEE. BREAK FREE THE BARS SO FREEDOM FLEES. GO I, GO WE, TO TRAVEL THEE THROUGH STONE AND IRON REVEAL TO THEE!" The witch paused but remained in a trance and began repeating the words "REVEAL TO THEE." The candlelight was flickering vigorously and then went out, leaving them all in darkness. The witch continued her chant and the bars began to rattle in the darkness. She swayed from side to side, holding on to the bars, then was thrown violently backwards into the air almost in slow motion, hit the back wall and slumped to the floor. The lanterns stopped flashing and the cell lit up with light from the corridor. Hertha ran to the witch to help her up off the floor. Berry stood amazed, looking at the cell doorway. The vertical bars had all been parted as though curtains had been opened. They were free.

"You did it," said Hertha as she helped the old witch up.

"Told you the stars were aligned," she replied, chuffed to pieces with her magic. "Now, let me see here. Ah yes, follow me," she said as she led them out. The corridor narrowed as they walked, sloped down slightly and was slippery with mould and mildew. "Careful as you go now," she warned as they both held on to the equally slippery stone walls for balance. She led them down deeper into the dungeons of Kingston Prison, through winding narrow corridors and into an opened darkened cell.

"What's this? What are we doing here?" asked Berry.

"Come on in and make yourselves at home," the witch replied as a lantern flared up as she entered.

"I don't understand," said Hertha. "I thought you were showing us the way out?"

"Yes, yes. All in good time." She sat down at her writing desk, picked up her quill pen and began scribbling frantically, dabbing it into the ink after almost every word.

"Well, which way do we go? Where's the way out of here?" asked Berry in frustration.

The witch did not reply and continued scribbling.

Hertha stepped forward, realising the witch was in a trance again. She cautiously walked over to her and gently placed a paw on her shoulder. This startled the witch who flung her chair back as she stood up and made a warning gesture with her slightly arthritic paws that she could so easily turn them into frogs or spiders. She claimed she hadn't seen these visitors before.

"WHO DARES TO ENTER JOSEPHINE'S REALM?" she asked.

"Oh well this is just great," said Berry.

"Lilly?" said Hertha, trying to snap her out of her trance.

This seemed to work. "Yes dear, Lillian Francis. How do you do."

"Lilly, you were going to show us the way out," reminded Hertha.

"Yes, yes goodness me. Forgetful in my old age, I am." She walked over to a shelf and reached up on tiptoes to retrieve a dusty old book. She handed it to Hertha. "Hold that will you?" she said, then reached up again for her jar of broken chestnuts. She placed the jar on her writing desk and unscrewed the lid. She then stretched out her paw to the side, signalling for Hertha to pass her the dusty moth-eaten book, whose pages she flicked through carefully. The book was bigger and heavier than she was. She found a page. "Ah, here we are," she said and began following its instructions. She tipped the chestnuts onto the desk and started shuffling the pieces around. "Hmm, yes," she said to herself, "Looks like we shall have to wait." She looked for her chair behind her – the one that had been flung to the floor – and said, puzzled, "oh what's that doing on the floor?"

"Wait for what? The stars to align again?" said Berry impatiently.

"No, silly – the moon."

"Lilly, what happens when the moon is aligned?" asked Hertha.

"The moon?" she asked, confused.

"Yes, you said we have to wait for the moon."

"Ah yes, the moon. Did you know we only see it

because of the sun?"

"Yes, I had heard that. Lilly, who is Peggy?"

"Peggy? Oh, she is a nuisance at times. Have you heard from her then?"

"No. Who is she, Lilly?" asked Hertha again as Berry began looking around at Lilly's trinkets and books.

"Peggy is my spirit guide," replied Lilly. Hertha saw Berry shaking his head and rolling his eyes.

"So, who are Josephine and Sylvie?" she asked.

"Oh goodness me, has Josephine shown her face? I'm surprised she has the audacity after what she did last time," said Lilly, reviewing the pages of the old book in front of her. "And Sylvie, you say? I have no idea who she is I'm sure." Hertha did not respond. Lilly could see that her visitors were confused. "My name is Lillian Francis," she said. "I'm not a witch but many think I am. Peggy is my spirit guide. She talks to me sometimes is all. She tells me things that others don't know. I seem to have a voice for others and am rather good at it. I had a profitable little business, you know."

"What do you mean?" asked Hertha.

"Well, there's money in knowing what's going to happen before it's happened. The only infernal problem with it is that folk don't always understand, and others don't always believe. I don't know what all the fuss is about, to be honest." Lilly tutted to herself, "Witchcraft."

"You were imprisoned for Witchcraft?" asked Hertha.

"Yes. Rather a lot of nonsense. I cannot be held responsible for ignorance, yet here I am counselling the 'non-believers'."

"People visit you?" asked Hertha.

"Yes, the very ones who imprisoned me, believe it or not."

"If you are showing us the way out, why don't you

leave?" asked Berry from the corner.

"Leave? And where would I go? I'm The Red Witch. No, I've been here so long, it feels like home to me now. I quite like it. I have free rein of the place because they know I won't leave the walls. Come and go as I please." She checked on the status of the chestnuts lying on the desk. "Ah here we go," she said, standing up from her writing desk, referring back to the book and then back to the chestnut pieces. "This way," she said as she walked out of her cell and back down the corridor. They travelled further into the deep, "Had to wait for the tides, you see," she called back to her visitors.

"The tides?" said Berry to Hertha as they both followed.

She took them down some crumbling old stairs where they could see algae, barnacles and seaweed stuck to the walls. It was damp and cold. The stone cobbled floor had now turned into slippery rock. The stairs led them to a cave deep under the prison. They could see the pattern of rippling water reflecting on the glistening walls and could hear the stream-like trickling of lapping water towards the back of the cave.

"Right, this is as far as I go," said Lilly. "I assume you know how to swim?" she asked as if the thought had not previously occurred to her.

Berry stood over the water's edge looking down into the murky seawater. "And if we don't?"

"You will be fine," she called out as she walked back up the stairs. "I'm a witch, remember." The two companions stood in silence looking down at the water, "Just follow your nose," she said, stopping halfway up the steps. They could only make out her silhouette. "And remember – look up when the wind blows."

## Chapter 9

 # NEVER INTENDED
# FOR THE DARK

T he hour was late in the village of Alver, the singing and
dancing had stopped, and the hedgehogs were starting
to clear away.

"It is time. It should be about now," said Lucius to
Morag as they walked together.

"She won't go with them, you know."

"I know."

Agatha was still watching from a distance, seated on a
log. Beaky came through the crowd with some leftovers he
was munching on. "So, are you from the Camp then?" he
asked.

"No. The Camp won't get me," she said, defiantly.

"But all the Reds are in the camp."

"Yes, including my father, my friends and everyone I
know."

"Yeah, I flew over it the other day. Loads of them there
are. All squashed in," he said, failing to realise the
sensitivity of the subject.

"I'm going to get them out," she replied with bravado.

"They're gonna be re-homed anyways."

"If that's what you want to believe."

"Morag said I should pick a side. I like this village.
Don't like it back at the Loft much, but I've got my orders."

"And what are those?"

"Well, you know – to see what's going on out here, but I told them nothing's going on. Not here anyways."

"So, what side are you on in that uniform of yours" she asked, nodding at his clothing.

"This?" he said, looking down at his badges. "I'm a soldier of the Gizor Army."

"You say that as if you're proud."

"I was proud. I am proud of who I am and what I've become …" He paused. "… and what I know now."

"And what's that?" she asked despondently.

"There are two sides in this world – a good and a bad. I know which side I want to be on."

Lucius and Morag came towards them, and Floppy came hopping out of the crowd at the same time. "I danced, I did. I was dancing, Lucius," he said.

"Yes you were, my friend."

Observing Lucius' familiarity with Morag, Agatha finally asked: "What's going on here?"

Lucius and Morag looked at each other. It was time. "We need to speak with yous, Agatha," said Morag.

"Lucius?" said Agatha.

"We must move forward, Agatha, before it is too late," he replied.

"I know that," she said, getting to her feet, "which is why we need to liberate the Camp."

"The Camp is just one small battle in a war that can't end unless we tackle it differently," said Morag.

"What do you mean?"

"Your friends in Kingston Prison have been released."

"Released?"

"Hertha, Hertha, Berry, Berry?" said Floppy, hopping with excitement.

"Aye. They've been released but they're still in great

danger, lassie. They're on Pompey soil, close to Gizor himself," said Morag.

"How do you know all this?" asked Agatha.

"Intelligence is scattered around. It always has been. Some make it their business to know," she said then added, "and some make it their business to protect."

Lucius placed a reassuring paw on Agatha's shoulder. "The Ark knights stand with you, Agatha," he said, "and the time has come."

Agatha stared into Lucius' eyes. "The carved acorn? Where is it?"

"It is close to falling into the wrong paws," said Morag, stepping forward so she was very close to Agatha. "We cannae allow that, lassie. It must be protected and brought back."

"Brought back from where?" asked Agatha.

"It was carved for the innocent and kind and must be saved by them also," said Morag, looking very serious. She glanced over at Floppy, who was munching on some leftover carrots.

Agatha looked over at Floppy. Why on earth should Floppy risk his life for an ancient acorn? "What we need to do is liberate the Camp," she said, dismissively.

"Aye, but we must also liberate ourselves and the only way to do that is to take back the power Gizor will hold if he gets his paws on the Ark."

"It's in Portsmouth?"

"Yes," replied Lucius. "The Ark rests under their very noses."

"So?"

Lucius and Morag could see they would have to try harder to convince this Resistance Fighter. Morag responded first: "Do you believe in magic, missy?"

"I do, Morag, I do," said Floppy, excited to contribute

162

to the conversation. "I like magic tricks, I do."

"Magic is just a trick," replied Agatha starting to walk away.

"I like the disappearing trick, I do," said Floppy.

"OK then. Do you believe in power?" Morag tried a different tack to bring the non-believer back. Agatha ignored her. "... Because Gizor believes in power above most things except one–he also believes in the Ark more than anything in his world and he won't be stopped until he finds it."

Agatha stopped in her tracks and turned around to face Morag. "Why does this matter?" she said, almost shouting in anger.

"It was never intended for the dark," replied Morag. "It was always intended for the good." She stepped closer to Agatha and placed both paws on her shoulders and peered into her eyes. Agatha could feel the hedgehog's breath on her face. "It does good, Agatha Mumby. Just like yous, which is why you and Floppy must retrieve it." Agatha broke eye contact briefly and looked behind Morag's spiky shoulders at the small gathering of comrades – Lucius, Beaky and Floppy. "It must be saved, Agatha. It must be saved by the kind and the good. It must be saved to save us all."

"I've heard enough of this," replied Agatha. "Come on, Floppy."

*

The fires hidden away in the Camp burned on, generating huge plumes of smoke and ash. The ash would soar high into the night sky, obliterating the moon and falling like snow to blanket the camp.

"Psst," said Doris Cruikshank to Lady Ellen as they lay

curled in their bunks. "Lady Ellen, do you think we will ever get out of here?"

Lady Ellen had lost a little faith herself (and a little weight) and didn't know how to respond to the young doe, so masked her doubt with her usual optimism. "Of course," she replied. "The important thing is not to let the barmy Pompey get us down."

Mary, from the top bunk, interjected with unusual positivity: "I do believe we shall be re-homed in no time. The process has clearly already begun."

Doris looked out of the window of their barracks and up to the sky. "It's snowing again," she quietly observed. The chatter between the animals all crowded into the barracks fell silent.

*

Agatha and Floppy reached the safety of their underground world of tunnels. The hour was very late, and Floppy was yawning uncontrollably. Agatha made sure she tucked him in and sat by his bedside as he fell asleep. Lucius entered the tunnel some twenty minutes behind them and was met in silence by Agatha. He stood waiting for some response from her. He would accept even anger.

Agatha was busy examining the pages of her notebook given to her by her father that she had filled with plans and sketches. She decided to break the silence as she couldn't stand it any longer and was still too angry to sleep. "Why lie?" she asked. "That's what I don't get. Why create an elaborate ruse to get us to the village? And as for that Morag …" She shook her head, baffled at what had happened.

"The Priory is a secret order," said Lucius.

"Then why tell me about it at all?"

Lucius sighed. "The Ark protects you, Agatha. We have been waiting for you both for a long time."

Agatha looked up from her notebook. "Me and Floppy?"

"Kindness is everything in life, and humility will save us all," said Lucius, knowing the words would resonate with Agatha whose father had said them to her.

She stood up from her chair in the corner. "What do you mean by that?" she asked, taken aback.

"Tell me, Agatha. What did your father study?"

Agatha didn't answer and was angered that he had mentioned him.

"A leader himself would be wise to teach humility and kindness – would he not – when forbidden to speak about the Ark of Rodentia?" Lucius was hoping he had said enough to indicate that her father was in some way involved with the Priory.

"My father is a peaceful man. He served the Federation, his Country and his Church."

"Yes, and he did so for freedom."

Agatha looked around the chamber, glanced at Floppy sleeping, and walked over to Lucius. "I will not go on some foolish crusade ..." She bit her lip, frantically thinking to herself, "... without freeing the Camp."

Lucius smiled to himself, knowing that their journey would be a difficult one. He looked down at the dusty floor and said: "Then we shall do both."

\*

Hertha and Berry began wading through the murky seawater underneath Kingston Prison. They held on to the slippery walls and travelled through the dark tunnels. As they did so, the water began rising.

"I don't like the look of this," said Berry observing the rise of the tide. "Moles are not great at swimming, you know."

"We can't go back now. We've got to keep going," said Hertha, determined to follow the tunnels to freedom.

They continued their journey, not knowing where it would lead them. At times they had to hold their breath and duck under the water to avoid low-standing rocks, emerging on the other side with their chests heaving. At other times there were shallow passages where they could rest for a couple of minutes and rub the water from their eyes with their paws. They had travelled all night, it seemed.

"So," said Berry, starting up a conversation as they travelled along a smooth stretch, "do you think she really was a witch?"

"Well how else do you explain it?" replied Hertha, her voice echoing.

"I can't. But I don't really believe in magic."

"Me neither, Berry. I think if we ever get out of here we keep it to ourselves or else we might find ourselves like her – locked up for witchcraft."

"Agreed."

Hertha looked ahead in the distance and could see a shimmering light. Daylight was reflecting on the water ahead. They both saw it and began wading more quickly towards the light. It was early morning and the sun was rising. The two unlikely characters found themselves approaching the shore and climbed out of a sewer pipe onto a pebble beach. They quickly took cover by the bank. "Where are we?" asked Berry, his wet black fur covered in seaweed.

Hertha looked out across the beach towards the open water. "Well either we're on the south coast of Portsmouth or Gosport's been blown up."

"Where do we go now then?"

"She said to look up and follow our noses," said Hertha, recalling Lilly's last words to them. "Let's get dried off first and head for that shed over there." The shed sat at the bottom of someone's garden and overlooked the shore.

\*

Admiral Gizor's motorcade travelled the distance from the dockyard and through the narrow streets of Old Portsmouth. It stopped outside the majestic cathedral with its stone tower and wooden cupula that overlooked the harbour to the west, the Round and Square Towers to the south, and Southsea Castle to the east. Sunday service would soon be starting and Gizor was in his military dress. The Bishop of Portsmouth Sedgrick Doyle and his Ministers were standing waiting at the entrance of the cathedral to greet their Admiral. The Bishop was a tall thin elderly mouse, terribly well-spoken and some might say sheltered from the realities of Portsmouth life and the life of the poor. Yet kind was he, despite his ignorance.

"My Lord," said the Bishop, bowing his head as he reached out his tiny paw to greet Admiral Gizor.

"I trust you are well, Bishop?" asked Gizor, as they both stepped into the cathedral.

"Very well thank you Admiral."

As Gizor entered through the bronze doors into the nave, he was greeted by a flock of peasants – the poor of Portsmouth. His entourage pushed them aside out of his way. Yet they continued to hold out their paws begging for food and money and wanting to greet the mighty Gizor. Pompey Lil' was there, of course, silently observing. She had taken her pew at the back of the nave and was wearing her moth-eaten Sunday best with a lovely bonnet covering her long grey greasy fur. She thought she was cleverer than the rest and quickly scrabbled a few pews closer to where Gizor had sat at the front.

"What's that smell?" he said to Prime Minister Denis Delaney who had joined him. In response, Denis signalled to one of the guarding soldiers to remove the old beggar squirrel. Pompey Lil' picked up a prayer book and pretended to observe service. The two soldiers shuffled either side of her down the long pew, grabbed her under the arms and escorted her out just as the organ struck up its pipes.

"My Admiral, my Lord, sir!" she cried hoarsely as she was being manhandled. "Spare a penny or two for an old squirrel – the squirrel of the night?" She continued begging as she was dragged out of the Cathedral. "Spare a penny, sir, for a wish? Perhaps some lucky heather?" The soldiers pushed her on to the Cathedral steps outside and she fell to the ground.

"Do you have no control over your peasants, Denis?" remarked Gizor as the service began. Denis did not reply.

*

Lucius woke to the sound of Agatha shuffling papers and the click of her claws as she paced up and down the chamber. "Agatha?" he said.

"Right – I've got an idea. I've been up most of the night."

"OK. Let's hear it."

"Well it was something Floppy said in the village," she said, rifling through old maps of Gosport.

"I like the village, I do," said Floppy who had also woken up and had started munching on some carrots for breakfast.

"But it's risky," she warned, "and we'll need help."

"The Priory will assist," replied Lucius.

"What did I say in the village, Aggy? What did I say?" asked Floppy.

168

"You like magic tricks, Floppy," she replied. "And so do I. In fact, I'm pretty good at them, as it so happens." She picked up a rucksack and placed it on her back. She then put another on Floppy's back and began stuffing it full of her maps and some supplies for a journey. "We need to go back to the village," she said.

The three travelled in broad daylight back towards Grange Farm. Lucius pedalled Agatha's old bicycle with Floppy and Agatha riding hidden in the basket trailer on the back. They approached the country lane that led to the farmhouse and Lucius decided to take the risk of running into Farmer Jack. He pedalled quickly along the lane then down the dirt track through the woods and into the village. Most of the villagers were hard at work farming the land for Farmer Jack. Morag stepped out to greet them. Agatha jumped out of the wicker basket and helped pull out Floppy, who was struggling with one foot over the side. Agatha meant business. She went straight over to a picnic table situated close to the watering hole. She took off her rucksack and Floppy's and began laying out her maps. Morag and Lucius followed her. She was focused and keen to begin her plans.

"OK. We're here and the Camp is here," she said, pointing at the map. "The tunnels are here and look there! There is one close to Priddy's! I can't believe I've never seen it before."

"What's this all about, lassie?" asked Morag.

"The workers at Priddy's – they're from the Camp. We get them out via that tunnel." She placed her paw directly on the spot and held it there. The tunnel from Priddy's would meet the Grange Chamber and a network of underground tunnels beneath Gosport – their headquarters.

"Oh, aye and how do you suppose we do that then?" asked Morag.

Agatha looked up from her map and over at Floppy, who was helping a hedgehog to fold some linen sheets. "A magic trick," she said.

*

It was a common or garden shed – nothing special. In fact, there were rows of them all backing on to the pebbled beach at Eastney. They were disused and full to the brim with clutter. Some even had old wooden rowing boats leaning up against them. They belonged to the terraced houses with their long narrow back gardens – probably owned by shopkeepers, industry folk or sailors. While they were not poor dwellings, they were also not very well kept and needed much repair. However, long tiring working hours with little pay would thwart any such plans a dweller might have.

"How the heck are we going to get from this shed to wherever that flamin' riddle tells us to go when we are practically on top of the Gizor grey – and you're a Red and I'm a mole?" Berry asked Hertha, who was once again studying the cloth given to her by Lucius. Ingeniously, it had dried out. (It was cloth, don't you know).

"Well we can't stay here forever."

"Well, I'm not going out there like this. They're bound to be looking for us – we've just broken out of a prison."

"We need to think, Berry. We need to pull all this together. Lucius gave us the cloth, the Red Witch helped us escape, but where do they want us to go?"

In response Berry just plonked himself on the floor of the shed, knocking into some shovels and buckets. A plant pot fell off the top shelf and landed straight over his head, "Marvellous!" he said, folding his paws in annoyance.

*

As yet the animals of the Camp were unaware of their fate. They knew they must work hard to avoid a beating and they hoped to be re-homed soon but knew nothing about Gizor's solution to the 'pest from the west' – his Red Squirrel problem. They knew the snow was not actually snow, but never spoke of it. They knew that the missing had not been re-homed, but never spoke of it. Deep down they dared not even think it, for fear that their worst nightmares were true. Anyway, the Gizor Army were simply burning their belongings. Yes, that would be it – nothing more.

Doris and others travelled to Priddy's Hard like they did every day – in the back of an animal truck – worn out from the previous day's work. They were ushered off the truck and immediately put to work. They knew the drill, and they all had their orders. Doris' task was to collect a sack of heavy items from another truck, take it to the store and unload it into massive containers. It was heavy work for such a small squirrel.

"Psst!" said a voice in the corner of the store.

"Agatha? Is that you?"

"Doris, we have a plan to get you all out, but you must listen very carefully," whispered Agatha from the shadows.

*

Once Agatha had finished at Priddy's, she clambered over the storage supplies and made her way undetected to the dock that – only a few months ago – she had started working on for Jane. She looked out towards Rats Island and took a deep breath. She didn't want to go back there but knew if the plan was going to work, this had to be part of it. She looked behind her to make sure no one was watching. The tide was pouring in to Forton Creek and she didn't have much time. She could barely see the sand dunes that joined

171

the mainland of Priddy's to the tidal island of ne'er-do-well rats. She almost flew over them to reach the rocky banks of the island. When she reached dry land, she quickly threw down her rucksack and emptied the contents, looking for a handful of notices. Of course, she had not gone undetected by the convicts and was once again bundled into a net and dragged through the woods to the centre of the island. She was counting on it. The island itself was only around 200 square feet when the tide is high but that was large enough to home a rabble of rat convicts.

Agatha was bundled out onto the mud and stood before the angry and hungry mob once again trying to grab at her.

"Well, well, well. Back for more?" said Weevil as he approached her. This time Agatha was less afraid. There were bigger fish to fry. Instead, she simply held out her paw to Weevil, handing him a notice. He snatched the notice from her in his talons and said: "What's this, you stinky scum?"

"I've come back to deliver a message," she said proudly.

"Let's cook her good and proper this time, Weevil," shouted a rat from the crowd.

"What's it say?" asked Weevil, pretending to be uninterested.

"It's a pardon."

"You what?"

"Read it for yourself. All you convicts will be pardoned."

"Listen here, you doe scum. We ain't interested in no pardon," he said to the cheers from the crowd.

"I'll fetch the spit iron for you, Weevil," shouted Bandicoot, running off.

"Your crimes will be undone," declared Agatha.

"What do you know about our crimes?" said Weevil,

circling Agatha with the notice in his skinny paw. "You ain't got a clue who you're messing with, little do-se-do? Our crimes can never be undone."

"You let me go last time and I know you'll let me go again," she replied bravely.

"Oh, is that right?" He was angered by her remark in front of his men, which suggested he was weak, so he grabbed her by the scuff of the neck and took her over to the fire pot. He pushed her face close to the flame, leant in and whispered: "Had ourselves a couple of grey ones we did, the other day – real tasty they were."

"Cooked them good and proper we did!" shouted a rat from the crowd.

"They'll be back," she replied in pain as the heat from the flame was scalding her whiskers.

"Ha!" he scoffed. "I don't think so."

"More will come," she replied.

Weevil pulled her away from the fire and pushed her into the crowd. The rats grabbed and pulled at her. "Read this!" he said as he handed the notice to another rat called Rodney.

The nerdy, scruffy-looking rat took the notice and read out loud:

> "By Order of the Resistance, your pardon will be pleaded with Gosport for deeds undone should you become an ally for others banished of free-will. On the fifth and sixth day of September 1939, your presence is requested to free your land and oppose annihilation."

Weevil grabbed the notice from the rat and looked at the writing. He couldn't read, so it didn't make any sense to him. Instead he scrunched the notice up in his paw and walked over to Agatha, pulling her out of the crowd. He towered over her. He picked her up by the scruff of her neck again and lifted her up off the floor so they were eye level. "Funny little doe, aren't you? Coming here acting all brave." Agatha remained silent. He threw her on to a large banquet table made of stone in the middle of their camp. "So you actually did run out of rat poison then?"

Agatha, lying on the table surrounded by rats trying to grab at her, frantically searched her pockets for a second note. She pulled out a folded piece of paper and chucked it at Weevil.

Rodney picked it up from the edge of the table. "It's a map, Weevil," he said. "Telling us what we've gotta do."

"No one tells us what to do. We makes up our own rules. Always have."

Agatha looked around at her predicament and decided that there was only one thing for it. She stood up on the table, took a deep breath and began her speech to the crowd: "If you value your land, this island, and your freedom, you will battle with us to save it. If not for Gosport, then for this land and your place on it. The Gizor Army will annihilate your world and mine. Don't like us? Fine. Don't want to fight with us? Fine. Fight for yourselves and freedom will be yours. Your crimes will be undone. Whatever you did will be forgiven in battle. Help us to save both our worlds. I beg of you."

The crowd stood in silence for a moment, shocked at the brave soul before them before bursting into hysterical laughter, chucking beer tankards, sticks and mud at her. As she ducked to avoid the avalanche, she had got closer to the table's edge. Weevil grabbed her and pulled her off the table. As the chaos continued, he dragged her out of the crowd and through the wooded area at quite a pace to the north of the island. When he reached the shoreline he threw her down the rocks and on to the shore. She landed in a seated position facing Priddy's Hard in the distance with her feet poking out of the shallow tidewater. She turned her head to seek out Weevil on the bank above, but he was nowhere to be seen.

*

Both Hertha and Berry had fallen asleep in the sanctuary of the shed on the edge of Eastney waters. Their slumber, however, was soon broken by the wailing sound of sirens in the far distance.

"What's that?" said Berry in a confused daze as he woke from his deep sleep.

"They're looking for us," said Hertha as she went over to the shed window overlooking the sea. "We need to get moving. It won't be long before they search the sewer pipe, and then this shed." She began searching around for makeshift weapons they could load up with for the perilous journey ahead of them.

"And where exactly do you suggest we move on to?" said Berry with his usual scepticism.

"Anywhere but here."

Just as they began grabbing what they could, they heard footsteps coming towards them from the garden. "Hide!" Hertha whispered. The shed door began rattling with someone on the other side turning its rusty stiff handle.

The door opened, and a figure blocked out by the morning sun could be seen standing in the doorway. "You will come with me," he said to the two comrades hiding in silence. They did not move. "Quickly!" he demanded. The figure walked out of the shed and looked out towards the beach, scanning the area. "Do you want to be caught? The Gizor are coming!" Hertha and Berry gingerly stood up from their hiding places and walked out into the back garden. "This way," he said as he led them back out on to the shore, up a narrow alleyway between two houses and bundled them both into the back of a waiting truck.

*

It was early morning and gruelling training was underway in the Alver Village.

"No, no, no!" shouted Morag, "You cannae do it that way. You're too heavy."

"She's right, you know," said Jasper, observing Agatha and Floppy trying to sit on Beaky's back.

"OK. What about one of us on his back and the other dangled by a rope?" suggested Agatha.

"Oh, aye that should reduce the weight all right," said Morag mockingly.

Agatha thought for a second. "Floppy, get on his back, and Beaky – try flying now."

Floppy hopped on to Beaky's broad back and held on to his neck.

"Keep low, Floppy," said Lucius. Beaky began walking backwards to get a good run-up before any take-off. He flapped his wings with all his might and managed a few seconds of 'flight' but crashed into some brambles and nettles at the end of the runway.

"This is no good. It's not gonnae work this way," said Morag as Beaky and Floppy walked out of the brambles, shaking off the twigs and leaves from their fur and feathers. As they did so, Agatha observed one of Beaky's feathers fly into the air and gracefully fall to the ground, landing in a puddle where the laundry was being scrubbed by two stout female hedgehogs. She watched as one pinned garments to the washing line to dry. She had an idea.

"Floppy, where are those maps I gave you?" asked Agatha.

Floppy ran to his backpack and pulled out several rolled-up maps. "Here are the mappies, Aggy." he said. "I had the mappies, I did."

"Excellent." She unrolled them.

"What're you thinking, missy?" asked Morag.

"Well if we can't fly over, and we can't swim or take a boat because of Gizor patrols, there is only one other way."

Second-guessing her plan, Lucius commented: "It is too dangerous and too long to go around, Agatha."

"I know that – which is why we're going to climb over it," she replied baffling her audience. "Look at this map of the Harbour." She pointed. "See how narrow the mouth is?"

"She's right, you know," said Jasper, looking over the shoulders of those following the map.

"It must only be about two hundred feet across. We could attach a rope to one end and Beaky could fly over to the other. We could climb across in the dark of night above the water, above the Gizor harbour master and reach the other side."

"Well, it's a solid plan, lassie," said Morag, looking impressed. "How's your climbing, Floppy?" she asked.

"I like hopping, I do. I'm a hopper."

"Aye," she replied, "that might be a problem."

Agatha scurried over to the washing line and untied it, apologising to its owner, then rushed over to a large tall tree just outside the village in the woods and tied the rope to it. She threw the other end to Beaky who wrapped it tightly round another tree opposite until the rope was taut. Although it was only a few feet off the ground, it made for good enough practice.

"Up you go, laddie," said Morag to Floppy. He struggled even to get on top of the line, let alone walk across it. "This might take a while," she said as she watched Floppy fall off the rope. "Why don't you have a go, lassie lou?" she suggested to Agatha. Immediately Agatha realised her plan – whilst brilliant – had not factored in her own weakness: she was a squirrel scared of heights and couldn't actually climb trees.

"Err, no I think Floppy needs to practice first," she said, hiding her fears. "How are the mock-ups going?" The mock-ups were to be an important part of Agatha's plan to liberate the camp.

"Oh aye, going well but it's a big task and a risky one," she replied.

"I know, but if it works – even just for a few – it'll be worth it."

"I don't imagine Farmer Jack would be too happy if he found out what the barn and stables were being used for, let alone his crops."

*

Berry and Hertha were driven only a very short distance when the truck came to an abrupt stop, knocking them sideways. Just as they regained their balance from the bumpy ride, the canopy was untied, and a figure emerged, jumping into the back with them. He was a good-looking young grey squirrel dressed in a short black leather jacket and scruffy trousers.

"Here, put these on," said the squirrel, handing them a jacket of their own. Berry's was obviously designed for a larger animal and when he put it on, it dragged on the ground. The squirrel then handed Hertha a tub of dazzle fur paint, which she quickly applied to cover up her red fur.

"I am Vincent Tudor," he whispered as he handed them a ration of fruit each. "We do not have much time. When we exit the truck, you must keep close and stay by my side at all times – do you understand?"

"Yes," they chorused.

Vincent Tudor jumped from the truck and lifted the canopy for Berry and Hertha to get down. They found themselves a short distance away from some Gizor officers and personnel parading the streets.

"Come," said Vincent as he led them away from the truck. A tannoy began blurting out the National Gizor Anthem for its soldiers to march to. "This way," he said as they walked between a couple of empty Gizor trucks towards a brick-built tunnel that sat beneath a huge grassy mound. They did not realise it until later, but they were entering Eastney Battery West – an abandoned stronghold that the Gizor Army had shown very little interest in but that was the home of the Gizor Resistance movement known as The Mary Rose. Vincent took them down a cobbled tunnel that appeared to lead straight out onto the beach. Yet halfway down the tunnel was a dark recess with a cast-iron barred door. They stopped in the recess and Vincent pulled them closer as a Gizor soldier walked past the tunnel entrance. Berry and Hertha were startled when they then heard the rattle of a key opening the door before them. They followed Vincent through as another squirrel locked the door behind them. The sloping passageway narrowed the deeper they walked through it. It was dark and damp and put them both in mind of the caponier back home. As the passage curved and sloped, they soon reached the end and were taken up some steps towards yet another door, which opened to reveal a huge chamber and a rabble of resistance fighters. Hertha immediately felt at home.

"Come, my friends," said Vincent as he led them to a couple of chairs placed around a table. Soon they were both provided with food and drink and were grateful for their safety. Hertha couldn't stop looking around at her surroundings, comparing it to the caponier base in Rowner Fort. She observed much planning and plotting with maps and sketches pinned on the walls and a rabble of animals that looked worn out from fighting many battles. She watched Vincent as he was called over to the corner of the room where an argument took place. She couldn't understand what they were arguing about, but an argument in any language is easy to spot. There were raised voices and harsh gesturing between Vincent and a burly grey squirrel.

"Apologies," said Vincent as he rejoined the two. "My friend here is not used to strangers."

"What language were you speaking?"

"Pompey. My friend does not speak English."

"And what exactly are we doing here?" asked Hertha.

"We are a small group – smaller still in recent days. They call us The Mary Rose – we are students from the university. We're motivated by a conscience of justice. We are here to help." He looked over to his comrade in the corner, who clearly did not agree with helping these two. "We work with Brother Lucius."

"You know Lucius?" questioned Hertha. "Where's Floppy?" she asked.

"Brother Lucius sent us to find you," said Vincent as his comrade scoffed at his response. "This is Eugene Conrad," he explained as Eugene muttered something in Pompey and turned his back to them in defiance. "We are here to keep you safe."

"It doesn't sound like a very popular idea," said Berry.

"It isn't. It is not safe, but we do what we can to sleep

at night," he said, mainly for the benefit of Eugene who glanced over. "We can help you get home but only so far. The rest you must travel alone."

"And Floppy – my friend. Do you know where he is?" asked Hertha again.

"I know nothing of Floppy."

\*

"That sounds very dangerous Doris," said Gertie Nicholson as Doris told a small group in the camp about Agatha's plans.

"Well, I for one won't play any part in it," said Mary Camper defiantly, folding her arms. "Besides, we shall be re-homed soon by all accounts."

"It didn't sound like they're planning on re-homing us. Mary." warned Doris.

"Well, I think we should give it a go," said Lady Ellen jumping up, clapping her paws together and eager to help with the plan. "Come on, troops – let's start making arrangements."

\*

As Floppy was busy practising his tightrope skills, Agatha was sitting with her back against a tree with her notebook charting the tunnels from Priddy's.

"We can't get all of them you know," said Morag as she sat down beside her.

"Maybe not but we can try."

"Aye, we certainly can, missy."

"We're running out of straw, boss," reported Jasper as he approached them. "Farmer Jack is gonna notice soon and we can't get to the back barn because it's locked."

"Aye," replied Morag.

"We need to start moving them into the tunnels," said Agatha, standing up and eager to start the liberation.

Morag was not entirely convinced by the plan but knew if the Ark was to be retrieved by Agatha and Floppy, she had to also support Agatha's plan to free the Camp. "You know Aggy, a small army can only fight battles and not win a war."

"Well that's where you're wrong. Wars are won by winning battles."

"You need a whole army," said Morag, "and we don't have one."

"We have Rats Island."

"That's if they choose to fight."

"They will," she said as if it was a certainty. "Plus, the more we save the bigger our army will become."

"You have a bigger heart than an army, Aggy. Don't get me wrong. I stand with ya, lassie. I just don't want you to be saddened."

"I will keep fighting with all my heart regardless of sadness. I will not stop," replied Agatha, walking towards Lucius who was helping Floppy with his balance. "We need to start loading, Lucius."

"Yes of course," he replied, holding on to Floppy's paw. "You're doing really well, Floppy." He released his paw and Floppy fell to the ground. Undeterred, Floppy began doing star jumps with Beaky.

"Pack them with soil and leaves if we need to," suggested Agatha to Jasper.

"Might be too heavy."

"We need more straw then. Can he be reasoned with?" asked Agatha, referring to Farmer Jack.

"I've yet to see it," replied Morag, "and I wouldn't try it myself, missy."

"How's his aim – improved much?" asked Agatha.

"His aim? Well, he's as blind as a bat but there's nothing wrong with his hearing. If he sees you at all, he'll wound you just enough that you're still able to feel the pain when he hangs you in the woods."

"I be scared of Rabbit Skin Jack, Agatha. I be scared of him, I be," said Floppy.

"Don't worry, Floppy, he never comes to the village," said Morag.

"Why is that?" asked Agatha.

"It's not his place. He doesn't need to. We serve the land for him and as long as we serve it well, there's no complaint."

"Then what does he do all day in that farm house?"

"Florence?" called Morag to the scullery maid who came running over. "Tell them what Farmer Jack does all day."

"Master Jack? He's a painter," said Florence.

"A painter?" queried Agatha. "But he can't see, he's half blind."

"Doesn't stop him though," said Morag, smiling to herself.

"What does he paint?" asked Agatha.

"The same thing he's painted for the last twenty-five years. The same sweetheart he's loved for that long."

"Who is she?"

"Oh, just someone who broke his heart and made him bitter. He does it from memory and it's a deep memory – a painful one at that. He cannae get over her." Morag paused, "His heart's almost as big as yours, lassie, but he will not show it. He's a broken man – a damaged one."

"Well broken or not, we need more straw," said Agatha walking off defiantly towards the farmhouse

"He'll hang you from a noose!" warned Morag.

"WE NEED MORE STRAW!" shouted Agatha. Her heart was pounding; she was not sure what she was going to say to Farmer Jack and couldn't quite believe her little legs were walking their way right up to the farmhouse door. She knocked and waited for a response. She suddenly had a tinge of foreboding and dove into the bushes to the side.

"Who's there?" shouted Farmer Jack as he swung open the door with his shotgun in paw. The old badger stood tall in the doorway. He stepped out into the clearing and raised his gun to the open space before him. Agatha quickly and silently scurried into the farmhouse behind him while Farmer Jack continued looking around his land for the intruder. Agatha needed the keys to the back barn if her plan was going to work. As soon as she entered she could see mountains of canvases lining the walls of the hallway and propped up against the walls – too many to count. The smell of oils was almost overwhelming and there were splashes of paint everywhere. She made her way to the back of the house towards the kitchen, but had to quickly jump into the reception room on the right as Farmer Jack returned to the house and shut the door behind him. He was muttering to himself.

"Coming here? Knocking on my door? Treading on my land?" He turned to the closed front door and shouted: "WE AINT OPEN FOR VISITORS" His raised voice made Agatha jump and bang her head on the table she was hiding under. She heard him pacing heavy-footed around his house. "Flamin' cheek, saying my apples are rotten," he said. "I'LL GIVE YOU ROTTEN, knocking on my door, I ain't no fool. I AIN'T A FOOL!" He was quite crazy, thought Agatha. She wanted to get to the kitchen, thinking the keys would be in there somewhere but was stuck under the desk for the time being. Her paws felt wet with what she thought was sweat but quickly realised was paint, as her left arm had brushed up against a canvas that was leaning against the footwell of the desk. She quickly leant the other way and hit another canvas with her right shoulder. Just as she began to panic, she heard the scratch of a needle hit the record on the gramophone in the room next door and a sweet, beautiful, but very loud song began to play. Farmer Jack had begun painting again. She crawled out from under the desk and got to her feet where she was able to look at the paintings for the first time. A familiar face was smiling back at her – a badger wearing a lily blue bonnet and dress, and crazy bright red lipstick. She looked closer – it was Lady Prideaux-Brune in her younger days, she was sure of it. It was Lady Ellen that Old Farmer Jack had been in love with all these years. Just as she realised who she was looking at, she heard the front door open and dived back under the desk. It was Florence, Farmer Jack's scullery maid.

"Just fetching your laundry, Farmer Jack, sir," a voice rang out. Agatha recognised it as belonging to Florence, the hedgehog who was one of the scullery maids.

"Hurry up!" he shouted back at her as he continued painting.

Agatha scurried out from under the desk and met Florence at the doorway. She ushered her into the kitchen at the back where Agatha quickly scanned the walls for the farmer's keys. Florence opened the back door for her and Agatha scurried off into the back garden, jumping over the picket fence and into the woods.

## Chapter 10
# A THREE-NIGHT WAIT

D rips of Portsmouth rain ran down the walls of Eastney Battery. The small group of resistence was unusually silent. Gizor troops were at the door. Hertha and Berry were ushered into a corner and covered up by old rags and sheets. Hertha strained to hear what was being said.

"The study of fools," said an officer in the distance.

"Of poetry. Hail Gizor the Mighty," replied Vincent Tudor.

"Hail Gizor," replied the officer who then walked away.

Hertha unravelled the blanket covering them. "What was that?" she asked.

"It is not safe here," said Vincent. "I have bought you a little time, that's all. There are patrols everywhere looking for you. We must leave." He handed Hertha the tub of dazzle fur paint to reapply, which she quickly did, handing it back to Vincent who bunged it into an old rucksack along with some bread, fruit and a drop of berry juice in a flask. He placed the rucksack onto Hertha's back and gave a similar one to Berry. He gave them each a cap to wear. "I will take you as far as the castle," he said.

"We don't wanna go back there," replied Berry, organising himself.

"Not that castle," said Vincent.

"Then where?" asked Hertha.

"Come! Quick!" said Vincent, ignoring the question. Hertha and Berry started walking towards the entrance. "No, this way," said Vincent as he directed them to the other side of the Battery. Some of his crew helped move a pile of tables and chairs to reveal a grating in the floor. He lifted it up and jumped down. "Jump!" he called up from the darkness.

"Reminds me of the shed," commented Berry as he lowered himself carefully down the hole.

*

Agatha and her gang waited for the cover of darkness to travel to the back barn in full view of the farmhouse. She struggled with the keys at first, trying to see which one would fit the lock. The villagers lined up patiently behind her with their wheelbarrows and baskets waiting for her to open the barn doors.

"GO! GO!" she whispered.

The operation was swift, and the villagers busied themselves collecting straw, fruits and nuts and ferrying it all away. As the last hedgehog left and scurried back to the village, Agatha picked up the last remaining strands of straw and headed for the door herself. She was met with a giant of a badger – Farmer Jack – lit by the moonlight standing in the doorway pointing his shotgun directly at Agatha's face. She dropped the remaining strands of straw and raised her paws in the air to surrender.

"I would like to know what it is you think you're doing 'ere?" asked Farmer Jack, pleased that he had cornered the pesky intruder.

Agatha didn't know how to respond. She shook her head with panic. "It's for … it's for the effort."

187

She fully expected to be shot dead but was grabbed by the neck and lifted into the air. She was getting mightily tired of being grabbed by the scruff, though acknowledged it was better than being shot. He spun her round and threw her on to the gravel path just outside the barn. She was on her back crawling away on her elbows from Farmer Jack who was following her, still menacing her with the gun.

"It's to end the war," she said, still trying to explain.

"Scrumping," replied Jack, "trespassing and stealing. You have exactly three seconds to get off my land."

"I know but wait. Please."

"ONE, TWO, THREE!" Agatha rolled out of the way as the gun went off, so the shot missed its target. Farmer Jack fired again and she rolled the other way. As she saw him reloading, she took the opportunity to scramble to her feet and saw the villagers running towards her.

"Whoa there, Master Jack!" shouted Morag.

"MORAG?" he shouted back.

"Aye, Master Jack. She means no harm, sir."

"We've got ourselves a thief, Morag" he replied, pointing the gun directly at Agatha.

"No, sir. She's an honest thief, Master Jack."

"I TRUSTED YOU, MORAG!" he shouted as another shot rang out.

"You can trust me, Master Jack."

"She's a thief."

"I mean to rescue Lady Ellen," declared Agatha with her paws still in the air and her back up against a wall.

"You should nay have mentioned her name, lassie," whispered Morag.

Farmer Jack's response was not the one Agatha was hoping for. Her name enraged him more. "YOU MENTION HER NAME TO ME?" he shouted.

"I'm sorry I mentioned her," said Agatha, conscious of

a panicky squeak in her voice. "Please, please. It's to liberate the Camp."

"Why do you mention her name?" he shouted again.

"She's been captured. She's in the Camp. The Gizor Camp," she tried to explain.

Farmer Jack was unsure. "Morag? Is this true?" he asked.

"Aye, Master Jack," she replied, walking closer to Agatha who was cowering against the wall, waiting for the final shot that she knew was still in the gun. Morag grabbed her arm and helped her up as Farmer Jack lowered his gun slightly.

"Ellen?" his voice softened as he questioned what he was hearing.

"Aye, sir," she repeated.

He thought for a moment and raised his gun once more. "NO YOU'RE LYING. She's a badger, not a Red."

"No, Master Jack. She's a heart of gold, sir. You know it to be true," replied Morag.

He lowered his gun once more. "My Ellen?" he asked again.

"Your Ellen, sir."

"Your Ellen," interrupted Agatha still slightly out of breath from being shot at, "my papa, my good friends, all our friends. They all lie in the Camp." She stepped closer to Farmer Jack. "Help us to help them, Farmer Jack."

Jack stared at Agatha for a moment and realised he was surrounded by all his villagers watching the crazy scene that had unfolded that night. He was a man of few words and all of them grumpy ones. "Take what you want," he said as he walked away towards the farmhouse. He staggered as if he himself had been shot, hobbled up the steps, and before closing the door behind him shouted: "And get off my land!"

"I tell you this, lassie, that doesn't happen every day," said Morag.

*

Hertha and Berry followed Vincent through the dark dank tunnel with barely any light to guide them, yet they trusted their guide. They had no choice. They were in Portsmouth territory – Gizor land.

"What's at the castle?" asked Berry, walking close behind Vincent.

"The Gizor," replied Vincent keeping a steady fast pace in front of them.

"What do we do when we get there?" Hertha asked, hoping there were further instructions or some sort of direction for them to take.

Vincent made a scoffing sound. "Run? Hide? Fight? You choose," he replied, "but you will only have moments at any sunrise to decide."

"Is there not another way?" asked Berry. "We don't stand a chance."

"No, this is the only way. I would suggest you make 'chance' your friend."

The small group travelled through the winding abandoned tunnels below the south coast of Portsmouth towards Southsea Castle where the enemy were organising. They began to hear muffled footsteps above them and suddenly Vincent stopped in his tracks. Berry almost walked into him.

"This is as far as I go, my friends," said Vincent.

"You what?" said Berry.

"Here," said Vincent, handing Hertha a notice that he pulled from the inner pocket of his jacket. "It seems like your friends have a plan of their own."

Hertha looked down at the notice and in the dim light could just make out the words "The Alvish Resistance of

Gosport'. It was Agatha's notice to the Federation. Clearly, Ethel had distributed it, and some copies had made their way to Gizor land.

"You wait here for three nights and leave at sunrise – this is very important," said Vincent as he handed them each a pistol and walked away back down the tunnel.

*

Gizor stood alone in his Semaphore Tower in Portsmouth Dockyard surveying his land, with his arms folded behind him and his chest puffed out. It was late, but his army of soldiers, sailors and air-crew were still busy in the dockyard. Not even a knock on the office door disturbed his concentration.

"Cousin, you sent for me?" said Roderick as he walked in and stood by Gizor's desk waiting for instruction.

"Yes, cousin," said Gizor, without breaking his gaze on the busy dockyard below him. "I hear word of a prison break. Is this true?"

"So I understand sir, yes."

Gizor turned to face his cousin. "Roderick, I want you to command the south. Take what arms you need. I will have no areas of weakness on my land."

"Weakness?" questioned Roderick. Gizor had in his paw a notice that he threw on to his desk for Roderick to examine. It was the Resistance message to the WWF. Roderick read it and commented: "Surely, our defences are stronger than any threat."

"I want OFFENCE in my army, Roderick. Defence is for the weak."

Roderick looked down at the notice again. "I will see to it that the south is armed and mobilised," he said.

*

A long line of hedgehogs from the Alver Village stood waiting in the tunnels beneath Bernard Hardway's land near to Priddy's. They were each dragging great big heavy sacks and had travelled far, deep beneath Gosport. Agatha was leading the way and Lucius and Beaky were following up the rear.

"In here!" she called as the hedgehogs began moving again. "We'll store them in here." She pointed to a large chamber deep beneath the land.

"I want no part in this, Agatha," said Jane Priddy as she handed her a rusty key to the outer door of the ramparts where she stored old beaten-up machinery and metals. It was a place she rarely visited.

"I understand Mrs Priddy, and thank you." Agatha began looking around the chamber at the various tunnels and rooms leading off it.

"These are heavy, these are," said Floppy, hauling a sack into the chamber. He was out of breath, dropped the sack and leant on a rickety old pipe that was wedged against lots of other clutter. The pipe snapped with his weight and fell to the ground, ricocheting on the concrete floor and making an almighty clang. The other half of the pipe then rolled towards Agatha's feet and knocked into a rusty cart which proceeded to roll into a couple of hedgehogs, knocking them off their feet and into the cart.

"I be as quiet as a mousey," said Floppy guiltily. "Like Hertha told me to be." He brushed off some of the dirt and dust from his white fur.

Agatha helped her comrades – who had curled into spiky balls in alarm – out of the cart and began examining it. She shook it a little to check its strength and sturdiness. "Hand me that rope over there, Floppy," she said, pointing. Floppy happily obliged, hopping over to a thick reel of old dusty unused rope. "Now take the reel down that tunnel back the way we came," she said as she began threading the end of the rope through the cart.

"Excuse me, excuse me," said Floppy, pushing through the remaining line of hedgehogs who were still ferrying the sacks into the chamber.

"Beaky, take these," she said, handing him a large box of old metal hooks, "and recruit two hedgehogs to help you. I need you to work your way back down the tunnel hammering the hooks into the walls as you go. The hedgehogs can stand on your back to do it. Then thread the rope through the hooks."

"Right you are," he replied, the hammer and hooks in his pocket making him waddle in a comic lopsided way. "Operation Hook-up," he said to himself.

"Florence, help me find some more wheels and planks," she ordered as they searched the clutter in the chamber.

"I'll grant you this, Lucius," commented Morag, watching Agatha take charge. "She's a driven little doe."

*

Morning came all too soon for the Camp prisoners. Work detail was being dished out on the parade line as usual. The older folk were given their usual detail of work in the barracks sifting through belongings, while Doris was ordered onto an animal transport truck as usual bound for Priddy's. The truck drove from the parade line towards the east gates, where Doris could see a small group of animals lined up outside a brick building. They were walking under orders down some steps into its deep bunker. She also observed the tall brick chimney above, billowing smoke from its top. As she left the Camp gates, just before going out of sight, she could see a scuffle between a red squirrel and a Gizor officer who dragged the squirrel down the steps and threw him into the bunker, then closed and locked the door behind him. The officer laughed as he walked back up the steps and noticed Doris watching him from the back of the truck. Doris turned and sat down. Beside her was a red squirrel called Joseph Muzzlewhite, pale, thin and weak from work. He looked exhausted and as though he had given up on life.

"You'll be OK, my friend," she whispered, placing a paw on his knee. "Not long now." Joseph did not reply and looked down at his paws, which were blistered and raw.

The truck – one of a convoy of ten – soon reached the gates of Priddy's. Each group were pulled out by Gizor soldiers and immediately put to work.

"Psst!" said Agatha, once more hiding in the store. Doris gave a quick glance across as she continued working. "Put this one back on the truck," Agatha whispered, gesturing to a crate near to her which had been stuffed full of heavy sacks. Doris nodded that she understood and continued working.

Agatha then positioned herself at the back of the work hall where she grabbed the paw of Joseph Muzzlewhite as he walked out the back door, as had been planned. He followed her through the undergrowth and towards the old ramparts situated at the north of Priddy's Hard.

"Go! Go!" she ordered as she quietly opened the door of the rampart and almost shoved Joseph into the dark. Following him was a group of twenty – maybe thirty – others being ferried secretly to safety by Agatha's crew of Resistance.

"That's the lot," whispered Beaky as he clashed his wings together, shaking off the dirt and twigs from the undergrowth and an operation well done.

"Where's Doris?" asked Agatha, looking ahead at the line of Camp mates standing in the tunnel.

"She's not coming," answered Lucius.

"What?" said Agatha, about to charge back out in to the yard. Lucius closed the door, preventing her from doing so.

"Maybe tomorrow," he replied.

"Tomorrow might be too late."

"Agatha, this plan can only work with sacrifice."

Agatha knew Lucius was right, shook off her disappointment and began tending to those she had helped to free. She would save Doris tomorrow, she said to herself. They put the Camp mates into the carts and onto long planks also attached with rope and with small wheels fixed to the underside. When they were ready, Floppy began heaving the pulley system that Agatha had rigged up that conveyed the ill and worn-out workers through the tunnels to safety.

It took about an hour to reach the safety of the Grange chamber – the Resistance base. Medical aid and sustenance was given, with hedgehogs rallying around helping those liberated.

"I must go back," said Agatha, staring at Lucius.

"Agatha, we will know if it worked by tomorrow," he pleaded.

Sighing with frustration, she started dishing out water, blankets and food rations to those around her.

\*

Doris travelled back to the Camp in the back of the truck and sat nervously waiting for it to stop. The disembarkation would be the riskiest part of Agatha's plan. Doris readied herself with a couple of others in the back and hoped her comrades would remember their positions. As the doors of the truck opened, she was greeted by Lady Ellen, Mary, and a few more of her Campmates. The Gizor Army had recently allowed the Campmates to support their tired 'co-workers' out of the trucks as they grew more and more weak and pathetic. Doris nodded at Lady Ellen who stepped briefly into the truck to assist the Camp mate that Doris was holding up, and the others followed suit. Lady Ellen and Doris carried their fallen comrade through the parade square with his arms draped over them for support. The creature looked in a state of complete collapse. All the Gizor soldiers did was mock them for their kindness to one another. They reached the relative safety of the barracks and closed the door behind them while one of their Camp mates, a small vole, stood on a box to peek out of the window keeping watch.

"You did it, Doris!" said Lady Ellen.

Doris collapsed onto one of the bunks with her fallen comrade collapsing into a heap beside her. No one ran to his aid, though. Instead, he was allowed to slump to the floor, his red scarecrow head rolling from his hood and disintegrating into straw.

"How many did we save?" asked Lady Ellen.

Doris shook her head, exhausted. "I don't know," she said, "about twenty or so."

"Tell us what happened?" asked another.

"They're heavy. I think they've padded them out with heavy cloth. It was hard work." She wiped the sweat from her forehead.

Mary began riffling through the straw of the disembowelled lump on the floor, collecting apples and other fruits and dishing them out to those in the barracks. "Here," she said sheepishly as she held out a juicy piece of apple for Doris to take.

"Thank you, Mary," she replied, bemused by Mary's sudden interest in the 'plan' that seemed to have actually worked.

\*

"I don't know about you, but I could murder one of Rosie's cupcakes right now," said Berry. He and Hertha were still hidden away under the ground of Portsmouth. They allowed thoughts of home to invade their desperate minds.

"He was brave to do that," commented Hertha, referring to Floppy's castle wall antics.

"Brave? He didn't know he was brave. He'll follow whoever leads him."

"He was still brave," she said, a little angered by Berry's reaction. "What do you mean by that anyway?"

"Well, he was always following you about, wasn't he?"

"I promised to look after him, you know that."

"Yeah? And me too, and what a fine job we did of that."

"He'll be safe – I know it," said Hertha trying to convince herself as much as Berry.

"I know, Hertha," replied Berry softly, trying to recover some of the hurt he had just dished out without thinking. "Not long now before sunrise."

"Why sunrise? That's what I don't get. Surely we should use the cover of darkness."

The two started packing their meagre supplies back into their bags and zipping them up tight. Hertha began reapplying her dazzle paint to cover up her red fur. Both were nervous but too busy checking their equipment to acknowledge it. They found themselves ready and looked at each other for a moment standing by themselves in the tunnel – as if they were the only ones left in the world. They gave each other a knowing nod before Hertha stepped on to the rusty rung of a fixed ladder that led up to a grating. Hertha stopped shy of the top as a truck went over the manhole and then a huge group of marching soldiers followed on behind it.

"We can't go up there," whispered Berry standing halfway up the ladder and hearing the marching feet.

"Shsh!" She moved slightly closer to the top to seek a better view. "They look like they're moving off."

The two waited a couple of minutes for the noise to fade into the distance before Hertha gently pushed the grating upwards and took a crafty peek before placing it back down in position. "It looks like they've gone. There's no one about. Come on." She lifted the grating up further this time, stuck her head out and looked at her surroundings. They were in the grounds of Southsea Castle. She lifted herself out of the hole and helped Berry out. They were completely exposed and realised that it would only be a second or so until they were discovered by the guards at the top of the lighthouse just across from them. They ran for immediate cover towards the central Keep and stuck close to its walls. They heard footsteps approaching from the south as they stood flat against the wall. Hertha signalled to Berry to follow her. She didn't know where she was going but needed to seek cover. They ducked round the front of the Keep and could see briefly ahead of them the back of an infantry line of soldiers crossing the moat away from the castle. She looked back up to the lighthouse and they took their chance, running for the entrance of the Keep. They scrambled up the stairs, hurried into the first chamber, then darted up the steps to the left and followed the many corridors around the Keep itself.

Berry stopped to catch his breath for a moment. "Where exactly are we going, H?" he asked.

She shrugged her shoulders – she didn't have a clue why they had entered the castle other than to escape the waiting Gizor. "OK, let's make our way back down and try to make a run for it," she said. As they turned back on themselves they heard footsteps coming up the stairs towards them. "This way!" she whispered and they headed further into the Keep. The footsteps continued heading their way. "In here!" said Hertha as she opened a door and prayed that no one was in the room that they were about to enter. They quietly closed the door behind them and listened for the guard, who walked straight past. They turned around to find to their amazement that they were in Gizor's war room. Hertha ran over to the table and examined the plans. Berry focused on the photographs and plans on the walls. "It's the whole of Gosport and Portsmouth," said Hertha, amazed at the detailed map before her. "Look – there's Camp Browndown and Priddy's, the airfield, everything." Berry didn't answer. "Berry, look!" she repeated. But Berry did not reply: he was still staring at the photographs and plans on the walls. Hertha scampered over to see for herself what had sparked his utter silence. She looked at the black-and-white photos and could see pictures of squirrels lined up in front of a brick building and plumes of smoke coming from a neighbouring tall chimney. Another photo showed heaps of charred animals and Gizor soldiers posing for their photo as if proud of their 'kill'. "But they were going to be re-homed," said Hertha, stunned.

"Looks like they've done away with that plan," said Berry, dryly.

Hertha scrunched her eyes up in frustration and anger, walked away from the wall and leant her paws on the table. "I should have listened to Agatha," she said. "We could have saved them."

"And exactly how would we have done that, H?" asked Berry, trying to be realistic.

"She was always saying we needed to liberate the Camp. I should have listened to her."

Berry didn't know how to respond. "Come on, H, let's

get out of here," he said as he grabbed her arm to prompt her to her leave. She shrugged him off and started furiously messing up the table before her, knocking off pins, running to the wall and tearing off the photos. She shut her eyes once more in pure anger and bowed her head to the floor. Berry just stood there. One of the photographs drifted serenely to the floor and as Hertha opened her eyes she picked it up.

"It's Rosie," she said. The image was a grainy one with captive squirrels all lined up waiting to be executed in the death chamber. One of the figures standing in a Camp uniform was indeed Rosie. Hertha was devastated. She scrunched up the photograph in her paw but then unravelled it, folded it nicely and put it in her jacket pocket.

"Come on, H, we've gotta get out of here," said Berry, tugging on her sleeve.

As they approached the door, they heard the soldier walking towards them. They quickly turned to seek another exit. They ran to the far corner and up some spiral stairs. They reached another door and hoped it would be unlocked. It was and they almost dived in. They placed a heavy wooden catch over the door to prevent anyone stepping inside. The room had no light but glittered with jewels, coins, trophies, silverware, rare paintings, and ancient ornaments.

"What is this place?" asked Berry in wonder.

"Gizor's loot," said Hertha, staring at the treasures.

"The admiral is crazy."

"The grey squirrel wants to rule his empire and everything in it."

"This way," said Berry, leading them through the piled-up loot towards the back of the room and up yet another set of steps.

They suddenly found themselves at the top of the Keep,

back into daylight and the smog of Pompey air. They now had a bird's eye view of Gizor's empire.

*

The streets of Portsmouth were swarming with animal folk, and Guildhall Square was crammed with Gizor's dedicated army of thousands waiting for their Lord Admiral. The doors of the Guildhall opened once more, and delegates, dignitaries, agents and officers spewed out. They too were star-struck by their Admiral and pushed and shoved to the front to stand in line next to the great Gizor himself. The roar of the crowd was enormous as Jean De Gizor – Admiral Grey, High Commander of the Fleet of Ratufinee – stepped out on to the steps and walked to his podium to address his nation. His arms outstretched to greet his adoring public and army, he began:

"Mine is the challenge of the west, and ours is the glory of victory. Their failure to recognise our internal scars is the same as those externally bestowed on them as a consequence. The annihilation is theirs. The collapse of the state will not ruin our industry but theirs. For twenty-five years we have been waiting and now we have reclaimed our harbour and fought tyranny with actions to bring our world, a new beginning. And we have done so with honour and promise. And if it has been possible, it has been possible because of you, the pure folk of Portsmouth." An almighty cheer erupted from the crowd. "No longer are we the victims of the Red World plot against our rights and our pure pedigree," he continued. "It has been our final solution to the west to re-join our harbour and rejoice in what is the common breed. The Gizor nation is the animals' nation, a society of pure blood and creed. There may be some who doubted my promise – the promise of a new era – but I say observe my actions and what I have given to you – I have shown you glory and trust. I promised a guide, and light has appeared – Heaven's path is revealed in my words, and I promise to always bear the flame so that you will always see. THIS GIZOR-GIVEN NATION. THIS NEW BEGINNING. THIS MIGHTY PORTSMOUTH!" A huge cheer and a chant of 'Hail Gizor' erupted once more.

As Gizor basked in his own evil glory and stood with his paws outstretched, listening to the adulation of the crowd, the cheers were replaced by panic as shots were fired into the crowd from the sidelines. The army charged at the attackers, but the Gizor Resistance was strong and threw grenades at the army on parade. Gizor was whisked off by his guards and took cover inside the Guildhall. The sound of firepower was immense from inside the Guildhall and its protective walls were shaken. The battle raged on in the streets outside.

"WHAT IS THIS?" shouted Gizor to his men as they manhandled him to safety.

"The Gizor Resistance, sir. They are more rallied than we anticipated," said one guard as they all took cover, preparing for the walls to cave in. "This way sir," said the guard, leading Gizor through the Guildhall and out through the back to a waiting automobile.

The huge plumes of smoke from the bombing and firing could be seen for miles.

"What's that?" said Berry, "Over there," pointing at the rising smoke some miles in the distance towards central Portsmouth.

"Keep low," said Hertha as they crouched down besides the parapet, undetected from the watch of the lighthouse. Attack sirens began to sound around the towns and slums. An army had been woken.

# PART THREE

## Chapter 11
# LAUNDRY LINES

T he chamber deep beneath Fort Grange was filling up fast with the tired and wounded. In just the space of a few days, they had managed to save hundreds of animals from Camp Browndown. Yet there was still no sign of Doris, or any of the Doe-hen Institute of Ladies – Agatha's old friends.

"You will continue, won't you, Lucius?" asked Agatha.

He placed a reassuring paw on her shoulder. "Of course, my brave friend."

"Don't worry, lassie," said Morag. "Jasper will take care of it for yous." She stood in the doorway of the chamber with her arm placed over Jasper the village woodpecker to demonstrate her absolute faith in him to finish the job. Agatha did not reply and turned to survey the chamber and the hundreds of animals she had already liberated.

"I won't force him," said Agatha as she watched Floppy chatting to animals in the chamber about his recent adventures.

"Aye, we don't expect you to," replied Morag.

"But you expect him to follow me nonetheless?"

Morag did not respond as she knew Agatha was right. Agatha broke the silence between them with a sigh and walked over to Floppy.

"Walk with me, Floppy," said Agatha. Floppy happily obliged, hopping over to her. "Can you tell me what our mission is?"

"Yes, I can, Aggy. It's to be as quiet as mousies," he said excitedly as they walked the tunnels. "We climb on a very long rope to the other side and we duck down really low, so no one sees us, and we be quiet as mousies. We then find a really old magical wooden acorn and bring it back to Gosport. But it's a secret acorn, isn't it Aggy?"

Agatha smiled to herself: she hadn't realised how much he did indeed understand. "Yes, that's right. It's a secret mission."

"Thought so," said Floppy, nodding. He scratched his ear with his back foot.

"It's also a dangerous one."

"But I am brave, aren't I Aggy? I'm a white rabbit."

"Yes. That's right but even the bravest get scared."

Floppy thought about this for a second, his foot still in the air. "That's why they are brave," he concluded.

Agatha was amazed at his wise words. "We don't have to do this mission, Floppy," she said.

"His Majesty the Gizor is a bad animal and bad animals shouldn't have magical acorns."

"Why not?" asked Agatha, wanting to know if he truly understood.

"Because he's greedy and unkind, and I don't think animals should be unkind to each other. I don't like it, I don't."

"So, if we do this mission – and retrieve the Ark – we stop Gizor from getting his paws on it?"

"Yes," replied Floppy as though he was teaching her, "and the world will be kind again. You see, lassie, if we all play a small part, the bigger our kindness can be."

"And if we should die?" asked Agatha, annoyed that he

205

had clearly been influenced by Morag.

"We shall die with honour and kind hearts," he declared, puffing his chest out as they made their way back to the chamber through the maze of tunnels.

*

Late afternoon was approaching fast, and the Portsmouth smog was still mixed with sulphur from the Guildhall raid that morning. Hertha and Berry could hear the bustle of Gizor trucks and personnel on the floor below and surrounding area.

"The Red Witch has a lot to answer for. We were safer in the prison," said Berry, chewing on a dried earthworm from a stash he had in an old tobacco tin. He offered some to Hertha who wasn't interested; she was once more studying the cloth given to her by Lucius that she had pulled from her boot. "And I'm getting cold," continued Berry.

"She said 'look up and follow your nose'," said Hertha.

"Well, all I see is a Gizor flag. And I'd give anything to smell some food instead of this rancid place."

Hertha held the cloth up by its corner and allowed it to blow in the wind like the flag before them. The sea air was pushing it northwards. She turned around, kneeling low, and peeked over the parapet towards the lighthouse. She caught a glimpse of the weathervane mounted at its highest point – but it wasn't a ship, as she assumed it would be. No, it was a fox. "A fox?" she murmured as she lowered herself back down to sit on the floor again with her back to the parapet. She began reading the riddle again:

*By design to aid our task*
*Travels the direction of our path*
*A mighty ship of glory be*
*Forged above the windy sea*

*Move first, the Fourth, elude deceit*
*And follow thee*
*Serves to glory those in need.*

Berry, bored by the riddle, heard her mumbling to herself. "And as for that riddle," he said, folding his arms, "that's certainly outfoxed both of us."

Hertha began smiling to herself. She had cracked the code. "Come on Berry, we have to start moving."

"You what?" he said, watching Hertha gather her backpack.

"Move first, the Fourth," she said, "It's the fourth night. That's why we had to wait. And that, my dear friend, is a fox," she said pointing to the weathervane on top of the lighthouse as she searched for a quick and safe way down from the roof. "Elude deceit," she said, smiling again.

"What are you chattering about this time?" Berry had never seen a fox in real life but had heard old stories about how mischievous and deceitful they were.

"You, my dear friend, are a genius. Come on!" She offered no explanation and headed towards the south end of the roof.

"Well naturally I am, yes, but where are we going, H?"

Hertha checked if the coast was clear below, dropped her backpack down a drainpipe and then flung herself down after it. Berry, not wanting to be left on his own, followed suit but still didn't have any clue as to why.

He crashed into her at the bottom in a heap with a thud. They moved west towards the inner walls of the castle and its entrance, hiding behind supply boxes and stationary trucks. "We're going for a swim," she warned him as they ran onto the footbridge and jumped into the moat with a splash.

They swam towards the west and scrambled up the

bank, stopping at the top and lying flat undetected on the grassy verge. "Where are we going, H?" asked Berry, out of breath from the swim.

"You can't outwit a fox, Berry, and foxes are deceitful," she explained. Berry scrunched up his face, now totally confused. She turned on to her back and gestured for Berry to do the same. "Look!" she said, pointing up at the lighthouse towering over them. "The fox is pointing to the south-east, so we need to go the other way,"

"Oh right," he said, still not understanding.

"Don't you see Berry, it's all been set up for us by the Resistance. The wind is blowing north, not south-east. And to 'elude' it, we must go the other way. It's a sign, Berry."

"Oh yeah," he said as he finally realised what she meant. "I am a genius, aren't I?"

"Yes you are, my friend. Let's head for that bandstand over there." She pointed across the field.

*

Gizor was pacing the floor of the Semaphore Tower in the dockyard while his aides ran about, packing up his desk and other belongings.

"Excuse me, sir," said a young grey squirrel who was frantically scampering about the office collecting Gizor's things – but Gizor was in the way and not in a mood to be asked to move. He grabbed the aide by the throat and flung him violently into the wall.

"My Lord," said Denis as he entered the office.

"WHAT IS IT?" he shouted, fed up with being surrounded by idiots.

"We think it best if you travel in the armoured vehicle instead, sir."

"YOU EXPECT AN ADMIRAL TO TRAVEL IN A TANK?"

"We just think that perhaps a decoy would be best," said Denis, stroking his whiskers nervously.

Gizor leant on his desk and bowed his head low, taking slow breaths to calm himself. "Let me see that I understand you, Denis. You not only want me to leave my office and my place of birth, but to do so you want me to travel IN A TANK?" He began flinging papers, boxes, and documents all over the office in pure rage.

"It is only for a short while, sir. While we rout out the vermin," said Denis referring to the Guildhall attack.

"Do you think I'm weak?" asked Gizor still leaning on his desk, his tail twitching in rage.

"Not at all, sir – we just fear there may be more strikes."

"MORE?" He picked up another aide and threw him across the room. "ON MY LAND. FROM WITHIN?"

"Yes, sir." Denis took a step back towards the door in fear of his Admiral. "They are more rallied than anticipated, sir."

"WELL UN-RALLY THEM THEN."

"Yes, sir. We are trying, sir. But the hills – they are the safest, sir." A note of pleading had crept into his voice now.

Gizor approached the window and looked out over his land to see smoke still billowing into the sky in the distance from the Guildhall raid. "And my treasures?" he asked.

"They will be moved, sir. They will join you at the Castle. I will see to it myself."

Gizor took a sharp intake of breath. "Resistance fighters, my foot! Just vermin! I will destroy them," he said, baring his teeth and banging his paw on the table.

*

Gosport was starting to feel gloomy despite the hundreds who had been saved from the Camp. The foreboding was palpable even in the deep tunnels. Agatha, Floppy, Lucius, Morag and Beaky were all walking the tunnels they had not fully explored before. Floppy was happy as muck, hopping along and peering into chambers and other dark corners of the underworld as they travelled.

Morag handed Agatha a sealed envelope. "Here it is, lassie. Don't read it yet. Not until you cross the water," she said as she closed Agatha's paw safely round the letter. As the others stopped for a short rest, she took Agatha aside. "There's a Garrison Church across the way – you'll be safe there," she said. "Find Brother Nicholas – he will guide you."

Agatha opened her paw and the letter slightly unravelled from its scrunched position. She looked down at its wax seal stamped with the outline of an acorn. "I don't believe in magic, you know," she commented.

"You don't have to, lassie. Some things reveal themselves without magic – just like yous and him." She nodded over to Floppy who was walking an invisible line on the floor practising his balance. The small group of unlikely travellers continued their journey through the tunnels towards the south lines of Gosport, passing underneath Stokes Bay Battery then Fort Gilkicker, and then Fort Monckton before reaching the underbelly of Fort Blockhouse located at the mouth of the harbour. They each took their positions and prepared in silence. Agatha helped Floppy on with his jacket, weapons and supplies and covered his white fur with mud to act as camouflage.

"He's too heavy," observed Beaky, looking at the amount of supplies Floppy was carrying.

Agatha agreed and immediately began chucking things out of the wicker basket they had brought along with them through the tunnels. Sometimes the solution is revealed when you actually need it and not before.

"OK," said Morag, "this way." She led the group through a tight opening in the crumbling wall of the tunnel and up a slope. It was the dark of night and they began to smell the sea air and hear the lapping of gentle waves against the stone walls. At the end of the tunnel they found themselves on a grassy ridge. The stone flank of the fort beside them was slightly angled and above them they could see a couple of patrolling Gizor soldiers walking the walls. They carefully and quickly ran passed each archway of the bastion until they reached a good vantage point looking over to the Round Tower in Old Portsmouth in the distance.

"Looks further than I've been practising, Aggy," said Floppy, surveying the journey ahead.

"Don't worry, Floppy, we'll make it," she replied.

"Right," said Morag. "Are you ready, Beaky?"

"I surely am, Morag – Operation Laundry Line in progress," he replied as he flew up to the Gizor guards on top of Fort Blockhouse. "Hail Gizor!" he said as he met the two gull guards, who looked startled at his arrival.

"Hail Gizor," they replied. "Which regiment are you in?" asked the larger one.

"Gull Bombers Loft D. I have orders from Flight Lieutenant Laraday that you are to report to him immediately."

The Gizor guards looked at each other puzzled. "But we have orders to maintain watch here."

"I have orders to remain here and keep your watch tonight," he replied to his peers.

"But what does he want?" asked the smaller guard.

"Of course I asked him lots of questions before shaking his wing and collecting my winnings from the game of poker we were playing," said Beaky sarcastically.

With that, the two guards marched off and disappeared into the fort to make their journey to Loft Daedalus. Of course, there were still a few Gizor soldiers scattered around in the fort but the first part of Beaky's mission had been successful – there was no one to see a small group of woodland animals scrambling up the wall.

"Well done, Beaky," said Morag as she reached the top: she proved to be a surprisingly good climber for a hedgehog. Lucius and Agatha were left to help pull and push Floppy up the remainder of the wall. It was a tricky climb for a rabbit and he slid back down several times in his attempt. Once on the ledge looking over the harbour mouth, Agatha grabbed a fishing spool from her rucksack and began unwinding it. It was very long and wiry – just the job for a makeshift pulley. Eventually, having unwound the spool completely, she found the two ends and tied them together securely. She then lassoed the loop over a flagpole and tugged on it hard to make sure her knot would hold. She grabbed the other end of the pulley and placed it over Beaky's scrawny gull neck, as if she were awarding him a medal. He flew up into the night sky and crossed the harbour with the near-on invisible wire around his neck, taking it to the other side. The group watched as he flew out of sight. Below them in the water they could see Gizor patrol boats guarding the entrance of the harbour. Beaky flew over to the Round Tower and dropped the loop of the wire around another flagpole. After a few minutes had passed, Lucius tugged on the line, and the line tugged back. It was a signal from Beaky that it was in position.

"It's ready," whispered Lucius.

Agatha tied a short rope from the wicker basket to the fishing line and another from her waist to the basket. Floppy scrambled in and Morag and Lucius then gently pushed it over the wall. They all gasped for a second as his weight made the line droop slightly, but it held fast. Agatha peeked over the wall at the murky water below. It must have been a

50-foot drop to the bottom. Lucius placed a paw on her shoulder as she continued making sure her rope line was secure. "Troubled waters, my friend, will calm," he said. Agatha did not reply. When she grabbed hold of the pulley it was the most afraid she had ever been. This was the time to conquer her fear, she thought to herself.

She edged out on to the wire and cautiously began her climb across the harbour entrance. She passed over the basket but lost her footing slightly when her line took up its full weight. She dangled for a second over the water, her back legs flailing, and glanced below. She swung her legs slightly to get back on top of the wire and as she did so a knife from her jacket pocket came loose and dropped into the water with a splash. Lucius and Morag ducked behind the wall, and Agatha clung on motionless in the air without taking a breath, waiting for a response from the Gizor patrol. There was none. They hadn't heard the splash. She began the slow and heavy journey across the harbour, pulling Floppy across in his wicker basket as she went.

"Are we there yet? Are we there yet?" came a tiny whisper from the basket.

"Quiet as a mousey, remember," she whispered back. As she did so, she immediately realised the pulley was drooping towards the middle of the harbour and before she could warn Floppy, the sheer weight of the basket made them hurtle to the centre of the harbour mouth with great speed. The momentum had knocked Agatha into the basket itself until it finally rested and bobbed up and down slightly. Gingerly she climbed the wire attached to the basket and reached up to the main line to make the difficult climb up the steep slope of the pulley towards the Round Tower.

She could see the end in sight and began to smell the Portsmouth air. Her heart was racing not only because she was heaving Floppy across the waters, but because she didn't know what they would find when they got there. She could just about make out Beaky's silhouette standing on top of the Round Tower. At least she hoped it was him. She looked ahead at the last few feet of wire in front of her, which seemed to slope at an even greater angle. She stopped for a second and gathered all the strength she had and began climbing with one paw over the other – it was a state of mind as well as a show of strength she didn't know she had. She reached the wall and was in touching distance when Beaky grabbed her paw in his beak and pulled her in the last few feet. The basket followed as Agatha tumbled to the floor of the Round Tower. She was exhausted. Beaky helped pull out Floppy from the basket and in turn he helped Agatha by propping her up against the parapet.

"We did it, Aggy. We did it," whispered Floppy, his eyes looking huge in his blackened face. Agatha smiled at him as she tried to catch her breath.

\*

As Hertha and Berry lay hidden in the Bandstand, they searched the rooftops for more weathervanes blowing in the opposite direction to the wind. "Look, there's one!" she said. "On that grand building – The Queen's Hotel." It was pointing westward whereas all others around it were pointing south. "Let's head for those trees over there," she said.

They scrambled to their feet and ran as quickly as they could, using the cover of darkness to reach the tree line. Hertha adeptly ran up the trunk of the first tree, almost forgetting that Berry was a mole and not a tree-climbing squirrel. She grabbed his paw and heaved him up to join her. As she did so, a huge line of armoured vehicles headed their way.

As the line headed past, towards Southsea Castle, they heard a familiar voice.

"I want more cannons! And hand me that sherry bottle!" It was Reckless Roddy, who they had first encountered at Portchester Castle weeks before. But what was he doing here? They had no time to think about this, because as soon as the convoy passed, Hertha resumed scanning the rooftops for further direction.

"This way," she said jumping to the ground.

*

The Round Tower was a formidable fortress that stood strong at the entrance of the harbour. The rooftop was unmanned, thanks to Beaky buying them time by repeating a similar ruse to that he had played out an hour ago. "Follow me," he said as he guided Agatha and Floppy down the staircase into the tower itself. "Better be ready, Miss Aggy," he warned. They both stayed close to Beaky, and Agatha had a pistol at the ready. Beaky looked at her and shook his head and pointed at the knife in his jacket pocket. A gunshot would attract attention.

"I don't have my knife. It fell out," she whispered.

"Here," he said, giving her his. Beaky was on home territory and had a new-found sense of confidence in himself. As he reached the bottom of the steps he heard some soldiers approaching. He signalled to Agatha and Floppy to stay put and entered the chamber himself.

"Hey Beaky, you Guller – thought you were in the Red lands?"

"I was, Spicey, but I've been sent on a mission," he replied, trying to hold his nerve.

"You, on a mission?" replied the Gull Guard. "They must be desperate." He laughed. Suddenly all Beaky's new-found confidence had gone in an instant. "So, what's the mission then, Beaks?"

"A secret one."

Spicey continued to mock him as he busied himself looking out of a peephole, seemingly on watch. "Ah go on, you can trust me. Besides I need a laugh."

"Why's that?"

"Ain't you heard? Gizor's on the run up north, and Roderick's come down 'ere to shackle the south."

"You what?"

"Yeah, we ain't never been so busy. Got magpies moving loot, starlings shouting orders, and the greys sitting pretty as a pedigree."

"Really?"

"Yeah, it proper spooked 'em, it has."

"What has?" asked Beaky.

"The raid yesterday mornin'. I'm just keeping my head down, I am. I've heard that Roderick is a drunken piece of evil work. He don't care who he bites and I ain't gonna be on the receiving end. No, sir."

"So, where has Gizor gone?"

"To the hills, we reckon. Anyway, gotta do me rounds," he said as he began walking off in the direction of the stairs.

"Err, I've just come from there. Nothing up there to report," he said, panicked.

Spicey stopped at the foot of the steps and turned to look at Beaky. "Part of your secret mission, is it?" As Spicey went to stand on the first step, a grey squirrel Gizor officer dressed in a military poncho walked into the Tower. "Hail Gizor!" They both saluted.

"What are you doing?" he shouted.

"Sir, doing me rounds, sir," said Spicey.

"And you?" he asked Beaky, who was standing to attention.

"Sir, doing the rounds, sir."

"Good. We are to prepare for the visit from Sir Roderick who will inspect the line tomorrow."

"Sir, yes sir." They both saluted their commanding officer who returned the salute and walked out of the Round Tower.

"Told ya we was getting busy," said Spicey as he continued walking up the steps to the rooftop. Beaky, his heart fluttering in his breast, followed the soldier up the steps so closely that he was brushing up beside him.

"What's ruffled your feathers?" he commented. Beaky did not reply and slowed his pace as they both reached the top. Beaky frantically searched the rooftop for his friends but there was no one there.

"See, nothing to be found up 'ere," said Beaky, puzzled as to where they could have gone.

"What's this?" said Spicey as he found the fishing line and basket attached to the wall. "Beaky? You've been acting funny. What is it?"

"Err, don't know."

"Part of your 'secret mission' is it?" asked Spicey.

"Nope, nothing to do with me," he replied. Spicey turned to Beaky and looked in his eyes, unconvinced, but could see he was not going to get any answers from him.

"Best inform the Master at Arms then," he said as he took himself down the steps leaving Beaky to continue his search for his friends.

"Psst!" he whispered, searching around the rooftop. "Psst!" There was no response. Then, as he continued looking over the walls into the murky water and surrounding area of Old Portsmouth Point, a pebble was thrown up and over the south side of the rooftop and landed near his webbed feet. He walked over to the edge of the south wall but still couldn't see his friends, who had hidden themselves in the bunker that lay below on the shoreline. "Aggy?" he whispered. Another stone was thrown from the dark below and hit him directly on his beak, nearly knocking him out. "Ouch!" he said in a whisper, pressing his wing to his beak to ease the pain and stumbling around. He lost his footing and fell over the parapet onto the pebble beach below. Aggy and Floppy emerged from their hiding place and ran over to their friend who was lying on his back with his wings outstretched. "That really hurt, that did," he complained.

"Come on, Beaky. Where do we go now?" asked Agatha, helping him up.

\*

Hertha and Berry followed the direction of the weathervanes leading them west towards Old Portsmouth. They reached a break in the tree line they had been using for cover and made a quick dash over the flat fields of Southsea Common towards an old church in the distance.

"Come on Berry!" encouraged Hertha. Berry never knew he could run so fast.

\*

"We need to head east," whispered Beaky to his friends as they moved along the narrow strip of pebble beach. The Old Portsmouth fortifications were impressive and intimidating. The walls reached high into the night sky when approached from the shoreline. They reached a square innocuous-looking hole in the wall, made their way through it, and ran along the ramparts and up some steps towards the Square Tower. From time to time they had to duck behind gunpowder barrels and coiled ropes to hide from the Gizor

Army patrolling the walls. Beaky slowed his pace and acted nonchalantly in front of his Army, whistling to himself, his wings folded behind his back as if he were patrolling the walls himself. They continued undetected along the rampart lines towards Southsea Common, then reached some steps that led down to Penny Street near a moat just across from the Garrison Church. Agatha and Floppy tucked themselves away under the ramparts overlooking a grand statue of Admiral Gizor while Beaky walked ahead towards the church to see if the way was safe.

*

"This way," said Hertha as she and Berry reached the church wall and ran crouched over towards the west entrance. They stopped at the corner and Hertha peeked round the side as Beaky made his way towards them. They crouched down lower and retrieved their knives from their pockets and waited. They watched as a Gizor Gull Bomber entered the roofless nave of the church – which had long been destroyed and left in disrepair. They silently followed him in, ducking behind the grand pillars to the side as he continued towards the chancel.

Hertha took her chance and charged at the Gull, whose back was turned to them. She let out a screaming war-cry as she pushed the Gizor Gull up against the entrance of the chancel. He called out in shock. Hertha grabbed him from behind and wrapped a rope tight around his beak, with Berry grabbing hold of his webbed feet at the same time. She turned him round to face her and pushed him back up against the wall of the nave. She gestured with her knife towards his face, snarled and said: "Let us into the chancel or I'll cut you dead."

The Gull shook his head and tried stamping his feet in

panic but Berry had a good grip on him. He began flapping his wings frantically but was well and truly pinned fast against the wall by his two captors. Berry, who was almost prone on the gravel floor holding onto the Gull's feet, was being bounced up and down by the Gull Bomber in sheer panic. The Gull, unable to speak, tried to gesture his intentions but was overpowered by the two. Berry pulled at his legs and he fell to the ground. "Tie him up!" said Hertha as she searched her surroundings to see if they had disturbed the peace.

"I'm trying," said Berry, struggling with the Gull Bomber twice his size.

"It's locked," she said as she tried the handle of the chancel entrance. She charged at the Gull with a look of menace. "You open it!" she demanded, believing he would have a key. He looked up at her and shook his head.

"Shush!" said Hertha, who had heard a noise approaching from outside. "Let's move him – quick!" They dragged the Gull into the corner of the nave and hid with him behind a pillar.

Agatha and Floppy had made their way into the church and entered the nave. Agatha signalled to Floppy to stay close as she bravely called out in a Pompey accent: "Where you at, Beaky?"

"Get down," said Hertha to Berry. She made her way up the side of the nave, hiding behind each pillar. Agatha, on the other hand, walked boldly down the middle of the empty nave, her paws making a skittering noise on its stone floor. She reached the centre with Floppy closely behind her. Hertha, hiding in the shadows could see the outline of the two figures. As the sun rose, light spilled through empty window frames and onto the two figures in the centre, revealing them to be two friends. "Floppy?" asked Hertha uncertainly, lowering her knife and trying to block the sun from her eyes to see. The rabbit was surely too dark to be Floppy: it was almost black.

"Hertha? Hertha!" he replied, hopping up and down in excitement and running towards the friendly voice.

"Hertha?" said Agatha, astonished and still standing in the centre of the nave as Floppy grabbed his friend in a big hug and spun her round with pure joy.

"Err, H?" called Berry who was still wrestling with the Gizor Gull in the corner. "I could do with some help 'ere."

Hertha, who was still buried in Floppy's tight hug, her feet off the floor, tried to clamber out of his grip. She dropped to the floor and hurried over to Berry, calling back to her friends. "We've taken a prisoner," she said proudly.

"That's Beaky, Hertha. That's Beaky, that is," said Floppy, gamboling over to the corner.

Agatha ran with him. "He's with us," she told Berry, untying Beaky's gag.

"Oh, of course he is," said Berry.

"Friends of yours, are they?" said Beaky, unimpressed, as he unruffled his feathers and climbed out of the rope that Berry had been wrapping round him. His beak was still hurting from where Agatha had thrown a stone at him earlier.

*

"I AM NOT LEAVING!" shouted Admiral Gizor from his office in the Semaphore Tower as he watched his armoured vehicle approach Victory Gate. He had so far led his troops and his country to 'freedom' by any means as he said he would, and those means were fierce and unyielding. He would not be stopped in his endeavours: he was a Grey Squirrel of pedigree and would not be motivated by fear, nor would his actions.

"Sir, the pockets of resistance are too great to predict," replied Denis Delaney, cowering slightly and turning his bowler hat round and round in his paws.

"I want the entire Fleet readied," said Gizor. "I want the ground troops to weed out the weak. I want more firepower, more guns, more cannons, and I want my fortresses impenetrable. Do you understand this, Denis?"

"Yes sir. I understand but …"

"But nothing, Mr Prime Minister. I am the mighty Gizor and I will have what I want. I want reports on the hour. One attack from within will not make me retreat."

"But, sir – there have been several attacks."

"WHAT?"

"Several, sir. We thought it best that you did not know, sir."

"WHAT?" he shouted again as he grabbed Denis by the scruff of the neck and lifted him up off the floor, dangling the vole in front of his eyes.

"I can see now that this was not the best plan, sir. We just thought it best at the time." He was struggling to breathe in Gizor's grip.

Gizor took a sharp intake of breath. "Have the troops parade in five minutes," he demanded as he threw Denis across the room and scurried out.

*

"And you crossed the harbour mouth on a fishing line?" said Hertha who was listening to Agatha retelling their journey. They were swapping their stories, huddled in the corner of the nave.

"I was brave wasn't I, Aggy?" said Floppy. "It was dark, and I was scared but we was brave wasn't we, Aggy? I missed you, Hertha," he said in the middle of his thinking.

"We missed you too, Floppy," said Hertha. "Any luck, Berry?"

"No," said Berry, who was trying to unpick the lock on the chancel door. We would have better luck if the Red Witch showed up."

"The Red Witch?" said Floppy, scared of the folklore.

"Here, let me have a go at the lock," said Hertha as she walked over to help.

"Morag said to find Brother Nicholas here. I don't understand why he's not here," said Agatha, frustrated at the vulnerable position they had all been left in.

"Well," commented Berry, "Perhaps the stars aren't aligned." Hertha looked at Berry and rolled her eyes.

"I'm hungry, I am," said Floppy to the sound of his stomach rumbling. The black dust with which he'd been coated to make his trip across the harbour was rubbing off now and he was beginning to look like his old self. Agatha reached into her jacket pocket to retrieve some fruit and passed it to Floppy. As she did so, an envelope fell from her jacket onto Floppy's feet. "What's that?" he asked as he munched on some bits of dried apple.

"I forgot all about it," she said, picking up the envelope. "What with everything going on. Morag gave it to me and said I could only open it when we had crossed the water." She carefully pulled apart the wax seal with its acorn motif and opened the folded paper. She read aloud what was written there:

*OF ABSENT COVER, the ASTUTE watch over you*

"Oh well that's just marvellous isn't it, another flamin' riddle to solve!" said Berry, dropping in frustration the pick that he was using to unlock the door.

*

223

As ordered, the Admiral's troops of grey squirrels lined up for parade in the dockyard square. Their High Commander entered the square and walked silently along the lines inspecting his glorious Army. He reached the front and stared at his troops in silence without a single word for a full ten minutes. The soldiers were frozen in place, not daring to move a muscle. Prime Minister Delaney who was standing beside Gizor, his neck still sore from where he had been picked up, was confused by the Admiral's utter stillness. Only a light breeze could be heard moving in the parade of many hundreds of soldiers. The silent calm was unnerving but still Gizor waited and waited without issuing a single command.

A piercing shot rang out so suddenly that no one had even realised that Gizor himself was holding the pistol, had raised it and instantly killed a soldier standing to the left of the line. There was a slight ruffle in the line in response and then utter silence again. The soldier squirrel was on the ground, dead. A further ten minutes or so passed in total silence. Gizor then stepped forward and walked towards the dead soldier. He glared at his dead body, bent over and with one paw grabbed the back of his uniform and flung him over the first line of troops and into the next. There was barely a shuffle, which pleased Gizor. He walked up the sidelines, peering down each row to check for order. There was order. No one dare be out of order or line. Two thirds of the way up the line, he stopped. He turned to look down it and stood again for many minutes in silence, watching his soldiers standing frozen and barely breathing in response.

Something caught his gaze. He began walking down the line and each soldier, as he passed them, silently sighed in relief. He walked to the centre of the line and stopped in front of a soldier who was shaking inside. He stepped close to him until he was no more than a foot away. The soldier, a young adult squirrel with round cheeks and well-kept fur, kept staring ahead trying not to make conscious eye contact with his Admiral. Gizor reached for his side pistol and raised it to the soldier's face, touching his nose. The soldier didn't even flinch as the cold metal met the damp black skin of his nostrils.

"Recite the oath!"

"Sir, I swear to the Lord this sacred oath, to the leader of the Portsmouth Empire and of all animals, Admiral Grey, High Commander of the Fleet of Ratufinee Jean De Gizor, that I shall render unconditional obedience and that as a brave soldier I shall at all times be prepared to give my life for this oath. Hail Gizor!"

Gizor said nothing to the soldier but handed him the pistol. Gizor stepped back and still said nothing. There were no commands. The soldier raised the pistol and pointed it at the back of the squirrel in front of him. He did not hesitate: he knew what his Admiral wanted him to do. He shot the squirrel dead without even a thought, then saluted his Admiral once more, handing him back the gun. Gizor gave a wry smile and then it dawned on him that his marching band was not playing.

"DENIS!" he shouted. Denis came skittering from the sidelines, holding onto his hat. "Where is my marching band?" Denis scurried off and within a couple of seconds the band was playing its ceremonial trooping anthem at the front of the parade. Gizor remained staring at the soldier before him. "You will do," he said as he walked away and back into the Semaphore Tower.

## Chapter 12
# SECRETS OF
# THE GARRISON

The small group of comrades tucked in the corner of the Garrison nave had given up trying to pick the lock and sat together waiting, with Beaky keeping watch in his Gizor uniform. Agatha and Hertha were trying to work out the riddle but failing miserably. Beaky, who was stationed at the entrance of the nave, suddenly squawked like seagulls do, signalling them to take cover. The four friends jumped up and hid one by one behind different pillars in the nave. They waited in silence.

Six monks and six nuns led by a Master began gliding through the entrance to the nave with their heads bowed and their arms folded as if in solemn prayer. The hidden friends watched the doors of the chancel open as if by themselves to let the brethren and sisters inside and close behind them. It was Morning Prayer time. The friends edged close to the door. They could hear the monks chanting from inside. The door was unlocked. Agatha looked back at Floppy and placed her paw to her mouth, signalling to him to be as quiet as a mousey again. Floppy nodded in agreement.

Hertha slipped in first undetected and saw that the monks and nuns were seated at the front of the chancel, close to the altar, in deep prayer. Agatha followed, then Floppy guided by Berry. Beaky remained outside, keeping watch for them. The group ducked down low behind the back pews. "Now what?" whispered Berry. The ceremony was beginning.

"*HUD-SONNN-ICUS, HUD-SONNN-ICUS, HUD-SONNN-ICUS*" they chanted in prayer.

The friends were waiting for something to reveal who Brother Nicholas was. It wasn't long before there was more movement from the monks and nuns, who rose to their feet and began lighting candles as they continued chanting. One of the monks, presumably the Master, then stood front and centre while the others returned to their pews. His head still bowed, dressed in an old habit and his hood draped over his head so they could not see what kind of animal he was, he began:

"Lord we pray, to thee our thanks. To thee we serve our strength to those in need. Today we worship and pray this Keep of peace and shelter from the sea. No passing fleet will go in need; no visitor will die of need. Our heavy hearts can carry more than wounded souls in battle by either foe. We pray to your Will. We pray for our keep."

The congregation began chanting in response: "*HUD-SONNN-ICUS, HUD-SONNN-ICUS, HUD-SONNN-ICUS.*" They continued as they filed out of the chancel in line, through to the vestry on the left and out of sight. The Master, however, stayed behind, his head still bowed. The four companions looked at each other, not knowing what to do.

"Children of Holozoa are sheltered by these walls. Come forth, my friends," said the Master in a slightly rasping voice. Floppy didn't have to be asked twice: he jumped up and before anyone could stop him, he was hopping down the aisle towards the monk.

"Hello," he said with his paw outstretched to shake the monk's paw. "My name's Floppy. What's yours?" The monk

227

did not reach out a paw to meet that of Floppy.

"Floppy!" called out the others in fear they had been betrayed.

"My friends, you are safe in the house of the Lord," said the Master, with his head still bowed.

The others slowly stood up from behind their pews and walked forwards. "Floppy – get back," warned Hertha. Floppy did as he was asked and hopped slightly back as his friends reached him.

"Who are you?" asked Agatha.

"I am Brother Nicholas of Domus Dei – the House of Hudsonicus – and you are safe here, my friends. Please allay your fears and warm yourselves in our church of peace. Take sanctuary and take rest," he said.

"Show yourself, then!" said Berry firmly: he was not going to be fooled by a holy charade like they had had at Portchester Castle. The monk obliged and slowly let down his hood to reveal a battered and scarred brown rat. The friends were taken aback.

"You're a ratty rat," said Floppy as he grabbed Agatha's paw tightly. Brother Nicholas replaced his hood in response to Floppy's reaction.

"Such a quest as yours will surely find a charity worthier of these scars and more," he said, "A journey so great will provide you freedoms beyond these walls and war of words. Perchance these walls may guide your quest." With that, he walked off towards the vestry.

"More flamin' mumbo jumbo," moaned Berry.

"But it's not," said Agatha who took the riddle from her pocket once more. "It's not mumbo jumbo. I can't carry a note that tells the enemy where to go, can I?" She sat down on the front pew and began reviewing the words on the sheet of paper. Floppy quickly hopped over and sat by her side to try and help.

"Read it out again," asked Hertha, scanning the walls and rafters of the church. Meanwhile Berry sat on a facing pew, sharpening his knife and reviewing their supplies.

"*OF ABSENT COVER, the ASTUTE watch over you,*" Agatha read.

"OK, let's think about this logically," said Hertha, taking the note from Agatha to read herself: "Of absent cover." She began looking around the church. "Is there something in this place without a cover of some kind?"

"Maybe you should call on Peggy for help?" said Berry mockingly, still sitting on his pew, his feet stuck out in front of him.

"The nave doesn't have a cover, does it Hertha?" said Floppy in a wondrous moment of cleverness. "It doesn't have a roof, does it?"

"Floppy, you are very clever sometimes. You are quite right. Come on!" said Hertha as Agatha and Floppy followed her back to the nave.

"But what are we looking for?" said Agatha.

Hertha looked back down at the note in her paw. "The astute watch over you". She looked up at the walls of the nave and the piercing morning sun. They had to be careful not to walk around too much within view of the entrance. "We need to find something that is watching over us."

"Beaky is watching over us," commented Floppy, spurred on by Hertha's praise. Beaky was at the entrance of the nave pacing up and down like a Gizor guard.

"What's going on?" he said, turning his head slightly sideways and talking out of the side of his beak to avoid attracting attention from elsewhere.

"We're looking for treasure," replied Floppy excitedly, running over to join him near the entrance.

"Floppy! Not so close!" shouted Hertha as she looked over at him. As she did so, something caught her eye high above the entrance. A wooden figure sat perfectly inside a two-barred small unglazed window high above the front entrance of the church. "Look at that!" she said, pointing.

"It's watching over us, it is," said Floppy cranking his neck upwards and folding back his ears. After a swift look around outside, Beaky flew up into the window recess. He flapped his wings furiously at first to stay on the ledge and then side-stepped around the wooden figure, leant against one of the stone mullions, stretched out his wings to steady himself and pushed the figure with both his feet. It fell through the window and onto the gravel, rolling slightly before coming to a stop at Agatha's feet. It was the size of Agatha herself and was heavy. Beaky flew back down and continued to keep watch as the others began rolling the wooden figure up into the chancel for examination.

By this time, Berry had placed his hat over his face to get some much-needed kip, but his nap was interrupted by a rumbling noise as the others rolled the massive wooden figure up the aisle. Thinking it was a surprise attack, he jumped to his feet, only to encounter Floppy.

"We found the watching one, we did," said Floppy. "He watches us, he does, from high above the world. And he wasn't covered. We found him, and we got him, and we rolled him in here."

"And?" said Berry, unimpressed.

"His name is Astute," added Floppy, proud of his new-found cleverness.

"What are we doing with our Mr Astute then?" asked Berry, stifling a yawn before helping them to lift the figure upright. The wooden statue appeared old and weathered. At first it was hard to make out what type of rodent the animal was until they brushed off some of the dirt and cobwebs. It was a squirrel dressed in the robes of a holy monk and was carved from solid oak. The figure was holding a book in his paw with an inscription on it that read: 'Builded here in effigy – the stars, the moon and the sun – watch over thee'.

"Look around!" said Hertha, "Look around for things with stars, the moon and the sun on them."

"This is ridiculous," said Berry, begrudgingly searching the walls of the church, which were adorned with hundreds of religious symbols, inscriptions, dedications and statues.

Agatha, who was searching the north side of the church, looked up at the stained-glass window as the painted silhouette of a rat had caught her eye. The window, with its intricate markings, shone with the haze of daylight. Below the picture of the rat was a similar sized statue to the one they had just retrieved. She stepped closer to it by balancing on the back of a pew to get a better look. She could just reach the feet of the statue. The carved figure, again of a squirrel, appeared to be of a noble knight carrying his shield in one paw and his sword in the other. On the shield Agatha could make out the markings of a crescent moon. "I've found one! I've found the moon!" she called.

Her friends came running over. They all struggled with its size and sheer weight but with Hertha standing on Agatha's shoulders, they managed to safely remove it from the ledge and drag it to the centre of the aisle. They continued looking for more. Hertha found the next one on the east side of the chancel behind the altar itself, again on a window ledge. It was another noble knight carrying his shield with the markings of a sun on its front. Again, they all scurried over to help retrieve it. They needed to find just one more – the stars. It was Berry's turn. He was searching the south walls and like Agatha, the stained-glass window caught his eye. There was a picture on it of a grand ship – *HMS Victory* – being guided by the stars. He stared at the image, imagining the waves crashing against the ship in a great storm. He tipped his head to the left and then the right,

231

hypnotised by the picture's splendour. His gaze then fell to the ledge below where the final noble knight was found, this time holding a shield with stars painted on its front plate.

"Stars," said Berry in the most apathetic way.

They now had all four wooden figures, which were in the aisle facing each other and almost ominously watching over their would-be rescuers ... but they didn't have a clue what to do next.

*

"There, there," said Florence the scullery maid, who was aiding the sick and injured in the Grange chamber as Morag and Lucius entered. They were in deep conversation.

"No shadow to the east will block the rise of the sun," said Morag. "Have faith, my brother."

"I do, my friend. But Agatha is working in the dark. She knows not her purpose, other than to guide the harmless," said Lucius as they walked around the outskirts of the chamber, which was crowded with wounded creatures from Browndown Camp.

"Aye, but look what she has already achieved. She is not a chosen one, but a destined soul. Her path may be blind for now, but her nature will witness her fate. Have no doubt, brother – Agatha Mumby will learn."

"Did you say Agatha?" asked a female squirrel who was sitting on the floor leaning against the wall. The squirrel grabbed Lucius' hand as he walked past. "You know Agatha?" she said, attempting to stand to her feet.

"Yes," said Lucius, helping her up. She was clearly very weak.

"Where is she? Is she OK?"

"Who are you?" asked Morag.

"Gertie Nicholson. Please tell me she is OK."

"Oh aye, I wouldnae worry," Morag replied.

"Where is she?" asked Gertie.

"We cannae tell yous that, missy, but rest assured she's OK."

"She saved us," said Gertie.

"Aye, she did."

"Well, really! It is astonishing!" came an indignant voice from across the chamber. "One cannot breathe in such cramped conditions." Mary was back to her old self as she dusted off an old chair to sit down on.

"Right then, ladies, let's get this place shipshape," came another familiar voice. It was Lady Ellen. "Gertie? Collect some of those blankets over there, and Elizabeth – put the kettle on."

"Ellen!" called Gertie. "These people know Agatha. She's safe."

"What's that?" said Ellen, absorbing the information. "Well that is jolly good news. Where is she? We must ..." Ellen stopped in her tracks as she noticed Morag standing next to Gertie.

"Lady Ellen," acknowledged Morag with a nod.

Ellen coughed with unease at being confronted by someone who she had not clapped eyes on for many years. She continued: "We must thank her," she said, ignoring Morag.

"They won't tell me where she is," replied Gertie, noticing the awkward exchange.

Ellen starred at Morag for a second and replied: "I'm sure she's fine. Come on, Gertie, help me dish out these blankets."

\*

The small group of comrades in the Garrison Church were still at a loss and had sat down to rest and think.

233

"Any ideas?" asked Berry, who had gone back to sharpening his knife.

"I liked that riddle, I did," commented Floppy.

"You were very helpful," said Hertha, who was lying on a pew staring up at the rafters.

"The roof didn't have a cover, did it Hertha?" said Floppy, wanting more praise.

Agatha was also lying flat on a pew, holding the note up in the air reading and re-reading it. "Wait!" she said, sitting upright. "There's more to this riddle than we think. Look at this: *OF ABSENT COVER,*" she read aloud.

"So?" commented Berry.

"It's still a riddle. We need to jumble it all up, the letters ..." She pulled out her notebook and pencil and began trying to scramble the letters around. Hertha stood up and joined her.

"OVER? Hertha suggested. "SENT? VETS? BASE? VETERAN?"

"FANE? FOE?" said Agatha.

"FONT!" they both shouted out at the same time. "FONT BASE!" they shouted again and ran towards the nave.

"What?" shouted Berry, who had been grooming himself and not really been listening. Floppy didn't know what was happening either but hopped with excitement, following his friends to the door of the chancel.

"There!" said Agatha, pointing to the far west corner of the nave. Near its entrance was a stone font exposed to the elements. They ran to the font, avoiding the centre aisle where they were exposed to the main entrance of the church, and quickly examined it for any clues or markings but could find nothing.

"Pass me the note for a second," said Hertha. "OF ABSENT COVER," she read aloud.

"FONT BASE COVER!" they both mouthed to each other at the same time. "It's in the chancel," said Agatha.

"Come on, Floppy, back we go," said Hertha.

All three ran back inside the chancel, nearly knocking over Berry who had decided to finally get up from his pew and find out what was going on. They ran towards the far end of the chancel near to the altar; on the stone floor to their right was a huge ornate font cover. It was made of heavy oak, circular at the bottom but with four carved sides as it rose. It was immensely tall and on its pointed top was a carving of a bird of prey in flight.

"I don't like those sorts of birdies, I don't," said Floppy, staring upwards at the cover.

"The ASTUTE watch over you," read Hertha, trying to work out the rest of the riddle. "STATE? SAT? TUE ... STATUE!" she shouted, her tail quivering with excitement. "OF ABSENT COVER, the ASTUTE watch over you."

"Look at the carvings around the sides," said Agatha. "See those alcoves?" There were four empty recesses, clearly made for an absent statue or two ... or four. "Come on," she said, running back to the statues they had left in the aisle. "Help us, Berry," she pleaded.

"If I must," he said, still fed up with everything. "But so what if they fit? It's not going to tell us anything we don't already have in front of us, is it? Unless you believe in magic?" As he said this he caught Hertha's eye and realised his stubbornness – it wasn't too long ago that they had both witnessed 'magic' for themselves. He grabbed the heavy end of one of the statues, grunting with the effort, while Agatha grabbed the head and Floppy pretended to help by gently carrying the weight of the middle.

"Wait," said Hertha. "They need to be in the right positions." She examined the cover for any markings.

"Err, H, do you think you could hurry up with whatever

you're doing?" said Berry struggling with the weight, "This is quite heavy for a small creature, you know."

Hertha ran over to the statue to examine it: it was the noble knight of stars. She matched the statue with some faint markings of stars on the south side of the cover. "Right, that one goes there," she said, pointing. "I'm sure of it."

They positioned the second and third statues in their corresponding slots until only the fourth one was left – the holy monk. They carefully carried it over to the font cover and glanced at each other, ready for something big to happen once they had slotted the statue into place.

"Ready?" asked Hertha. They all nodded. "One, two, three …" They lowered it gently and quickly stepped back. Hertha shielded Floppy with a protective paw to his chest as they all stared at the font cover.

"Was something supposed to happen?" asked Berry into the silence that followed.

Hertha frowned and sighed. Agatha scratched her head puzzled, and Floppy did the same, copying his frustrated friends.

"Told ya it was a waste of time," said Berry in his usual jaded voice, returning to his seat and worn out from all the lifting.

Hertha and Agatha stepped closer to the font cover to observe any change. Agatha pushed on the shoulders of the monk to see if it was securely in place. It wasn't, and as she pushed, it clicked into position and the bird of prey began to move above them. She immediately stepped back and looked up, as they all did. The bird began turning slowly to the right and made several complete turns before coming to a stop with its head looking downwards in line with the monk. They could hear a series of clicks and clonks from inside the font cover itself and a whirring sound began.

"Stay back, Floppy," warned Hertha.

The noise was getting louder as the whirring sound got faster. Just as it was reaching a crescendo, a small panel above the monk's alcove clicked open and the noise came to a sudden halt. It was a secret drawer. Hertha and Agatha ran over to it and Agatha, on tiptoes, peered inside. She retrieved a scroll from the drawer, unfurled it and placed it on the altar steps.

**SHIP** to **ROW**, as space **TRAVELS** so
Towards the **HATED LARC**

"Marvellous!" said Berry in classic form.

"Another riddle!" said Floppy, hopping up and down, "I like riddles, I do."

*

Seated in the corner of the Grange chamber, Lucius and Morag were deep in conversation. Lady Ellen was in the opposite corner with Mary and Gertie, starring at Morag.

"I do so hope Doris will be OK," said Gertie.

"And Agatha of course," remarked Mary, rather uncharacteristically showing concern.

"Hmm," said Lady Ellen, still focused on Lucius and Morag. "Well, let's find out, shall we?" She stood up from the table and made her way over to them. "I demand you tell me where Agatha is!" she said, interrupting their conversation without apology.

Morag remained silent, leaving Lucius to respond. "Agatha has more strength than she realises," he said gently. "She is safe, my dear."

"Don't you 'dear' me. I demand you tell me where she is!" She raised up her head and looked quite fearsome.

Neither Lucius nor Morag replied, so she thrust her face closer to Morag. "You owe me the truth," she said.

Morag stood up and attempted to take Ellen's arm and lead her away to avoid a scene, but Ellen easily shrugged her off. Morag sighed with regret. "You can only know that she has a greater task, Miss Ellen," she said.

"Another pointless crusade then, no doubt?"

"There is a chance to end this conflict, Miss Ellen," replied Morag signalling the badger to follow her into the darkened corridor away from the chamber.

"I sincerely hoped that you had changed, Morag, after all these years. Yet I see you remain entirely of the same character – reckless."

"This is different, Ellen," she hissed, feeling her quills rising. "You have me wrong."

"I don't believe a single word that comes out of your tiny hedgehog mouth, Morag."

Morag sighed again. "I cannae take back what was done all those years ago," she said, "but I can make the future right. And so can Agatha."

"Her father wouldn't want this. Not like this."

"Well Peter's not here, and she is the only one who can do it. Now, you can sit here cleaning up your bed space for the night, or you can help Agatha by being part of something."

Ellen did not reply but continued to look at the hedgehog before her with caution.

"Be part of something for once," said Morag, "instead of being proud and proper like you've always been."

Ellen still said nothing, sniffed loudly and walked back into the chamber.

Lucius joined Morag in the corridor. "It is almost midday, my friend. They are coming," he said.

*

Jane Priddy was in discussion with a Gizor officer at the gates of Priddy's Hard. "If you want more to sell, more is required to be built and we simply don't have the workforce," she said in a reasonable tone.

"You will work them harder," replied the officer, an unpleasant-looking grey squirrel with a disconcerting squint in one eye.

"Perhaps you should've stopped killing off the workforce in the first place," said Jane, who for her trouble received a solid slap around the face for insubordination, knocking her off her feet. As soon as his paw struck her face, a group of Gizor soldiers came running from the back of the yard, yelling. The officer confusedly thought it was something to do with his slap.

"What are you doing?" he shouted, but they ran past where he was standing, uttering panicky yelping cries. He watched as they fled, then turned to face the yard to see what had spooked them. A huge rat with an ugly face and exceedingly bad breath grabbed the officer by the scruff of the neck and lifted him clean off the ground. The officer's back legs wheeled helplessly in the air. The rat laughed, displaying a random collection of yellow teeth.

"I'm Weevil," he said. "You'll want to remember my name." He threw the officer to the ground and stood over him as he tried to scramble away on his back. He looked over to his soldiers for support, but most had fled and others were being pulled apart by Weevil's motley rabble of rats in the yard.

"Ain't nice to be left on your tod, is it?" said Weevil who stepped closer to the officer, picked him up again and threw him to his crew of ravenous rats.

"Come quick!" said a young squirrel boy who had run all the way through the tunnels from Priddy's to the Grange chamber. "They're taking over the yard!"

239

"Who are?" replied Mary, standing up in a bit of a panic.

"Monstrous rats."

"Oh my! What on earth can be going on?"

Lady Ellen turned to glance over at Morag as everyone began filing out of the chamber and making their way back to Priddy's. Morag nodded back. As the animals reached the tunnel entrance of Priddy's and began emerging into the yard itself, they found it deserted of Gizor soldiers and observed hundreds of rats lined up behind Weevil who was standing waiting.

Morag wriggled through the crowd and walked over to Weevil, who stepped forward. "It's true then?" he said.

"You know the plan, Weevil," she replied with a certain familiarity.

"Yeah, and I know you too. Ain't gonna be disappointed now, am I Morag?"

"It will be done – you will all be pardoned."

Weevil stepped forward, pushing his nose right into Morag's face. "You and I both know that I ain't usually accustomed to being this accommodating," he said, "but unlike you, I am true to my word."

"It will be done," she repeated.

"It better had be, or else you'll have rolled your last," he said, referring to what hedgehogs do when scared. "Right, you scum bags, get moving!" he yelled at his men.

"Oh my!" said Mary, who had watched the spectacle along with Ellen and Gertie. Ellen walked over to Morag. "How can we help?" she said. They chatted for a few minutes before Ellen returned. "Right, ladies, come with me. We have a job to do."

Gertie subserviently followed Lady Ellen, leaving Mary standing alone. A rat from the Island then approached her from the side. "'Ere – you aint seen my toothy peg, have ya missus?" said the rat.

Mary looked at him: he was smelly, scrawny and scruffy looking. "Ugh, how uncouth," she said, holding a paw in front of her nose.

"No, missus, it's me tooth," said the scruffy rat, misunderstanding Mary's words.

"I beg your pardon?" She took a step backwards.

"It fell out while I was munching on one of them grey squirrel things over there – real tasty they are, by the way."

"I'm sure I don't know what on earth you mean," replied Mary, turning her face away in disgust. She then saw her friends at the back of the yard in the distance. "Coo-ee!" she called over. "Wait for me!" She waved as she hurried over to them.

"It's alright, missus," called out the rat cheerily enough, "I'll keep looking."

Mary approached her friends who were walking over to the docks. "I cannot believe you left me behind, Gertie," she said, her heart still fluttering.

When they reached the dock, Lady Ellen walked onto the pebble shore and untied one of the many rowing boats moored to the dock itself. "Right, here you go," she said, handing Mary a sea-soaked rope line. "Hold that." Mary had little choice as Ellen had thrust it into her paw. She daintily held it by her claws as if it was a delicate lace handkerchief. "And this one," said Ellen as she gave her another. The badger then began wading into the water to untie the other boats.

"Please be careful, Lady Ellen," said Mary nervously.

"Make sure you hold on tight to those lines, Mary," she said, noticing that Mary did not want to get her paws wet. "Here, Gertie – take these ones."

As Ellen continued to move the boats about in the water with Gertie and Mary standing on the shore holding their respective lines, she was almost chin-deep in the murky seawater of Forton Creek. As she moved one of the boats it accidentally knocked into the boat whose line Mary was holding, causing her to be tugged into the water. She splashed about, coughing and spluttering. Lady Ellen tried to smother her giggles. "Sorry, Mary – my fault!" She looked at Gertie who chuckled.

"I hope you don't think I can row?" Mary asked prissily.

"Of course not. Don't worry, Mary, we just need to move them east of the yard and let them go."

"Let them go?" asked Gertie.

"Yes, push them out into the harbour."

"Why on earth would we do that?" Mary asked.

"A magic trick," said Lady Ellen, untying the last rope and walking them round towards the east like badger cubs on leads. As the boats moved off, a huge line of rats scurried into the water, crossing the creek past their island and onto Clarence Yard heading for the Town Borough.

*

The midday sun shone through the broken windows of the nave and spilled onto the gravel floor. Beaky was still guarding the front entrance while Agatha, Hertha, Floppy and Berry were busy inside working out yet another riddle.

> ### *SHIP to ROW, as space TRAVELS so*
> ### *Towards the HATED LARC*

They had worked out that SHIP to ROW, when unscrambled, was 'worship' but were struggling with the rest. As their attention flagged, Berry told Floppy a story about witches and folklore.

"Legend has it that the Red Witch only has to look at you to turn you into a worm," said Berry.

"But I don't wanna be a worm," said Floppy.

"You won't have a choice, Flophead. Once they decide to turn you into bird food, you're done for," he said, playing with him.

"But I don't wanna be bird food, Berry."

"Stop winding him up," called out Hertha.

"Well ..." said Berry, "... we're getting bored over 'ere."

Hertha gave Berry a disapproving look and shook her head at him. Just then the vestry door opened and Brother Nicholas serenely walked out, his hood over his head, followed by six monks and six nuns. They all quickly scrambled to their feet and rushed towards the door to the nave. The bells of the church chimed twelve.

"Worship with us, my friends," said Brother Nicholas calling to them.

"We are grateful for your kindness but have been here long enough," said Agatha standing at the end of the aisle nearest the door.

"The Domus Dei church will always shelter you," he responded.

"Come on," said Agatha to her friends, ushering them out of the chancel and into the nave – which they immediately realised was a mistake. They froze in their tracks as they came face-to-face with a Gizor officer, a smartly uniformed grey squirrel who wore the peak of his cap very low over his eyes

"They are my prisoners, sir," said Beaky, waddling down the centre of the nave behind the officer.

The officer looked the 'prisoners' up and down. "Take them to Kingston. Use the truck," he said, barging through the centre of them and entering the chancel.

"Come on, prisoners," said Beaky, not very genuinely.

"I don't want to go to Kingston Prison, Hertha," said Floppy.

"We just have to pretend, Floppy," whispered Hertha. "Put your paws up like this and do what Beaky tells you to do."

"OK." Balancing on his back legs, Floppy hopped out of the nave and into the sunshine of Old Portsmouth.

Beaky stopped just short of the truck. "Err, I don't know how to drive," he said. Berry quickly shoved him into the driver's seat and sat on his back to see above the dashboard, while Agatha jumped into the rear hold, pulling Floppy in with Hertha's help. As this was happening, an officer and his men walked over to the church. The officer walked with a swagger and was pushing berries into his mouth from a stash held in his paw. He glanced over at the truck as it slowly pulled away and stalled. Berry was not that great a driver himself. As the officer entered the nave of the church he turned back to see a fluffy white tail sticking out from the rear canopy of the truck. In the church he was greeted by the officer who Beaky had outwitted.

"Hail Gizor," said the officer, saluting smartly.

"What was that?" He gestured at the truck.

"Prisoners, sir. Would you like to see the chancel?"

"Not really."

"It would be an honour for me to show you, Sir Roderick."

"Hmm." Reckless Roddy gestured to his men to stay outside.

He was less than impressed with the church. "Why can I smell rabbit?" he asked.

"One of the prisoners, sir, was a rabbit."

Roderick paused. "A rabbit? A white rabbit?"

"Yes, sir, and a couple of reds and a ..."

"… mole," he answered for him.

"Yes, sir."

Roderick immediately took out his pistol and shot the officer in the chest. "After them!" he shouted to his soldiers as he ran from the church, only to see the truck disappear out of sight around the corner towards Portsmouth Point.

The ride was bumpy over cobbled streets and the friends suddenly heard gunfire ricocheting off the tin sides of the truck. "Keep low, Floppy. Head and ears down," said Hertha. They drove down the wrong road as Berry didn't know where he was going, past the Round Tower and on towards Spice Island – a dead end – but they had evaded capture. They abandoned the truck, which had been torn to shreds, and ducked down an old alleyway. Portsmouth Point, known locally as Spice Island, was full of seedy taverns, sin, depravity and debauchery. As they hid in the shadows of the cobbled dank alleyway between empty cider kegs and beer barrels, they watched peasants and sailors – weasels, voles, squirrels and stoats – staggering past, drunk and weary in broad daylight.

"Still bored, are we?" said Hertha sarcastically to Berry.

# Chapter 13
# THE ALLEYS OF OLD PORTSMOUTH

D enis scampered from his office along the corridor and up the stairs of the Semaphore Tower. He burst into the room. "Sir, my Admiral, sir!" he shouted in panic, tripping over as the handle on his umbrella got caught on the door. He picked himself up and couldn't immediately see Gizor, who was outside on the balcony looking over at Old Portsmouth. Nor did he see the sailor – handpicked by Gizor himself – standing in the office in silence to the side of the door. Denis quickly joined Gizor outside. "Sir?" he prompted, needing to interrupt his master who was peering through his binoculars. Gizor, as usual, casually ignored the Prime Minister. "Sir, I have news of Priddy's. Terrible news."

Gizor immediately moved his magnified gaze towards the north west of the harbour, trying to locate Priddy's Hard. "What is that smoke?" he asked.

"Priddy's, sir. It has been taken, sir."

"Taken?"

"Most unfortunate, sir."

"'Unfortunate? Why do people not understand that my army will not be taken, Denis?" He paused. "By whom?"

"It appears by several hundred rats, sir."

"RATS?" he shouted as he lowered his binoculars.

"So say the reports, sir. I really feel we must leave as I fear more strikes."

"So say who?"

"Sir they appear more rallied than we expected."

"Rats, Denis, do not rally behind an inferior breed," he replied, moving round to peer down into the dockyard at his military power.

"But the Mary Rose Resistance appears quite strong also, sir, with daily, hourly attacks."

"The M.R.R. couldn't rally a race let alone a breed, and yet you stand here and tell me they are strong."

"They do appear responsible for the bombing of Guildhall Square, sir."

"And the rats?" asked Gizor, turning his head to face Denis who did not have all the answers.

"Unknown, sir. But I really feel it would be safer to head to the hills." He took a step backwards towards the door of the balcony, fearing his Admiral's response. Gizor did not reply at first and continued to stare down at his busy dockyard. "Your leadership will not diminish in the hills, sir," said Denis nervously, fiddling with the catch on his umbrella.

"My rule," said Gizor firmly, "is as far-reaching as fear pretends to be. A ruler does not flee their kingdom, and a leader does not respond to fear. No breed of rat nor the Mary Rose will challenge me to a duel." He walked from the balcony back into his office and over to the soldier in the corner who was being measured by a seamstress mouse. She stood on a stool with a mouthful of pins adjusting the sailor's grand uniform, which appeared to have elevated him to the rank of Admiral. Gizor walked round the sailor, inspecting the uniform.

Denis, baffled by Gizor's intentions, carried on with his message. "The convoy is ready, sir," he said and no sooner were the words out of his mouth than gunfire could be heard outside the gates. The dockyard was under attack.

*

Weevil's rabble of rats had crossed Forton Creek from Priddy's Hard and positioned themselves in Ferry Gardens directly opposite the dockyard across the harbour. The army of rats had travelled through Clarence Yard – a disused supply depot – to get there, and on their way had half-inched some rusty old cannons and a mountain of round-shots to use. Once positioned at the ferry gardens they began loading them up.

"FIRE!" ordered Weevil. The rats all put their fingers in their ears. The first fusillade began.

Meanwhile, Lady Ellen, Mary and Gertie, as soon as they heard the first shot fired, let the empty boats drift off towards Portsmouth to reinforce the 'rallied' army.

*

Floppy leant over and stuck his head into an empty barrel: the alcohol fumes were quite overpowering. They remained hiding in the alleyway beside a tavern called The Coal Exchange. While Beaky and Berry tugged at Floppy's back legs to pull him out, Agatha and Hertha were trying to plan their next move.

Floppy popped out of the barrel and fell to the floor. "I like cider, I do," he said, hiccupping.

"The attack has started," said Agatha, hearing the bombs in the distance. "We have to get going."

"Sounds like your rats came through," said Hertha, impressed with Agatha's planning.

"Ratty rats? I don't like rats, I don't [hiccup]," commented Floppy.

As they tried to sober up Floppy, Portsmouth Point was getting more and more busy with Gizor trucks whizzing past, and soldiers and sailors marching to their positions. Amid all this were the drunk and brawling, the poor and peasant, and the sinner clothed in gentlemanly attire. They were startled by an innkeeper who burst out of the side door of the tavern, throwing out another empty barrel and starting to sweep the alleyway they were hiding in. He was a grey squirrel with a wooden leg and was wearing an innkeeper's tunic, an old moth-eaten waistcoat and a filthy cap. Hertha's motley crew stayed silent and low while the innkeeper continued sweeping. From the side door was spilling out the sound of sea shanties and the clinking of tankards and roughhousing from inside.

Without looking at the small group in hiding, the innkeeper called out: "You best not be afoot round 'ere." He continued sweeping.

The group did not reply, and Berry was holding a tight paw round Floppy's mouth, preventing him from doing so. "The Gizor be looking," he said, turning and walking back inside. "Best come in where it's safest," he called out behind him, leaving the door ajar.

"I don't think we should go in there," said Berry, releasing his grip over Floppy's mouth.

Hertha looked down the alleyway at all the Gizor personnel scattered around Spice Island. "Well, I'm out of ideas and we can't stay here," she said as she reapplied the coverall paint and passed it around. "Floppy, you need to be as quiet as a mousey again, OK?" Floppy hiccupped and nodded in agreement.

They entered the tavern by the side entrance and walked into a bustling rabble of drunken soldiers, sailors, peasants and flea-ridden misfits, drinking, smoking and singing at their top of their voices:

249

*"On the westward fallen shores, come the brave and
mighty sailors
And again, we tread the waters, on the seas of
Portsmouth Harbour"*

The sea shanty followed a hasty little beat that
increased as the rabble of drunken customers banged their
tankards to the rhythm.

"What can I get you, my darlin's?" said a voice from
the bar. Berry cleared his throat and approached the busty-
looking mole.

"Err, can we have four jugs of apple cider and a carrot
juice please?" he replied, blushing. She was a particularly
attractive wench.

"Of course you can, my lovely," she said, caressing his
cheek endearingly from behind the bar. "You sit yourselves
down and I'll brings 'em over for you, my darlin'."

They found a table at the back of the inn and plonked
themselves down. "We shouldn't be here," said Agatha. "It's
too risky."

"'Ere you are, my lovelies," said the busty bar mole,
bringing over their drinks. "Don't get too many handsome
moles like yourself in here." She squeezed Berry's paw.

"I likes it here, I do's," said Floppy, sipping his carrot
juice.

"Where exactly are we, though?" asked Agatha. At this,
Hertha began looking around at the walls of the decorated
and cluttered inn. Without a word, she stood up and walked
through the crowd of singing sailors and quickly returned
with a framed map of Spice Island and Old Portsmouth that
had been hanging on the wall. She placed it on the table and
blew the dust and cobwebs off it and into Floppy's face.

"Here!" She pointed, "We must be here. Look, there's
the Garrison Church and you drove us down to this point.

250

Look, there's the inn."

"Well, that's all fine and dandy but we still haven't got a clue where to go," said Berry, drinking his cider.

"OK," said Agatha, reaching in her pocket and getting the riddle out. "We need to work this out." They all huddled over the table reviewing the map and the riddle while drinking and listening to the sea shanties. Just as one had finished, a mangey old fox who was sitting in the corner struck up the accordion with a more solemn tune, and the bar-mole swayed and danced into the centre of the inn and began singing to the crowd. Floppy saw the fox and hid in Hertha's lap.

"Is that what I think it is? Is it a foxy, Hertha?" he said, his voice muffled.

"Don't worry, Floppy. He looks too far gone to be interested in chasing rabbits."

The customers began calling out the bar-mole's name with excitement, encouraging her to sing. "Go on, Vera!" they shouted, and as she began her song, she circled the tables, caressing the animal folk as she went including Berry, placing an affectionate paw on his shoulder as she passed,

*'I once knew a poor man, a gentleman too*
*Too kind to the many, so mean to so few*
*But I was a young lass of only sixteen*
*And I was in love with a beautiful king*

*Lord of his manner, and reckless was he*
*Too lazy to work hard, too greedy for me*
*So I travelled far, to be rid of this sin*
*And I met a boy so much stronger than him*

*He taught me of kindness and love did I him*

> *But he went away travelling west with the wind*
> *A sea storm would follow and cast him away,*
> *And I am left lonely and bitter this day.'*

She repeated the song with the pace quickened and everyone joining in, "*You once knew a poor man, a gentleman too*".

"I think I'm in love," said Berry.

"Snap out of it, Berry, we've got work to do," said Hertha.

"Sorry, H. She really is pretty, though."

"'The hated Larc?' It's not spelt right. Arc? Late?" said Hertha to Agatha as they sat working it all out.

"Silly riddles," commented Floppy, repeating the attitude of Berry before him.

"OK, what about 'travels space'," said Agatha, going back to the other word.

"Ravels, lave, leave, real, vest," said Hertha

"VESTRAL," they both shouted at the same time.

"What's a vestral space?" asked Floppy.

"Lovely heather for you, my sweet?" said a voice. It was Pompey Lil trying to sell her many knickknacks.

"Do you know what a vestral space is?" Floppy asked innocently before the others could answer him.

"Find it in the cathedral, my sweet," she replied.

"CATHEDRAL!" shouted Hertha and Agatha. "Thank you, miss," said Hertha as she stood up, encouraging the others to grab their belongings and finish their drinks. They left the framed map on the table.

"Leaving so soon, my sweets?" asked Pompey Lil with a smile.

Beaky placed some money in the old beggar woman's paw. "Thank you for your kindness," he said because 'kindness is everything in life' he thought.

"What's that?" asked Floppy looking at a trinket on a chain around Beaky's neck. "It's pretty."

Beaky pulled the chain over his head with his beak and gave it to Floppy. "It's for luck," he said.

As they walked towards the front entrance of the inn, they saw Reckless Roddy and a couple of sober soldiers walk into the pub, clearly looking for them. "This way," said Hertha as they ducked through the crowd and out of the side door.

"Goodbye, my love," called out Berry to his beloved bar-mole as Hertha pulled him away by the arm.

They ran down the alleyway and out onto the crowded cobbled streets of Portsmouth Point where they moved through the bustling crowd of beggars and sellers, paupers and prostitutes. There were hecklers and sailors, and market traders selling berries, herbs, and spices but most of all fish from the harbour. It had a distinct and horrible smell. The streets were busy with trade and netting and buckets from the fresh catches of the day.

"ALL THEM GOOSEBERRY-A-POUND!" shouted one trader, holding a bunch of gooseberries in the air.

"LOVELY LUCKY HEATHER FOR YA!" shouted another, probably a rival of Pompey Lil's.

"FRESH CARP. GET YOUR FRESH CARP 'ERE!" yelled another. It was far from fresh.

Undetected, they followed the west shore of Spice Island through the smelly crowd and headed for the Round Tower.

"*I once met a poor man, a gentleman too, too lazy to work hard, so mean to soooo few,*" sang Floppy, happily mixing up his words.

\*

253

The Great Hall of Winchester stood majestically as the head of the World Wildlife Federation, the cornerstone of democracy, a champion of peace. Yet it also stood many miles from Gosport and far from the sounds of a raging war and threat from the east. It was never more needed than it was right now by the animals of Gosport. The Great Hall, built of flint and stone, housed the many united flags of the federation and was presided over by its faithful leader Lord Arthur, a Grand Knight of the Federation itself. He was a humble and fair red squirrel, reasonable to the core, trusted without question, and good to all animals.

Small footsteps on the slate floor clacked towards the Great Hall itself where Lord Arthur was presiding over a council meeting. The knock on the grand door, despite only being a small scratching sound, nevertheless echoed to the rafters. A little mouse scurried in and over to Lord Arthur without saying a word. Lord Arthur looked down at the mouse, who handed him a letter, bowed at his leader and scurried out of the hall. Lord Arthur was elderly and slightly overweight, but always impeccably dressed, right down to his hat. He puffed on his pipe as he opened the letter and began to read. It was Agatha's notice that Ethel had posted to the Federation. His shoulders drooped.

"Trouble, Arthur?" said one of his Council officials, a mournful-faced badger.

"It would seem so, my old friend," he replied with sadness.

*

"I rather enjoyed that," said Mary, who was watching the empty boats drift off towards Portsmouth and was soaked up to her waist. "What next then, Lady Ellen?"

"I think we should join the forces, don't you?" she replied.

"Well," commented Gertie, "I must say, I think we are rather good at it." All three were innocently proud of their efforts to push the boats into the harbour.

"What say we join our comrades at the Gardens?" Lady Ellen suggested as they watched the smoke and flames rising up in the distance.

"Well, why not? Nothing else to do," said Mary, who seemed to have acquired a new-found sense of duty. "If my husband could see me now, he would think I'd gone quite mad."

They took one of the remaining boats and the three of them rowed over to Clarence Yard, and headed towards the Ferry Gardens to 'support the effort'.

"'Ello, missus," said a scruffy rat as the three of them walked towards the busy outpost on the banks of the Harbour. "I found my toothy peg in the end." He held it up, all blackened and dirty.

"Oh well, that's jolly good," said Mary, slightly repulsed and not wishing to know where he had found it or indeed what he was going to do with it. The firing resumed and all three friends covered their ears.

"Right you rat bags, listen up!" shouted Weevil to his men. "I need more fire power on the cannons, and the rest of you get your seafaring legs on for tomorrow. We're going for a swim, boys." His crowd of followers cheered with excitement and hunger.

*

The once bright summer's day was turning to grey, and the skies appeared heavy with acidic rain as clouds loomed over the dockyard. The bombing continued over the Harbour, and Gizor's soldiers were struggling to rally their cannons to fight back to the same degree. They had been arrogantly unprepared for an attack. With his bowler hat at just the right angle and his umbrella to his side, the Prime Minister walked quickly and purposefully out of the Semaphore Tower and on to the streets of the huge dockyard itself, ducking slightly every time a shot hit its target. He scurried past running personnel who were attempting to fight back, headed up Stony Lane turning north towards Victoria Road until he reached a huge hangar at the top of the dockyard itself. He tipped his hat to the officers guarding the entrance and walked into the building. At the back of the hangar he approached a group of well-dressed menfolk in the corner sitting on crates, muttering to themselves. One of the men – a water vole – saw Denis approach and walked to greet him.

"Prime Minister, my friend," he said.

"Theodore," replied Denis, greeting him warmly and shaking his paw with both of his own. It was First Minister Forton from Gosport, with his Ward ministers sitting behind him. "A convoy has been readied to convey his Admiral to the hills," said Denis, checking for watchful ears around him. Theodore nodded with relief. "It should not be long now, my old friend."

"Bless you, Denis," he replied.

Denis stayed for ten minutes or so talking to Theodore before making his way back towards the Semaphore Tower. The rain began to fall heavily and the sun disappeared into the night sky. As he approached the entrance of the tower, he saw Gizor walking out dressed in the uniform of a lowly deckhand. Denis stretched out his paw, guiding his Admiral to the waiting convoy.

A sailor came rushing over to them to report the sighting of an armada of vessels in the harbour heading their way.

"The mark of a leader is to visit all of his lands, Denis," said Gizor as he stepped into the armoured vehicle and the door closed behind him. Denis saluted and watched the convoy move off and leave the dockyard.

"And a coward will always protest too much the power he thinks he has," he said to himself as he turned to look upwards at the balcony of the Semaphore Tower where he could see Gizor's phony standing tall and proud in his place.

*

Hertha and her band of Resistance fighters travelled through the streets of Old Portsmouth, checking behind them for signs of pursuit. The light had faded into night and the crowds were dispersing as the streets were now lit by flares.

"This way," said Hertha as she directed them down Tower Street towards the Round Tower.

"We're completely exposed 'ere, H," said Berry.

"*I once knew a poor man, a gentleman too ...*" began Floppy again.

"QUIET, FLOPPY!" they both yelled at him as they all came to a stop in a narrow alleyway. They heard running footsteps coming from West Street behind them, so they turned to keep heading south but heard footsteps coming from Tower Alley in front of them too. They were going to be cornered with no way of escape. Agatha frantically banged on an old oak door with a sign declaring it to be the Blackhorse Tavern c1657 but there was no response. Opposite, however, an old grey squirrel with a long white beard stepped out of his house and ushered them all in. They quickly ran in, shut the door behind them and heard the soldiers running past.

"Thank you for your kindness," said Floppy, holding his paw around the trinket Beaky had given him.

"Welcome to my humble home," said the old man.

257

"Don't touch my things," he added as he tapped Floppy's paw, who was indeed touching his things. They found themselves to be in Tower House – a grand town house yet cottage-like and cosy within. The old man walked them through to the sitting room and began pouring them some tea. "Please rest your weary bones," he said. "I suspect a Captain amongst you. No?"

The small company sat down on an old moth-eaten sofa. All around them were paintings of grand old ships, maritime knick-knacks, compasses, maps, rope knots, handheld telescopes, and brass trinkets. It was a treasure trove of marine equipment and antiques. Hertha stood up. "We travel on a mission, sir," she said.

"Hmm, a seafaring mission no doubt," commented the old man, walking over to an easel and attending to an imperfection on the painting that rested there by brushing it with his long beard.

"Well not exactly, sir."

The old man peered over his spectacles. "But you are a Captain?"

"Well …" Hertha was about to reply but Agatha stood up.

"Yes, sir. A Captain of Resistance," she said.

"Told you so," he replied, proud of his observation and returning to his painting, "I can always tell a Captain from a deckhand. Wyllie's the name."

"Hello, Mr Wyllie," said Floppy getting up and hopping over to the old boy to shake his paw. "My name's Floppy." He knocked over a jar of water which had various paintbrushes in. Wyllie did not respond and just looked the rabbit up and down while holding a paint palette in his paw.

"Apologies, Mr Wyllie," said Agatha, righting the toppled jar and pulling Floppy back from the old man. "As we are indeed on a seafaring mission, could we trouble you

258

for a map of this fine port?"

"If it's a map that you require, you've come to the right place, me hearties." He rummaged through some old maps in the corner of the sitting room. "Ah yes, here we are, Old Portsmouth. Looking for anything in particular?"

"We're looking for the ..." said Floppy, whose words were quickly muffled by Agatha's paw over his mouth.

"Just the fishing docks, sir," replied Agatha.

"Well, they're easy to find," he said, handing the map to them, continuing his painting and every so often peering over his glasses at the group studying the map.

They whispered their words and tried to locate the Cathedral and come up with a plan. Floppy, however, wandered off and started looking around the old squirrel boy's treasures. He walked behind Wyllie and looked at the painting, "That's a lovely ship, sir," he commented.

"Victory is a grand old ship. She commands the winds and the weather, you know. She should be free on the seas and not set back on the dank dock," he proclaimed as he added some froth to the waves with his brush.

Hertha and Berry looked at each other and mouthed "the dank?" Hertha reached into her boot and pulled out the cloth once more:

*Scattered rust and wood of rot*
*We wait the dank*
*Shored by the dock*

"HMS Victory?" Hertha questioned.

"The flagship of Admiral Gizor," replied Wyllie, continuing his brush strokes.

"Here," said Agatha, pointing at the Cathedral on the map. "We're not far."

"Let me see," said Hertha, who was looking for *HMS*

259

*Victory*. She thought for a second. "OK, here's the plan," she said as they listened to their 'Captain'.

*

"I'm knackered, Weevil," said a scrawny little rat resting up against the sea wall of the Ferry Gardens. Firing on both sides had eased as night had fallen.

"Rest up, boys," said Weevil to his men. "We got a job to do in the mornin'."

"I say, Lady Ellen, these cannon balls are very heavy," said Mary rolling one close to the cannon itself. It rolled away on its own as soon as she took her paws off it and she had to chase after it.

"I got it for ya, missus," said the rat that appeared to have taken a shine to Mary. He struggled to stop it rolling away, as it was bigger than him. Yet he picked it up and carried it awkwardly back to the cannon with his rat friends laughing at him.

"'Ere Squidge, fancy a flying lesson?" called out one of the hecklers.

"You what?"

"I reckons you could fit in that cannon and reach the other side."

"I reckon so too," said Bandicoot, joining in.

"He aint brave enough," said Yersinia.

"I am too, I tell ya," replied Squidge, naively climbing head first into the cannon while the others looked at each other mischievously.

"What on earth are you thinking?" said Mary, rushing over and pulling on Squidge's grubby legs that were poking out the end of the cannon.

"What's going on?" said Weevil.

"Nothing, guvnor, just a bit of fun," said Waldheim, who had started the dare.

Weevil watched as Mary helped Squidge down from the cannon. He looked at the pranksters before him and grabbed Waldheim by the scruff of the neck. "You want a Pardon, do ya?"

"Weevil," he grovelled, "I was just playing, guv. Didn't mean nothing by it."

"Well, let's just see if you're right, shall we?" He carried the rat with ease over to the cannon and loaded him up. Without any hesitation he pulled the cannon cord, which fired the grovelling and very sorry rat through the air and over the harbour. The rats cheered at his misfortune.

"Cor blimey, I reckons he cleared the other side," said one of them, trying desperately to see in the dark.

"Get some kip, the lot of ya's. We got work in the mornin'," ordered Weevil.

"Thank ya's, missus," said Squidge to Mary, tipping his cap in gratitude and scampering off.

*

Portchester Castle was in silent darkness with the hour late and the monks in quiet solitude tucked up in their cells sleeping. Yet the bell rang out, waking them from their slumber as the Admiral's convoy pulled up to the gates.

"Sire," said Pontius Perseus walking briskly through the rain to greet his Lord Admiral.

They could all hear the faint echo of explosions in the harbour with the sound resonating around the castle walls. Gizor's men marched into the castle grounds and surveyed for resistance. There was none. They paved the way for their Admiral to continue his journey into the Keep itself. His hood up to protect his fur from the torrential downpour, he entered the banquet room and sat down at the table. One of the monks took Gizor's mac, shook off the raindrops and hung it up. Another quickly provided him with a plate of food and a goblet of wine, bowing to his Lord Admiral as he walked away. Gizor looked at the food before him and pushed the plate away. He took a pensive sip of his wine and spat it out. He stood up again and began examining the decorated walls with their hangings and holy artefacts.

"I understand that you were charged with the holding of three prisoners, Brother Perseus?" said Gizor as he wandered around, touching the various artefacts as he went. One was a sword attached to the wall of the Banquet Room. He teased the blade with his paw as if to remove dust from its surface.

"Sire, it was with regret and sorrow that their escape confounded us," said Perseus, grovelling.

"Hmm. Regret is a misleading word, would you not agree?"

"Sire." The little vole hung his head in shame.

"It is with regret, Brother, that I am faced with a sorrow greater than yours. You see, weakness is no virtue. There are times when we cannot forgive those who are regretful, and there are times – such as these – that sorrow has no place. Not in my world." He pulled the sword from its place on the wall and turned sharply round to face Pontius Perseus. "And this is my world, Brother," he said as he pushed the sword into Perseus' stomach. As he drove it deeper, he leaned in closer to the monk's face and whispered: "I will pray for you, Brother." Gizor released his hold on the sword and Perseus slowly dropped to his knees, his paws holding the hilt of the sword with which he had been impaled. He fell sideways to the floor, dead. Gizor stepped over the dead body, sat back down at the table and began eating the food he had previously pushed away.

## Chapter 14

# A FISHERMAN'S TALE

*I*t was early dawn and the Resistance crew lay asleep together on Wyllie's old sofa in the Tower House of Old Portsmouth. Floppy was up early, however, and was busy talking to Wyllie while learning to paint.

"Sister Nunna at the orphanage always said the fishes don't wanna be caught," said Floppy, dipping his paintbrush into the jar of water.

The old man ignored the comment and said: "Caught me a fish as big as a carrot once."

"A carrot? I likes carrots, I do."

"Aye, little sailor. As big as ten carrots it was."

"That's a lot of carrots."

"It is when your boat is only the size of three. Caught it in a storm and made a rug from its skin and an easel from its bones."

"Wow!"

"Aye, little sailor, a fisherman makes his own rod to catch his own fish," he said, nodding over to the fishing rod proudly hung on the wall.

Floppy stood up and walked over to the rod. He saw a perpetual brass calendar dial on the mantelpiece, which he couldn't help but pick up. "What's this, Mr Wyllie?" he said, weighing it in his paw.

"That, my sailor friend, will tell you all the days of your life."

"And this?" he asked, picking up another trinket box on the shelf.

"Well that contains the ramblings of another adventure," he explained. "You see, we sailors aren't born to one port, little kit. No, we sailors sail all the ports in all the lands, and in there are the stories of a few. To map the world is an adventure, Master Floppy."

"I like adventures, Mr Wyllie."

"So do I, little sailor kit," he replied as the cuckoo clock sounded on the other side of the room. "Right, I best be gathering my things."

The striking of the clock had stirred the others from their slumber. "Not yet, I'm nice and comfy," murmured Berry, rolling over on to his side. He opened his eyes and came face to face with Beaky who was unintentionally hugging him. Berry jumped to his feet, coughing and puffing his chest out, quite embarrassed.

"Things to do – you best be on your way now, me hearties," said Wyllie, collecting his fishing rod, tackle and bag. "The wind is a steady north today," he added, grabbing his sailor's cap, which was hung on a hook in the hallway. Hertha jumped up and rubbed her eyes.

"Guess what, Hertha? Guess what?" said Floppy, hopping up and down. "He once caught a fish as big as ten carrots, he did."

"You best be leaving out the back, my Captain," said Wyllie as he walked through the hallway to his back yard. The group followed.

"Thank you for your kindnesses, Mr Wyllie sir," said Beaky as they all spilled out into the closed yard, which was full to the brim with fishing nets and equipment. They watched as Wyllie dragged his rowing boat into the fresh harbour water. Without saying a word, he tipped his cap to the group and rowed away into the misty morning sea, whistling to himself a sailor's sea shanty.

Hertha began reviewing the map she had taken from the old boy. "The cathedral is north east. That way," she said, pointing.

"And how do you propose we get there then, Hertha?" said Berry, peering over the rickety fence into the opposite alleyway. The morning markets were opening, and Portsmouth Point was once again starting to bustle with trade oblivious to the war – it seemed a world of its own.

"Can we go back to the tavern, Hertha?" asked Floppy, beginning to sing again.

"No. We have work to do, remember," said Hertha as she looked around the yard for supplies. "Look at this!" She grabbed what appeared to be tarpaulin but was in fact the cloth of an old sail used long ago on some epic seafaring adventure, no doubt. "Beaky – your knife," she said as she stretched out her paw. "Floppy – hand me some of that rope over there." Agatha was left holding the map and studying it carefully. Beaky, on the other hand, was at the water's edge dipping his webbed feet in ever so carefully and peering into the water to see what he could catch for breakfast. Berry was standing behind him to see if he fancied the fresh catch.

"OK," said Hertha. "Remember the plan everyone? We head for the cathedral and to get there we use the cover of disguise." She handed out her makeshift monks' habits made from the leftover hessian sail. They each took their costumes and began putting them over their heads and tying them at the waist. Floppy needed help with his, which was slightly oversized but which hid his tail effectively.

"You look great, Floppy," said Agatha.

"Yeah, almost holy," mocked Berry, pointing out the holes in his costume. Beaky, being a Gizor officer, was relieved that he didn't need a silly costume and continued searching the shores for some breakfast for them all. He was quite successful and dug out some worms for Berry, some cockles for the rest of them, and fish for himself.

They stood in line at the rear gate of the yard. The Round Tower loomed over them. "Remember to look the part," said Hertha to her rabble of kin. "Look holy, Floppy."

"Like Brother Nicholas?" said Floppy, waving his arms about trying to find his paws in the long sleeves.

"On my mark we walk serenely out in line," said Hertha. "Remember – follow me, look down to the ground and don't say a word. We are holy members of the cloth."

"I like this game already," replied Floppy.

"Agatha? You head up the rear behind Floppy. Beaky, you walk beside us."

"Right you are," he said saluting his Captain and picking at a half-eaten fish.

Hertha opened the side gate and led the group down towards Broad Street past the Round Tower where Floppy, Agatha, and Beaky had landed via zipwire the day before, and headed towards the Square Tower. Their pace was slow as they passed traders and beggars, soldiers and sailmakers. The misty sea air and the foreboding of war would not see Portsmouth Point differ in its enduring endeavours. War didn't matter to these desperate livelihood seekers – they had to live somehow. The group followed the road towards the Square Tower, a place not immediately familiar to Hertha and Berry, especially as they were attempting to look holy by looking at the ground in solemn prayer. Hertha, who was leading the line, suddenly stopped in her tracks as she saw the shadow of the tall stone wall hitting the roadside.

She looked up and saw the bust of Admiral Gizor himself sitting proudly in the hollow of the wall. The group continued walking and bumped into Berry and Hertha as they had stopped.

"What have we stopped for?" asked Agatha from the back of the line.

"Sorry," said Hertha. "This way." They crossed the road onto the lush green lawn of the cathedral and hid behind one of the tall oak trees surrounding the building, almost protecting it.

"Oh, I forgot my painting," called out Floppy, as if to turn and head back. Agatha grabbed him by the scruff of his habit and pulled him to the ground as Gizor trucks whizzed by.

"It's too late, Floppy" she said. "Remember, we are on a mission,"

"I like missions, I do," he said, easily distracted by the prospect of an adventure.

They moved from the cover of the trees and headed towards the main entrance of the cathedral. Hertha pushed the door open and guided the others in. The cathedral was grand and tall, full of riches set amongst the poorest of Portsmouth dwellings. They entered the nave from the south door and were met with solemn silence from the scattered congregation deep in solitary morning prayer. Hertha guided them to the left – the south ambulatory – towards the rear of the nave.

"Now what?" asked Berry, whispering to Hertha at the front of the line.

She looked at her surroundings: they needed a place of cover so they could discuss their next move. To her left at the back of the nave she spotted an alcove leading to some stone steps. The short line of would-be monks followed her and disappeared up the stairwell. The steps spiralled round to the right and continued far up into the rafters, yet Hertha ducked into a doorway halfway up and reached a platform overlooking the nave itself. There were lots of discarded chairs all piled up in a messy state. They closed the door behind them and began upturning the chairs and huddling close together. They needed a plan.

*

The World Wildlife Federation, born of the mighty Country of Winchester, had rallied to answer their call of duty. A mighty army driven by the commands of Lord Arthur – who had put all his faith in a single note written by Agatha and delivered by Ethel – travelled the 30 miles to the borderlines of Gosport. They reached Titchfield Abbey first, unaware of Gizor's breach into nearby Portchester or the surrounding hills of the South Downs. Lord Arthur had assigned General Henry Palmerston to lead the army – a powerful figurehead in the WWF. Affectionately known as Pam, he was the type of otter who stood up to bullies, opposed slavery and thrust his opinions of morality upon whoever would listen. A creature of good faith and trust whose ideas were akin to a philosopher of peace rather than an animal of war. Yet he would always fight the 'good fight', one that needed fighting when peaceful remedies were exhausted. Pam had reached the fortress gates where the Abbeystocracy were seated in session. The rain began beating down the cobbled path that led to the portcullis. Pam ordered the gates be opened for his army to rest and survey any intelligence.

"Brother Thomas," said Pam as he bowed his head to the monk, a small water vole, approaching. "What view from Portsmouth?"

"Ours is not to interfere, General," replied the monk.

"Rather then, your order is of ignorance?" he said sharply.

"It is a limited view of rumour only. Our abbey walls have not been breached."

"So, it's true then that ignorance is blind?" said Pam, twitching his whiskers in annoyance. "You sit here, with rumour in your paw, and hear nothing on which to act? Yet, you are party to the Federation and sit in comfort?" Pam stared in silence for a moment at the monk standing before him. "Perhaps these walls have not been physically breached," he continued, "but I would challenge that a rumour has ruptured your duty, and I would place upon here a curse if I could because if true, your limited views have destroyed this place and my faith in you."

Brother Thomas could not immediately respond to the General and simply bowed his head as the army marched away in disgust. He then rushed to catch up with the General to offer what he could: "Lucius will know!" he said.

Pam stopped. "Lucius is probably dead," he said, turning to face the monk. "And you, Brother Thomas, will have killed him with your comfortable ignorance."

\*

The fires of the ovens raged on in the Camp. The Gizor officers no longer cared if the prisoners knew what would become of them, or noticed their dwindling population, or even that the snowy ash fell upon their feet. They continued to work them hard, and did not even realise that the Camp's population had been halved by the rescue efforts of the Resistance and not by their animal furnace. There were still plentiful vermin in the yard to work or burn – however they chose. The distant noise of bombing only spurred the Gizor on to burn them quicker. Great steel tubing – forged at Priddy's – was attached to the chimneys of several brick bunkers where poison was pumped into the chambers, killing those who thought they were having a flea bath. Of course, in the early days, they tricked the prisoners by actually giving them flea treatment to reassure them. The bodies of the poisoned were then transported to the furnace – another huge brick building where the chimneys smoked morning, noon and night and where ash rained down like snow. The Gizor officers presiding over the atrocity would pose for photographs standing next to their proud 'kills' – the annihilation of an entire race, the Red Squirrel and its sympathisers.

Doris was still worked hard at the Camp by the Gizor but had worked even harder to help release her comrades. Yet she knew that the plan could not include her, because for it to work, some animals must be sacrificed, and by facilitating the plan she felt it wrong to choose another to stay behind.

"Why are you so calm, Peter?" she asked Agatha's father who was sitting reading his journals in the barracks.

"Fate," he replied without looking up at her.

"Fate? And what is ours?"

"Well, that is a question that does not matter, young Doris, because it will happen whether we know it, want it, or understand it," he replied as he closed his book.

"I would rather know it," she reflected as she peered out of the barracks window and looked up at the clouds and ashy snow.

*

"We need to think," said Hertha, which prompted Floppy to cross his legs and place a paw to his chin as if to concentrate really hard. "We need to work out what a vestral space is and how to find it."

"Sister Nunna always said that I should wear a vest in

the winter, but I never did and then I got cold," said Floppy.

"It's a vestral, not a vest."

"She said I should hide from vestrals. Nasty birds."

"You're thinking of a kestrel, Floppy. A vestral space is somewhere the priests hang up their robes – a vestry. Maybe a secret room."

"Why are we looking for it?" he innocently asked.

"Good question," said Berry, folding his paws, once more fed up with riddles and secrets.

Agatha was leaning over the balcony, looking down into the sparsely populated nave. "It's got to be over that way somewhere," she said, pointing.

"I could go and have a look," suggested Beaky, still dressed in his military uniform.

"No," said Hertha. "We all go together."

They left the room and walked back down the steps to the rear of the nave, walking solemnly in line towards the north ambulatory. Agatha, who was walking behind Floppy, had to quicken her pace at one point to pull his habit over his fluffy white tail which was sticking out as he hopped along, blissfully unaware. They walked the length of the north ambulatory looking for anything resembling a little room. As they did so, the great organ struck up with a piercing note that startled the comrades: they had inadvertently found themselves directly under the organ, which sat alone in a loft above. The organ played its morning medleys to a dwindled congregation as the Bishop of Portsmouth, Sedgwick Doyle, stepped up to the podium.

"We pray with heavy hearts this morning, each a blessing we shall give to our Lord who keeps us safe and does not rest. For Gizor remains our light, our strength, our guide," intoned Sedgwick.

"Tsk," said Berry under his breath. "Gizor's light shines out of his backside, more like!" This comment sent Floppy

271

into a fit of giggles. Hertha and Agatha had to quickly wrestle him to the floor and place a paw over his mouth.

"Shut up, Berry," warned Hertha. "Hush now, Floppy, quiet like a mousey remember?" Floppy couldn't reply with Agatha's paw tightly covering his mouth, so he simply nodded. "OK, this way," she said, leading the group to the back of the cathedral. They walked towards the Chapel of St Thomas and found a small quiet room to the left behind a heavy oak door. Hertha ushered in her band of resistance, except for Beaky who she asked to keep watch outside the cathedral.

"What are we looking for, H?" asked Berry.

Hertha didn't know what they were looking for, so ignored Berry's question. Instead she took stock of the space before her. It was dusty and clearly barely used, full of tattered old books, religious knick-knacks and Orders of Service. There was an ironing board, an ancient-looking iron and a tall wardrobe full of moth-eaten robes. At one end of the room was an altar with a single candle with the words carved above it in the stone wall: 'Heaven's Light, Our Guide'. Beneath was the Crest of Portsmouth also carved in stone with a crescent moon lying at the bottom like a hammock and a star above it.

Agatha stepped forward to take charge. "We need a sign. We've found the Vestral Space – we now need to find out what's in it and why we are here."

"Oh, well why didn't you say it was that easy?" said Berry, rolling his eyes. Floppy followed his lead.

Ignoring Berry and Floppy, Agatha walked over and placed the riddle onto the table:

**SHIP** to **ROW**, as space **TRAVELS** so
Towards the **HATED LARC**

"We need to put all this together somehow," she said. "Hertha, where's your riddle?" Hertha pulled off her boot and reached inside for the cloth Lucius gave her and handed it to Agatha who put it down it next to hers. "Any ideas?"

"I've got a brilliant idea – why don't we just head home?" suggested Berry.

"SHUT UP, BERRY!" shouted both Hertha and Agatha.

\*

"Oh, my head hurts," said Mary holding her paw to her forehead.

"'Ere you are, missus," said Squidge, helping her up. "Got yourself a 'eadache 'av ya?"

"FETCH ME MORE SHELLS!" shouted Weevil to his crew as the bombing continued over the water.

Just as Mary was pulled to her feet by Squidge, an incendiary device flew over her head and into a couple of rats attempting to fetch more cannonballs to fire. Mary ran for cover, almost falling on top of Lady Ellen and Gertie on the sidelines.

"They're running low on ammunition," commented Gertie, trying to hold her hat pins in place while ducking for cover.

"If only I knew where my brother kept his blasted supply," said Lady Ellen. Brigadier Brune was an avid gunpowder and weapon enthusiast.

"One big bang would do the trick," commented Mary.

Lady Ellen, struck with an idea, called over to Weevil who raced over. "At this rate," he said, "we ain't got enough to cross the water."

"Would more cover help?" suggested Lady Ellen.

"Yer, but I don't know where you'll get it from," he replied, bent over taking cover from the relentless blasts from Portsmouth.

"There is a way," said Lady Ellen, "but I need some sewer rats."

Weevil stared blankly at Lady Ellen, and put his paw out, gesturing across the battlefield for her to survey his weary soldiers. "Take your pick," he said.

*

Hidden within the disused vestry of the cathedral, Agatha and Hertha studied the riddles and looked around the small dark room for clues, while the others sat and rested.

*By design to aid our task*
*Travels the direction of our path*
*A mighty ship of glory be*
*Forged above the windy sea*
*Move first, the Fourth, elude deceit*
*And follow thee*
*Serves to glory those in need.*

*Scattered rust and wood of rot*
*We wait the dank*
*Shored by the dock*

*Of our path, our puzzle be*
*We seal these walls*
*And start with thee*

"Where's Peggy when you need her?" commented Berry who was sitting on an old pew resting his weary back on the arm-rest. Floppy was at the other end copying him.

"Yeah where's Peggy?" asked Floppy, who didn't know who Peggy was. "Who's Peggy?"

"A witch," said Berry folding his arms and legs like the grump he was.

274

"A witch!" he said, startled at this revelation as if being told it for the first time.

"Don't worry about it, Floppy. He's winding you up again," said Hertha shooting Berry a stern look.

"Good job we're safe in here, then, if there's a witch about," replied Floppy.

Agatha snatched the cloth from Hertha. "We seal these walls," she read aloud, "And start with thee." She looked up and around the room towards the door. "Floppy," she said, "make sure the door is closed." Floppy jumped up from his pew and hopped to the door. He tugged and pulled at it, making sure it was securely shut.

"Yep, it's proper locked, it is," he said chuffed with the task he had been given.

"LOCKED?" replied the others in unison: even Berry, who was slightly alarmed, sat bolt up from his perch.

"How can it be locked?" asked Hertha.

Berry immediately stood up and rushed over to Floppy who was standing at the door. "Let me see here," he said as he pushed and pulled at the handle in disbelief. He turned to face his crew. "Yeah so, the door is locked," he confirmed in his usual fed-up manner.

Hertha walked over to the door, pressed her ear up against the wood and quietly tapped on it. "Beaky?" she softly called out. "Beaky?"

"I knew we shouldn't have trusted a Gizor Gull Bomber," commented Berry.

"I sent him to keep watch outside the cathedral," said Hertha.

"Gizor soldiers will be swarming this place in no time."

"Have a little trust."

"Beaky's my friend, Berry. He's a friend, I tell you. I trust, Beaky. I do," said Floppy, unhappy with Berry's remarks.

Berry leant on the door and crossed his ankles and said: "Well we'll soon find out, won't we?"

Agatha, still sitting at the table studying the cloth and searching the room with her eyes, ignored Berry's jibes. "It isn't locked," she commented without looking up, "it's sealed."

"And the difference exactly?" asked Berry.

"We're in the right place. We're meant to be here." She stood up and searched the walls of their 'cell'.

"Oh, must be magic then."

"And you don't believe in magic then, Berry?" said Hertha, referring to their time spent in Kingston Prison.

"Oh, well forgive me then," he continued. "Let me just pray to Gizor The Great and Powerful to get us out. He'll be here in a minute anyway." He plonked himself back on to his pew.

Agatha glanced at Berry and rushed over to the wall where the candle stood alone on the mantle below the stone carving of 'Heaven's Light, Our Guide'. She ran her paw along its letters and looked down at the candle. "I need a match," she said.

The group searched their pockets and bags but couldn't find a match, until Berry came forward, "Here," he said, reaching out a disinterested paw in the direction of Agatha. Hertha quickly grabbed the matches and ran back to Agatha. She took a match and struck it on the wooden mantle. It made a crackling sound as matches do, and she carefully lit the virgin candle. Nothing happened.

"Oh, so nothing's happened," said Berry. "That's a surprise."

Hertha had just about had enough of Berry's taunts and squared up to him in pure frustration, grabbing him by the scruff as he sat on his pew and lifting him so that his back legs dangled in the air.

"Yeah, well I've just about had enough of all these games, to tell you the truth," he said in response. Just as they were about to square up to each other, Floppy hopped over to the engraved stone and followed the letters with his paw, feeling each indent as he read aloud.

"Heaven's Light, Our Guide," he said.

Just as he had finished, the carved Portsmouth Crest under the mantle began to rattle and shifted slightly further into the wall itself. Dust from its recess fell to the floor. Hertha and Berry stopped in their tracks, with Hertha still holding on to the scruff of his neck. They both turned to face Floppy. Agatha quickly crouched down to examine the recess.

"Floppy – you did it!" she said as she felt around the edges of the recess.

"No such thing as magic then Berry, hey?" mocked Hertha, releasing her grip and chucking him back on to his pew.

"What is it Aggy? What is it I found?" said Floppy, crouching down and resting his front paws onto his knees in awe of his discovery.

"I don't know, Floppy, but it's something that only worked for you," replied Agatha. "Here, help me push." Berry reluctantly rose from his pew and joined in. All four pushed on the stonework as hard as they could and it began to shift further back into the wall. It was arduous work. Just as it began to get easier, the crest slid sideways ever so quickly into the wall, leaving them all to tumble forwards onto the dusty cold floor in a heap. They coughed and spluttered, and let their eyes focus on what they had found. A passageway. At first it looked like a short recess with nothing in it – a dead end. But as they re-focused their eyes to the dark, they saw it led towards some craggy twisted steps leading downwards, deep under the cathedral itself.

277

Agatha led the way, Floppy behind her, then Hertha, and Berry taking up the rear.

The steps led them to a huge chamber, ancient and full of dust. The walls were carved with numerous stone statues of monks, soldiers, scholars, peasants and fishermen, towering over the room itself. They were oversized mice, squirrels, rats and badgers. They lined the great chamber, and each held an acorn in their cupped paws. Their faces were all pointed to the centre of the dark chamber. The small group of four walked silently past the parade of statues towards the centre of the chamber where they could see what looked to be an ancient stone font.

"This place gives me the creeps," whispered Berry.

"I be afraid, I be," said Floppy, holding on to Hertha's paw for comfort.

"Me too, Floppy," she replied, keeping a watchful eye on the eerie statues towering over them.

Agatha walked slightly ahead of the group and reached the font first. She peered bravely into it. It was empty. In the bowl were some very fine, very faint markings, which she couldn't make out. They appeared as light scratches in the stonework.

"Now what?" asked Berry "I tell you something, I'm not heaving any of these statues around. No sir-ee."

"I don't want to heave anything anymore, Hertha," said Floppy "I've got achy bones, I have".

"Let's rest up a little then," suggested Hertha.

*

"Where are we going, Lady Ellen?" asked Mary as the small group of unlikely soldiers raced through the tunnels under Gosport between Priddy's Hard and who-knew-where. In tow was Gertie, Jane Priddy, Squidge and a gaggle of other 'sewer' rats.

Ellen was sprinting ahead holding a map as she went. She ignored Mary's question. "Are you sure this map is correct, Jane?" she asked.

"Of course, it is. My late husband loved these tunnels and mapped out all of them over the years," she replied, following close behind while the others struggled to keep up.

"We've been travelling for miles, Lady Ellen, and I for one have blisters on my paws," said Mary, appalled by the conditions.

"Not far now," replied Ellen, ahead of the group, examining some white fur she found stuck to a crevice in the damp wall. "Onwards, my band of lovelies – tally-ho!" she said, marching on.

\*

Portchester Castle stood strong in the gusty winds that rolled up the harbour. Gizor stood proudly on the top of the Keep overlooking his empire.

"As an advisor, my Lord, it is felt by the Council that a move to the hills is in order," suggested a meek, windswept squire stoat standing behind Gizor.

"If Denis wishes to advise me, I suggest that the Prime Minister addresses me himself," replied Gizor without turning around.

"Last night's shelling and this morning's have been quite relentless, sir," the squire replied.

"Puh!" scoffed Gizor. "My army will destroy them. I am not concerned about the shelling."

"Still, sir, for an empire to be ruled, it requires a ruler." Gizor turned to face the little squire. "The hills, you say?" He was impressed with the little figure before him and for a split second wondered why he had not noticed him until now, before returning to his thoughts of deluded grandeur. The little squire was right, he thought: his empire needed a ruler, and the ruler must be protected at all costs.

*

"Well, I've checked every one of these statues," said Berry. "They don't move. Not one inch. Nope. The font is dry, I've run out of fruit, quite frankly this place stinks like a library, I'm thirsty, and to top it all off, I've just found a flea!" he said picking at his shoulder.

"I'm thirsty too, Berry. I am," said Floppy.

"Well it's a good job one of us isn't so grumpy and can see the wood for the trees," said Hertha, standing near to the statue of a squirrel fisherman. Beside the prominent stone figure was a stone bucket for his fresh catches of the day. The bucket was full of water where the rain had seeped through the cathedral walls and through its floor into the chamber. Hertha scooped some of it up from the fixed bucket and rushed over to Floppy who drank the last few drops from her paws. Berry raced over and began almost shovelling it down his throat, scoop after scoop.

"Wait!" said Agatha, who had been leaning up against the font. She rushed over to the stone bucket, which was fixed to the wall. She too scooped some up with her paws, ran to the font and threw the remaining drops into its well. She raced back to retrieve more to do the same. The others looked at her perplexed.

"She's finally gone mad," said Berry.

"No," replied Agatha. "Look," she said, pointing at the font, which now had a small layer of water covering the base. They all peered over the bowl. The water had magnified the scratches at the bottom of the font, which were now readable:

*Only two shall travel, and*
*Only one shall find*
*The rest will follow*
*Forwards on time*
*Tall ships will sail above windy seas*
*And light will reign eternally.*

Agatha looked up at the tall ceiling of their chamber and found directly above the font, the crest of Portsmouth – a crescent moon and a star. She looked again around the room at all the statues lining the chamber. "Look for something like a ship," she told the group as she frantically examined the huge stone figures. The group, including Berry, began searching.

"Anchor," said Floppy, pointing to the north wall of the chamber. He had found a squirrel sea captain carved into the wall, with an anchor resting beside him. The captain was holding something in his paw. Agatha climbed onto a slight stone ledge to look: it was an old nautical timepiece fixed to his paw. While she tugged at the timepiece, the others held her up, to stop her falling off the ledge. The timepiece suddenly popped open to reveal a mechanical clockface. Berry caught her as she fell backwards. They then heard the clockwork mechanism moving and all shuffled quickly back from the wall. The whirring became louder and more intense and a rumbling began in the chamber. A deluge of dust began to fall from the hundred or so statues in the room. They moved even further to the centre of the chamber for safety.

"I be afraid, I be," said Floppy, holding onto Hertha's paw once more.

Suddenly they watched as the eerie figures from around the room begin to move their stone-carved heads in the direction of the sea captain. The figures each then lifted a single arm slowly to point at him. The group of friends were speechless and continued to watch the stone captain, who began to shudder and shake in the wall. The figure was driven backwards like a door opening inwards, revealing a wooden staircase within the walls.

"Let's go," said Hertha, rather more bravely than she felt.

The group entered the passageway and began their climb up the creaky wooden stairs. It wasn't long before they reached what they thought would be the floor of the cathedral but the stairs led them still further. In fact, they were now near the ceiling of the cathedral itself and had reached a wooden hatch. It was stiff to open and they had to push on it with their backs to get it to move. Hertha luckily caught the rope handle, avoiding it crashing open and alerting folk below to their presence. Once it was open they could hear the morning choir in the cathedral singing 'Heaven's Light, Our Guide'. They could also hear the faint noise of shelling in the nearby streets. Hertha popped her head up through the hatch to check their surroundings. They were on some sort of abandoned balcony– an unreachable redundant corridor, a quirky architectural flaw to those who could see it from below. The narrow corridor was bound by great arches, giving a view of the congregation below. Hertha turned to face her crew and signalled to keep low and quiet as they crawled out of the hatch and followed her lead. The balcony acted like a bridge standing tall over the north side of the cathedral. They crawled along until they reached an alcove at the end that hid them completely from view and which led into a square room.

"Where are we?" asked Berry, dusting himself off.

"I think we're in the clock tower," replied Agatha, looking up and around the quite ordinary and sparse room. To each side was an embrasure overlooking the north, south, east and west sides of the cathedral and Portsmouth itself. They were high up, but Agatha realised there was still further to travel – and she and Floppy must travel alone. On the south-facing wall, they could see a rusty ladder fixed in position and attached to the wooden ceiling where there was yet another hatch. The ladder did not reach all the way to the floor: Hertha ran and jumped at it to catch the bottom rung but missed. She gave it several tries. Each time she landed back on the floor, adjusted her bandana and her jacket and tried again. Finally she was successful – she grabbed tight to the bottom run with her paws, her back feet dangling off the ground.

"Wait!" said Agatha. "This isn't right!" She grabbed at Hertha's feet to pull her down.

"Hey!" said Hertha. "What are you doing?"

"Only two shall travel."

Hertha again smoothed her jacket but more forcefully this time, in anger at being pulled down. She stared at Agatha in silence for a moment. She didn't want to admit that Agatha was probably right.

"OK, then," she replied defiantly. "Me and Berry will go."

They both knew that this wasn't correct either, and that it should be Floppy with Agatha. There was silence between them, and both turned to look at Floppy who was staring up at the hatch in a world of his own.

"We don't know what's up there," said Hertha, worried about the decision they were having to make. Agatha took a step towards Hertha, placed two reassuring paws on her shoulders and looked her straight in the eye. Hertha returned her gaze, as if to relinquish her caring role and place the responsibility for Floppy's safety onto Agatha.

Floppy looked at the exchange between his friends and hopped slowly over to Berry who was standing at the window looking down on to the street below. He put his paw affectionately over Berry's shoulder and said: "I want to be brave and strong like you, Berry." Berry briefly turned to look at his friend and then back out of the window where he could see Beaky marching up and down outside the entrance of the cathedral. He hadn't been a traitor after all.

"Then we do it right," he declared in response. "If magic is real, then you are a powerful wizard, Floppy."

"I like magic, I do."

## Chapter 15
# MAGIC LIGHT

W ithin the great Keep of Portchester Castle was a room with a single desk and chair, waiting for the Lord Admiral. Upon the table was a radio broadcast system and a 'suited and booted' mole holding ready a microphone and twiddling some dials.

"Sire, your empire awaits," he said as he brought the microphone closer to Gizor, who stepped into the light and sat down at the table.

He began:

"It is within this day, and in this hour that I, Admiral Grey, High Commander of the Fleet of Ratufinee, Jean De Gizor speak to you in victory. Resistance has been crushed. Mighty Portsmouth reigns the Harbour, and Gosport is of new power under my rule. It has been a bloody war and there have been many losses. In our victory we will remember them and the sacrifice made for our freedom under what was the tyranny of the Red rule. No more. Our pure pedigree survives and will go on, untainted by the Red Squirrel.

"There will be some that have doubted me and my resolve. I hereby forgive this transgression and there will be a place for you in my empire as we rebuild our mighty Portsmouth. Victory is ours. Hail Gizor!"

The radio address was heard across the two nations, in

the streets of Gosport and the outside spaces of Portsmouth. From the Alver Village to the tunnels beneath Priddy's, from the Coal Exchange Inn to the dockyards and beyond. He may have fooled some with his premature declaration of victory, but there was a strong band of peaceful peoples scattered across 'his empire' spurred on with determination to overthrow this madman.

Following his address, Gizor left the castle and by convoy travelled towards the hills like a coward.

*

The tunnels beneath Portsdown Hill were chalky to the touch as they travelled deeper into them. Lady Ellen was taking up the front with her band of 'lovelies' following obediently behind. The sewer rats were dragging up the rear apart from Squidge who was helping Mary navigate the uneven path beneath her paws. The muffled radio sounds from Gizor's address were still echoing along the walls of the tunnel – 'Hail Gizor'.

"'Watch out for that rock there, missus," said Squidge, pointing out a protruding piece of chalk while chivalrously holding her paw.

"Why thank you, Squidge," she politely replied. "How much further, Lady Ellen?" she called out.

"Not far at all – just up here I believe," she said. Ellen suddenly stopped in her tracks and threw her back up against the chalky rock in a star-like position with her arms outstretched flat against the wall. Her long tartan pleated skirt caught the wind and blew slightly back into the tunnel. She looked at her group and placed a paw to her lips to silence them. They had reached the end of the tunnel and just round the bend was the opening. She signalled for them all to move closer to her position but to do so quietly.

"Where does it lead, Lady Ellen?" asked Jane as she crouched down low which – given her size – was hardly necessary.

"If my calculations are correct, we should be directly under the centre of Fort Nelson," she said. The group looked at each other, not really understanding Lady Ellen's plan. "Now, if my bumbling old fool of a brother is correct, and your late husband knew his left paw from his right, then at the entrance of this fort is the biggest cannon ever made."

"You mean to say we are going to drag it through the tunnels back to Gosport?" asked Mary, bewildered by such an impossible thought.

"No, Mary. We're not going to drag it anywhere," she replied crouching down and peering round the bend of the tunnel. "We're going to fire it."

"Oh, dearie me," said Gertie.

\*

"Are we ready?" said Agatha, watching Hertha tie a rope tightly round Berry's waist.

"Err, well, I may have failed to mention that I … err … don't really like heights. Particularly dangerous heights involving big drops and bombs going off at the same time. Just thought I would mention it."

"You'll be fine, Berry," replied Hertha, tugging on the rope, "and besides, it's not the fall that'll hurt, it's the landing. Just keep your feet flat, knees bent and don't look down."

Berry climbed up onto the embrasure ledge and began edging out backwards very slowly. "I'm not even sure I'm going to fit, to be perfectly honest with ya," he said.

Hertha snuck a peek over Berry's flat body, which was now half in and half out of the window. She looked over at

Beaky who was still marching up and down outside the entrance to the cathedral, then glanced over at a soldier who was marching passed the Square Tower in the distance. She watched as he saluted the bust of Gizor sitting in the wall. She turned to face Floppy and Agatha who were standing watching them both.

"Right," she said. "No time for goodbyes. We'll see you at the bottom. We'll be waiting in position." She took a last glance at Floppy, then at Agatha who nodded in agreement. "Be brave, Floppy," she said.

"I be as brave as all of us. I like adventures, I do."

Hertha nodded to him affectionately, shoved Berry's shoulders with her paws, and climbed out the window behind him. Agatha and Floppy rushed to the window to see if their friends had made it to the ground safely. They had lowered themselves to the pitched roof of the cathedral, slid down its tiles and landed side by side on the grass flat on their backs. Berry raised his paw to signal that they were OK. Both, however, were a little dazed by the far-from-gracious fall. Hertha picked herself up and yanked Berry up to hide in the nearby shrubs. Gizor personnel were still everywhere.

Agatha turned and walked towards the rusty ladder. She made several attempts to jump and reach the bottom rung but, like Hertha before her, she struggled. She made one more attempt and as she did so she felt paws around her waist lifting her that bit higher. Floppy was, of course, taller than all of them and could easily reach the ladder.

"Grab my bag, Floppy," said Agatha as she pulled herself up higher. Floppy hopped over to Agatha's rucksack that she had left in the corner and rushed over to lift it up to her. "Got it," she said as she swung it over one shoulder. She edged up to the ceiling where the hatch was. She moved a paw over to her right to grab hold of an angled rafter for balance and with a gentle push on the hatch she took a quick peek at their destination. Sunlight poured through. "Come on, Floppy," she said, pushing the hatch open and scrambling up. She immediately turned back to help him up the ladder and through the hatch.

"Where are we, Aggy?" asked Floppy, making the remaining distance himself.

They found themselves to be in the disused empty bell tower of the cathedral. It was hexagon shaped and each side window was covered by white wooden shutters. Agatha looked around and could see no way out other than the hatch they had entered by. She stood in the middle of the floor looking up, slowly circling the room. Floppy began to do the same.

"I'm dizzy, I am," he said as he copied Agatha at a slightly quicker pace.

Agatha could see several small portholes in the domed roof and began manoeuvring herself around the room standing on the window ledges to see if they would be able to reach them. Unsuccessful, she knelt to open her backpack and pulled out the last remaining rope. Floppy helped her untangle it. As Floppy was taller than her, she asked him to try and lasso the rope over a thin metal joist in the roof. It took him several attempts, but he managed it. Agatha tied the other end to one of the shutters and tugged on it to see if it would be secure enough. As she did this, she saw Hertha and Berry through the shutters in the distance on the ground, running in their monks' habits towards Beaky.

*

"Psst!" said Hertha to Beaky while ducking for cover in the bushes to the side of the cathedral entrance. "Psst!"

"Missy?"

289

"Beaky, it's us," she whispered from the shrubbery. "Do you think you could get us over to the Square Tower?" Beaky looked around and in the distance, he could see the Tower to his right.

"Is it a mission?"

"Yes. A top secret one."

"Say no more," replied Beaky, giving a salute to the bushes.

*

Still crouched in the tunnel beneath Fort Nelson, the small group followed Lady Ellen quietly towards the daylight. They could hear nothing: no sign of commotion or soldiers. Nothing. They edged closer and closer to the end of the tunnel, which was barred by a rusty gate. Lady Ellen tugged on it, but it was padlocked.

"Squidge?" she called out. Squidge came running from the back with a few of his cronies. They jumped onto the padlock and started gnawing at its rusty old locks. It didn't take long until the chain broke free and fell apart. Lady Ellen grabbed one end, tugged the lock away and pulled open the gate. She poked her head out slightly to check for any Gizor troops and could see no one. She signalled to the rest of her group to follow her, edged out and found herself at the centre of a gully opposite the Redan and would-be barracks. They made their way west towards the entrance of the Fort itself to be greeted by an enormous lime green wooden gate towering over them. They kept checking behind them for intruders and prying eyes.

"It seems to be empty, Ellen," commented Mary.

"Don't be fooled," said Lady Ellen, yanking at the door. "Keep your wits about you. They'll be coming soon." They all began to pull on the heavy gate, which began to shift and get easier as the hinges remembered their job. Once opened, an awe-inspiring sight was revealed – they could see the whole of Portsmouth, the whole of Gosport and the Harbour. The group, standing in an unintentional row, were silenced by what they were seeing: the smoky dens of Portsmouth, the fires raging from the bombs, and Gosport – a green and pleasant land.

"My, we have travelled a long way," said Mary.

In front of them stood proud the rustiest, most enormous cannon, painted grey and overlooking the Harbour itself.

"Quick," said Lady Ellen, "load up those cannonballs over there." She pointed as she pushed the cannon with all her might towards the direction of Portsmouth.

\*

Pretending to be holy and deep in chanting prayer, Hertha and Berry followed their escort towards the Square Tower along the open streets of Old Portsmouth, amid military convoys and scattered Gizor soldiers on duty.

"'Ere you are, Hertha," said Beaky as he stopped at the north-facing wall of the Tower.

Hertha fell to her knees in front of the wall and nudged Berry to do the same. They began to pray as Gizor personnel marched past:

*"Lord Admiral Gizor, emperor of our lands*

*May we guide and protect you and keep you safe from the ills of Red kind."*

"H, what are we doing?" whispered Berry, his paws clasped together.

"Beaky," said Hertha, "I need you to fly up there and push Gizor off his perch."

\*

Having rigged up a pulley, Agatha was hauling on the rope with all her might, raising Floppy slowly up to the high metal joists of the domed-shaped green roof. He grabbed hold of the bar and shifted himself along to one of the portholes. He pushed one of the small round windows with his back leg and climbed out on to a thin ledge. He then flung the rope back inside and pulled up Agatha with ease. He helped her crawl safely out of the window and onto the ledge to join him.

"What now, Aggy?" asked Floppy, as they both leant against the hot copper domed roof.

"Up there, Floppy," she replied. They couldn't see the top of the roof itself or what they were looking for, but Agatha knew they were close. They both made several attempts to climb the incline before successfully gaining some leverage on some of its protruding bolts. As they climbed and clung to the hot roof, a glorious bronze ship acting as a weathervane came into view. It stood tall and magnificent at the highest point of the Cathedral overlooking Portsmouth.

"A ship, Aggy! A ship!" said Floppy.

"You might say it sails above windy seas," said Agatha, knowing they had found what they were looking for. There was, however, still one more obstacle to overcome. The weathervane sat proudly on top of a small enclosure.

They reached the enclosure and took stock of their surroundings.

"We're really high up, Aggy. I can see Gosport – look!" he said, as he pointed west. They could hear the faint sound of air raid sirens going off in the distance across the water as the bombing continued.

"Are you ready, Floppy?"

"I'm ready." As Agatha began to make her climb up the outside of the enclosure, Floppy pulled her back. He looked at her with eyes she had never seen before. "I'm ready, Agatha," he said, gazing warmly into her eyes. "Only two shall travel, and only one shall find – remember?"

Agatha looked back into his beautiful eyes and gently whispered: "I remember." She watched him climb up the outside of the enclosure to the weathervane itself.

\*

Lady Ellen and her Band of Lovelies rallied about the grassy entrance of Fort Nelson, rolling the heavy cannon balls over to the cannon itself.

"How on earth are we going to fire this monstrosity, Lady Ellen?" asked Mary.

"I'll fire it, missus," said Squidge.

"We'll be blasted through that back wall if you ask me," commented Jane.

"We can't possibly do this then," said Mary, sitting down.

"I'll fire it, missus," repeated Squidge, pushing the cannon ball into the chamber.

Gertie looked over their vantage point, observing the relentless firepower of Portsmouth bombing Gosport and the meagre but mighty efforts of the bombs being flung back by the rats in Gosport. 'To pardon was a promise', she commented to herself.

Mary looked at her friend and back over to Squidge, who began to light the wick of the cannon.

"Squidge!" she called out.

\*

Beaky flew up to the recess of the wall, scrambled behind the bust of Gizor and pushed with all his might. The statue began to shift as Hertha and Berry readied themselves below to catch it.

"Do you believe in magic?" she asked, with a grin.

*

Floppy continued his careful climb up to the very highest point of Portsmouth Cathedral. The wind began to whirl around his large ears and he lost his footing a couple of times, but managed to keep his balance. He straddled the tall thin vertical pole that supported the weathervane, wrapping his paws round it like he was climbing a rope. He edged higher and higher until he was able to grab tight the deck of the ship and pull himself above it. Agatha watched from below, biting at her claws in anxiety.

The bronze ship was three times the size of Floppy who was now clinging onto it. He looked at the ship's markings and read softly but aloud the words 'HMS VICTORY'. "Like Mr Whyllie's painting," he said to himself. The deck was level with his white fluffy chest as he began rooting around it with his paw. He noticed the captain's wheel in the centre and began spinning it. As he did so, the sails of the bronze ship unfurled and blew gloriously with the west wind. The wheel continued spinning and suddenly the ship itself spun, along with Floppy, until it faced Gosport. The wheel then stopped spinning, leaving Floppy to cling on tight with the momentum. Resting his back paws on the W of the weathervane itself, which sat below the ship, he propped himself up against the port bow and noticed the figurehead at the front of the ship. It was Hudsonicus Holozoa, holding a coat of arms that depicted the crescent moon and the stars. At the bottom of the crest were the words, *Heaven's Light Our Guide*. Floppy reached out his paw and touched the coat of arms, which immediate pinged open like an awkward-shaped drawer on a spring. Floppy was no longer surprised by all these secret drawers and passages. He reached his paw into the drawer above him and fiddled around in it to retrieve a small wooden box. He brought it closer to him as he clung onto the ship's side, careful not to drop it. He re-adjusted his position to free his other paw to examine the item, wrapping himself around the weathervane pole to do so. The lid of the wooden box was intricately carved with oak leaves twisted and woven around each other and an inscription that read: 'Apple Dumpling Bridge'. Floppy followed the engraved letters with his paw and then slowly began to lift the lid of the box. The interior was cushioned with velvet and resting upon it was an ancient carving of an acorn. It was the Ark. He'd found it. He'd found the Ark. He hesitated for a moment before reaching inside to place a single paw on it as if to stroke it gently.

\*

"CATCH!" said Beaky, with his wings outspread like an eagle against the recess in the wall and with one leg giving one last push on the bust of Gizor.

\*

"FIRE!" shouted Lady Ellen as the cannon blasted into the Harbour.

\*

A glorious and blinding light filled the whole world. Its brilliant rays let out a chorus note, piercing the air so loudly that the ground shook. Barely anyone could see: the good and the bad all covered their eyes and stopped in their tracks. The force of the light and the ethereal sound blew Floppy's ears backwards and he closed his eyes tight. It was as if all the wind in the world was concentrated on him. He found himself holding the Ark, his paws clenched tightly around it. Agatha cranked her neck up from her position in the enclosure, clinging on to its sides with the wind attempting to push her back in. She was almost blinded by the light and attempted to call out to Floppy, but no words could leave her mouth. He was still consumed with brilliant noise and brilliant light, and still holding the acorn carved by Hudsonicus Holozoa – the animal God. He found himself holding the acorn in one paw and reaching up to the sky with the other. His feet began to leave the weathervane, but he was not falling, he was rising. His whole body began to lift and twist gently in the air around the ship while the raging wind spun around him like a storm.

*

Doris, frantically scrubbing pots and stacking them under the eye of the G.C., was almost blinded by the brilliant light reflecting off the hot tin she was holding. She turned to face the parade square where soldiers and prisoners alike had stopped in their tracks, looking up at the sky. Her gaze fell to the horizon where a line of prisoners continued to walk the dreaded path towards the gas chambers of the Camp. A frail looking red squirrel stood still at the back of the line and raised his paws to the sky as if he was free before being ushered down the steps into the chamber. It was Peter Mumby.

*

Floppy's body disappeared entirely from the weathervane as the sound began to echo away and the brilliant light began to fade. Gizor soldiers began running in fear and panic down below. Agatha recovered and looked up again at Floppy but he had disappeared. She then felt a presence behind her in the enclosure. She whipped round to find Floppy lying on the floor motionless. She rushed over to him and placed a paw on his fluffy white fur to stir him. He sat up immediately. "Hello, Agatha," he said. "I found it, I did. I found the Ark."

*

Lady Ellen and her Band of Lovelies lay motionless on the grass next to the cannon – knocked clean off their feet by the blast.

"Goodness me," said Gertie mildly, brushing the dust out of her fur.

"Squidge!" called Mary, running to the back of the cannon. "Where is he, Ellen?"

Ellen turned to face the front wall of Fort Nelson. "There!" She pointed at his lifeless body lying in the distance. The group quickly ran across to him.

"Oh Squidge!" cried Mary, kneeling on the grass beside him and trying to rouse him.

"I hope I helped ya, missus?" he mumbled in pain.

"Oh yes, you helped us all, my dear friend," she replied, gently lifting his head and placing it on her lap as a pillow for him.

"Ain't never been a friend before, missus," he said as he slowly closed his eyes, still holding onto Mary's paw.

"Oh Squidge!" said Mary, shedding a tear for her friend as she cradled his lifeless body.

"He died a hero," commented Lady Ellen, "an innocent rat."

Mary remained on the ground with her friend as the

others surveyed the damage they had done. They stood on top of Portsdown Hill looking out over the Harbour. It had been a direct hit – Portsmouth docklands and its great barrier wall was severely damaged, and the relentless shelling of Gosport had paused for a moment.

"Pass me the binoculars," asked Ellen to Jane, who hefted them across to the badger. Something in the Harbour water had caught Ellen's eye. It looked like a huge school of fish. She soon realised it was Weevil and his rats swimming across the Harbour to continue their assault on the Docklands.

"Well I never expected such a heavy blast of light from the cannon," said Ellen, peering through her binoculars.

"We must move now," warned Jane, trying to gather the group together.

"Yes. Yes, quite right. Let's go, my Band of Lovelies. Back through the tunnels."

"We can't just leave him," Mary said as Gertie grabbed her arm to pull her up off the grass.

Gertie hovered over her friend and looked down at Squidge, his head resting on Mary's lap. "Once this is over, we shall come back for him, Mary," she said.

Mary looked up but still didn't want to leave Squidge.

"Listen to me for once, you old bag!" shouted Gertie for the first time in her life. Mary was completely taken aback and Gertie had even stunned herself for a second. They stared at each other, both equally startled, "You boss me about often enough – now it's time to listen to me" she said. "In about thirty seconds, this place will be swarming with the enemy." She reached out her paw again to Mary. "Now do you want to die along with Squidge or live to tell his tale?"

Mary was in total shock. "Well, I …" she began.

"Now get up and stop being so silly," said Gertie as she

yanked Mary up.

"Knew you had it in you, Gertie," said Lady Ellen, winking at her as they ran back towards the lime green gate of the fort.

They all piled back into the tunnel and scampered through as quickly as they could. As they rounded a bend, where the tunnel forked – left to go back home or right to go into the Fort itself – they were running so fast that they bumped straight into a group of Gizor officials, all grey squirrels. Mary ran straight into one of them with such force that it knocked him clean off his feet. The other officers quickly rallied to his side and pulled him up off the floor. Both groups were stunned by the incident and stood in silence for a couple of seconds. The officer who had been helped up off the floor was adorned in maritime regalia and stood much taller than the others. It suddenly dawned on Mary and the group that she had not just knocked any old Gizor officer off his feet, but Gizor himself. Without thinking, Mary threw a punch with her right arm straight into Gizor's face and he was immediately knocked back into the arms of his guards.

"THAT'S FOR SQUIDGE!" she shouted. They took the opportunity of surprise to run like the wind past the guards and down through the tunnels back towards Gosport. The guards, panicked for their fallen admiral, let the group run out of sight and into the darkness.

Ellen chuckled as the group ran through the tunnels.

"I don't know what came over me. I really don't," said Mary.

*

As Berry and Hertha caught the bust of Gizor, staggering under its weight, the brilliant light faded and their eyes

299

recovered. Beaky flew down to the ground to join them. The force of the catch had blown their hoods away from their faces, revealing their identity.

"We've got company," said Berry, nodding towards a group of soldiers.

"Run!" shouted Hertha, struggling to carry between them the heavy bronze bust. But run with it they did, albeit awkwardly, down White Hart Road then behind the cathedral.

"What about Floppy and Aggy?" said Beaky, half flying and half running on behind them.

"We'll come back!" shouted Hertha. As she turned slightly to shout towards Beaky, she saw that it was Roderick leading the troops. The two friends ran towards the fishing wharfs of Old Portsmouth, hearing an almighty gunfight erupt behind them. She risked a second glance back: it was the Mary Rose Resistance group led by Vincent Tudor. The gunfight bought them time to hide and as they looked for a place of safety, they saw Floppy and Agatha in the distance running across the south gardens of the cathedral towards them.

"Quickly!" Hertha said. "This way!"

The re-united group of friends scampered towards the fishing boats and along the docks, frantically looking for a hideout. Suddenly, in all the chaos, they heard a calm whistling from below – a sea shanty. It was Captain Wyllie sitting in his rowing boat, sifting through his fresh morning catches. His boat was moored to the side of the dock, hidden by the low tide. Floppy peered over the edge.

"Hello Mr Wyllie," said Floppy, squatting down and leaning on his knees to greet his friend, oblivious of the anxiety of his friends, who kept looking behind them for signs of imminent attack.

"Well hello there, Master Floppy."

"Hello, sir," said Hertha. "Can we trouble you for some assistance?"

"A captain on dry land is like a boat without its crew," he said as he stood up, ushering the group down to him. It was only a small rowing boat full of netting, buckets, rope lines and smelly fish. Floppy needed no encouragement and quickly clambered down the rusty ladder attached to the dock wall. Beaky flew down and perched on to the stern of the boat. He quickly gulped down a wriggly fish that was lying in one of the buckets.

It was Agatha's turn next. She jumped onto the ladder and began her climb down. "What is that?" she said, looking unimpressed at Hertha and Berry standing on the dockside holding onto the bust of Gizor.

"A keepsake," said Hertha proudly as she reached for some netting strewn over a barrel on the dock. With one paw she quickly wrapped the netting round the bust and she and Berry began lowering it down to Captain's Wyllie's boat. Wyllie didn't notice the bust at first until he turned to face his boarding passengers.

"A curse upon this land, is what that is," he said as the bust was dropped the remaining few feet into the boat, rocking it violently from side to side. Berry and Hertha jumped on board as Gizor troops ran past their hidden position.

"A curse?" whispered Floppy to his captain.

"Aye," he said, stroking his beard. "To remove him is to curse this place a dreaded fate. That's what you've done."

"Well," said Berry, "I hope that's true. Couldn't happen to a nicer place."

"What will happen, Mr Wyllie sir?" asked Floppy.

"Some believe, little sailor, that if you move the bust from the Square Tower, awful happenings will occur."

Floppy edged away from the bust, not wanting to be

anywhere near it.

Ignoring the scaremongering, Hertha looked over to Agatha. "What happened?" she asked, but Agatha did not respond other than to shake her head. The group was silenced as gunshots continued raging on above them, and a single pair of footsteps could be heard slowly approaching.

They all looked up at the edge of the dock, waiting for their fate. They felt helpless in the little rowing boat, which was still rocking from side to side with the tide and hitting the mouldy damp wall. A shadow fell on their position and without warning, a young grey squirrel wearing a leather jacket jumped to sit on the wall and dangle his legs over the side, looking down at them.

"I see 'chance' became your friend," he said, as a small battle continued behind him.

"Vincent!" called out Hertha, happy to see a friendly face.

"Who's that Hertha? Who's that?" asked Floppy.

"A friend," she said. Vincent, startled by the battle behind him drawing closer, jumped with precision into the boat, landing on his back feet without losing his balance. He placed a paw to his mouth to silence the group.

*

"Swim, you bunch of sewer rats!" shouted Weevil, who was leading his rabble across the choppy Harbour waters against a strong current.

"I can see him, Weevil!" shouted one of his men as they swam closer to Portsmouth dockyard. Gizor's selected phony was still standing on the balcony of the Semaphore Tower, feeling completely out of his depth. He was frozen with fear as he watched hundreds of rats crossing the harbour towards him. He paced up and down in a panic, watching Gizor's men below him run around the dockyard like headless chickens.

"What would Gizor himself do?" asked Prime Minister Denis Delaney who was standing inside the tower watching the soldier lose his nerve. The soldier began tearing off his robes and running for the door of the office, but Denis slammed it shut and pushed the soldier backwards into the room with his umbrella. He picked up Gizor's uniform from the floor, threw it around the squirrel's shoulders and shoved him out through the double doors onto the balcony. Although the solider was much bigger than him, Denis was still able to push his umbrella against the squirrel's neck in a chokehold, forcing him back against the balcony rail. Denis was angry but maintained a calm demeanour. "What would Gizor do?" he repeated. The soldier shook his head in panic and fear. "Would he shoot his comrade in the back to save himself?"

Weevil reached the mucky shoreline and entered the gates of the dockyard with his men behind him. They were ruthless and wild, biting and gouging at the enemy who were scrambling about in fear. Weevil himself stood just inside Victory Gate and looked up at the Semaphore Tower.

"Hand me that pistol," he said to one of his rat crew, who pulled it from a dead Gizor sailor lying on the floor.

Denis, still angry, stared at the pathetic creature before him. The squirrel could barely breathe so Denis released some of the pressure on his throat from the umbrella to allow him to speak. "HAIL GIZOR!" he said croakily as a shot rang out at the same time. Weevil had shot him dead from below. Denis fell back slightly with shock and dropped his umbrella on the floor of the balcony. He reached down to retrieve it and peered over the balcony. He saw Weevil staring back at him from below. He touched the rim of his bowler hat in gratitude and watched Weevil continue his battle in the docks.

## Chapter 16
# A MIGHTY SHIP OF GLORY BE

C amp Browndown seemed to stand calm amid the
bombing. An eerie place that had consumed death and
revelled in evil, it simply didn't matter that on the other side
of the Harbour, Gizor's homeland was being attacked. Their
mission continued just the same. Orders were orders, and
theirs were to exterminate an entire race and rid the empire
of the Red vermin squirrel and its sympathisers. The
furnaces raged and grew hotter with red tinder. The
chimneys bellowed great plumes of smoke out into the
midday sun. The Campmates were never more depleted –
only a few hundred scattered around each barrack remained,
attempting to look indispensable in order to be spared the
fate of their fellows. The air was black and white, and the
ground covered in thick snowy ash. While others fruitlessly
hid, Doris stood at the doorway of the barracks waiting. An
officer who was gathering the remaining prisoners at
gunpoint onto the parade ground, scurried over to Doris,
grabbed her by the arm and marched her quickly on to the
square. She didn't resist. The officer – a young grey squirrel
with a thin face and a haunted expression – looked slightly
unnerved, as did they all.

The prisoners were lined up in single file and marched

the long walk towards the Gas Chambers at the edge of the Camp. As they marched, Doris observed Colonel Fratton standing in full Gizor military uniform, outside the Chamber, his arms crossed behind his back, observing the spectacle with pride and madness. The officers began hastening the line of prisoners, shouting and whipping them, pushing and shoving them. There appeared suddenly now some urgency to their deaths.

Just as quickly as she had observed the Camp leader Colonel Fratton, Doris heard an almighty clash of metal verses motor. The line of prisoners fell to the ground as Gizor guards began running in all directions. Some attempted to preserve some order, but not very successfully. The prisoners scattered quickly around the camp in all directions. Shots were being fired and Gizor guards were falling to the ground. Colonel Fratton remained arrogantly still at the entrance to the Gas Chamber. The allied army from Winchester, led by General Henry 'Pam' Palmerston, had crashed through the gates of Camp Browndown. Any resistance from the Gizor Army was met immediately with death, and those who looked timid were quickly captured as prisoners of war. Doris, who stood in the middle of the parade square – shots being fired around her – watched on as an allied officer of the WWF approached Colonel Fratton, shackling his feet and binding his arms. He arrogantly and symbolically saluted with a 'Hail Gizor' gesture, twitching his tail in defiance.

Henry Palmerston surveyed the liberation and spotted Doris standing alone, still on the parade square, numb and exhausted. He walked calmly over to her. She did not look at him and was staring blankly at the Gas Chambers in the distance.

"What's happened here?" asked Henry, who saw how weak and thin Doris was.

She turned her head slightly, breaking out of her trance to look at him. "Fate," she said, echoing the words of her wise old friend, the late Peter Mumby.

*

His ego still shaken from the punch to his face, Gizor was ushered by his men through the tunnels of Fort Nelson.

"My Lord, we must retreat further," said his aide, a portly weasel, ushering him down some crooked steps deeper underground and into the secret passageways hidden in the chalky hills themselves.

"My treasures?" he asked, as he submitted to being pulled along by his men to safety.

"They will follow, my lord," said his aide, trying to hurry him along.

*

Still hidden from view, Captain Wyllie's fishing boat laden with passengers continued to bump against the wall of the dock. Shots continued to be fired and bombs continued to rage. Gizor troops were still hunting the White Rabbit and his companions – known to be a red squirrel and a mole.

"We could row it," suggested Berry, looking across the small fishing inlet out towards Gosport.

"Don't be silly, Berry," said Hertha. "We'd never make it. They've got the Harbour patrolled, and besides if we cast away here, they'll shoot us dead from the dock." Hertha looked over at Floppy who was sitting low, huddled next to Agatha at the back of the boat – neither of them saying a word. Vincent watched on and knew his part to play in this adventure.

"The Mary Rose can grant you passage," he said as he

stood up and peeked over the flat of the dock. "You must follow the winds on land." With that he jumped up onto the floor of the dock and charged at the enemy.

"Come on," said Hertha, ushering the group onto their feet to climb the ladder.

"Little sea captain," said Wyllie to Hertha who turned to face him while she nimbly ran up the ladder. He stood up on his little fishing boat, which rocked in the water, and pointed above the dockside. "The wind is north this noon," he said.

Hertha nodded her appreciation as she helped the others up. They quickly moved behind a huge pile of fishing buckets, ropes and netting on the dockside.

"Bye-bye, Mr Wyllie," said Floppy, waving as he watched him row out into the harbour. Berry grabbed Floppy and pulled him lower to hide as his long ears protruded from behind the pile of buckets.

"Where are we heading, H?" asked Berry as they watched the Mary Rose Resistance fight the enemy around them.

"You heard him," she replied. "The wind is blowing north." She pointed up at the tall roofs of the buildings that surrounded the dock. Berry was puzzled, licked one of his paws and held it up against the wind.

"It's not, you know. It's blowing west as far as I can tell."

Hertha did not reply but instead placed a paw around his shoulder and pointed up at a weathervane standing proud on top of one of the buildings. It too had a bronze ship as its signature and was pointing north. They chose their moment carefully and hid behind other buckets, the corners of buildings, and seedy alleyways as they made their way north.

"They're broken, I tells ya," observed Berry.

307

"They're friends," said Floppy. The weathervanes weren't following the wind at all; they were deliberately guiding their path north, navigating their treacherous way and helping them to remain undetected.

The group ducked and dived, weaved and sheltered, being guided by the mock breeze that was their new friend.

"Wait!" shouted Hertha. "Gizor's head!" She looked as if she was about to run back to retrieve it.

"His ugly head is the least of our worries," said Berry, pointing at Roderick in the distance charging on their position. "Run!" he shouted. They soon reached a gated fortress known locally as Gunwharf and looked for cover by running under the Vernon Gate – a grand entrance with turrets and an arch. As they ran through, more of the Resistance had been rallied and from their hidden position revealed themselves to stop the enemy by throwing stones, arrows and shots from above the gate.

"KILL THAT RABBIT!" ordered Roderick, who had caught a glimpse of Floppy's fluffy white tail going through the gate. He was firing indiscriminately into the crowd of soldiers and resistance.

Hertha was looking for a way out of the fortress, which sat on the water's edge. Berry looked up at the old buildings surrounding them and spotted another weathervane on top of Vernon Gate – pointing north. They followed the walls of the old fortress and past some brick railway arches that carried an old train line above it: the arches contained artillery shells and storage, a cobbler's keep, a stonemason's, and a makeshift inn for the sailors of Portsmouth. Berry spotted that one of the arches appeared to exit onto a main street. They immediately ran to it and took shelter. Completely out of breath, they checked on each other.

"Now where?" asked Berry, panting and spluttering as

he rested his paws on his knees trying to regain his breath. Hertha snuck a peek from the side wall of the entrance to find Gizor troops running around in a frenzy. Bombing was still relentless from both sides of the war and incendiary devices were going off left, right and centre. They all covered their heads when a blast from above struck the railway line, the walls of the arch rattled and bricks fell about the ground. Berry shook the dust off his head and patted himself down. "All limbs intact," he said in classic form. "Got a ringing in me ears and annoying rubble in me boots but all good."

"We need to keep moving, keep light on our feet," said Hertha, turning around to kneel and empty some of the heavier items from her rucksack. "Beaky, front and centre," she ordered.

"Right you are," he said, running from one end of the arch to the other for his orders.

"I need you to check the coast is clear," she said as she tied a red bandana round his head.

"I can do that, yep," he said, excited about his mission, "I've done reconnaissance before, I have." He marched out of the archway into the busy street then turned to face his crew and ushered them out like a policeman: "Go! Go! Go!"

"Keep close, Floppy," said Hertha as she watched Agatha grab Floppy's paw. Hertha looked up at the row of old taverns lining the coast. Every weathervane she could see was pointing to the dockyard. "Head for the dockyard, Beaky!" she shouted. As they edged ever closer, a huge crowd of troops were running out of the dockyard, but they weren't doing so to attack them: they were running in panic – fleeing Weevil's rabble of rats.

Hertha and her crew ran towards them and through Victory Gate – the entrance to the dockyard itself. The troops brushed shoulders with the Red enemy but offered no resistance. Weevil was hot on their tails with his rats biting and snapping their necks as they fled.

The small frightened group kept running as fast as they could through the gate and into the dockyard. Beaky hopped and skipped through and bumped straight into Weevil who grabbed his neck and held him high in the air – his wings flapping ferociously.

"Weevil!" shouted Agatha, "NO!"

Weevil looked behind the squawking seagull and spotted Agatha running towards him. He looked back at Beaky, saw he was wearing a red bandana and gently released his grip, lowering him to the ground.

"Ain't never seen me such an odd bunch of frightened rabbits," he said, looking at the unlikely group of friends – two red squirrels, a mole, a seagull and a white rabbit. Floppy hid behind Agatha.

"Ratties scare me, Aggy," he said, gripping her paw tightly as Weevil gave him a menacing stare.

"It's OK, Floppy. This is Weevil. A king of rats."

Floppy edged out behind Agatha and held out his paw to Weevil. "Hello, Mr Ratking. My name's Floppy." Needless to say, Weevil did not shake his hand and continued to stare at him.

"Bit far from your dank warren, ain't ya?" asked Weevil. "Lucky I ain't hungry," he added, which sent Floppy hopping immediately back behind Agatha.

Berry, who was standing behind the group, began muttering in panic. He had spotted Roderick running towards the gate. "Err, so we'd … err … better RUN!" he shouted.

"CHARGE!" shouted Weevil to his men.

The group scampered down Main Street past Gizor's Semaphore Tower towards the docks. "GO! GO! GO!" shouted Agatha. They ran through the crowd of rats, dodging shots, shelling, smoke and fire. As they raced down the long street they entered a large square where they were greeted by some tranquil calm amid the raging battle, and a crescent line of gentlefolk standing beside a magnificent tall ship – *HMS Victory*. It was Prime Minister Denis Delaney with the Alverstocracy of Gosport dressed in their bowler hats and carrying their umbrellas by their sides.

\*

*HMS Victory* stood alone in the dockyard, moored with thick rope lines to the dockside. It stood gloriously almost as if to say '*I can keep you safe*.' It was a magnificent ship and a magnificent sight. It was their way out, their way home. Made of ancient wood and painted ochre and black, its cannons prominent and unused for more than a century. Its masts towered over the taverns and old buildings of Portsmouth. The gangplank was down and all the animals of Gosport who had been captured by the Gizor and released by Weevil's rats were making their way on board, as if it were an ark.

"They wait the dank," said Hertha to herself.

"Shored by the dock," added Berry, standing in awe.

Floppy stood in the centre of his friends, Beaky at his back, Hertha and Berry either side of him and Agatha at the front: from above they formed an unintentional star standing in front of a crescent moon composed of Denis Delaney, Theodore Forton and the Alverstocracy. Hertha looked up at the main mast, which was flying the Portsmouth flag, flapping in the wind. The wind was indeed blowing west towards Gosport.

"My friends," said Denis as he stepped forward from the line and held out his paw, guiding them to the gangplank.

The friends said nothing but hesitantly walked towards

the gangplank holding paws for the first time in a line. They watched the last of the freed animals walk up, and then followed Denis up the steep ramp. Floppy, who was at the rear, was halfway up when he turned to face the docks below. He looked over to his left and saw Mr Wyllie in the Harbour water in the distance.

"Mr Wyllie, sir!" he called out, waving frantically, his words drowned out by the continuing sound of bombing.

"Floppy!" shouted Agatha as she had reached the top of the gangplank and realised he had broken free of her paw. "Floppy! Come on!" But Floppy had jumped down from the gangplank and was heading to Mr Wyllie's boat, which was in trouble in the water. Peppered with bullet holes, it was sinking fast with the weight of Hertha's forgotten souvenir. Floppy reached the edge of the dock and the port bow of the mighty *Victory* to watch with horror as Mr Wyllie stood in his rowing boat saluting his friend as he went down. He was lost, together with the bust of Gizor, in the middle of the Harbour waters.

"Mr Wyllie?" he mouthed to himself.

His despair was broken by his friends shouting at him to get back to the ship. Floppy turned with tears in his eyes, which he wiped away quickly with his paws and began running back to the ship. To his right coming down Main Street was Weevil, running with his rabble of remaining rats. The rats clambered and jumped onto the ship, which had begun to pull away from the dock.

"Floppy!" shouted Hertha and Agatha, watching from the deck. Hertha couldn't stand it any longer and began running towards the gangplank, only to find it had already been pulled up.

"Wait!" she shouted, struggling to get off the ship to get to Floppy, who hopped faster, looking for a way to get on board.

Someone on board shouted that the main line was still tied at the stern.

"Floppy – go to the stern!" shouted Hertha, "Untie the rope and climb up!"

Floppy struggled with the huge rope because it was so heavy, thick and oily. He hopped around it, heaving and tugging with all his might. Eventually it came free and slopped into the water with its sheer weight.

"Floppy!" shouted his friends, "jump onto the rope!"

Floppy took a few steps back as if to run, hop and skip onto it, but lost his nerve with each attempt. The ship was moving further and further away from the dockside with every minute.

"Hertha! Hertha!" cried Floppy standing alone and small on the dock below. His friends were scrambling about on the ship trying to find a way to get back to him.

"STOP THE SHIP!" shouted Hertha. "TURN BACK!"

"Turn back?" queried one of the rats who was steering the ship. "Are you crazy?"

"Turn the ship around!" she demanded, trying to grab the wheel. The rat was much stronger than her and pushed her to the deck.

"We're all dead if we turn this thing around," he warned. "Look!" He pointed at the docklands. Hertha scampered to the port side of the ship to see Roderick – very much alive though injured from being gnawed at by Weevil and his rats – charging towards Floppy and firing his pistol.

"RUN, FLOPPY!" she shouted. Floppy did as he was told and ran along the side of the dock parallel to the ship. Hertha and Berry pushed a rope over the side of the hull for Floppy to grab. He ran along the side of the ship trying to grab hold but had no hope of reaching it. It was just too far.

"The rabbit is mine," warned Roderick to his men as he noticed that Floppy was now trapped on the pier alone.

Without a second thought, Beaky flew down from the ship and swooped at Roderick, who shot at him. Hit in one of his wings, Beaky flew manically high into the sky for a second or so before falling back onto the ship with a thud.

"FLOPPY!" shouted Hertha and Berry from the ship as they watched in horror.

Roderick trained his pistol once again on Floppy who closed his eyes tight, reached into his jacket pocket and then held out his cupped paws towards Roderick.

"I told you I would get you, White Rabbit," said Roderick, but Floppy kept his eyes tightly closed and his paws stretched out. Roderick pulled the trigger, but nothing happened. He shook the pistol in his paw and tried again, but still nothing happened. He gave it a last shake to get it to work and aimed it at Floppy's chest.

"THOU SHALT LIE ABOVE THIS HATE," declared Floppy as he opened his outstretched paws. As he did so, a brilliant light rose into sky once more.

Roderick's pistol went off with a loud bang. Everyone on board the ship dived for cover except Agatha who was standing on the deck with a pistol in her paw: she too had fired, striking Roderick dead. The brilliant light immediately disappeared, and the world was silent for a moment. Hertha and Berry stood up from their crouched positions and looked over at Agatha who was still aiming her pistol at the dockside – standing motionless like a statue. They leant over the side of the ship to see Roderick on the ground, surrounded by a pool of blood, and Floppy lying on his side with only the gentle wind blowing his fluffy white fur.

"FLOPPY!" they shouted. The ship was moving towards the ruins of the harbour gate. They ran to the stern to stay closer to Floppy who was getting further and further away from them. Denis Delaney and the Alverstocracy of

Gosport stood next to Agatha in silence, lining the port side of the ship and looking down at Floppy.

"He ain't moving, H," said Berry as they looked helplessly at their fallen friend. The docks were still frantic with panicking Gizor troops fleeing the scene. As they watched Floppy's lifeless body on the dock, small and all alone, a hooded figure walked calmly through the crowds and onto the pier. "Look!" said Berry, pointing.

The hooded figure in moth-eaten clothes, a grubby red tail protruding from its cloak, approached Floppy's body, crouched down and spun its cloak around Floppy, shielding his body and them from view.

"Is that …?" asked Berry.

"The Red Witch," said Hertha.

They watched as she swayed and chanted over his body. Her words drifted across the water to the ship: "REVEAL TO THEE, CHART THE STARS TO SEE, OUR GREAT, OUR MIGHTY, COME TO THEE. REVEAL TO THEE. REVEAL TO THEE." The witch looked up at the sky and her hood fell back to reveal her old haggard squirrel face, "REVEAL TO THEE!" she commanded. They watched as she fell violently backwards onto the dock a few feet away from Floppy who was still lying motionless.

"FLOPPY!" they shouted. They watched as his paws began to twitch. He suddenly shook his head and with his hindleg began scratching his ear. He then sat up, facing the Red Witch.

"Hello," he said. "My name's Floppy." He jumped to his feet and like a gentleman hopped over to the witch to help her up.

"FLOPPY!" called out Hertha from the ship.

"Those are my friends," he said. "Will you be coming with us?" The witch did not reply. She simply replaced her hood, turned and walked calmly away.

"FLOPPY!" they shouted, "THE ROPE!" Hertha and Berry pointed to the end of the pier where the ship was making its way through. The sails unfurled gloriously to catch the wind and the rats on the yardarms began to sing a sea shanty. Floppy ran to the end of the pier and grabbed the rope that was dangling over the side. He struggled to climb it and was still dangling there when the ship broke free from the dockyard itself and into the choppy waters of the Harbour. Hertha and Berry began tugging at the rope, trying to pull him up, "CLIMB, FLOPPY!" shouted Hertha desperately, as she watched Floppy swinging his legs trying to gain some leverage. No one noticed Roderick reaching for his pistol as he lay dying on the dock.

"I told you, you were mine," he muttered as he grabbed the pistol and with one remaining bullet and one remaining breath fired it at Floppy. The shot rang out across the harbour. Floppy was still holding on to the end of the rope. Hertha quickly climbed down the rope, grabbed Floppy's paw and dragged him up onto the deck.

"You did it, Floppy!"

"Well done, Floppy," said Berry, patting him on the shoulder.

"I did it, Hertha. I did it, I did," said Floppy, briefly standing on his feet before collapsing sideways.

Hertha saw the blood on his back, staining his white fur. She backed away for a second, wanting to change what was happening in front of her, before edging closer and crouching down beside him. She grabbed his paw. "Someone help me!" she shouted.

Berry quickly knelt and tried to stem the flow of blood from Floppy's back. The crowded deck of the ship parted around Floppy with only his friends around him trying desperately to save him.

Agatha looked on, feeling helpless, as Berry and Hertha

frantically tried to stop the blood.

"I feel dizzy I do, Hertha," said Floppy now resting his head on Hertha's lap. "Tired, I am."

"I know, Floppy, but you have to stay awake for me, my brave friend." She tried to stop her eyes from welling up.

Floppy was growing confused and drifting in and out of consciousness. "I be as quiet as a mousey, I be," he whispered.

As the friends fought to keep him alive the mighty tall ship floated effortlessly and gloriously into the centre of the harbour for all to see. While the bombing had stopped, and the war seemed to have been won, a deep thud was suddenly heard from the hills to the north and a huge plume of smoke could be seen. A great cannon had been fired from the hills. It missed *Victory* but only by a few yards. As the shot hit the water, the ship rocked and the waves crashing over its starboard side. All the animals on board fell to the deck and rolled to the port side, the water knocking them off their feet.

"RALLY THE CANNONS!" ordered Weevil to his men who began scurrying around the decks. "FIRE!" he shouted. But nothing happened. The cannons were so old and rusty that they could never work, yet Weevil would not give up. "FIRE!" he yelled again, but still the cannons did not fire.

Another deep thud from the hills could be heard, then another, and another. The waves were enormous, and the grand old ship rocked from side to side with each huge blast, knocking one unfortunate rat off the crow's nest, his body crashing to the deck. The bombing was unrelenting: all aboard either ran below or scurried about the top deck running for cover.

"HOLD ON TIGHT" shouted Weevil. He watched as

one of his bedraggled rats flew from one side of the ship to the other and over the side. Weevil caught him by grabbing his tail and swinging him back round, making him barrel-roll to safety across the decking and down a hatch. The bombing from the hills continued. Weevil grabbed the ship's wheel from another rat who was struggling to keep a steady course.

"WHERE ARE MY CANNONS?" shouted Weevil.

"They ain't working, Weevil," said one of the rats, trying to pull the cord but losing his footing.

Hertha and Berry, soaked through, had been pushed to one side of the ship with Floppy still cradled in their arms. Agatha had fallen to the deck and had wrapped one arm firmly around a rope line to stop herself sliding down the ship as it tipped and rocked. Her other paw was holding Beaky steady who was also lying on the deck, his wing broken.

The cannon fire from the hills was deafening and suddenly things began to play out in slow-motion. Weevil's men were scrambling about everywhere – slipping and sliding, yelling and screaming. Agatha looked over at Weevil shouting his orders, but couldn't hear a thing. She thought she would pass out from fear. One almighty wave struck her in the face so hard that her head was flung back and hit the ancient wooden planks. She shook her wet face and held on tighter to the rope. She lay on her side wishing she was home; wishing this was all over.

Amid the chaos and the waves, a single pair of white feet could be seen serenely walking towards the starboard side of the ship. Agatha looked on as the figure made its way towards the cannons. Unable to wipe the seawater from her eyes, she blinked and batted her eyelids to see. Still without sound and in total slow motion, Floppy could be seen facing the hills, standing strong against the force of the water and the wind. She watched as he raised his arms and stretched them out to his sides. He looked up to the sky. He stood there for a moment holding his position while others around him were losing theirs. She watched as he slowly pushed his arms forwards as if to grab the north hills for himself, and as he did so all the cannons from the starboard side of the ship went off in unison with an almighty BOOM, hitting the side of Portsdown Hill in the distance. A huge plume of chalky smoke rose into the sky and a massive part of the grassy hill front fell away like an avalanche, leaving a newly formed chalky cliff face. The bombing from the hills was no more and Gizor's tunnels had crumbled away.

As the mighty *Victory* began to settle in the harbour and the seawater began to drain away over its sides, Floppy could be seen still standing facing the hills. Hertha called out his name as she clambered to her feet, and as she did so, Floppy collapsed. They rushed to his side.

"I enjoyed our adventure, Hertha," said Floppy in a weak voice as he lay on the deck with Berry holding his paw, and his head resting on Hertha's lap. Agatha stood over him. The friends looked at each other, helpless and desperate.

"You're the bravest of us all, Floppy," said Berry, letting a tear escape from his eyes and roll down his face.

"Hello, Mr Wyllie," he said, confused. "I once knew a poor man, a gentleman too. Too kind to the many, so mean to so few," he sang. "Yes, I would like a custard cream, Rosie. I was brave, wasn't I, Hertha?"

"So brave, my friend," she replied, stroking his forehead.

"Aggy?" he called out. Agatha knelt to hold his other paw. "I see him, I do."

"Who, Floppy?" she asked.

"I see them all, Aggy. I see all the ones before you, and

the ones before them, I do." He paused. "I'm not in pain. They want me to go with them." He turned to look up at Hertha who was holding his cheeks in her paws. "I promise I be brave, Hertha."

"I know you will. "

"I know why I'm here. If I go with them, Hertha, can you come too?"

Hertha's eyes were heavy like rain. "You're not going anywhere, Floppy."

"Come with me, Hertha," he said again.

A single tear broke free and rolled down her cheek, dissolving into her red fur. "I can't, Floppy," she said, choked.

"Then I be brave like you. I be brave and kind for all of us," he said as he moved Agatha's paw so that it was touching Hertha's and then let go, his paw falling to his side.

Time seemed to stop for the three friends surrounding Floppy's lifeless, empty body, as is often the way when you want the world to rewind and things to begin again. Berry cried like a child, he was inconsolable, shaking his head and letting out great gulping sobs. Hertha and Agatha sat holding paws with their eyes closed tight. Floppy was gone.

*

Berry remained at Floppy's side for the entire voyage. Beaky's wing had been bandaged up and he placed his good wing over the mole's shoulder to comfort him. Hertha stood at the stern of the ship looking over at Portsmouth where the smoke and fires were still raging. She heard footsteps coming towards her from behind and tried discreetly to wipe away her tears. She turned her head briefly to the side to see who was approaching. It was Agatha who had come to share the view. They didn't look at each other.

"What was this adventure all worth?" asked Hertha. Agatha did not immediately reply. "He died believing in it and died because of it." Hertha turned her head sharply to look at Agatha. "So tell me," she said. "Why did he have to die?" She wiped away an angry tear and turned back to face Portsmouth to hide her vulnerability. Agatha still did not respond.

They stared over at the skyline, watching the smoky clouds form patterns in the fading early evening light. They followed the west coast shoreline with their eyes moving from the destroyed docklands, past the Semaphore Tower, and down towards the waters of Old Portsmouth Point and the fishing docks of the south. They both caught sight of a single star – the brightest in the sky – still waiting for the dark. The star shimmered above the great dome of the Cathedral and their gaze fell to the Red Witch – Lillian Francis – standing like a ghost on top of the weathervane, dancing deliriously hand-in-hand with Mr Wyllie.

They could barely hear the celebrations behind them. The rescued animals had gone up onto the deck of the ship and were dancing for joy.

"The war is over!" cried one of the revellers.

"Gizor is dead!" cried another. "We're free at last!"

Hertha and Agatha turned to face them. The mighty *Victory* was sailing closer to the shores of Forton Creek and Priddy's Hard, with its mainsail blowing them home. Agatha turned to look at her friend standing beside her.

"This world isn't theirs anymore," she said, referring to what a Gizor officer had once proclaimed to her.

\*

In the days following the end of the war, great celebrations took place in the Country of Gosport with huge street parties on every corner bringing the animal folk together once more with lashings of food and wine, music, singing and dancing. The war was over, the animals were free, yet the loss was great – some sixty thousand red squirrels and their sympathisers had been exterminated by the Gizor army in their evil quest for a 'pedigree' society. The land was changed for ever, with buildings and homes destroyed and loved ones gone. Yet, the world carried on. It had to.

Among the celebrations, in the little village hidden in the woods of Alver, another party was taking place, hosting a different crowd. These were the animals who the rest of the Country were unaware of – the ones who had actually ended the war. The campfire was burning, pocket whistles were playing, and soft drums were beating. The village was repairing its heart. Beaky could be seen dancing around the fire, his broken wing in a sling, his webbed feet stamping the dirt ferociously in one spot like seagulls do. Hertha, Berry and Agatha were seated at a picnic table drinking their elderflower wine and watching Beaky and some village hedgehogs and Weevil's rats dancing into the early evening – the sun beaming rays through the canopy of trees. Lady Ellen Prideaux-Brune, Mary Camper, Gertie Nicholson, Jane Priddy and Doris Cruikshank were watching the spectacle on the other side of the campfire. They all smiled as Beaky ran over to Mary and put his wing around her, pulling her into the dance. She stood there for a while, not knowing how to dance and not wanting to be made to look a fool. Beaky carried on dancing with his village friends. Gertie got up and joined Mary, drawing her further into the dancing crowd.

She whirled Mary round and said: "come on, my old friend, dance with me!" and with that Mary let herself go and danced like no one was watching her. Lady Ellen was overjoyed and clapped her hands as she too stood up and joined them. Jane and Doris followed.

Agatha watched Hertha staring into the fire looking at nothing but the flames.

"Ask me," said Agatha.

"Ask you what?" replied Hertha.

"Ask me why I didn't shoot Roderick sooner."

"Well? He was standing right there. You had a pistol in your hand and you could have saved Floppy."

Agatha looked Hertha straight in the eye, a deep burden on her mind. "Roderick never killed him," she revealed. "He didn't die on the docks, Hertha, and he didn't die on the ship." She glanced at Berry. "He died on the weathervane, he died at the cathedral." Neither Berry or Hertha said a word. Agatha looked through the dancing crowd and could see Weevil through the fire standing on the other side, staring at her. She stood up and left her friends and walked through the crowd, declining offers to dance and join in.

"What will you do now?" she asked, standing next to Weevil as they both looked at his rabble of grubby, scruffy, smiling rats dancing with the villagers.

"Ain't never been free," he replied.

"Are you going back? Back to your island?"

"Might try me a different island, across the harbour." He glanced at Agatha. "Up for grabs, I hear," he said, allowing a little smirk to show on his face. "And what will you do?"

Agatha couldn't reply because she didn't know what she would do, other than go back to her cottage without her papa and carry on working on her inventions while repairing damaged buildings and finishing Jane's dock at Priddy's. What else would she do?

"The smallest of light will burn your eyes," commented

Weevil, glancing behind them at Morag and Lucius.

"Agatha Mumby!" called out Morag. Agatha turned and walked towards them. They were standing near to the village well at the far end of the lane. As she approached the pair, Denis Delaney, Theodore Forton and the rest of the Alverstocracy stepped out into the lane to greet her. She knew what they wanted.

Lucius stepped forward. "You have a path, Agatha. A destiny. Your father gave it to you."

"I don't want it."

"But it's yours, lassie," replied Morag. "You're the one that must carry it on."

"I don't want it," she repeated.

"But you are the Grandmaster now, Agatha," she said.

Agatha shook her head. "I will not be its keeper."

"But you must," said Morag, astonished.

"I realise now that my father was obsessed with the Ark. It all makes sense now. I won't be the keeper of his burden. It's not mine. He died for it and so did Floppy. How many more will die, and for what?" She shook her head, "No, no more. It will have no keeper, no Grandmaster, no one following to protect it. It belongs to the trees and the earth." With that she turned around and began walking back to the party.

Morag was desperate. "Where is it, Agatha?" she cried, but Agatha did not respond. "The rabbit will return," said Morag, trying to pull at her heartstrings. She was wrong to do so.

"HE HAS A NAME!" she shouted back. "His name is Floptiers," and with that Agatha turned and walked into the crowd. She grabbed Beaky, pulled him out of the dance and headed towards Hertha and Berry who were still sitting at their table absorbing what she had told them. "Come on," she said as she began walking out of the village. Lady Ellen

324

saw the commotion and signalled to the others with a nod of her head to follow. Mary, Gertie, Jane and Doris followed behind.

Agatha led them past Farmer Jack's house and through the woods to the south. They travelled over the ruins of the old motte and bailey, reached the River Alver and followed along its banks to a clearing, where there was a bridge.

The group were silent as they watched Agatha walk to the centre of Apple Dumpling Bridge. They stood on the bank looking at their friend – the Grandmaster of the Ark. Agatha reached into her jacket pocket and took out the small wooden box. She held it in her paws for a moment before bringing it close to her lips and kissing it. She looked back at her group of friends. "Kindness is everything in life," she said, holding out her paw over the river and

releasing her grip on the box, which fell into the water. It bobbed up and down for a second or so before slowly sinking. As it did so, the lid of the wooden box opened, and an incredible ray of light was released. The brilliant light scorched the waters of the river, charting its entire path through Gosport. As the box – and its contents – sunk deeper to the riverbed, the light began to fade, leaving the river tinged with a dark black loam. The small group of comrades – the only observers – bowed their heads in honour of their friend, Floptiers Burrows-Warren the Third.

\*

Floppy was buried in a quiet ceremony in Rowner churchyard, next to Agatha's cottage, with a headstone that read:

HERE LIES
FLOPTIERS BURROWS-WARREN THE THIRD.
A HERO WHO DIES IS FREE
AND KINDNESS THERE,
RESTS HIS SOUL TO THEE

As *Victory* had sailed into Forton Creek and the animals had disembarked, with Hertha and Berry carrying Floppy's dead body down the gangplank, Agatha had remained on board alone. She could hear the water lapping against the great ship; a ship that had carried them to safety and brought Floppy home. Her gaze had fallen to the deck, still damp with seawater, where Floppy had lain. She saw something shimmering between the wet wooden planks, picked it up and held it in her paw – it was her father's trinket. Kindness really was everything in life, she thought.

**THE END**

If you enjoyed this book,
why not visit the website
(appledumplingbridge.co.uk)
and follow K. L. Knowles on
Facebook?
An ebook version of
**The Road to Apple
Dumpling Bridge**
is also available for all
ebook platforms